Literary Lives

General Editor: **Richard Dutton**, Professor of English, Lancaster University

This series offers stimulating accounts of the literary careers of the most admired and influential English-language authors. Volumes follow the outline of the writers' working lives, not in the spirit of traditional biography, but aiming to trace the professional, publishing and social contexts which shaped their writing.

Published titles include:

Literary Lives
Series Standing Order ISBN 0–333–71486–5 hardcover
Series Standing Order ISBN 0–333–80334–5 paperback
(*outside North America only*)

You can receive future titles in this series as they are published by placing a standing order. Please contact your bookseller or, in case of difficulty, write to us at the address below with your name and address, the title of the series and one of the ISBNs quoted above.

Customer Services Department, Macmillan Distribution Ltd, Houndmills, Basingstoke, Hampshire RG21 6XS, England

Mary Wollstonecraft

A Literary Life

Caroline Franklin
Reader in English
University of Wales, Swansea

First published 2004 by
PALGRAVE MACMILLAN
Houndmills, Basingstoke, Hampshire RG21 6XS and
175 Fifth Avenue, New York, N. Y. 10010
Companies and representatives throughout the world

PALGRAVE MACMILLAN is the global academic imprint of the Palgrave Macmillan division of St. Martin's Press, LLC and of Palgrave Macmillan Ltd. Macmillan® is a registered trademark in the United States, United Kingdom and other countries. Palgrave is a registered trademark in the European Union and other countries.

ISBN 0–333–97251–1

This book is printed on paper suitable for recycling and made from fully managed and sustained forest sources.

A catalogue record for this book is available from the British Library.

Library of Congress Cataloging-in-Publication Data
Franklin, Caroline.
    Mary Wollstonecraft: a literary life / Caroline Franklin.
        p. cm. — (Literary lives)
    Includes bibliographical references and index.
    ISBN 0–333–97251–1
        1. Wollstonecraft, Mary, 1759–1797. 2. Women and literature–
    –England—History—18th century. 3. Authors, English—18th century–
    –Biography. 4. Feminists—Great Britain—Biography. I. Title. II. Literary
    lives (Palgrave Macmillan (Firm))

    PR5841.W8Z675 2004
    828'.609—dc22
    [B]
                                                          2004044368

10   9   8   7   6   5   4   3
13 12 11 10 09 08 07 06 05

Printed and bound in Great Britain by
Antony Rowe Ltd, Chippenham and Eastbourne

For Mike

Contents

Preface

Fiction, imaginative work that is, is not dropped like a pebble upon the ground, as science may be; fiction is like a spider's web, attached ever so lightly perhaps, but still attached to life at all four corners. Often the attachment is scarcely perceptible; Shakespeare's plays, for instance, seem to hang there complete by themselves. But when the web is pulled askew, hooked up at the edge, torn in the middle, one remembers that these webs are not spun in mid-air by incorporeal creatures, but are the work of suffering human beings, and are attached to grossly material things, like health and money and the houses we live in.

(Virginia Woolf, *A Room of One's Own*)

This literary life aims to give a detailed description of the intellectual, publishing and political coteries with which Mary Wollstonecraft was connected during the ten years she was a woman of letters. Although she was hailed by contemporary admirers as an original thinker and an intuitive Romantic 'genius', with the hindsight of history it is possible to detect those threads attaching her works to their material and cultural contexts, forming webs of correspondences between writers, which shaped language and literary genres.

The underlying theme of the book is just how emancipatory print culture was seen to be at the time, especially by an autodidact like Wollstonecraft. An aspiring female intellectual such as Wollstonecraft could take advantage of the clubs, salons and meeting-places the Enlightenment public sphere had opened up to women, where social barriers were broken down so that books and ideas could be discussed. Communicating with a network of like-minded friends also entailed writing and reading letters, and it was the letter in the form of polemical epistle, advice book, travelogue and conversational story which would remain central to her published works. The influence of the wealthy Dissenters made publication available to the women in their circles at this exciting period when their campaign for religious toleration was turning into an argument based on rights.

A latitudinarian Anglican with much in common with Rational Dissenters, Wollstonecraft joined these outsiders in the suburbs North of

London. Their geographical location indicated the history of such oppositional thinkers: for a hundred years they had criticized the Establishment. Though numerically small, the Dissenters were well-connected in the world of publishing and education, and hospitable to women intellectuals. Disenfranchised like them, Wollstonecraft was inspired to spread Enlightenment thinking through the power of print. Passing on literacy had traditionally been the Protestant mother's business, and Wollstonecraft was one of many women who professionalized the role of educationalist by becoming a children's author and moralist.

When she became a full-time woman of letters, Wollstonecraft worked for Unitarian publisher Joseph Johnson, the most important distributor of late Enlightenment scientific, philosophical, and religious publications, and also a pioneer publisher of early German and British Romanticist writing. A reviewer in the most prestigious oppositional periodical of the day, *The Analytical Review*, Wollstonecraft became politicized by the French Revolution and one of the most prominent contributors to the most important pamphlet war since the civil war period. Her *Vindication of the Rights of Woman* was a reasoned yet passionate defence of female intellectual equality, which repudiated the false dichotomies now arising between the public world of action and the private world of conscience.

In republican France she joined the Girondin salon society, where writers predominated and whose belief in the power of print to achieve reform was messianic in its fervour. However, when the influence of newspapers began to unsettle the authority of the National Convention itself, her belief in the ideal of an unregulated press was shaken. Wollstonecraft experienced the Terror: she learned the hard way that public opinion could be manipulated by those controlling the media; that idealists became corrupted by power and money. Nevertheless, Wollstonecraft continued to believe that the role of print culture was to question the authority of all hierarchies and argue for a community of equals. Still impelled by this ideal, she travelled to Scandinavia, viewing the progressive regime as promising some hope for social reform without the bloodshed she had witnessed in the Terror in France. The fact that she was writing a 'feminist' novel when she died shows that she hoped, even in the darkest days of reaction and anti-Jacobinism, to spread her ideas to the reading public at large through popular culture.

This study hopes to problematize the assumption of critics such as Gary Kelly and Isaac Kramnick that Wollstonecraft can be grouped together with all those 'Bourgeois' writers who criticized feudalism and court culture and distanced themselves from the lower classes. Though her grandfather had been a merchant, Wollstonecraft's father became indigent and had to be supported by his children. Wollstonecraft herself had no property or income, except what she earned, and belonged to a heterogeneous social group of artists, intellectuals and bohemian writers living by the pen. Wollstonecraft's arguments against gender distinctions were only part of her thoroughgoing egalitarianism. Wollstonecraft's occasionally snobbish remarks about servants should not blind us to the fact that her criticisms of landed property and suggestions for land reform put her at the most radical end of the political spectrum.

Feminist critics such as Anne Mellor and Mitzi Myers, in order to trace a specifically female literary tradition, have also sought to homogenize all women writers at the cost of eroding the ideological differences between them. It is important to situate an intellectual like Wollstonecraft amongst the whole range of writers and thinkers, male and female, with whom her texts engaged, for she played her part in the public sphere and not in a separate women's arena. Close scrutiny of the intellectual scene shows that differences of religious opinions split women writers and shaped the way they saw their role, and that this healthy debate and rivalry demonstrated their confidence in their right to write.

Suggestions for further reading

For those who would like a fuller account of Wollstonecraft's life, which concentrates more on her personal and family relationships, see Janet Todd's recent well-researched *Mary Wollstonecraft: A Revolutionary Life* (London: Phoenix Press, 2000). A shorter and livelier general biography is Claire Tomalin's *The Life and Death of Mary Wollstonecraft* (London: Weidenfeld and Nicolson, 1974). Gary Kelly's *Revolutionary Feminism: the Mind and Career of Mary Wollstonecraft* (London: Macmillan – now Palgrave Macmillan, 1991) is a meticulous and scholarly account of Wollstonecraft's intellectual development, in which she is perceived as typifying the temporarily radicalized bourgeois professional classes.

Wollstonecraft did not write her vigorous and informal letters with an eye to posterity, but even in her own day they were admired and published as literary productions in their own right. Janet Todd has edited a new edition of *The Collected Letters of Mary Wollstonecraft* (London: Penguin, 2003), which came out just as this book was being revised for the press.

The standard edition of *The Works of Mary Wollstonecraft*, 7 vols (London: Pickering, 1989), used here, is lightly annotated, but for fuller textual commentary, I would recommend an edition of *Vindication of the Rights of Woman* edited by D.L. Macdonald (Ontario: Broadview Press, 1997); see also Carol H. Poston's edition of *Vindication of the Rights of Woman* (New York and London: Norton, 1988); *A Short Residence in Sweden* and William Godwin, *Memoirs of the Author of "The Rights of Woman"*, edited by Richard Holmes (Harmondsworth: Penguin, 1987), and *Mary* and *The Wrongs of Woman* edited by Gary Kelly (Oxford: Oxford University Press, 1976).

For a clear-sighted exposition of Wollstonecraft's political thought, see Virgina Sapiro's *A Vindication of Political Virtue: The Political Theory of Mary Wollstonecraft* (1992, Chicago: Chicago University Press). The historical context is explicated in Jane Rendall's *The Origins of Modern Feminism: Women in Britain, France and the United States, 1780–1860* (London: Macmillan – now Palgrave Macmillan, 1985). The centrality of religion to Wollstonecraft's idealist blend of reason and passion is explored in Barbara Taylor's important study, *Mary Wollstonecraft and the Feminist Imagination* (Cambridge: Cambridge University Press, 2003).

Good introductory books on Wollstonecraft from the literary point of view are Jane Moore, Writers and Their Work Series, *Mary Wollstonecraft* (Plymouth: Northcote House, 1999) and Harriet Devine Jump, *Mary Wollstonecraft: Writer* (New York: Harvester Wheatsheaf, 1994). *Women's Writing* 4 (1997) was a special issue on Wollstonecraft. *The Cambridge Companion to Mary Wollstonecraft* (Cambridge: Cambridge University Press, 2002) offers a stimulating collection of essays by the foremost scholars on Wollstonecraft, covering most genres in which she wrote. Two recent specialist studies are Ashley Tauchert, *Mary Wollstonecraft and the Accent of the Feminine* (Basingstoke: Palgrave Macmillan, 2002), which uses the theories of Luce Irigaray to examine Wollstonecraft's representation of female subjectivity; and Saba Bahar, *Mary Wollstonecraft's Social and Aesthetic Philosophy: An Eve to Please Me* (Basingstoke: Palgrave Macmillan, 2002), which examines Wollstonecraft's aesthetic strategies in figuring female virtue.

Acknowledgements

This book would not have been able to be completed without a Research Leave Award from the Arts and Humanities Research Board, and I am most grateful to them and to my colleagues for making it possible for me to devote my time solely to this project in 2002–03. My thanks are also due to Professor Ian Bell and the Department of English, University of Wales, Swansea, for assisting with travel expenses to enable me to make a research trip to the Beinecke Library in April 2001. I quote from the Abinger Papers deposited in the Bodleian Library, Oxford with the permission of Lord Abinger, and I am grateful to Senior Assistant Librarian Dr. Bruce Barker-Benfield at the Department of Special Collections and Western manuscripts for his expert help. I would also like to acknowledge the Carl H. Pforzheimer Library, whose microfilm of Mary Hays' letters I consulted in the New York Public library. Librarians at the Beinecke Library, the Sterling Memorial Library, Yale, the British Library and University of Wales, Swansea have all helped in my research. Particular thanks are due to Helen Braithwaite, John Turner, Barbara Taylor, Nigel Leask and Mike Franklin who read and commented on portions of the manuscript, as well as to the series editor, Richard Dutton, and editorial and copy-editing staff at Palgrave Macmillan.

List of Abbreviations

WMW   *The Works of Mary Wollstonecraft*, 7 vols., ed. Janet Todd and
       Marilyn Butler (London: Pickering & Chatto, 1989).

MAVRW *Memoirs of the Author of A Vindication of the Rights of Woman*,
       ed. Pamela Clemit and Gina Luria Walker (Ontario and
       Letchworth, Herts: Broadview Press, 2001).

CLMW   *The Collected Letters of Mary Wollstonecraft*, ed. Ralph M. Wardle
       (Ithaca: Cornell University Press, 1979).

Chronology

Life

27 April, 1759 Birth in Primrose Street, Spitalfields

20 May 1759 Christened at St Botolph's Church.

1763 Family moved to Epping Forest, Essex.

1765 Grandfather, Edward Wollstonecraft, died; leaving bulk of his estate to Mary's father, and an inheritance to her brother Ned.

October 1768 Family moved to a farm near Beverley, Yorkshire. MW attended a day school there.

1773 First extant letter to Jane Arden.

1774 Family moved to Hoxton, London. Elder brother Ned articled to a lawyer. MW befriended by Revd and Mrs. Clare. Friendship with Fanny Blood.

1776 Family moved to Laugharne, West Wales.

1777 Family moved to Walworth, London, lodging with Thomas Taylor 'the Platonist'.

1778 MW took post as paid companion to Mrs Dawson of Bath. Visits Bath, Windsor and Southampton.

1780 Wollstonecraft family moved to Enfield.

1781 MW summoned to Enfield, Middlesex, to nurse mother.

1782 19 April Mother died. Father remarried and moved to Laugharne. Sisters Eliza and Everina went to live with Ned and his wife and MW lodged with the Blood family.

20 October Eliza married Meredith Bishop.

1783 10 August birth of Eliza's baby.

1784 MW helped Eliza to leave her husband and baby who subsequently died. MW set up school at Newington Green, North of London, with Fanny, Eliza and Everina. Friendship with Dr Richard Price and his circle. Death of Eliza's daughter.

January: 1785 Fanny Blood sailed to Lisbon and married Hugh Skeys. Autumn, MW journeyed to Lisbon to nurse Fanny in childbirth.

November: Death of Fanny and MW returned to London by December.

Events

1759 George III succeeded to the throne.

Published: Samuel Johnson, *Rasselas*; Sarah Fielding, *The Countess of Dellwyn*.

1768 Sir Joshua Reynolds is elected first President of the Royal Academy.

Published: Laurence Sterne, *A Sentimental Journey*.

1774 Louis XVI succeeded to the throne of France.

Published: Goethe, *The Sorrows of Young Werther*.

1776 Declaration of Independence of American colonies. Cook's third voyage to the Pacific.

Published: Adam Smith, *The Wealth of Nations*; Thomas Paine, *Common Sense*.

Richard Price, *On Civil Liberty*

1780 Gordon riots.

Published: Arthur Young, *A Tour in Ireland*.

1782 Negotiation of peace between Britain and America

Published: Jean-Jacques Rousseau, *Confessions*; Frances Burney, *Cecilia*; William Cowper, *Poems*; William Gilpin, *Observations on the River Wye*; Joseph Priestley, *A History of the Corruptions of Christianity*. Henri Fuseli, 'The Nightmare' shown at the Royal Academy.

1783 First ministry of William Pitt the Younger.

Published: Catharine Macaulay, vol.8, *A History of England, from the Accession of James I to that of the Brunswick Line*; George Crabbe, *The Village*.

1784 Pitt's India Act puts East India Company under parliamentary control.

Published: Charlotte Smith, *Elegiac Sonnets*. William Blake, *An Island in the Moon*.

1785 Founding of the Sunday School Society.

Published: William Cowper, *The Task*; James Boswell, *Journal of a Tour to the Hebrides*.

Life

1786 MW closed school and in August took up post of governess with Viscount and Lady Kingsborough's family in Mitchelstown, County Cork, Ireland.

September: visits Eton on way to Dublin. Winter in Dublin.

1787 January or February: *Thoughts on the Education of Daughters* published by Joseph Johnson, and MW gave her payment of 10 guineas to Blood family. Excerpts published in *Lady's Magazine*.

June: travelled to Bristol Hot Wells with the Kingsboroughs and wrote *Mary: a Fiction* and 'Cave of Fancy'.

August: MW began work in London for publisher Joseph Johnson, having been dismissed from governess post.

September: moved to 49 George Street, Blackfriars.

1788 Began translating Lavater's *Essays on Physiognomy* but overtaken by Thomas Holcroft. Organized Everina's trip to Paris. Summer: launch of the *Analytical Review* and MW helped editor Thomas Christie run it and wrote reviews. *Mary: A Fiction, Original Stories from Real Life* and MW's translation of Necker's *Of the Importance of Religious Opinions* published. Refused an acquaintance's offer of marriage. Took in seven-year-old orphan, Ann.

1789 Compiled *The Female Reader*, published under name of Mr Cresswick.

1790 Translated Maria van de Werken de Cambon's *Young Grandison* and Salzmann's *Elements of Morality*, illustrated by William Blake.

29 November published anonymously *A Vindication of the Rights of Men* in answer to Edmund Burke's *Reflections on the Revolution in France*. 18 December second edition published with author's name. Became a regular member of Johnson's circle including Henry Fuseli, Anna Barbauld, Thomas Paine, William Godwin, Thomas Holcroft.

1791 Second edition *Original Stories* published with illustrations by William Blake.

April: Death of Dr Price. William Roscoe commissioned a portrait of MW. MW moved to Store Street.

November: MW met Godwin at Johnson's dinner party. Everina refused marriage proposal of George Blood.

Events

1786 Published: William Beckford, *Vathek*; Robert Burns, *Poems Chiefly in the Scottish Dialect*; William Gilpin, *Observations of Picturesque Beauty in Mountains and Lakes of Cumberland and Westmoreland*; Helen Maria Williams, *Poems in Two Volumes*.

1787 United States Constitution ratified.

Published: Clara Reeve, *The Progress of Romance*; Ann Yearsley, *Poems on Various Subjects*.

1788 Mental illness of George III; impeachment of Warren Hastings.

Published: Final volume of Edward Gibbon, *The Decline and Fall of the Roman Empire*; Immanuel Kant, *Critique of Practical Reason*; Hannah More, *Thoughts on the Importance of the Manners of the Great to General Society*; Charlotte Smith, *Emmeline*.

1789 Recovery of George III.

14 July: Storming of the Bastille and outbreak of French Revolution.

August: Declaration of the Rights of Man approved by French National Assembly.

Dr Richard Price's sermon 'Discourse on the Love of Our Country'.

Published: W. Blake, *Songs of Innocence* and *Book of Thel*; Charlotte Smith, *Ethelinda*; Sir William Jones, translation of *Sacontala, or the Fatal Ring*; Erasmus Darwin, *The Loves of the Plants*.

1790 Parliament retains Test and Corporation Acts.

Published: Edmund Burke, *Reflections on the Revolution in France*; Helen Maria Williams, *Julia*; and *Letters written in France*; Ann Radcliffe, *A Sicilian Romance*. Anna Laetitia Barbauld, *Address to the Opposers of the Repeal of the Corporate and Test Acts*.

1791 Rejection of William Wilberforce's motion to abolish the slave trade. Anti-Jacobin riots in Birmingham. Louis XVI captured attempting to leave France.

Published: Elizabeth Inchbald, *A Simple Story*; Thomas Paine, *The Rights of Man*, Part 1; Ann Radcliffe, *The Romance of the Forest*; Anna Laetitia Barbauld, *An Epistle to William Wilberforce*; James Boswell, *Life of Johnson*; Charlotte Smith, *Celestina*.

Life

1792 January: *Vindication of the Rights of Woman* published. MW met Talleyrand. Second revised edition *Rights of Woman* published. MW in love with Henry Fuseli. Summer MW met Mary Hays. August MW, Johnson and Fuselis departed for Paris but turned back on hearing the King's palace stormed. Crisis with Fuseli.

December: departed for Paris alone. Joined Girondin circle including English supporters Helen Maria Williams and Tom Paine.

1793 MW fell in love with Gilbert Imlay.

June: MW moved to Neuilly. August: MW pregnant.

September: returned to Paris. GI registered MW as his wife at the American Embassy.

1794 MW moved to Le Havre.

May: Fanny born. GI returned to Britain.

December: *An Historical and Moral View of the French Revolution* published.

1795 April: MW returned to London. Suicide attempt on learning of GI's infidelity.

June: MW travelled to Scandinavia with Fanny and maid to attempt business negotiations for GI.

Sept: MW returned to London via Hamburg.

October: Attempted suicide by jumping off Putney Bridge but saved by passer-by. Lived in Finsbury Square.

1796 January: *Letters Written During a Short Residence in Sweden, Norway and Denmark* published. Third edition *Rights of Woman*. Moved to Cumming Street.

March: final meeting with GI.

April: met WG again at Mary Hays' home. Began *Maria, or The Wrongs of Woman*.

Summer: relationship with WG began. Death of Christie.

December: MW pregnant.

1797 Portrait painted by John Opie.

29 March: MW married WG at St. Pancras Church. MW moved to the Polygon, Somers Town.

30 August: birth of daughter Mary.

10 September: death of complications following childbirth. Buried at St Pancras Churchyard.

1798 *Posthumous Works* published as well as WG's *Memoirs of the Author of A Vindication of the Rights of Woman*.

Events

1792 Louis XVI and family imprisoned. September massacres. Abolition of the French monarchy. April: France declared war on Austria and Prussia.

Published: T. Paine, *The Rights of Man*, Part 2; Thomas Holcroft, *Anna St. Ives*; Charlotte Smith, *Desmond*; Mary Robinson, *Vancenza, or, The Dangers of Credulity*; Samuel Rogers, *The Pleasures of Memory*.

1793 January: Execution Louis XVI. War between Britain and France. Assassination of Marat. September: 'Terror' in Paris. Execution of Marie Antoinette. Execution of Girondins.

Published: William Godwin, *An Enquiry Concerning Political Justice*; William Blake, *Marriage of Heaven and Hell, America, Visions of the Daughters of Albion*; William Wordsworth, *An Evening Walk* and *Descriptive Sketches*; C. Smith, *The Emigrants*; and *The Old Manor House*; Hannah More, *Village Politics*.

1794 Habeas Corpus suspended. State trials of leaders of London Corresponding Society end in jury's refusal to convict. July: Execution of Robespierre, Danton, St Just.

Published: W. Blake, *Songs of Experience, Book of Urizen, Europe*; A. Radcliffe, *The Mysteries of Udolpho*; W. Godwin, *Caleb Williams*; T. Paine, *The Age of Reason*, Part 1; R. Southey, *Wat Tyler*; William Paley, *Evidences of Christianity*; C. Smith, *The Banished Man*; Mary Robinson, *Poems*.

1795 'Two Acts' passed against seditious meetings and treasonable practices. Speenhamland system of poor relief introduced.

Published: Maria Edgeworth, *Letters for Literary Ladies*; H. More, *Cheap Repository Tracts*; T. Paine, *The Age of Reason*, Part 2; Robert Southey, *Poems*; W. Blake, *The Book of Los, The Book of Ahania*; C. Smith, *Montalbert*.

1796 Threat of French invasion; French occupy Northern Italy.

Published: Mary Hays, *Memoirs of Emma Courtney*, F. Burney, *Camilla*; Samuel Taylor Coleridge, *Poems on Various Subjects*, Robert Southey, *Joan of Arc*; M.G. Lewis, *The Monk*; Robert Bage, *Hermsprong, or Man as He Is Not*; Elizabeth Inchbald, *Nature and Art*; Jane West, *A Gossip's Story*.

1797 Peace between France and Austria..

Published: A. Radcliffe, *The Italian*; W. Wordsworth, *The Borderers*, M. Robinson, *Walsingham*; R. Southey, *Poems*; Harriet and Sophia Lee, *The Canterbury Tales*; Thomas Spence, *The Rights of Infants*.

1

'A genius will educate itself': Mary Wollstonecraft as Autodidact

By *self-taught* we only mean that they have not gone through the formal discipline of Academies and Universities. They have been educated, not by *teachers*, but by circumstances, not in particular schools but in the great school of the world. And this kind of education, if one were sure of its being properly applied, is of all the best and most effectual.

(Thomas Christie, *Miscellanies: Literary, Philosophical and Moral*, 1788)

Mary Wollstonecraft was born in Primrose Street, London, on 27 April 1759, the second child and eldest daughter of Edward and Elizabeth Wollstonecraft. Her mother's maiden name was Dickson; she was an Irish Protestant from Ballyshannon. If Mary's secondary status in the eyes of her parents through her sex and age was calculated to sting Wollstonecraft into proving herself, then her loss of economic and class status as a young woman would be another spur. Her grandfather had been a wealthy silk merchant in Spitalfields who had left £10,000 to his son, but Mary's father tried to distance himself from trade and set up as a gentleman farmer first in Essex, and then near Beverley in Yorkshire, quickly ruining himself and the whole family through extravagance and incompetence.

Childhood memories

Both Wollstonecraft and her husband William Godwin were fascinated with childhood and the way early experiences formed the character of an individual. Godwin tells us he 'felt a curiosity to be acquainted with the scenes through which [his friends] had passed, and the incidents

1

which had contributed to form their understandings and character. Impelled by this sentiment, he repeatedly led the conversation of Mary to topics of this sort; and, once or twice, he made notes in her presence ...'.[1] A pioneer of the burgeoning genre of biography, after his wife's death, Godwin wrote *Memoirs of the Author of the Vindication of the Rights of Woman*: the source of most of our information on Woll-stonecraft's early life. The Abinger archive also contains some notes he made on his own early life, his upbringing as son of a High Calvinist minister. He remembered being reproved for the sin of picking up the cat on a Sunday and haunted by fear of the Devil. Introspection and the Protestant tradition of spiritual autobiography were obviously mutating into a secularized but still moralized life-writing, at this time, and this is evident in Wollstonecraft's fiction too, for she had used her own name or variations of it for the heroines in both her novels, her children's stories, and even her translated books for children. This implied to readers that the texts drew on the author's experience. Mary Wollstonecraft's family had been feckless not religious, but she, too, had suffered a lack of parental love:

> She experienced in the first period of her existence, but few of those indulgences and marks of affection, which are principally calculated to sooth the subjection and sorrows of our early years. She was not the favourite either of her father or mother. Her father was a man of quick impetuous disposition, subject to alternate fits of kindness and cruelty. In his family he was a despot, and his wife appears to have been the first, and most submissive of his subjects.
>
> (*MAVRW*, p. 45)

The need for and loss of maternal love would become a recurring theme of Wollstonecraft's fiction. Her elaboration of the mother's ideal role in socializing the next generation of women would inspire her educational works. Godwin cites incidents from Maria's life story (written for her baby daughter) in chapter seven of Wollstonecraft's unfinished novel, *The Wrongs of Woman or Maria* as autobiographical. These tell of Maria's mother's 'extravagant partiality' for her eldest son, the 'deputy-tyrant of the house', to the detriment of all the rest of the children, and her extreme strictness over her eldest daughter:

> continual restraint in the most trivial matters; unconditional sub-mission to orders, which, as a mere child, I soon discovered to be unreasonable, because inconsistent and contradictory. ... Such indeed

is the force of prejudice, that what was called spirit and wit in [my elder brother], was cruelly repressed as forwardness in me.[2]

In *Mary: A Fiction* the daughter's unsatisfied desire for the mother's love produced 'a kind of habitual melancholy' (*WMW*, 1: 11). For the rest of her life, Wollstonecraft was subject to depression.

Godwin commented that where 'the reproof or chastisement of her mother' was the only thing capable of curbing Mary's own strong passions, 'the blows of her father...instead of humbling her, roused her indignation:

> The quickness of her father's temper, led him sometimes to threaten similar violence towards his wife. When that was the case, Mary would often throw herself between the despot and his victim, with the purpose to receive upon her own person the blows that might be directed against her mother. She has even laid whole nights upon the landing-place near their chamber-door, when, mistakenly, or with reason, she apprehended that her father might break out into paroxysms of violence.
>
> (*MAVRW*, p. 46)

The publisher of the *Memoirs*, Joseph Johnson, was understandably nervous about the unprecedented frankness of the first version of this account. He altered the word 'blows' to 'severities' on p. 9 of the MS to try and mitigate the effect of the portrait of Edward Wollstonecraft as a wife-beater, for the latter was still alive when the *Memoirs* were published, as were Mary's siblings. Though Godwin resisted this change, arguing that 'severities' could be interpreted as a whipping which presumably might be thought a more calculated act than the blows of temper, he had to submit to Johnson's alteration of the phrase 'blows directed against her mother' to 'blows that might be directed against her mother'. Godwin complained that the reader might now think the idea was merely in Mary's mind '& not as a thing actually existing'.[3] The published version therefore refrained from categorically stating that Edward habitually hit his wife. Wollstonecraft had herself avoided depicting actual blows in *Mary: A Fiction*: the heroine's father 'was very tyrannical and passionate; indeed so very easily irritated when inebriated, that Mary was continually in dread lest he should frighten her mother to death....She was violent in her temper; but she saw her father's faults, and would weep when obliged to compare his temper with her own' (*WMW*, 1: 10–11). Both Wollstonecraft and Godwin use their portraits of her family to demonstrate that both parents connived in reproducing the unequal valuing of male and female children, and that their gendered expectations of the temperaments of each sex were calculated to encourage male 'despotism' and female supine passivity, the breeding-ground of domestic violence. Both had good reason from their own upbringings to attack the family as a tyrannical and patriarchal institution in their political writings and to dispense with sentimentalising childhood.

Beverley

Wollstonecraft's memory of her Yorkshire girlhood as the time when she learned to love nature inspired her heroine Maria's reminiscence of:

> the healthy breeze of a neighbouring heath, on which we bounded at pleasure....And to enjoy open air and freedom, was paradise, after the unnatural restraint of our fire-side, where we were often obliged to sit three or four hours together, without daring to utter a word, when my father was out of humour from want of employment, or of a variety of boisterous amusement.
>
> (*Wrongs of Woman, WMW*, 1: 124–5)

Up until the age of fifteen when the family left Beverley, Mary occasionally attended the day schools of the town, but Godwin speaks dismissively of the education which they provided as having had no part in shaping her later eminence. Contemporary advertisements for girls' schools make it clear that embroidery and needlework were considered the most essential skills for a middle class girl, who only received a basic elementary-school grounding in literacy, Bible studies and household accounts: insufficient for business or enterprise but thought adequate to prepare her for household duties and motherhood. French and drawing were extra 'accomplishments' for wealthier pupils. When she later thought of opening a school, Wollstonecraft was haunted by the inadequacy of her own education: 'As to a school my want of knowledge with respect to the French language would be an impediment' (*CLMW*, p. 108); and when she became a governess she knew her lack of embroidery skills and 'fancy works' might be frowned upon (*CLMW*, p. 120). She panicked that her pupils already 'understand several languages, and have read *cart*-loads of history' (*CLMW*, p. 126).

The female autodidact

Disinherited both economically and emotionally, Wollstonecraft had to make her own way in the world and education was essential for this. Since the Reformation the spread of print culture had taken control of the written word away from priests and into the public domain of capitalism. While university degrees and offices under the crown could still only be conferred on male members of the national church, thus controlling entry into the professions, others such as Dissenters, the lower-classes and women had to educate themselves. Dissenters and women did set up their own seminaries. But many, like Wollstonecraft, became autodidacts, who learned through reading and by participating in the 'public sphere' created by the Enlightenment, which, though mainly bourgeois, had many different overlapping circles of participants. In the metropolis and provinces alike, informal and formal discussion groups, public lectures and clubs proliferated, circulating libraries made books affordable and coffee shops offered the latest periodicals and newspapers. Women were accepted into many such eighteenth-century cultural arenas, for the necessary improvement of female education was a commonplace of the *philosophes* in England, Scotland and France.

The contrast between the education of Godwin as a Dissenter and Wollstonecraft as a female, is striking. Though his Fenland family was 'poor' in middle-class terms, Godwin knew from a young age that because he showed extraordinary intellectual promise he was to follow his father and grandfather into the ministry. The Dissenting community and its wealthier members would sponsor such a boy if his family could not. At the age of eight Godwin was sent to a day school and then at eleven as a special privilege he was sent to Norwich to live for three years as sole pupil to the strict Sandemanian pastor, the Revd Samuel Newton, to prepare him for further studies. In 1773 Godwin was awarded a bursary of £18 to study at the Hoxton Dissenting Academy, the nonconformist equivalent of a university. The hours of study and standards expected in the examinations system in the more progressive Academies were far more rigorous than at Oxbridge. In the top liberal academies of Warrington, Manchester College and Hackney New College (associated with Rational Dissent) the syllabus was broad and modern. Science was taught by luminaries such as Joseph Priestley in Warrington, and modern teaching methods stressed the practical application of ideas as well as abstract theory. The only slightly less stellar Hoxton was Congregationalist and its Divinity students underwent a thorough training in the classics, theology, philosophy and Hebrew. But because

Hoxton was forward-looking theologically, its syllabus was progressive enough to also include science and a range of modern languages.[4] It provided lay education for fee-paying students not intending to become ministers to help subsidize free education for divinity students like Godwin. These Dissenting academies educated some of the top minds of the age. Godwin left aged twenty-two after a long apprenticeship in writing essays, sermons and translations; defending his views in argument and expressing himself through preaching.

Girls, however, were traditionally educated at home, and if the indolent mothers of Wollstonecraft's *Mary* and *Wrongs of Woman* are any guide, then Elizabeth Wollstonecraft did not provide much intellectual stimulation while 'Her father always exclaimed against female acquirements' (*Mary: A Fiction, WMW*, 1: 10). The protagonist of *Mary* is taught to read by the housekeeper, and neglect provides a blessing in disguise as she acquires the autodidact's independence of mind, so prized by Jean-Jacques Rousseau:

> As she had learned to read, she perused with avidity every book that came into her way. Neglected in every respect, and left to the operations of her own mind, she considered every thing that came under her inspection, and learned to think.
>
> (*Mary: a Fiction, WMW*, 1: 10)

Bright girls like Wollstonecraft who had to educate themselves often found male mentors. At Beverley, she attended the public science lectures of John Arden, and formed an intense friendship with his daughter Jane. Whilst the Arden family stayed at Beverley Mary was taught by Jane's father the use of the globes and to argue philosophical problems alongside her friend. Wollstonecraft's earliest extant letters were written to Jane Arden, who informed Godwin after Mary's death that she had 'carefully preserved [them] as valuable marks of her friendship at that time' and that he could publish them, 'as I think it a pity that any of the writings of such a genius should be buried in oblivion'.[5] Wollstonecraft too remembered their friendship fondly: '[W]e used to laugh from noon 'till night' (*CLMW*, p. 77). Wollstonecraft was high-spirited. Indeed, the teenage Mary in *Original Stories* who 'had a turn for ridicule' was probably a self-portrait (*WMW*, 4: 361).

The first extant letter written by the fourteen year-old Mary to Jane is woven around several pieces of verse in heroic couplets. The second line of the first gobbet is from Dryden's *Aeneïs*, Book 1, 949; the second piece is a couplet from Pope's *Essay on Criticism* (ll. 362–3); the third chunk also has as its third line a quotation from the *Essay on Criticism* (l. 526), sandwiched between William King's lines from *The Art of Love: In Imitation of Ovid De Arte Amandi* (1709), pt. 8, ll.1; 12; the next passage begins with a couplet from Ovid's *Metamorphoses*, (7.29–30; tr. Nahum Tate), continuing with three couplets from Dryden's *Oedipus: A Tragedy*, III.i.678–83.[6] This precocious teenager was obviously steeping herself in Pope, Dryden and translations of the classics, and she and her friend were enjoying quoting their favourite authors to each other and trying to emulate them.

Mary reminds her friend to translate a French song she wants and promises to show her some 'aenigmas' of her own composition about Beverley and on a friend. The letter also includes the copy of a comic song 'Sweet Beverley', obviously full of local references to known individuals, and mentioning 'Thursday's club' as much superior to fashionable meeting-places elsewhere, and celebrating the 'Driffield bards' as choice entertainment. This was a local circle of poets centred on William Mason, a clergyman poet/playwright and biographer of Gray. Mason was an early enthusiast for his clerical friend William Gilpin's tours of the British countryside in search of the picturesque, the manuscript of which he had (unsuccessfully) urged him to publish as early as 1771.[7] A subsequent letter thanks Jane for sending her an acquaintance's verses on the death of Hugh Bethell the High Sheriff of Yorkshire; and returns the favour by enclosing the local clergyman's riposte to 'Sweet Beverley'; while her next includes a Mr Rudd's verses on 'the Beverley Beauties'.

This correspondence suggests that the girls belonged to a typical provincial literary circle, in which light-hearted occasional and extempore poetry-writing was performed and circulated. Wollstonecraft's liking for such Popeian battles of wit would be lasting: sharpening her caustic barbs against conventional femininity in her future writing, to the extent that she has even been accused of misogyny by a modern feminist.[8] Such local literary groups were particularly valuable to young women, not only in encouraging their cultural education but also in giving them the confidence to write for an audience in a permitted domestic setting. Many women of the period who became published poets began writing in provincial clubs: for example, Anna Seward in Lichfield, Elizabeth Hands of Coventry and Amelia Opie of Norwich.

Young ladies who could not afford to buy books not only copied out the amateur versifying for each other, as in this letter, but also made collections of handwritten extracts from books they borrowed for their commonplace books. Mary thanks Jane's father for 'the Essay on friendship...I have copied it for it is beautiful' (*CLMW*, p. 62). Friendship through shared intellectual interests had already become the light in her life. Writing letters to her friend was a literary as well as an emotional outlet, and the young Wollstonecraft was aware of her deficiency in the art:

> I have just glanced over this letter and find it so ill written that I fear you cannot make out one line of this last page, but you know, my dear, I have not the advantage of a master as you have, and it is with great difficulty to get my brother to mend my pens
>
> (*CLMW*, pp. 54–5).

Women were sanctioned to write privately in diaries and letters – and satirized for their prolixity. From her earliest epistles to her intimate friend Jane as for the rest of her life, Wollstonecraft wrote in the 'feminine' style – which had been borrowed by sentimentalist epistolary novelists such as Richardson and Rousseau – informally, frankly and with a tendency to analyse her own emotions.

Hoxton

Though Wollstonecraft was baptized and brought up an Anglican, this may have been the result of her father's misguided attempt at gentrification, for the silk merchants of Spitalfields were of the wealthy entrepreneurial class dominated by nonconformism. Whatever the case, when the family returned to London in 1775 it was to the Northern suburbs of London where nonconformists' strongholds clustered around certain meeting houses. They settled in Hoxton with its Dissenting Academy, coincidentally where Wollstonecraft's future husband, William Godwin, was at that very time being educated. Here the 'wild, but animated and aspiring' sixteen year-old Mary found new mentors in the next-door neighbours, the Revd Clare and his wife. Revd Clare was a diminutive reclusive clergyman, lame like Pope, and who also loved poetry and was a 'humourist of a very singular cast' (*MAVRW*, p. 49). Wollstonecraft wrote to Jane that 'They took some pains to cultivate my understanding (which had been too much neglected) they not only recommended proper books to me, but made me read to them' (*CLMW*, p. 66).

Fanny Blood

Through Mrs Clare she was introduced to a young woman two years her senior, Frances Blood, who was to become the emotional centre of

Wollstonecraft's life for the next ten years. She passionately described her to Jane Arden as 'a friend whom I love better than all the world beside, a friend to whom I am bound by every tie of gratitude and inclination: to live with this friend is the height of my ambition' (*CLMW*, p. 67). Fanny was an artist who illustrated botanical publications. She became a role-model for the younger girl, for 'she sung and played with taste', 'read and wrote with considerable application' and 'drew with exquisite fidelity and neatness; and, by the employment of this talent, for some time maintained her father, mother, and family' (*MAVRW*, p. 50). Fanny Blood's family was even poorer than Mary's; of Irish extraction, and also drained by a ne'er-do-well father. Like Mary, the elder sister was expected to care for and educate her siblings. Fanny was also a consumptive, whose delicate health called forth all her new friend's protectiveness.

The two friends were much separated as the Bloods lived far off in South London, and then in 1776 the Wollstonecrafts moved away completely – to Laugharne in West Wales, probably to escape their creditors. All the intensity of Wollstonecraft's emotions were doubtless poured out into what Godwin dryly called 'an assiduous correspondence'. But Fanny had what Wollstonecraft termed 'a masculine understanding' (*CLMW*, p. 67), and:

> Mary found Fanny's letters better spelt and better indited than her own, and felt herself abashed. She had hitherto paid but superficial attention to literature. She had read, to gratify the ardour of an inextinguishable thirst of knowledge; but she had not thought of writing as an art. Her ambition to excel was now awakened, and she applied herself with passion and earnestness. Fanny undertook to be her instructor; and, so far as related to accuracy and method, her lessons were given with considerable skill.
>
> (*MAVRW*, p. 51)

The ability of Fanny to earn her living inspired Wollstonecraft to think of leaving her unhappy family and obtaining employment. Indeed, she once found herself a situation and was preparing to move out when her mother begged her with tears and entreaties to stay. So, to keep her looking after her siblings, when the family returned to London in 1777 they chose lodgings at Walworth so she could easily visit Fanny and allowed her a room 'exclusively her own' and 'the other requisites of study' (*MAVRW*, p. 52). They lodged with an unusual young couple: Thomas Taylor 'the Platonist' and his wife. Mary became friends with them and began to read Plato, which influenced her ardent religiosity. Taylor was in the process of establishing himself as a translator of and commentator on Plato and the Neoplatonists, and he championed Greek philosophy as superior to modern thinking. He moved in radical circles and was a friend of William Blake. In later years he would satirize Wollstonecraft's *Rights of Woman* by bringing out *A Vindication of the Rights of Brutes* (1792) in the form of a *reductio ad absurdum*, though paradoxically 'he almost certainly believed the Pythagorean arguments he used for abstaining from animal food'.[9]

Bath

By the time she was twenty Wollstonecraft, though nicknamed 'the Princess' by friends for her sometimes haughty manner, had to take the demeaning position of paid companion to a rich lady in Bath, for as she explained to her childhood friend, Jane Arden, 'my father's affairs were so embarrassed by his misconduct that he was obliged to take the fortune that was settled on us children; I very readily gave up my part; I have therefore nothing to expect, and what is worse depend on a stranger' (*CLMW*, p. 66). Her employer was a widow in Bath, whom Godwin wryly described as having 'great peculiarity of temper'. Mrs Dawson 'had had a variety of companions in succession, and...no one had found it practicable to continue with her' (*MAVRW*, p. 52). But Mary Wollstonecraft had a self-assertiveness at least equal to that of Mrs Dawson and established the relationship on her own terms. Nevertheless, we have some insight into the humiliating nature of the job from her chapter on the 'Unfortunate Situation of Females, fashionably Educated, and Left Without a Fortune' in *Thoughts on the Education of Daughters* (1787). She wrote to a friend about this passage: 'I felt what I wrote!' (*CLMW*, p. 161):

> Few are the modes of earning a subsistence, and those very humiliating. Perhaps to be an humble companion to some rich old cousin, or what is still worse, to live with strangers, who are so intolerably tyrannical, that none of their own relations can bear to live with them, though they should even expect a fortune in reversion. It is impossible to enumerate the many hours of anguish such a person must spend. Above the servants, yet considered by them as a spy, and ever reminded of her inferiority when in conversation with the superiors. If she cannot condescend to mean flattery, she has not a chance of being a favorite; and should any of the visitors take notice of her, and

she for a moment forget her subordinate state, she is sure to be reminded of it.

(*WMW*, 4: 25)

She amassed material for future writing in caustically observing the follies of fashionable society, while distancing herself from it by proudly embracing an exaggerated Puritanism: 'I am going to sup *solus* on a bunch of grapes, and a bread crust; – I'll drink your health in pure water' she declaimed dramatically to her friend (*CLMW*, p. 75). The heroine in *Mary: A Fiction* practises a nun-like asceticism akin to anorexia:

> In order to be enabled to gratify herself in the highest degree, she practised the most rigid oeconomy, and had such power over her appetites and whims, that without any great effort she conquered them so entirely, that when her understanding or affections had an object, she almost forgot she had a body which required nourishment.
>
> (*WMW*, 1: 17)

Wollstonecraft only gave up the post in 1781 when summoned home to nurse her dying mother in Enfield, where her parents had moved. The family then broke apart, as, within months of Elizabeth's death, her husband married the housekeeper and returned to Laugharne. At last Wollstonecraft could achieve her dream of living with her beloved Fanny. She moved in with the impoverished Blood family and threw her all energies into supporting them as well as her own younger sisters who were living temporarily with their elder brother and who faced an uncertain future.

Leading the sisterhood

Godwin summed up Mary's innate qualities as 'exquisite sensibility, soundness of understanding, and decision of character' (*MAVRW*, p. 45). She had a very strong will and 'to her lofty spirit, scarcely anything she desired appeared hard to perform' (*MAVRW*, p. 58). She was dogged throughout her life by a tendency towards melancholy and nervous illness, but in company she was often high-spirited and vivacious. Her failure to earn her mother's love may have given her a lasting insecurity for she could be too demanding in relationships. Their parents' marriage seems to have put all the Wollstonecraft sisters off matrimony, for Everina chose to remain a spinster; and Mary did not succumb until, at the age of nearly 38, she discovered she was pregnant by Godwin. The prettiest sister, Eliza, did marry in 1782 but the relationship proved unhappy, and after a difficult childbirth, she suffered a severe post-natal breakdown with 'raving fits'. Wollstonecraft was galvanized into action, first in nursing her and then in organizing the secret flight of her sister from her husband. Eliza's baby, Mary, who was left behind, subsequently died. This traumatic experience would be combined with other real-life stories of women and fictionalized as Maria's flight from her husband and separation from her baby in Wollstonecraft's unfinished novel, *The Wrongs of Woman or Maria*.

Wollstonecraft now set about idealistically planning an all-female community of herself, Fanny and Eliza, living together on money earned solely through Fanny's painting and their needlework. Fanny was rather more realistic, writing to the youngest Wollstonecraft sister, Everina: 'The very utmost I can earn, one week with another, supposing I had uninterrupted health, is half a guinea a week, which would not pay for furnished lodgings for three persons to pig together.' She knew the Wollstonecraft girls thought themselves above the piece-work that would be all they could expect. She explained that her own mother 'used to sit at work from *four* in the morning 'till she could not see at night' to earn a pittance; and 'Mary's *sight* and health are so bad that I'm sure she never could endure such drudgery'.[10]

Newington Green

Wollstonecraft hardly considered Fanny's modest suggestion of borrowing from Mary's hated elder brother Ned to set up a haberdashery shop. She entertained grander notions and had the drive to carry them out. For by now Mary was the dominant of the two bosom friends by virtue of her greater assertiveness and intelligence. Wollstonecraft, Fanny and her two sisters set up a school in the Northern suburbs of London early in 1784. The options of middle-class women were limited and Wollstonecraft and her sisters would try most of them in time, but, if they were to be teachers, then running their own establishment would at least give them some autonomy. However, after the event she would comment caustically, 'A teacher at a school is only a kind of upper servant, who has more work than the menial ones' (*WMW*, 4: 25). Fanny's skill as an artist would be a selling-point, as was Mary's bookishness. The friends doubtless devised the curriculum and taught the older children. Wollstonecraft probably reasoned that her sisters could combine completing their own educations with supervising the younger pupils. Hannah More's sisters had set up such a school in Bristol with great success thirty years previously, and Anna Barbauld ran a school with her husband at Palgrave in Suffolk from 1774 to 1785. Perhaps Ned lent his sisters some capital, but, as he was usually distinctly unwilling to help support them, it is more likely that Wollstonecraft accepted a loan from one or other of the mentor figures to whom she attached herself in Newington Green.

Wollstonecraft was strongly religious and, according to Godwin, 'she may be said to have been, in a great degree, the victim of a desire to promote the benefit of others' (*MAVRW*, p. 55). The choice of first Islington and then Newington Green as the location of the school suggests that, although she continued to attend Anglican services, she had already come under the influence of Rational Dissent. To move in such intellectual circles, the cream of the English enlightenment, was the equivalent of a university education for this female autodidact.

As the nineteenth-century local historian William Robinson commented, ever since the seventeenth century, the hamlet of Newington Green, three miles north of London, had been known as the 'habitation of ejected and silenced ministers'.[11] In 1782 the village of Stoke Newington was recorded as having about 195 houses, of which about 40 families were Dissenters, who attended its meeting house. Nearby, Newington Green 'forms a square of respectable houses chiefly inhabited by gentlemen and merchants', having its own 'meeting house belonging formerly to the Presbyterian Dissenters, but now to the Socinian Independents' [Unitarians] (p. 11). Four houses had been built at the beginning of the eighteenth century specifically to house Palatinates, or Protestant immigrants fleeing persecution. The village had a reputation both as a nonconformist educational centre and home to progressive thinkers. Daniel Defoe had been educated there, as had the educationalist Thomas Day. Famous former residents included hymnwriter Isaac Watts and prison reformer John Howard. The late James Burgh, author of *Political Disquisitions* (1774–75), one of the most influential books for the development of political radicalism, had been master of an academy first at Stoke Newington then at Newington Green before his death in 1775. His widow Sarah now became a surrogate mother to Wollstonecraft. Thomas Rogers the banker was the treasurer of the meeting house, and his poet son Samuel, the future author of *The Pleasures of Memory*, was amongst the wealthy and cultured circle who met at fortnightly suppers. But the heart of Newington Green intellectual life was the distinguished Welsh philosopher, mathematician and political pamphleteer the Revd Richard Price who, with his invalid wife, had lived in the village since 1748 and who had been the minister until 1783. Soon

Wollstonecraft was a friend and disciple and attended his occasional sermons. She was also befriended by the Bible scholar Revd John Hewlett and his wife, and mentions in her letters acquaintances such as the naturalist and artist James Sowerby and Quaker philanthropist John Lettsome who had set up botanical gardens (*CLMW*, p. 93). Through her new circle of mentors she was even introduced to the elderly Dr Johnson who had a long conversation with her and 'desired her to repeat her visit often' (*MAVRW*, p. 60).

Religion

Godwin himself had in the intervening years gradually abandoned his High Calvinist beliefs, though in his private memoranda he recorded that he was 'not a complete unbeliever till 1787' following correspondence with Joseph Priestley.[12] Perhaps we should therefore be slightly sceptical when in the *Memoirs* he gives exactly the same year as the date from which Wollstonecraft's attendance at public worship became 'less constant and in no long time was wholly discontinued' (*MAVRW*, p. 57). The rationalist Godwin firmly repudiates any thought that Wollstonecraft had any 'superstitious adherence' (i.e. belief in the divinity of Christ) to Dr Price's doctrines of Rational Dissent, any more than she believed in Calvinist predestination or hellfire.

Godwin describes Wollstonecraft's religion as 'almost entirely of her own creation', and allied to her spritualized love of nature: 'When she walked amidst the wonders of nature, she was accustomed to converse with her God' (*MAVRW*, p. 56). This is supported by the descriptions of the protagonist's religiosity in the presence of the sublime in *Mary: A Fiction* (*WMW*, 1, 11; 16–17; 26, 29, 57, 63, 70). It indicates that Wollstonecraft was an advocate of natural rather than revealed theology, like those latitudinarian clerics within the Established Church who believed that 'the essentials of Christian revelation could be confirmed by the study of nature which made manifest the mind of its Creator'.[13] She had been influenced by their Christian Platonism. Latitudinarian Anglican theologians at Cambridge, such as Richard Watson and William Paley, also called for greater ecclesiastical and civil liberty. Paley's utilitarian *Principles of Moral and Political Philosophy* (1785) was recommended by Wollstonecraft to her sisters in 1787. But one of this group, Theophilus Lindsey, left the Church to found the first Unitarian chapel in Essex Street, North London, later to be joined by another cleric, John Disney, and subsequently about eight more. Such ex-Anglican Unitarians were close in their views to Rational Dissenters such as Joseph Priestley and associated with them whilst remaining a distinct group.[14] They were attacked by both High Church critics and the Low Church Evangelicals within the Church of England, because, like the Rational Dissenters, they were seeking to accommodate Enlightenment thought with Christian theology. The development of Wollstonecraft's feminism in the 1790s was not secular in origin: it stemmed not from her emancipation *from* religion but directly from this attempted philosophical integration.[15] Though she never formally embraced Unitarianism, it was Rational Dissent which had a particularly strong influence on the development of first her educational and then her political thinking. What was more, as an autodidact Wollstonecraft empathised with the Dissenters' ethos of self-help and improvement through print culture: their immersion in the republic of letters to which anyone literate could belong.

Rational dissent

Dr Price's theology had particular appeal for an autodidact as it stressed that the individual should by the rigorous exercise of his reason determine for himself what was moral law and thus practise virtue.[16] He gave back a sense of autonomy to humanity by rejecting Calvinism's insistence on the arbitrary will of an all-powerful God. Price rejected the doctrines of original sin and the predestination of the redemption of the elect, and even the key Protestant doctrine that man is justified by faith alone. He argued that the existence of virtue presupposes and necessitates complete liberty of conscience – including the freedom to choose evil. The 'superstitious doctrines' to which the now-atheist Godwin referred were probably his Arianism, for unlike the Socinians (Unitarians) Price did believe Jesus was more than human, though not to be prayed to as a God, as did the orthodox Trinitarians. Nevertheless, Price certainly relegated the importance of the traditional Christian theology of revelation, grace and the interposition of the saviour in favour of man's individual agency. A rationalist but also a Platonist, he argued not only with orthodox theologians but against empiricist Enlightenment philosophers Francis Hutcheson and David Hume who lessened human agency by positing the influence of the environment in shaping the understanding through its evocation of various contingent sensations and feelings within the mind. For Price every individual has a right to use his reason to ascertain where his duty lies; to subject laws and precepts to sceptical criticism; and he is right to follow his conscience if sincerely convinced, even if later proved incorrect.

The Honest Whigs

It is obvious that such doctrines have major political implications. Price's concept of liberty of conscience included the right to resist abuses of power, and he advocated religious toleration for all creeds and the dissociation of State and Church. Most importantly, he believed that as a servant of God, man must not only work his personal salvation but must also take responsibility for the condition of the society in which he lives. The exercise of virtue thus has a civic and even political dimension. Price therefore saw it as his duty as a minister to expound his political views from the pulpit. He was a member of the club of 'Honest Whigs', a group dominated by Nonconformist ministers many of whom were also fellows of the Royal Society, and which included Thomas Avery who had been preacher at Newington Green, James Burgh, Benjamin Franklin, Andrew Kippis, Sir William Jones, Theophilus Lindsey, and Joseph Priestley. The 'Glorious Revolution' of 1688 was unfinished business for this club, who campaigned for equal civil rights for Dissenters and the extension of political rights in order to enable individuals to work for more effective improvement of society. James Burgh's *Political Disquisitions*, 3 vols (1774–75) was 'one of the most influential documents in the history of radicalism and the development of representative government'.[17] A statistical analysis of the political system, it convincingly argued the need for a more extensive suffrage, abolition of rotten boroughs, a redistribution of seats in metropolitan and commercial districts and shorter parliaments. Burgh's call was supported by Price. Both were statisticians, and Price was an expert on insurance and finance. Price even pioneered a projected system of social insurance and state aid for the relief of poverty.

An important member of the 'Honest Whigs' was a woman: the celebrated Whig historian Catharine Macaulay. Macaulay's *History of England from the Accession of James I to that of the Brunswicks*, 8 vols (1763–83), underpinned by unprecedented use of contemporary documents, took a republican point of view of the English revolution, in opposition to Hume's Tory *History of England*. This helped the case that reform was needed if the true spirit of the 1688 constitutional settlement was to be implemented.

Few of the Honest Whigs went as far as Major John Cartwright, founder of the Society for Constitutional Information, in endorsing universal male suffrage. It goes without saying that political rights for women were not thought of. Nevertheless, the intellectuals of Rational Dissent inherited a long tradition of promulgating female education.

Women such as Catherine Macaulay and Anna Barbauld were not merely tolerated, they were respected as equals in discussion. The Rational Dissenters' linking of the mental development of the ability to reason with the capacity to make moral choices enhanced the intellectual aspect of the pseudo-maternal role of teacher, and thus increased the status of women. This would provide an entry into the public sphere and even into the world of print culture for Wollstonecraft.

Teaching

Though he gave a rosy picture of her 'more than maternal qualities', Godwin admitted that Wollstonecraft could be 'severe and imperious' and 'express her censure in terms that gave a very humiliating sensation to the person against whom it was directed'. But he maintains that she only showed these defects of character to her equals and never to children or servants. She was 'little troubled with scepticism and uncertainty' and easily inspired the confidence and respect of her pupils (*MAVRW*, pp. 59–60). Wollstonecraft had certainly had practical experience in helping to bring up her younger siblings; she was genuinely interested in educational theories and manifested the dynamism to launch the school successfully and to keep it afloat for two and a half years. Though she was still remedying the defects of her own education at twenty-five, she managed to attract pupils from wealthy Dissenting families such as the Disneys.

Portugal

In January 1785 Fanny left the school to marry the Irish businessman Hugh Skeys and settle with him in Lisbon. The match had been delayed for some time but Fanny's health had not improved. She was soon pregnant and by the Autumn, despite her sisters' protests, Wollstonecraft borrowed some money and set off for Portugal to attend her beloved friend in childbirth. She was not a moment too soon. Fanny was in labour and gave birth to a baby boy. But as Mary had feared, Fanny was herself already dying and lingered only a few days more. The death of her friend was the greatest tragedy of Wollstonecraft's troubled early life. Even as late as 1796 she was still mourning, writing in *Letters From Norway*: 'The grave has closed over a dear friend, the friend of my youth; still she is present with me, and I hear her soft voice warbling as I stray over the heath' (*MAVRW*, p. 61).

Independence

When she returned, the school had foundered in her absence and she was too plunged into grief to rescue it. By the following Summer it collapsed and she was up to her ears in debt. In August 1786 she would take up the temporary expedient of a post as governess to the children of Viscount and Lady Kingsborough in Mitchelstown, County Cork. But Godwin tells us that Wollstonecraft already had her sights fixed on a literary career:

> Independence was the object after which she thirsted, and she was fixed to try whether it might not be found in literary occupation. She was desirous however first to accumulate a small sum of money, which should enable her to consider at leisure the different literary engagements that might offer, and provide in some degree for the eventual deficiency of her earliest attempts.
>
> (*MAVRW*, p. 64)

From the middle of the century writing had become an increasingly respectable profession for women, for they made sure they were no longer associated with the risqué plays and romances of pioneers such as Aphra Behn by taking the lead in establishing newly-moralizing fiction and improving educational works. Wollstonecraft was one among many, for the mid-1780s saw a surge both in the number of female authors and in their rate of production far in excess even of that of the 1720s, when Eliza Haywood was at her most prolific.[18]

Thoughts on the Education of Daughters: with Reflections on Female Conduct, in the More Important Duties of Life

In fact Wollstonecraft had already taken up the pen. By 1 May 1786 she had obtained ten guineas for a conduct book, *Thoughts on the Education of Daughters*, which was published the following January or February. This was generous payment for a first (and slim) volume by an unknown author. Though declaring 'My debts too haunt me like furies' (*CLMW*, p. 105) Wollstonecraft gave the money to Fanny's impoverished parents to fund their passage to Dublin. The Revd Hewlett had helped her by negotiating with his own publisher, Joseph Johnson, on her behalf. 'You never saw a creature happier than he was when he returned to tell me the success of his commission – the sensibility and goodness that appeared in his countenance made me love the man' she recalled to

Fanny's brother George (*CLMW*, p. 105). She tried to return the favour by writing to Johnson on 5 December 1786 for 'a dozen of Mr Hewlett's spelling-books [and] His sermons ... and a few copies of my little book if it is published' to distribute among her aristocratic employers and their friends (*CLMW*, p. 130). Though a second edition was not called for, *Thoughts* was sufficiently successful to be excerpted in three parts in the *Lady's Magazine* (*MWRL*, p. 77).

Conduct and advice books as a genre had been adapted by Protestant culture from renaissance guides to courtly behaviour and etiquette. They now served the needs of the aspiring bourgeois individual. Schoolteachers often distilled their expertise. For example, Newington Green's James Burgh in his *Youth's Friendly Monitor, or the Affectionate School-master* (1754) condensed the advice on the dangers of vice and dissolution he gave to his upwardly mobile pupils when they left him to embark upon careers in business. In his *Thoughts on Education, Tending Chiefly to Recommend to the Attention of the Public, Some Particulars Relating to that Subject; Which Are Not Generally Considered with the Regard Their Importance Deserves* (1747) Burgh had addressed parents, advising them on the sort of syllabus and educational method they should provide for their offspring's rational Christian upbringing. His syllabus is designed to be useful to those in commercial life, so it emphasizes English language and literature, orthography, grammar and punctuation rather than traditional knowledge of the classics (Greek may be necessary for reading the scriptures in the original but heathen poetry must be avoided). Mathematics, accounts, geography and astronomy are particularly important. Burgh follows Locke's *Some Thoughts Concerning Education* (1693) in stressing that the child must be guided through conversation to test out intellectual precepts for himself. But Burgh's greater stress on moral choices and active Christian virtue in civic life leads him even further away from conventional conduct book conformism, when he asserts that the young should be encouraged to 'question common opinions' even including the social structure of society itself:

> That we see the most laborious, industrious, and useful part of mankind generally treated with neglect and contempt, and at the same time the idle, the inactive and most useless part of the species, I mean the rich, who feed and riot, and fatten on the labours of their fellow-creatures, adored as gods upon earth. That we see mankind admire learning, wit and courage in men, and outside beauty in the other sex, and all the while neglect the less ostentatious, but infinitely

more valuable virtues of humility, meekness, prudence, benevolence, patience and mortification.[19]

Burgh also questions the conventional dismissal of the female intellect. He describes the usual 'accomplishments' taught to girls as:

> [T]rifling and contemptible in themselves, serving only as ornaments or trappings, which may a little (and but a little) set off the less conspicuous but infinitely more valuable beauties of the mind . . . it is of great consequence to the youth of both sexes that they be early led into a just and rational way of thinking of things.
>
> (pp. 53–4)

Wollstonecraft's book takes up this latter point and develops it further. The title indicates this by reflecting that of Burgh, also published by Johnson. Wollstonecraft also acknowledges the influence of both Locke's ideas and Rousseau's *Emilius and Sophia* of 1762 (*WMW*, 4: 11). She expresses the autodidact's overestimation of education as the supreme power for change, having taken on board the exciting Lockean notion of the child's mind as a *tabula rasa* and Rousseau's view of the learning process as both cultivation and preservation of 'that beautiful simplicity' of innate 'principles of truth' (*WMW*, 4: 9) with which s/he is born. Nevertheless, Wollstonecraft declares she realizes 'perfection cannot be attained' (*WMW*, 4, 9) and 'the mind is not, cannot be created by the teacher' (*WMW*, 4, 21). Her Preface acknowledges other treatises which dealt specifically with female education. She was probably thinking of such as male-authored classics as James Fordyce, *Sermons to Young Women* (1765) and John Gregory, *A Father's Legacy to His Daughters* (1774), but also Sarah Pennington's *An Unfortunate Mother's Advice to Her Absent Daughters* (1761) and Hester Chapone's *Letters on the Improvement of the Mind* (1773). Indeed, the number of conduct books specifically written for women now 'surpassed in quantity and variety those directed at men'.[20] Despite these, she feels that 'much still remained to be said' (*WMW*, 4: 5).

Wollstonecraft struck a melancholy authorial pose, admitting her 'reflections will, by some, be thought too grave'. She envisages her implied reader as one whom 'sorrow has made heavy' (*WMW*, 4: 5). The implication is that her predecessors have not taken female education seriously enough, and that a more rigorous approach will be perhaps most likely to interest those who have suffered (like the author) from a life circumscribed by lack of opportunity. 'Reason' and 'rational' are the buzz-words throughout. But whether a more rational education will prove emancipatory for girls, or whether its moral training will merely help them repress their inevitably doomed yearnings for fulfilment is left uncertain.

Like Locke, Wollstonecraft lays much emphasis on inculcating good habits through firm discipline, though – remembering her own upbringing – she does not want the child's spirit to be broken, for 'it is only in years of childhood that the happiness of a human being depends entirely on others – and to embitter those years by needless restraint is cruel' (*WMW*, 4: 8). For the mother, too, 'maternal tenderness arises quite as much from habit as instinct' (*WMW*, 4: 7); and, like the parent of an adopted child, she need only perform the correct role of a mother 'to produce in herself a rational affection for her offspring'. A child's moral sense would be confused if she were punished for accidents or 'giddy tricks' not maliciously intended. But Wollstonecraft had not yet abandoned Anglican authoritarianism, for the child must learn 'a proper submission to superiors'. She still assumed girls should be particularly submissive, declaring: 'I am quite charmed when I see a sweet young creature, shrinking as it were from observation'(*WMW*, 4: 11). Because the girl must develop her rationality, she must always be spoken to rationally, and not allowed to romp in the kitchen, listening to servants' 'improbable tales, and superstitious accounts of invisible beings which breed strange prejudices and vain fears in their minds' (*WMW*, 4: 10).

In spite of this puritan suspicion of the fantastic, reading is given pride of place as 'the most rational employment' for it is important for 'the mind to have some resource in itself, and not to be entirely dependant on the senses for employment and amusement' (*WMW*, 4: 20). 'A relish for reading ... should be cultivated very early in life', and little stories 'which amuse and instruct' are recommended, such as Dorothy Kilner's *The Life and Perambulations of a Mouse* (1783) and Anna Barbauld's *Hymns in Prose for Children* (1781) which may 'cultivate the good dispositions of the heart' (*WMW*, 4: 10). Nevertheless, Wollstonecraft is nervous about the volatile power of literature to inflame the passions. Older girls must avoid 'productions which give a wrong account of the human passions', where 'sensibility is described and praised': novels where gallantry 'is made the only interesting subject'. The moral allegories of Dr Johnson's periodical *The Adventurer* (1752–54) are preferred, for 'Reason strikes most forcibly when illustrated by the brilliancy of fancy' (*WMW*, 4: 20). Without intellectual stimulation 'the mind is confined to the body, and must sink into sensuality' so reading is essential for the adult woman. However, in another conventional touch, she is warned,

'No employment for the mind is a sufficient excuse for neglecting domestic duties' (*WMW*, 4: 21).

The second half of the book broadens out to consider how best women may achieve 'active virtue' (*WMW*, 4: 24), and becomes much less conventional. Though women need Christian 'gentleness and humility' this should not be confused with 'indolence' or 'weakness of mind':

> She who submits, without conviction, to a parent or a husband, will as unreasonably tyrannize over her servants; for slavish fear and tyranny go together'
>
> (*WMW*, 4: 23).

Early marriages are rejected for they condemn women to a life rooted in the physical:

> If we were born only "to draw nutrition, propagate and rot", the sooner the end of creation was answered the better; but as women are here allowed to have souls, the soul ought to be attended to'
>
> (*WMW*, 4: 31).

A wife may read but she has few opportunities for active virtue in the public sphere.

> Men...are forced to see human nature as it is, and are not to dwell on the pictures of their own imaginations. Nothing, I am sure, calls forth the faculties so much as the being obliged to struggle with the world; and this is not a woman's province in a married state.
>
> (*WMW*, 4: 32).

So woman can only exercise her reason in the service of virtue by participating in the virtual world: the public sphere of print culture.

> In a comfortable situation, a cultivated mind is necessary to render a woman contented; and in a miserable one, it is her only consolation.... Of what importance, then, is intellectual improvement, when our / comfort here, and happiness hereafter, depends upon it.
>
> (*WMW*, 4: 32–3)

Here we see Wollstonecraft anticipating twentieth-century existential feminism in her awareness that a purely traditional gender role based on her reproductive capacity condemns woman to a life of immanence rooted in the physical. Only through exercising her intellect can she exist as a moral being.

Wollstonecraft's personal bitterness erupts when she considers the fate of single women 'fashionably educated and left without a fortune'. They have not even adequate modes of earning a subsistence, especially as 'the few trades which are left are now gradually falling into the hands of the men'. Teachers and governesses are treated as servants, and their meagre earnings will not provide for their old age:

> How cutting is the contempt she meets with! – A young mind looks round for love and friendship; but love and friendship fly from poverty: expect them not if you are poor!
>
> (*WMW*, 4: 26)

Her flashes of indignation however are at war with, and are eventually quelled by, her Pauline religious conviction of 'The Benefits which Arise From Disappointments', which is the title of one of her chapters. For earthly suffering will be rewarded in a future existence:

> The difference between those who sorrow without hope, and those who look up to Heaven is not that the one feels more than the other, for they may be both equally depressed; but the latter think of the peaceable fruits which are to result form the discipline, and therefore patiently submit.
>
> (*WMW*, 4: 35)

As Gary Kelly has commented, religion functions here as 'a way to heroize women's impossible social position'.[21] Thus, though 'Reason is indeed the heaven-lighted lamp in man', Wollstonecraft counsels girls against associating with 'those who have no fixed principles' in religion and warns that 'improper books' have sent young men adrift in a sea of Deist speculation. Religious scepticism would take away woman's only consolation. There is thus an awkward mismatch throughout the book between the ardent belief that cultivating the intellect will be woman's salvation (deriving from Rational Dissent) and fear that woman's special penchant for melancholy religious sensibility will die if exposed to the harsh light of reason.

Hannah More and the Bluestockings

The Anglican Hannah More had also attempted to balance the claims of reason and religion in female education ten years earlier in her *Essay on*

Various Subjects, Principally Designed for Young Ladies (1777). More resolved the question by affirming Christian egalitarianism in the equality of souls, male and female, while conceding that women were innately intellectually inferior. More validated sexual difference as part of God's hierarchical scheme: declaring the 'distinctions between the sexes cannot be too nicely maintained'. She conceded that women were inferior in science and strength of intellect.[22] However, from the suitably modest position of a footnote she reminds the reader that 'this nation can boast a female critic, poet, historian, linguist, philosopher, and moralist, equal to most of the other sex'(p. 12). For More was a leading light in the Bluestocking coterie of women intellectuals who dominated cultural life in the1770s, and this book was dedicated to its patron Elizabeth Montagu, 'Queen of the Blues'. In 1779 Richard Samuel would paint the group portrait entitled 'The Nine Living Muses of Great Britain', comprising: the artist Angelica Kauffman, the linguist Elizabeth Carter, the poet Anna Barbauld, the singer Elizabeth Sheridan, the historian Catharine Macaulay, critic Elizabeth Montagu, novelist Charlotte Lennox, and playwright and Evangelical campaigner Hannah More herself. More had risen from humble beginnings as a schoolmaster's daughter and was on the way to becoming the most best-selling woman writer of the period.

So overwhelming was women's contribution to the arts that in 1766 a biographical dictionary of distinguished women was published, and articles had appeared throughout the 1770s on the phenomenon. One even raised the question of giving learned women honorary degrees.[23] More resolves the apparent contradiction she has raised regarding her validation of the traditional belief in women's intellectual inferiority by asserting roundly that the female geniuses she cited 'only stand as exceptions against the rule, without tending to invalidate the rule itself'. She gains all the more authority therefore to relegate the rest of her sex to their rightful place.

By further conceding that it is likely that the wisest *average* woman will only reach the level of a school boy, More can safely mount her own argument for the importance of female education: 'Next to religious influences, an habit of study is the most probable preservative of the virtue of young persons' (p. 23). Because girls are not distracted with the 'masculine' subjects of science and the classics (both potentially anti-religious, as deriving from Enlightenment materialism and the pagan past) their limited education better prepares them for religious duties. However, women are needed to reform society and must not be shut away: 'They have useful stations to fill, and important characters to sustain' (p. 36). But this campaign to get women into the world is contingent on essentializing their gendered social role. Acknowledging their secondary status in turn necessitates conduct book self-repression: 'That bold, independent, enterprising spirit which is so much admired in boys, should not, when it happens to discover itself in the other sex, be encouraged, but suppressed. Girls should be taught to give up their opinions sometimes, and not pertinaciously to carry on a dispute, even if they know themselves to be in the right' (p. 145). Religion is particularly important to 'the female character' because it encourages self-abnegation. Also souls have no sex, so women's intellectual inequality and lower social status are thus represented by More almost as a tactical advantage in helping them to focus on their spiritual equality and true vocation as reformers within and without the home.

Wollstonecraft was in the process of developing views in direct opposition to these, but no less driven by religious fervour. Both women were inspired by the vision of active Christianity projected by the religious revival. But whereas More devoted her energies to shoring up and extending the influence of the Church of England, Wollstonecraft was developing her own philosophy of moral individualism in which the intellect or reason had an important part to play in developing the soul, and required independence incompatible with authoritarian religious institutions.

In her greatest work, *Rights of Woman*, Wollstonecraft would throw down the gauntlet to older women of letters such as the Anglican More and the Unitarian Anna Barbauld who smugly reinforced their own exceptionality by conceding women's innate intellectual inferiority to men. In the late 1790s, More would ride the crest of a huge tide of popularity in the reactionary backlash against democratic ideals produced by the war against France, which attempted to consign Wollstonecraft to oblivion. But, in the long term, because More had legitimized Christian women's participation in 'domestic' issues of social amelioration such as housing and education, paradoxically she prepared the ground for an eventual acceptance of women's civic and political participation later in the nineteenth century, when these became the subject of governmental policy.

Ireland

When she took up the post of governess to the children of Lord and Lady Kingsborough in Summer 1786, at forty pounds a year, Wollstonecraft was forced to return to dependency. Mary Poovey has seen both her early life and writing as driven by two conflicting desires, for familial love but also for emotional and financial independence.[24] Her post as governess was particularly frustrating in that she was in the centre of a family but marginal to it; supporting herself yet a shabby, debt-laden dependent. Nevertheless, the insights she gained into aristocratic life were to prove invaluable. Lord and Lady Kingsborough had been married in their mid-teens and were the largest landowners in Ireland. Wollstonecraft experienced aristocratic life in Mitchelstown Castle at the centre of the vast desmesne. Her employers had called in the agrarian reformer Arthur Young to help them run their estates profitably but without undue exploitation. They provided the workers with a model village complete with school and library (*MWRL*, p. 85). The family also had a town house in Dublin, where there was a round of balls, masquerades and concerts. Wollstonecraft was scornful of the affected and rouged mistress of the house who petted her dogs, while her own children were kept at a distance and were afraid of her. The governess formed a close bond with the eldest daughter, the future Lady Mountcashel, who later wrote of her childhood:

almost the only person of superior merit with whom I had been intimate in my early days was an enthusiastic female who was my governess from fourteen to fifteen years old, for whom I felt an unbounded admiration because her mind appeared more noble and understanding, more cultivated than any others I had known – from the time she left me my chief objects were to correct those faults she had pointed out and to cultivate my understanding as much as possible. [25]

Wollstonecraft's feelings of inferiority manifested themselves as jealous rivalry with the beautiful Lady Kingsborough, both over the affections of her charges and the attentions of George Ogle, a poet and MP, who was a friend of the Viscount's, and she was eventually dismissed in August 1787.

However, as Ralph Wardle comments, when she was a governess in Ireland and removed from her own family dependents, Wollstonecraft had probably found more time to read than at any other time in her life, having the resources of the castle library at her command (*CLMW*, p. 33). She had studied French hard, by reading the Countess de Genlis on education and the Baroness de Montolieu's 'prettiest' novel *Caroline de Lichtfield*; as well as indulging her taste for wit and paradox in La Rochefoucauld's *Maxims*, Louis Sebastien Mercier's comedy *Mon Bonnet de*

Nuit, and the fiction of Le Sage. She had also told her sister she was improving herself by reading 'philosophical lectures and metaphysical sermons' and found Hugh Blair's *Lectures on Rhetoric and Belles Letters* (1783) 'an intellectual feast' (*CLMW*, p. 138). She had asked Johnson to send her the melancholic poetry of Cowper and the *Elegiac Sonnets* of Charlotte Smith. Most of all, she was reading Rousseau, thinking of his *Confessions* and enthusing over *Émile* (1762) 'He chuses a common capacity to educate – and gives as a reason, that a genius will educate itself' (*CLMW*, p. 145). It is significant that she appropriated the phrase as her own in describing her next publication on 13 September 1787 when she wrote to her friend the Revd Gabell: 'Spite of my vexations, I have lately written, a fiction which I intend to give to the world; it is a tale, to illustrate an opinion of mine that a genius will educate itself. I have drawn from Nature' (*CLMW*, p. 162).

Mary: A Fiction

Godwin tells us she had written the novel in the Spring when staying with the Kingsboroughs at Bristol Hot-Wells (*MAVRW*, p. 66). By early November she had given it to Johnson (*CLMW*, p. 166) and by May 1788 it was published (*CLMW*, p. 174). Nine years later she was ashamed of it, 'I consider it as a crude production, and do not very willingly put it in the way of people whose good opinion, as a writer, I wish for' (*CLMW*, p. 385). By then Wollstonecraft was writing a second novel. Godwin, out of curiosity, read the earlier book, *Mary: A Fiction*, in August 1796. He however rated it highly:

> This little work, if Mary had never produced any thing else, would serve, with persons of true taste and sensibility, to establish the emin-ence of her genius. The story is nothing. He that looks into the book only for incident, will probably lay it down with disgust. But the feel-ings are of the truest and most exquisite class; every circumstance is adorned with that species of imagination, which enlists itself under the banners of delicacy and sentiment. A work of sentiment, as it is called, is too often another name for a work of affectation. He that should imagine that the sentiments of this book are affected, would indeed be entitled to our profoundest commiseration.
>
> (*MAVRW*, p. 66)

Slight and undeveloped though it undoubtedly is, the novel was bold and experimental. As Godwin admits, in some ways it was an anti-novel, being more concerned with ideas than plot. It refused even to call itself a novel: defining itself self-consciously as 'a fiction' suggested the narrative was not intended as light entertainment but had a serious purpose. The author satirically suggests only in a fiction could 'the mind of a woman who has thinking powers' be displayed (*WMW*, 1: 5) yet describes the tale as 'artless' or realistic. Paradoxically, though published anonymously, it wore its author's name on its sleeve, thus signalling, at least to intimates, its autobiographical elements.

The transition from conduct book to novel of education was a natural step as the genres overlapped. From the time of Eliza Haywood and Charlotte Lennox to that of Frances Burney, scores of women's novels had focused on the upbringing of a heroine, and 'a young lady's entrance into the world' when courtship gave her a brief period of autonomy before the closure of marriage. But *Mary: A Fiction* offers a new protagonist, neither the male-authored fantasy of 'a Clarissa, a Lady G-, nor a Sophie' nor even a naïve but spirited Evelina, but an alienated female intellectual portrayed as trapped by an arranged marriage and seeking fulfilment outside wedlock. 'I will work, she cried, do anything rather than be a slave' (*WMW*, 1: 55). On the very last page she is prevailed to overcome her physical disgust of her commonplace husband and live with him, sacrificing herself like Rousseau's Julie for the social good: 'She then retired to her house in the country, established manufactories, threw the estate into small farms; and continually employed herself this way to dissipate care.' Nevertheless the defiant last sentence looks forward to Mary's release by death into 'that world *where there is neither marrying*, nor giving in marriage' (*WMW*, 1: 73). This text therefore can be categorized as 'dysphoric' for the protagonist is not truly reconciled to society.[26]

Wollstonecraft sought to create a female *bildungsroman* based on the Romantic concept that the 'genius' of individuality is retained and developed through an interaction with society which is largely negative. Neglect in the family, a perfunctory education and social oppression challenge a girl to think for herself instead of conforming: '...she indulged herself in viewing new modes of life, and searching out the causes which produced them.... She had not any prejudices, for every opinion was examined before it was adopted' (*WMW*, 1, 29). Self-reliance develops both Mary's intellect and her capacity for passion to an exceptional degree:

> she entered with such spirit into whatever she read, and the emotions thereby raised were so strong, that it soon became a part of her mind.

Enthusiastic sentiments of devotion at this period actuated her; her Creator was almost apparent to her senses in his works...

(WMW, 1: 16)

Because she is insufficiently socialized she is doomed to unhappiness. Yet this very unhappiness triggers spontaneous effusions which punctuate the novel and which she is later depicted as writing down (*WMW*, 1, 51, 57, 59, 60). This indicates that Mary is a poet in the making so that the novel is also a *kunstleroman* or portrait of the female artist. In a sublime landscape of mountains Mary reads Thomson, Young and Milton (*WMW*, 1, 15). She may be a tragic isolated figure but her story and the originality of her 'fragments' of art will be instructive in pointing our society's flaws:

Poor solitary wretch that I am; here alone do I listen to the whistling winds and dashing waves; – on no human support can I rest – when not lost to hope I found pleasure in the society of these rough beings; but now they appear not like my fellow creatures; no social ties draw me to them.

(WMW, 1: 49).

Here then in embryo we have the novel of sensibility turned against marriage to hymn the alienated female artist. This formula would be perfected twenty years later in Germaine de Staël's *Corinne, ou L'Italie* (1807), that seminal text of both Romanticism and of nineteenth-century women's writing.

Though reading has been the key to the autodidact heroine's development, Wollstonecraft testifies to the dangerous power of print by exhibiting the ubiquitous eighteenth-century fear of the effects of novel-reading on the young female reader. Woman had become 'the epitome of the misguided reading public', easily swayed and liable to lose her reason to romance.[27] She attempts to distance *Mary: A Fiction* from other sentimental novels, by satirizing the heroine's mother, whose romances are merely 'substitutes for bodily dissipation'. Wollstonecraft singles out two recent publications which disguise adulterous fantasy by calling it Platonic love: *The History of Eliza Warwick* (1778) and Mrs H. Cartwright's *The Platonic Marriage* (1786). This defensive strategy strives to differentiate the Platonism of Wollstonecraft's own novel from vulgar titillation. Indeed, *Mary: A Fiction* is structured to unfavourably contrast the disgusting physicality of marriage with the purity of romantic friendship.

Barbara Taylor has pointed out in her recent monograph on the subject that we should not over-emphasize the rational in Wollstonecraft's personal religion, which was imbued with *eros*, particularly derived from Rousseau but also strongly influenced by Milton and the Cambridge Christian Platonist tradition.[28] Wollstonecraft gives a picture of this in her heroine's communion with her maker through nature, the novel's valorisation of human love as one of the channels which links mankind with the divine, and the representation of the passions in dialectic with the intellect in developing the protagonist's moral psyche. Though her first fiction, like her conduct book, still gloomily counselled stoic resignation and looking toward the afterlife as consolation for lack of fulfilment, Wollstonecraft would develop a more optimistic theodicy. From the Unitarians she would learn to view the passions as intrinsic to the divine purpose in the development of virtue.[29]

For now the originality of the novel lies in the fact that pride of place in the novel's hierarchy of values in given to female friendship. The heroine undergoes an arranged marriage but her love is reserved for Ann (a fictionalized Fanny Blood) and, after the latter's death, in a more muted way for her sensitive male friend, Henry. Prioritizing friendship and, in particular, female friendship over marriage was an unusual emphasis in novels of sensibility though it had been a theme of women's poetry from the time of Katherine Philips. The psychological complexity of the shifting balance between desire and power in Mary and Ann's relationship constitutes the novel's greatest strength. Initially the older Ann is the intellectual superior, but while Ann retains 'a delicacy truly feminine' (*WMW*, 1: 18) in her tastes, Mary gradually outstrips her by her bolder questioning of convention. '[Ann] often wondered at the books Mary chose, who, though she had a lively imagination, would frequently study authors whose works were addressed to the understanding' (*WMW*, 1: 19). While Mary's all-consuming love for her friend 'resembled a passion' (*WMW*, 1: 25), the relationship is only of secondary importance for Ann whose illness is exacerbated by grief for a male lover's death. Yet when Mary achieves her greatest dream – to live with Ann – she finds herself unaccountably disappointed: 'Ann and she were not congenial minds'. Only when she is nursing her dying friend does Mary achieve the power and authority over her she desires, albeit disguised as a feminine role of self-abnegation.

As with de Staël twenty years later in *Corinne*, Wollstonecraft's insistence on Mary's uniqueness and the novel's pessimistic fatalism tend to undermine the potential political radicalism of its analysis of the effect of environment on the construction of female sensibility. This was picked up by the *English Review*:

> We by no means, however, approve of that dismal philosophy, or rather gloomy superstition, which pervades this volume, and which tends to render man unhappy, by teaching him to believe that he was made to be miserable in this world, and that the earth is a vale of tears, where all our business is to weep, and to merit by our sufferings a state of bliss in a future order of existence.... If we examine rightly, we shall find that our misery is the work of our own hands, and that human ills are not so much the inevitable consequences of natural imperfection, as that they flow from the impure source of false opinion, and wrong systems of education, government and laws.[30]

Nevertheless, the reviewer's overall judgment was favourable:

> The sad tale is told with no common portion of pathos, and the sentiments display an original turn of thought, much superior to the vulgar combinations of similar productions.

The writing of the novel seems to have had a cathartic effect, for 1787 marked a turning point in Wollstonecraft's life. When she returned to London she gave up traditional female employments like companion and governess, and even gradually renounced her attempt to be a mother-substitute to her sisters. She turned her feet towards St. Paul's Churchyard, the area where the bookshops, publishers and printers' businesses clustered, declaring to her sister her determination to survive by writing alone: 'I am going to be the first of a new genus' (*CLMW*, p. 164).

2

'When the voices of children are heard on the green': Mary Wollstonecraft the Author-Educator

Is the concept of a separate state of childhood a modern invention? The influential thesis of Philippe Ariès' *Centuries of Childhood*, tr. Robert Baldick (1962) suggests it is. In mediaeval society children were dressed like the adults alongside whom they worked, played and listened to stories, in the mixed-age kinship groups of feudal times. But by the eighteenth century, children had become the highly-valued particular focus of the bourgeois nuclear family, and began to be treated as a distinct group, as for several hours they were educated together in nurseries or schools. The new consumer society underlined this by producing toys, clothes and entertainments specially designed for children, who began to be thought of as 'innocent' and in need of protection from adult culture. This was the context in which the book written specially for children came to the fore: with proliferating sub genres like the textbook, the reading primer, the school story. Specialist bookshops and publishers sprang up to provide them, while periodicals were founded to advise on purchase.

Sociologists such as Lawrence Stone, have seen this as evidence that in the eighteenth century newly affectionate family relationships blossomed. Instead of callously accepting high infant mortality or beating the original sin out of their surviving offspring, parents became more humane. But it seems doubtful whether medieval parents had ever been quite so uncaring as historians with a Whig view of history have painted them. What is undeniable, though, is that from the seventeenth century onwards there was an intellectual outpouring of abstract *theory* about training the next generation. As Linda Pollack comments, 'It is possible that these developments were related more to the growth and spread of literacy as well as increasing expertise with writing as a form of communication than to any significant transformations in the parent–child relationship.[1] For it was the Protestant obsession with literacy which produced the extension of the period of education for a larger proportion of the population, resulting in the modern concept of childhood. Literacy had been snatched from the hands of priests and a latinized elite, but its emancipatory power was so dangerous that the Church of England still felt it had to be passed on only as a mode of internalizing biblical authority. Enlightenment philosophers argued instead that a 'liberal' (that is, moral) education could guide a child to train his/her own conscience to take moral decisions instead of merely obeying commandments. All were agreed in dismissing oral folktales and pedlar's chapbooks as mere entertaining trash.

Locke and textuality

A tradition grew up of advice books designed for parents and teachers, and the most influential of these was the philosopher John Locke's *Some Thoughts Concerning Education* (1693) which stressed the developmental training of the child's rationality as the chief goal of education, in order that the passions may be curbed and virtue cultivated. The object was to socialize the individual, to become a fit member of civil society. Reading the Bible was central to the Protestant internalization of moral discipline, so that even a liberal educationalist like Locke, who recommended child-centred learning, repeatedly used the imagery of printing and textuality when talking about the way a child's mind works:

> there ought very early to be *imprinted on* his Mind a true notion of God ... [P]reserve his tender Mind from all *Impressions* and Notions of Sprites and Goblins'.[2] [My italics]

In *An Essay Concerning Human Understanding* (1689) the empiricist Locke had also used the famous analogy of the mind as a sheet of 'white Paper, void of all characters' (Book II, Chapter 1).

If the child's mind was a potential text then it must be open to scrutiny by God; s/he must think of her/his life as the narrative of his/her soul's journey. The link between monitorial surveillance and textuality was overt in the best-selling children's book *Divine Songs Attempted in Easy language for the Use of Children* (1715) by Dr Isaac Watts , whose Song 9 is entitled 'The All-Seeing God':

> There's not a sin that we commit
> Nor wicked word we say,
> But in thy dreadful book 'tis writ,
> Against the judgement day.

This followed on from song 8, where the child praises God for learning to read:

> That I am brought to know
> The danger I was in,
> By nature, and by practice too,
> A wretched slave to sin.

Song 28 took up the Lockean metaphor of the child's mind as a potential text:

> O write upon my mem'ry, Lord,
> The texts and doctrines of thy word . . .

In Watts' *On the Education of Children and Youth*, textuality is portrayed as sacred : 'Writing is almost a divine art, whereby thoughts may be communicated without a voice and understood without hearing.' All children should be taught to read so that 'everyone may see with his own eyes [. . .] what God requires of him in order to [obtain] eternal happiness'.[3]

The children's book trade

John Newbery, who often cited Locke's name in his prefaces to attract parent customers, is usually credited with launching the commercial children's book trade with his *A Little Pretty Pocket-Book* (1744). He provided cheap and cheerful ABCs, chapbooks, and miscellanies and in 1751 launched the *Lilliputian Magazine*. He commissioned authors such as Oliver Goldsmith and Christopher Smart but controlled the whole publication process himself. Reading was itself the subject of many texts, and in Newbery's most successful title, *The History of Little Goody Two-Shoes* (1765), the heroine teaches herself and others to read. Literacy was always associated with rising in the world in these bourgeois stories, where both aristocrats and the lower classes were frequently represented as ignorant and boorish. Newbery's motto was 'Trade and Plumb-cake for ever, Huzza!'[4]

Children's verse, animal stories, primers, hymns, and textbooks: all appeared in the course of the eighteenth century, often well-illustrated. But the profusion of genres produced for every pocket from that of children themselves to their parents, teachers and schools by the expanding and sometimes vulgar book trade produced a corresponding unease amongst the Church and intelligentsia. For it was clear that reading was becoming thoroughly secularized and commercialised; also that books and newspapers were so readily available in circulating libraries and coffee houses that they could be read by (and more importantly to) anyone. The fear that reading would dangerously inflame the passions of the young – especially gullible females; that reading fiction would become addictive and cause the reader not to be able to distinguish reality from romance; became so commonplace that it inspired comic novels like Charlotte Lennox's *The Female Quixote* and theatrical stereotypes such as Sheridan's Lydia Languish.

Literacy, religion and women

The tension regarding expanding literacy was centred on the role of women. Young women epitomized the giddy reader-as-consumer in the literary marketplace, yet it was also the mother's traditional role to teach her children to read. Harvey J. Graff points out that those places with near-universal levels of literacy in the seventeenth and eighteenth centuries were intensely religious and usually Protestant: Scotland, New England, Huguenot parts of France and areas of Germany and Switzerland.[5] Reading (but not necessarily writing) was part of a religious system of control and regulation, often sponsored by a state church and predicated on literate mothers whose special role was to induct children into Bible study at home. So it should come as no surprise that some of the most important British women writers of the eighteenth century sprang from puritanical religious circles. Wollstonecaft's intellectual forcing-house was the Dissenting culture of the North London suburbs; Anna Letitia Barbauld (née Aikin) had been brought up in the Dissenters' premier 'university', the Warrington Academy; and Hannah More belonged to the religious revival within the national church which had all the evangelizing zeal of Methodism. Such women were the product of the association of motherhood with the induction of literacy within Protestantism and their entry into print culture could thus be justified as an extension of their familial role. All were professional teachers as well as creative artists, and all produced pedagogic books as well as texts in other genres.

Women writing for children

From the middle of the century onwards women writers came to the fore in an attempt to replace Newbery's fanciful successors to the chapbook with more improving fare. They learned from Newbery how to make their moralizing wares attractive. *The Juvenile Magazine* was launched in 1788 to provide stories by popular authors such as Dorothy Kilner and educational aids like sheet music and folding maps.[6] Women also began producing books specifically for the older female reader: conduct books and novelised versions of them in the Richardsonian tradition which held the field until the time of Scott, and thereby laid the foundations of F.R. Leavis's 'Great Tradition' of moralising fiction.

These women writers sometimes produced fictionalized versions of the conduct book especially for younger girls: thus accepting and per- petuating a gendered division in child readership. This may be seen as implicitly endorsing different behavioural codes and stricter self-repression for girls under the name of femininity. But girls' fiction also provided the opportunity to bring out into the open and even question the gendering of education. Wollstonecraft, in her own fiction for children, was drawn to the new genre of the school-story. Sarah Fielding's *The Governess or Little Female Academy* (1749) had pioneered it, providing stories of magic alongside the girls' own accounts of their real-life experiences. It was followed by others such as Eleanor Fenn's *School Occurrences: Supposed to Have Arisen Among a Set of Young Ladies Under the Tuition of Mrs Teachwell* (1782), and Ann Murry's *Mentoria, or The Young Ladies Instructor [Sic] in Familiar Conversations on Moral and Entertaining Subjects: Calculated to Improve Young Minds in the Essential as well as Ornamental Parts of Female Education* (1778). Wollstonecraft particularly liked the feminocentric collection of plays *The Theatre of Education* by the Countess de Genlis, translated from the French in 1783.

In pointing out the importance of children's literature to the founding of a female literary tradition, Mitzi Myers downplays the ideological differences between Romantic-period writers such as Sarah Trimmer, Anna Barbauld and Mary Wollstonecraft, in order to demonstrate how the genre as a whole empowered women by fantasizing the Christlike power of the female mentor figure.[7] Gary Kelly also lumps them all together when he comments that writing for children 'gave women a role in the bourgeois cultural revolution promoting defence of middle-class youth from corruption by court culture and contamination by lower-class culture'.[8] But it is only possible to ignore the deep ideological rifts between these women writers by viewing their texts through contemporary secular eyes which perceive class and gender similarites but not religious differences.

Children's literature and its largely female authors were central, not peripheral, to a war in the public sphere over enlightenment, religion and the control of knowledge which would last until the concepts of both democracy and state education were accepted in the nineteenth century. In the 1780s, the Anglican Church was fighting a rearguard action to regain control over education, particularly from Dissenters, who, since the Toleration Act of 1689, had set up their own academies, soon leading the way in terms of Enlightenment curriculum and pedagogy. Unitarians such as Anna Barbauld were dangerous because their writing sometimes expressed a scientific view of the creation; while Richard Price's disciple, Mary Wollsonecraft, trained children to use their own moral judgement instead of obeying authority. When the well-connected Sarah Trimmer and Hannah More set up Sunday Schools and published tracts and chapbooks for the poor, they were acting for the Church in trying to contain the spread of the Dissenters' moral individualism on the one hand and commerical print culture on the other. Both these developments were leading inexorably to democracy and a free press subject to the control only of market forces.

The Anglican loyalist Sarah Trimmer established her own *Family Magazine* (1778–89) for newly-literate servants which was 'designed to counteract the pernicious tendency of immoral books'. The January 1789 issue, for example, was a typically jolly number, containing: 'A poem upon Death', Isaac Watts's 'The Dying Christian's Hope', and a meditation by Bishop Hale 'Upon the sight of a grave digged'. In *The Oeconomy of Charity* (1787) Trimmer described it as the patriotic duty of middle-class women to use literacy to socialize unruly lower-class children and thus prevent class war: 'It is evident that unanimity does not at present subsist in this country and the consequences are dreadful to society' (p2). She hoped Sunday Schools would bring 'restoration of that harmony' by keeping uncouth juveniles in control on their one day off from the factories and mills. She went on to launch the *Guardian of Education* (1802–04), which, as its name implied, alerted parents to fiction which was theologically suspect or simply too secular, like Maria Edgeworth's. There was 'a conspiracy against CHRISTIANITY and all SOCIAL ORDER', according to Trimmer, in which revealed religion would be abandoned and replaced by so-called 'new philosophy', all 'through the medium of Books of Education and Children's Books'.[9]

The bellicose patriotism of Sarah Trimmer and Hannah More emanated from their belief in the sacred mission of the Church of England to anoint Britain's monarchs and guard secular authority from incursion by Dissenters or Catholics. In her commentary and catechism on Isaac Watt's *Divine Songs*, written for use in Sunday Schools for the poor, Trimmer particularly commended nos 3, 5, 6 and 7 as they would 'enforce some essential doctrines'.[10] These songs hymn the British as God's chosen people. For example:

> 'Tis to thy sov'reign grace I owe
> That I was born on British ground,
> Where streams of heav'nly mercy flow,
> And words of sweet salvation sound.

(Song 5, verse 2)

> Lord I ascribe it to thy grace,
> And not to chance as other do,
> That I was born of Christian race,
> And not a heathen, or a Jew.

(Song 6, verse 1)

Wollstonecraft and education

On 7 November 1787, after she had been dismissed as a governess, Wollstonecraft returned to London and announced proudly in a letter to her sister Everina:

> Mr Johnson whose uncommon kindness, I believe, has saved me from despair and vexations I shrink back from – and feared to encounter; assures me that if I exert my talents in writing I may support myself in a comfortable way. I am going to be the first of a new genus ...
>
> (*CLMW*, p. 164).

Wollstonecraft was setting up as an author-educator and obviously saw herself as a pioneer woman of letters, for she was shortly to become chief reviewer of educational works in her publisher Joseph Johnson's new periodical, the *Analytical Review*. She had already published *Thoughts on the Education of Daughters* (1787) and written a *bildungsroman*, *Mary: a Fiction*, which she now gave to Johnson, who would install her in a house in George Street near enough for her to visit his shop daily. More of this later.

Johnson particularly specialized in publishing religious works appealing to Protestant Dissenters, and the title of his review indicates it aimed to appeal to the more intellectually advanced nonconformists who subscribed to Rational or New Dissent. So, although he was Sarah Trimmer's publisher, he needed a progressive female educationalist rather than a conservative of Trimmer's type, to advise the journal's middle-class readership how to discriminate between the multiplicity of children's books. Wollstonecraft's reviews demonstrate an anti-Calvinist liberal view of the child as naturally good. She disapproved of William Jones's *The Book of Nature* for teaching children that 'the human heart is naturally depraved', but praised the Unitarian Anna Barbauld's *Hymns in Prose for Children* (1781) which attempted to convey in simple words joyous wonder at the natural world as God's handiwork (*WMW*, 7: 35). She much preferred the Rousseauistic and lively Countess de Genlis to the vapid moralism of Eleanor Fenn (*WMW*, 7: 123); and warmly recommended Thomas Day on female education, for 'he wishes to see women educated like rational creatures, and not mere polished playthings, to amuse the leisure hours of men' (*WMW*, 7: 176).

Wollstonecraft approved of Sarah Trimmer's scheme for Sunday Schools for the poor and recommended her children's fiction. Indeed, she had told her sister 'I spent a day at Mrs Trimmer's, and found her a truly respectable woman' (*CLMW*, p. 166). But the fact that her own modern educational philosophy was in complete opposition to Trimmer's traditional Christianity is demonstrated by her extremely long and enthusiastic review of the radical Deist David Williams's *Lectures on Education* (1789). Williams blamed the religious tradition of education for instigating a bullying use of punishment and fear of future damnation, and advocated instead a modified version of the developmental programme described in Rousseau's *Émile* (*WMW*, 7: 141–52).

Original stories from real life

Wollstonecraft had been meanwhile hard at work composing her own 'book for young people, which I think has some merit' (*CLMW*, p. 166). *Original Stories from Real Life* (1788) was her greatest commercial success. It was carefully revised for a second edition in 1791, and Johnson commissioned William Blake to make ten designs and to engrave six of them to illustrate the book. Blake did not often produce original designs for other authors and this may have been the first time he did so.[11] We do not have any proof that author and artist met but it is virtually certain, for both attended Johnson's regular literary dinners; were close friends of artist Henry Fuseli; and knew of each other's work. The originality of the text (flagged in the title) together with its striking illustrations made this a very handsome publication to attract the middle-class progressive parent. The book was reprinted three times by Johnson in the 1790s; there was a Dublin edition in 1799; a French edition in 1799 including copies of Blake's plates by an anonymous engraver; and German and Danish translations also (*MWRL*, p. 129). Its popularity outlasted Wollstonecraft's respectability. Posthumous editions such as those of 1820 and 1835 were anonymous.

Wollstonecraft graphically announces her aim to expunge false consciousness in the young by likening her book to 'medicines' designed to purge, replace and counteract the influence of their pleasure-loving wealthy parents (*WMW*, 4: 359). The fictional spoiled children, Caroline and Mary, embody the implied child reader: 'If they had been merely ignorant, the task would not have appeared so arduous; but they had caught every prejudice that the vulgar casually instill' (p. 361). She describes her openly contemptuous attitude to rich parents – the book's purchasers – as unvarnished 'sincerity': 'I aim at perspicuity and simplicity of style; and try to avoid those unmeaning compliments, which slip from the tongue...'. She had stubbornly refused her publisher's request to change this rude Preface, declaring: 'I hate the usual smooth way of exhibiting proud humility' (*CLMW*, p. 167).

We even begin to feel a glimmering of sympathy for Lady Kinsgsborough as we get some insight into the way her strong-willed governess took the moral high ground and thereby reversed the usual power relationship between employer and employee. Since the professional has to come in and clean up the mess the indulgent parents have made, her 'cruel necessity' is to prematurely explain the 'nature of vice' to the next generation. So two wealthy but neglected children will no longer be left to hear the servants' folktales, created out of the wish-fulfilment of the poor, using romance conventions such as luck and magical transformations of poverty into riches. Their governess, Mrs Mason, reverses the process by shocking them with gruesome 'real-life' stories of ordinary people's lives destroyed by poverty. Often the root cause is found to be grasping landlords – those of their parents' class. These were doubtless based on actual incidents, some probably derived from Wollstonecraft's experience of poverty in Ireland. Soon after arriving at the castle, she had written to her sister that rather than telling her about the clever conversation of the Lords and Viscounts, 'I would sooner tell you a tale of some humbler creatures Intend visiting the poor cabbins as Miss K, is allowed to assist the poor I shall make a point of finding them out' (*CLMW*, p. 124).

The story of crazy Robin, however, is a fictionalized version of a notorious case of a farmer and ex-miner ill-used by his landlords 'who dug a cave for himself by the seaside, at Marsden Rocks, between Shields and Sunderland, about the year 1780'. His many visitors included Thomas Spence, a radical artisan, later to become a campaigner in London for a communitarian scheme for land reform. Notes to his broadsheet ballad 'the Rights of Man', explain that, 'Exulting in the idea of a human being, who had bravely emancipated himself from the iron fangs of aristocracy, to live free from impost, he [Spence] wrote extempore with chaulk above the fire place of this free man, the following lines:

> Ye landlords vile, whose man's peace mar,
> Come levy rents here if you can;
> Your stewards and lawyers I defy,
> And live with all the RIGHTS OF MAN.[12]

In 1788 Spence was a poor printer's deliveryman in London, and had not yet obtained his own bookstall selling radical propaganda.[13] It is unlikely Wollstonecraft knew of him, but the fact she too was inspired by the *cause célèbre*, as well as other stories highlighting property relations, undermines the conventional labelling of *Original Stories* as mere bourgeois liberalism. On his side, the artisan radical was as interested in literacy as Wollstonecraft. Spence wanted to spread reading among the poor by way of his scientific phonetic alphabet, which he used to print reading primers and the story of Robinson Crusoe, and he pioneered an early pronouncing dictionary.

As Susan Khin Zaw notes, Wollstonecraft, unlike contemporary children's writers Dorothy Kilner and Anna Barbauld, uses reasoned discussion of everyday situations to inculcate morality rather than the threat of violent punishment to exact unquestioning obedience to authority.[14] Nevertheless, Wollstonecraft's refusal to sentimentalize the innocence of children, and girls in particular, was carried to lengths shocking to today's readers, more familiar with Wordsworth and Blake's Romantic child. As much violence and death can be found in *Original Stories* as in many a robust folktale. On the first page the governess avoids treading on a snail in her path. But in case the reader thought this evidence merely of feminine delicacy, only two pages later she deliberately crushes the head of a wounded bird under her foot (to spare its pain). For women's virtue must be tough as well as tender. The girls, too, must endure bodily pain without complaint: 'The Almighty, who never afflicts but to produce some good end . . . sends diseases to children to teach them patience and fortitude', while occasional 'cold and hunger . . . make us feel what wretches feel' (p. 438). They must not be protected from the facts of life and death but confronted with them.[15]

While we find no Rousseauistic idealization of the child's primitive wisdom in *Original Stories*, its style of social realism derives from a para-doxical attempt to provide a simulacrum of learning from real experience. Wollstonecraft acknowledged in the preface that this was a regrettable compromise with Rousseau's educational theory as expressed in *Emile*.[16] She wrote to Johnson: '. . . for, what are books – compared to conversations which affection inforces!' (*CLMW*, p. 167). The frame story of Mary and Caroline's everyday life in a country village gives Mrs Mason opportunities to make them conscious of their power to act morally within a fallen world of unequal power relations. These are the 'conversations calculated to regulate the affections and form the mind to truth and goodness' of the title.

Human power over animals is highlighted in these quotidian conver-sations, and linked to the capacity of even children to exercise virtue by choosing whether or not to inflict pain and death on insects, birds, pets and farm animals. The catalogue of horrific acts perpetuated often by youngsters thoughtlessly and casually – puppies drowned, guinea-pigs callously rolled down roofs for fun, larks carelessly shot, a pregnant dog killed in anger – exceeds even the brutality of *Wuthering Heights*. But, unlike Mrs Trimmer's *Fabulous Histories*, these discussions are counter-pointed with longer case-stories told by Mrs Mason of the physical and mental suffering of humans, usually caused by the abuse of power, such as the local madman who lived in a cave when dispossessed of his farm, or a prisoner in the Bastille baited by sadistic guards. Gradually the girls are taken to meet some examples of the suffering poor in person.

Original Stories sets out to shock the wealthy reader with the sordid 'reality' of the lives of the poor by including repellent physical details of barbarity, illness or injuries, a characteristic rarely found in polite children's literature, but more often associated with 'low' forms such as journalism, grotesque Gothic ballads or the folktale. The madman Robin's crazy rantings would terrify the girls if they encountered him;

they progress to actually meeting Jack (who tells his own story) and whose loss of an eye and a leg presumably repelled them like the deformed woman at whom they had stared on the way.

The shocking catalogue of deaths and horrors derives from Wollstonecraft's attempt to avoid the clichés of sensibility in contemporary literature where the poor are merely picturesque bit-players brought on to induce middle-class emotionalism. Saba Bahar has drawn a useful comparison between Anna Barbauld and Wollstonecraft in their views on representing poverty. In 'An Enquiry into those Kinds of Distress which Excite Agreeable Sensations' [from J. Aikin and A.L. Aikin, *Miscellaneous Pieces in Prose*, second edn, 1775] Barbauld argued that literary depictions of deformity and violence and 'real poverty' only shock and repel instead of producing the desirable emotion of pity, though she concedes that romanticized accounts evade 'the common incidents of life'. Yet the climax of Wollstonecraft's book has Mary and Caroline taken to visit a windowless filthy London garret, to experience the 'bad smells' and the appalling sight of two naked, emaciated children who 'seemed to come into the world only to crawl half formed – to suffer, and to die' (p. 445). As Bahar comments, in *Original Stories* Wollstonecraft 'refuses to produce the aseptic and romanticized vision of poverty', though she asserts that in other respects *Original Stories* conforms to the usual focus on middle-class subjectivity as poverty only figures as inscribed within the education of the two wealthy children.[17]

It is certainly true that the starving mother had handily presented herself as 'an object in distress' seized upon by Mrs Mason as a teaching aid (p. 444) for Wollstonecraft's stories are overtly designed to re-educate the wealthy. But in fact Wollstonecraft avoids dwelling on the girls' emotions and focuses instead on the dignity of the poor and their capacity for endurance. This sometimes leads her into bathos. The conclusion of sailor Jack's account of his woes – blinded, gaoled, shipwrecked, crippled – is his stoic 'Indeed we are very happy'. Blake couldn't resist ironizing this in his illustration, which shows Jack making this statement framed by the ambiguous sight of his wife behind him covering her face and in the shadows his son contorted with strong emotion, while the two girls weep.[18]

The stories are also explicitly designed to link the materialism and conspicuous consumption of the rich with the unequal distribution of wealth, and even the children are made to take the responsibility for adding to a shopkeeper's debts by not paying quickly, or spending so much they are not able to relieve the destitute: 'Oeconomy and self-denial are necessary in every station to enable us to be generous, and to act conformably to the rules of justice'. Charity is common to all didactic literature of the period, but Wollstonecraft analyzes the causes of poverty rather than merely castigating idleness: she explains that the father of the London family was thrown out of work because foreign competition had driven his employer to lay off the hands; that the place is filthy because all the family's strength is used in a fruitless search for 'the necessities of life'.

To conclude this consideration of poverty in *Original Stories*, consider an earlier more distanced view of poverty in children's literature. Isaac Watts' Song 4 begins:

> Whenever I take my walks abroad
> How many poor I see?
> What shall I render to my God
> For all his gifts to me?
>
> Not more than others I deserve,
> Yet God hath giv'n me more,
> For I have food while other starve,
> Or beg from door to door.

Mrs Trimmer in her commentary on the *Divine Songs* felt it was necessary to point out to the poor children who attended Sunday School: 'Remember, that God seldom keeps quite without food, any but the *idle* and the *wicked*' (p. 15). It would take the transformative experience of the French Revolution before Blake's speaker could blaze forth to denounce the detachment of such as Watts never mind the Calvinistic condemnation of poor people by such as Trimmer:

> I wander thro' each charter'd street,
> Near where the charter'd Thames does flow
> And mark in every face I meet
> Marks of weakness, marks of woe.
>
> In every cry of every man,
> In every Infants cry of fear,
> In every voice; in every ban,
> The mind-forg'd manacles I hear.

'London', *Songs of Experience*

Wollstonecraft's stories brought to the representation of poverty a bitter disillusion with both the romanticization of sentimental litera- ture and the complacency of the religious right which anticipated *Songs of Experience*. In 1788 she had yet to cast off her own 'mind forg'd manacles': her religious reliance on the next world to right inequities in this one. Yet the most disconcerting features of her style, the sordid detailing of social realism, and fear-inducing representations of divine and social power point to the evolution of didacticism into social protest.

The sublime

Mrs Mason's interpolated stories of the poor have outdoor settings to induce a mood of awe in accord with the Burkean sublime. The story of crazy Robin is told to the sound of a mountain torrent while the girls contemplate his cave within a craggy ivy-covered mountain; the history of the shipwrecked Jack is told when they take shelter in the sailor's cottage after a violent thunderstorm and hurricane during an evening walk by the cliffs, where they see the raging sea dashing against the rocks and fear for their lives. This demonstration of natural power leads to thoughts of the ultimate in the sublime: the power of God before whom, says Burke, 'we shrink into the minuteness of our own nature, and are, in a manner annihilated before him'.[19] Mrs Mason assures the girls: 'I fear not death! – I only fear that Being who can render death terrible, on whose providence I calmly rest' (p. 394). Her own Godlike authority and ability to punish is shown mutating into the internalized consciences of the children. For after the girls know they have been self-indulgent yet have not been reproved, Mary says: '"I declare I cannot go to sleep, . . . I am afraid of Mrs Mason's eyes – would you think, Caroline, that she who looks so very good-natured sometimes could frighten one so?"' (p. 389). The sublime scenery and sombre tone of the stories reinforce the implication that the reward of virtue will be in the next life not the here and now.

Yet the Gothicism of these tales is calculated to work on the subjectivity of the child reader to engage the emotions in developing their moral idealism away from mere personal salvation and towards the good of society. A good example is the account of a ruined mansion-house at twilight. Anticipating Edgar Allan Poe, Wollstonecaft allows the degen- eracy of the aristocracy to be communicated through the imagery of the eerie place which seems to exude its own claustrophobic atmosphere, signalling the fearful response the implied reader should have by the girls clinging to their governess as they view it:

> A spacious bason [sic], on the margin of which water plants grew with wild luxuriance, was overspread with slime; and afforded a shelter for toads and adders. In many places were heaped the ruins of ornamental buildings, whilst sun dials rested in the shade; and pedestals, that had crushed the figures they before supported. Making their way through the grass, they would frequently stumble over a headless statue, or the head would impede their progress. When they spoke, the sound seemed to return again, as if unable to penetrate the thick stagnated air. The sun could not dart its purifying rays through the thick gloom, and the fallen leaves contributed to choke up the way, and render the air more noxious.
>
> (pp. 402–3)

This dream landscape whets the auditors' appetite for the explanation of the tainted atmosphere. Charles Townley, the owner, had negligently allowed his friend to die in gaol and the friend's daughter then married a vicious old rake just to escape destitution. Fanny became mad and was locked up in a lunatic asylum, until Charles rescued her and brought her to his mansion where she was cared for, while he destroyed himself with remorse, becoming a long-bearded recluse and letting the garden run wild. The symbolism of the woman hidden or imprisoned for years in a gloomy mansion would recur in *The Wrongs of Woman*, and feature in the popular 1790s novels of Charlotte Smith and Ann Radcliffe. But Wollstonecaft was suspicious of the sentimentalism inherent in the formula of passive female victim and Gothic villain. She thus has the child auditor ask the governess why Fanny married the rake, so the contemptuous answer 'timidity' can be given .

Woman's role

The harvest supper now symbolically suggests the near maturity of Mary and Caroline when they become 'candidates for my friendship' (p. 449) rather than pupils, as Mrs Mason relinquishes her position of authority over them; signalling too the approaching Autumn of her own life. As Zaw has argued, Wollstonecraft's 'method of moral education is an attempt to recreate human nature so that it will allow relations of dominance and subjection to be replaced with disinterested friendship between equals'.[20]

This new egalitarian relationship is reflected in the way the next story, that of the Welsh harper, is told. For the first time Mrs Mason not only acts as an observer of social ills, but depicts the story as a personal reminiscence, incorporatinging indications of her thoughts and feelings. When her carriage overturned in Wales, Mrs Mason had followed the sound of the 'national music' of the harp at dusk and come upon a picturesque scene which functions as obvious political symbolism: a peasant's hut built on to the ruins of a medieval tower. The castle had formerly belonged to the harper's family before he was first reduced from an aristocrat to a farmer, and then became a mere peasant, vindictively persecuted by the squire. Mrs Mason muses:

> While he was striking the strings, I thought too of the changes in life which an age had produced. The descendant of those who had made the hall ring with social mirth now mourned in its ruins, and hung his harp on the mouldering battlements. Such is the fate of buildings and families!
>
> (p. 420)

This moment of poignant awareness of life's transience and the emotions produced by the harvest celebration precipitate a confessional revelation of the inmost state of the governess's mind. It proves to be shockingly melancholy:

> The pleasure the sight of harmless mirth gave rise to in Mrs Mason's bosom roused every tender feeling, and set in motion her spirits. She laughed with the poor whom she had made happy, and wept when she recollected her own sorrows; the illusions of youth – the gay expectations that had formerly clipped the wings of time. She turned to the girls – I have been very unfortunate, my young friends; but my griefs are now of a placid kind. Heavy misfortunes have obscured the sun I gazed at when first I entered life; early attachments have been broken; the death of friends I loved has so clouded my days; that neither the beams of prosperity, not even those of benevolence, can dissipate the gloom; but I am not lost in a thick fog.
>
> (p. 422)

Thomas Pfau convincingly argues that the passage inspired Blake's 'Nurse's Song', from *Songs of Experience*.[21] Blake rewrote the character sceptically: presenting the nurse's utilitarian dismissal of 'play' and need to strip out 'disguise' and illusions as emanating from her own jealousy and disappointments in life:

> When the voices of children, are heard on the green
> And whisprings are in the dale:
> The days of my youth rise fresh in my mind,
> My face turns green and pale.

> Then come home my children, the sun is gone down
> And the dews of night arise
> Your spring & your day, are wasted in play
> And your winter and night in disguise.

To underline the point, the illuminated plate 'is a parodistic variant of the plate Blake designed and engraved for the frontispiece' of *Original Stories* with the Christ-like governess taking the children haloed by their sunhats outside to exalt in God's creation.[22] In the *Experience* version, the nurse exercises control over nature by combing the boy's hair, while she is implicitly mocked by the prodigality of the vines escaping restraint and heavy with fruit. Of course Blake's questioning of the authoritarian nature of education in *Songs of Experience* and foregrounding of the child's innate vision in the *Songs of Innocence* is itself subject to the ironic qualification that his rejection of commercial publication, and painstaking production by relief etching and hand-colouring, made his illuminated books into expensive collector's pieces rather than art which could be put into the hands of real children.

The voices of many of the *Songs of Experience* are bitter and angry because, like Wollstonecraft, they articulate social critiques. But the dialectic with the *Songs of Innocence* signals their lack of a Utopian perspective: the capacity to imagine a better world. Indeed, the abrupt turn in Wollstonecraft's *Original Stories* from didacticism to lyric melancholy itself displays the cracks in its apparently confident ideology. Pfau understands this stylistic eruption of melancholy as 'the aesthetic expression of the loss of history that has produced the middle class'; the governess has no authentic being and her authority is solely invested in her professional function.[23] One could argue the exact opposite is the case: that now that her maternal and pseudo-maternal roles are over, Mrs Mason's sorrow expresses a frustrated desire for a *more* powerful and meaningful role in the public sphere to bring about change. The governess also signals that we may identify her with the author when she gives the book itself to her pupils, so her self-pity is doubly authenticated when demanding sympathy from the reader. Mrs Mason turns to the pubescent girls on the verge of womanhood and admits that even a relatively wealthy woman's life has its own tragedy – lack of fulfilment.

To enforce the point, *Original Stories* continues with the story of high-spirited schoolteacher Anna Lofty (another self-portrait) whose mother died when she was eighteen and whose father 'insensibly involved himself in debt' before being killed in a pointless duel. 'She had her father's spirit of independence, and determined to shake off the galling yoke [which she had long struggled with], and try to earn her own subsistence.... "When I am my own mistress, the crust I earn will be sweet..."' (p. 428). But the only role available is pedagogic: she too becomes a teacher. When Mrs. Mason returns to her confessional revelations of the tragedy of losing her husband and child in one Winter, seeing the 'wide waste of trackless snow...and the heavy, sullen fog' as an image of her own mind she recalls finding some alleviation of her solitary state in recognizing her affinity with others of her sex: a poor but dignified widow woman, and a motherless child, Peggy. As with the critiques of poverty, this observation of woman's constriction leads to no enabling political vision. All Mrs Mason can do is teach more girls to struggle but to expect disappointment in this 'vale of tears' (p. 424).

The female reader

The success of *Original Stories* must have built up over a year or two, for Johnson did not capitalize on Wollstonecraft's name when he published her next educational text, an anthology for girls' recitation, *The Female Reader* (1789). In fact, he conferred masculine authority upon it by attributing it to 'Mr Cresswick, Teacher of Elocution'! The extensive reading she had to do to make her selections, like the translations she undertook at this time, helped her combine her own self-improvement with her literary work. Demand had risen for such advice books since Newington Green educationalist James Burgh had produced *The Art of Speaking* (1761). The fact that Johnson already published the best-selling William Enfield's *The Speaker* (1774), a textbook designed for Warrington Academy, as well as the philologist John Walker's *Elements of Elocution* (1781), shows the importance bourgeois nonconformist culture placed on elocution: in helping the young to rise in the world by demonstrating how to speak correctly and confidently, using standard pronunciation and accent. There was also a moral aspect to elocution, for 'ethos' or the power to persuade through the respect due to one's character was a central concern of eighteenth-century rhetorical theorists such as Hugh Blair.[24]

Most elocution texts only considered males, as they alone were being trained for public life. Women were routinely satirized for their incorrect use of language. The ignorance of the best-known caricature, Mrs Malaprop, in R.B. Sheridan's *The Rivals*, was perpetually horrifying the choleric Anthony Absolute, presumably based on the playwright's own father Thomas Sheridan, author of *A Course of Lectures on Elocution* (1762). Though educationalists such as Hannah More and the Countess de Genlis had written plays for performance by girls in schools, it seems that Wollstonecraft was a pioneer in producing an elocution manual. This may explain the attribution of its authorship to a male expert and the conservatism of its selection.

Enfield's *The Speaker* had doubled as an anthology of *belles-lettres* which imparted polish by providing ready-made taste in polite literature. The rise of the anthology as a genre was itself testament to the expansion of print culture which spawned editors and canon-makers who selected the grains of moral beauty from the chaff of vulgarity, frivolity and obscenity for the less well-read reader. Anthologizing was felt particularly necessary for the female reader who was increasingly considered in need of being shielded from anything shocking. Commercially, it functioned as a taster for the consumer, for the compiler often included extracts from books on the publisher's list which were advertised in the end pages of the volume. Patricia Michaelson also suggests that performing *belles-lettres* helped widen the linguistic range for women in the art of conversation.[25]

Like Enfield, Wollstonecraft selected mainly English literature, and like him she included extracts from the *Spectator, Rambler, Guardian,* Thomson, Dr Johnson, Young, Collins, Barbauld, and Shakespeare. Wollstonecraft, however, had several passages from the Bible; more extracts from conduct books such as Gregory's *A Father's Legacy to His Daughters* (1774) and her own *Thoughts*; copious amounts of Cowper (published by Johnson); and also included a generous selection of the most morally improving women writers. As well as Mrs Barbauld (who is quoted at length in the preface), there were Charlotte Smith, Sarah Trimmer, Hester Chapone, Sarah Pennington, Elizabeth Carter and the Countess de Genlis.

Like Enfield, she has an entire section devoted to moralistic pieces, and another with a stress on sensibility or 'pathetic pieces'. But it would be difficult to detect the future feminist in the selection and preface if we had not both Godwin's and Joseph Johnson's word for her editorial role, and the fact that extracts from her own works are included. For Wollstonecaft omits Enfield's 'Argumentative' section as well as 'Orations and harangues', as 'Females are not educated to become public speakers or players', and asserts that 'diffidence and reserve ... [are] the most graceful ornament of the sex' (*WMW*, 4: 55). In their place are more devotional pieces including four prayers of her own composition: for women who have not the distractions of business or pleasure in the public world particularly need religion to 'still the murmurs of discontent'. The preface warns sternly that they must therefore 'fix devotional habits' for 'Obedience is the only daily incense pleasing to the Supreme being' (*WMW*, 4: 57). Her young readers are discouraged from the unfeminine display of reciting to an audience: '[I]t is not necessary to speak to display mental charms – the eye will quickly inform us if an active soul resides within; and a blush is far more eloquent than the best turned period' (*WMW*, 4: 59).

When Anna Barbauld brought out her own *Female Speaker* in 1811, also published by Johnson, she at least allowed that bashfulness should not prevent a young lady reciting 'by her father's fireside, amidst a circle of her friends, a passage of twenty lines from Milton or Cowper' (p. v). *The Female Reader* rattled no cages and thus was accepted into print culture's proliferating merry-go-round of extracts and recommendations, being quickly included in the list of recommended reading in a new edition of Pennington's *Advice to Her Daughters*.[26]

Adaptations, translations, reviews

The following year Wollstonecraft produced her own versions of two popular European children's books. Johnson told Godwin after her death 'a translation from ye Dutch of young Grandison was put into her hands which she almost rewrote'.[27] The Rev. John Hall had translated Madame Maria Geertruida van de Werken de Cambon's Dutch Richardsonian epistolary novel *Young Grandison* and Wollstonecraft's two-volume abridgement 'with alterations and improvements' was published in 1790. The advertisement declared in unmistakeably robust style: 'The author has judiciously interspersed little introductory hints relative to natural philosophy; which, as they tend to awaken curiosity, lead to reflections calculated to expand the heart. Indeed any production which has not this tendency will be found not only useless but pernicious.... It would be needless to point out the alterations that have been made, they were, in the editor's opinion, necessary' (*WMW*, 2: 215).

On 15 September 1789 Wollstonecraft wrote to a friend, 'I am so fatigued with poring over a German book, I scarcely can collect my thoughts' (CLMW, p. 184). She was learning German by making a free translation of Christian Gotthilf Salzmann's *Moralisches Elementarbuch* (1782). This was not her first translating work as she had already been improving her French by translating Jacques Necker's *De l'Importance des Opinions Religieuses*. Here the financier discusses the vital role of religion in an *ancien régime* culture vitiated by aristocratic corruption and philosophical scepticism. Wollstonecraft's translation came out in 1788 and she reviewed it herself for the *Analytical*. Two volumes of *Elements of Morality* were ready to be published in 1790 and the complete three volumes appeared in 1791. It was revised for the second edition, which was illustrated with designs engraved by Blake, and the unillustrated first edition reprinted in 1793. Salzmann later returned the compliment by translating *Rights of Woman* and Godwin's *Memoirs* into German (*WMW*, 2: 2). He had corresponded with Wollstonecraft at some point. Wollstonecraft showed her authority as a fellow author by pronouncing on the original, condescendingly remarking that she was pleased to find it 'a very rational book', and declaring that had it not been 'a very useful production' she would not have gone on with the translation. She admired and emulated 'the simplicity of style and manners' of the original and its adoption of pictures from 'real life' like her own *Original Stories*.

The frontispiece shows a mother with children at her knee and Salzmann apostrophizes the mother as the best person to read his didactic tales, as 'the properest person to form the character of thy children is thyself' (*WMW*, 2: 11). The stories don't specifically mention Jesus Christ, but see his purpose as 'to redeem us from the law' by giving us the freedom to make moral choices rather than obey orders, and therefore aim to alert children to their capacity independently to choose virtue in everyday situations. The progressive aim of the book is to 'root out of our little posterity the number of prejudices, which prey like poisonous insects, on human happiness' (*WMW*, 2: 14). In a passage which would much later be seized upon by Wollstonecraft's detractors, Salzmann explains that he would have liked 'to speak to children of the organs of generation as freely as we speak of the other parts of the body' (*WMW*, 2: 9) but has had to bow to public opinion. There are stories where a child learns that he was wrong to think all Jews are evil for we all worship the same God; one where the servants of a family are called away suddenly and everyone has to knuckle down to all the unpleasant household tasks. Undoubtedly that with the strongest personal resonance for Wollstonecraft must have been that of the innkeeper who beats his wife and child. It is explained to the child reader that this man is to be pitied like a cripple for his lack of control. The psychological cause of his disorder is analyzed for the children as what the twentieth-century would term an inferiority complex. His wife holds him to blame for losing her fortune; he is a failure at business; his children have no affection for him, they prefer their mother. Wollstonecraft extended the progressive agenda of the book by adding one tale of her own on racial prejudice. Little Charles had got frightened when he was lost in the woods and imagined he saw a frightening black man. So Wollstonecraft incorporated the story of a soldier in America who had been humanely cared for by a native American after panic at the appearance of the face of a 'savage' caused him to fall from his horse. He thus learned that 'the same blood warmed it which mounts to beautify a fair face' (*WMW*, 2: 28–9), and noted that the 'savage' prayed to the 'Great Spirit'. The story implies that fear distorted the little boy's ability to find his way out of the wood, and in the same way fear of black men and natives is also irrational.

Joseph Johnson had a sufficiently strong list in children's literature by 1789 to publish *A Catalogue of Books Composed for Young Persons, and Generally Used in the Principal Schools and Academies in England* featuring 26 titles.[28] As the leading publisher of the Unitarians he had strong links with the Dissenting Academies, which had taken the intellectual revolution of the Enlightenment on board and now outstripped Oxford and Cambridge. Their tutors were in the forefront of their fields and published textbooks for their own use and that of other schools. The modern subjects of science and natural history were strongly represented, in books by Dr John Aikin and others; an arithmetic textbook was for sale by the mathematician John Bonnycastle. Utilitarian guides to trade and business were included, for many Dissenters spearheaded commerce as they were barred from the professions. Indeed, this was why education was so vital to them. The list shows a stress on elocution and the study of the English language rather than the classics: one of the grammars was by Joseph Priestley. As one would expect, there were included religious and conduct books by nonconformist ministers such as James Burgh. There is a notably strong cohort of women writers: as well as Wollstonecraft, Sarah Trimmer and Anna Barbauld were published by Johnson as would be Maria Edgeworth.

Women writers and didacticism

It is sometimes assumed by modern critics that writing children's books was just hack-work as far as Wollstonecraft was concerned, or that adopting and adapting the maternal role amounted to a regrettable compromise with oppressive domestic ideology. In fact, Wollstonecraft and her sister author-educators were all profoundly committed to professionalizing the maternal role of inducting literacy and training the next generation. A connection between didacticism and Romantic individualism is common throughout the Protestant literary tradition, but the intense didacticism of Georgian children's literature reflects anxiety over the enormous power of literacy itself to change society.

The theological emphases we hardly notice today were most apparent to contemporary readers of this children's literature, between a radical influenced by Rational Dissent such as Wollstonecraft, and the Evangelical conservative Hannah More, or a mainstream Anglican loyalist such as Sarah Trimmer, secular moralists exemplified by Maria and Richard Edgeworth or Unitarians Anna Barbauld and her brother John Aikin. So whether children were being trained to be obedient to parental and religious authority; to develop rigorous self-examination; or to prioritize social benevolence (as in *Original Stories*) was of crucial importance.

Wollstonecraft and Barbauld's didacticism was ironized by Blake, who, like Rousseau, idealized the individual child's natural joy and visionary imagination to such an extent that he regretted any socialization at all. However, as Alan Richardson has pointed out, a conservative fear of the empowering of the working-classes through education underlay some male Romantics' criticism of modern children's literature and reactionary idealization of the primitive world of folklore, at the beginning of the nineteenth century.[29] For example, when Charles Lamb, in a famous letter to Coleridge, violently denounced Anna Barbauld's books for children, he saw the Rational Dissenters' pioneering of science and natural history textbooks[30] as eroding that unquestioning religious belief which he associated with poetic vision:

> Science has succeeded to Poetry no less in the little walks of Children than with Men. – Is there no possibility of averting this sore evil? Think you what you would have been now, if instead of being fed with tales and old wives fables in childhood, you had been crammed with geography & Natural History.? **Damn them**. I mean the cursed Barbauld Crew, those **Blights & Blasts** of all that is **human** in man & child.'[31]

Lamb was probably referring to Coleridge's memories of how fairy tales stimulated his imagination when a child, as when he had reminisced to Thomas Poole in a letter of 16 October 1797, and expressed fears that scientific education would develop a materialist view of the world in the next generation:

> Should children be permitted to read Romances, & Relations of Giants & Magicians, & Genii? – I know all that has been said against it; but I have formed my faith in the affirmative. – I know no other way of giving the mind a love of 'the great', & 'the Whole'.[32]

Noone would today disagree with the Romantics' validation of imagination, but Richardson points out that Georgian children's literature was not bifurcated into reason and imagination according to a generic division between didactic story and fairy tale. For both genres – like the novel itself – partook of both realism and romance, and, indeed, both could be didactic.[33]

Education had been the subject of Wollstonecraft's first publication; her most important work, *A Vindication of the Rights of Woman* would focus particularly on equal education for both sexes; and amongst her posthumous works, published in 1798, were a draft on the care of infants and *Lessons for Children*, a first primer written for her little daughter which was also published independently by Johnson as a sixpenny pamphlet. As Mitzi Myers has remarked, though Wollstonecraft never wrote a memoir, her works are full of self-referential aspects like the obsessive use of her own name and reworked anecdotes culled from her own experience.[34] We should see didactic works such as *Thoughts on the Education of Daughters* and *Original Stories from Real Life* as reflections on her own experience both as a daughter and a mother-surrogate; while her novel written at the same time, *Mary: A Fiction*, fictionalized her own life in order 'to illustrate an opinion of mine, that a genius will educate itself' (*CLMW*, p. 162). Lockean educational theory and Rousseauistic primitivism both engendered a particular respect for the individual and the history of self-development. When the fictional subject was female, the stories of self-making trembled on the brink of cultural critique.

3
'The first of a new genus': Proud To Be a Female Journalist

> How few authors or artists have arrived at eminence who have not
> lived by their employment?
>
> > (Mary Wollstonecraft, *Letters Written*
> > *in Sweden, Norway and Denmark*)

It was to 72 St Paul's Churchyard where her publisher Joseph Johnson
lived above his shop that Mary Wollstonecraft had made her way in
August 1787 after she had been dismised as a governess. She had frankly
explained to him her intention to live by the pen. 'After a short conversation, Mr Johnson invited her to make his house her home' and by the
end of September he had found her a house in George Street on the
South side of Blackfriars' Bridge. She lived there for the next four years.
As Johnson's protégé, she worked her literary apprenticeship: described
by the publisher to Godwin as 'the most active period of her life'
(*MAVRW*, p. 67).[1] Godwin gave a negative picture of her 'miscellaneous
literary employment' which has remained the conventional judgement
ever since. Hack writing tended to 'damp and contract...the genius';
because answering 'the mere mercantile purpose of the day...touched
[the author] with the torpedo of mediocity'. The 'daring flights' evident
in *Mary: A Fiction* evaporated and Wollstonecraft even stooped to 'homily-
language' (*MAVRW*, pp. 69–70). But Godwin preferred the sentimentalist
to the polemicist in Wollstonecraft. He underestimated what a morale-
boosting achievement it was for a female autodidact to keep herself
entirely by the pen in the eighteenth century. This formative period
was crucial in the making of Wollstonecraft as a writer. And Joseph
Johnson, who published every one of her books, was to become her
lifelong patron.

Grub Street

From before the time of the fire of London, the area around Paternoster Row including St Paul's Churchyard, Little Britain and Duke Street had been packed with booksellers, printers, print shops and allied trades. Grub Street, to the north-east, had once been infamous for the poverty of its starving hacks: literary prostitutes who scrabbled for a living in the early eighteenth century. However, by the 1780s the publishing trade had increased so steadily in wealth and respectability that the balance of power had changed, and there was now a demand for new authors. Acts of copyright in 1709 and 1774 had established authors' ownership of their intellectual property for 14 years which could be further extended to 28. The publishing trade was tightly controlled by a relatively small number of publishers who cooperated in congers – an eel-like string of shareholders spreading the risk in expensive projects, and which also prevented undercutting by interlopers and by operating as a limited monopoly, gobbled up the profits. Aristocratic patronage had been replaced by the sponsorship of these publishers whose premises now rivalled bluestocking salons as meeting-places for scholars and intellectuals. The practice of paying acceptable rates of payment in exchange for copyright had been regularized throughout 'the Trade'. Dr Johnson was held up as an example that authors could earn a living by the pen while keeping their independence. It was now possible to earn a respectable living fom 'miscellaneous employment' while making one's name as an intellectual.

In fact the last quarter of the eighteenth century seems to have been something of a golden age for authorship as the nineteenth-century publisher Charles Knight estimated that Gibbon's profits in 1777 were 59 per cent higher than they would have been later in 1840.[2] By the 1780s the price of books had risen in response to the high demand from 10s or 12s to a guinea for a quarto, and from 5s or 6s to 10s or 12s for an octavo. They were therefore a luxury item, for a schoolmistress earned £12 p.a. and a labouring woman under a shilling a day. The days of mechanization and mass-production were as yet far off. But circulating libraries and literary clubs proliferated so that the cost of books could be shared by many readers. Inexpensive reprints and cheap chapbooks sold by pedlars abounded, and a trade in secondhand titles grew up, so that even illiterate farmworkers or artisans could listen as one of their number read aloud while they were at work or by the fireside. By the end of the century the number of new titles being published was almost four times the Augustan norm of 100 new books a year.[3]

Joseph Johnson and the publishing trade

72 St Paul's Churchyard was the largest commercial premises in the street. It was a quaint place built on a trapeziform floor plan on three floors, with none of the walls at right angles.[4] Here Johnson, a reticent, asthmatic bachelor held open house on Tuesdays and Sundays for his authors, and an inner circle of intimates, including Wollstonecraft, was invited to stay to dinner. The food was notoriously plain: boiled cod, veal and vegetables, rice pudding. But the company was second to none. It would be Wollstonecraft's university.

In his reminiscences of literary London, Thomas Rees, whose brother Owen had been a partner with Longman, divided the 20 booksellers in the vicinity in 1780 into three types. There were the publishers who sold only their own productions; then there were general book-merchants who dealt as wholesalers with country booksellers as well as publishing and selling their own books and periodicals together with some works printed by others; and lastly a humbler class of retail traders who sold secondhand books and chapbooks from booths, and sometimes printed small pamphlets for authors, including popular street ballads and radical tracts. Joseph Johnson was of the second eminently respectable category. He acted as a distributor as well as a publisher of texts for Dissenters; and occasionally used provincial printers to produce his own authors' books and pamphlets.[5] He was especially a conduit for publications produced in the Liverpool area, from where he hailed and where the Warrington Academy was located. But many nonconformists were in trade, and this gave him connections with other expanding manufacturing centres, such as Manchester and Leeds; as well as in Birmingham, where the Lunar Society of scientists was to be found; and Norwich where Dissent was particularly strong. In fact, Johnson's shop constituted the communication centre of all the Dissenters' provincial networks: where letters could be collected, messages sent, texts ordered, meetings arranged.

Rees remembered Johnson as generous to his authors, adding extra money to what had been agreed originally when a book sold well (giving Maria Edgeworth £1000 extra for *Tales of Fashionable Life*), and having reputedly paid the fabulous sum of £10,000 for Hayley's *Life Of Cowper*. Only when incarcerated for six months for selling a controversial pamphlet by Gilbert Wakefield in 1798 did enforced idleness lead him to check his ledgers and call in his debts, so that he realized a large amount of income on his release from prison![6] Nevertheless he was a sufficiently astute businessman to make such good profits on certain publications (for example, the works of Cowper) that they subsidized his patronage of risky ventures; and he was well known in insisting on using cheap paper and plain bindings to keep down costs. He preferred to provide affordable books for the many to luxury items for the wealthy.

Carol Hall calculates that in his forty-eight years as a publisher Johnson put out 2700 titles, averaging 56 a year.[7] By 1788, when he took Wollstonecraft on, Johnson's annual output had reached 75 separate titles and for 1789 it would peak at 79. Gerald P. Tyson estimates his productivity for these years to be 50 per cent greater than that of his nearest competitor, Cadell.[8] Letterpress copies of his correspondence show him dealing with foreign dealers and printers as far afield as Hamburg, Philadelphia, New York and Bombay.[9] Religion was the largest category of texts he published, followed by 'literature' (in the broad sense of miscellaneous *belles-lettres*), then medical, political and scientific books.[10]

The chief publisher for the academics of the Warrington Academy, Johnson was a figure whose significance for the development of Romanticism has not been sufficiently recognized. The nonconformist circles for whom he was chief publisher constituted the spearhead of the later English Enlightenment. His press was at the heart of an intellectual revolution whereby the rationalist progressives of the Dissenting community were subjecting both society and the natural world to scientific enquiry. This scientific revolution bolstered the concept of natural rights, which would democratize liberal politics in the French Revolution. But the growing acceptance of empirical rationalism also provoked religious artists and poets of these circles to respond with a Romantic revisioning of man's sacred relationship with the natural world.

Johnson published the theology, the science, the polemics and the literature produced by and in reaction to this wide-ranging intellectual revolution. His list included the work of scientists and thinkers Joseph Priestley and Benjamin Franklin; theologian and mathematician Richard Price; chemists Humphrey Davy and Antoine Laurent Lavoisier; the New England theologian Jonathan Edwards; the evangelical former slave-ship captain John Newton; philosophical anarchist William Godwin; his antagonist the political economist Thomas Malthus; poet and naturalist Erasmus Darwin.[11] Johnson was simultaneously at the forefront of medical advances, launching the first medical periodical, *Medical Facts and Observations* in 1791; and publishing George Fordyce on the treatment of diseases; John Hunter on anatomy; Alexander

Monro on the nervous system; Thomas Beddoes on respiration; John Haygarth on small-pox.

Johnson had long encouraged women writers, having published Mary Scott's *The Female Advocate* (1774) and the poems of 'Theodosia' (Anne Steele).[12] Later important female authors, other than Wollstonecraft, included poet Anna Barbauld; educationalist and novelist Maria Edgeworth; children's writer Sarah Trimmer; and feminist novelist Mary Hays. His literature list was innovative, too, in including the new poetry of sacred nature by William Cowper, William Wordsworth, and Samuel Taylor Coleridge. Proto-Romantic literary currents were also evident in the Gothic novels of William Beckford; while Johnson's closest friend, Henry Fuseli, the Swiss artist, was the first major commentator in English on Rousseau. Johnson set up in print William Blake's *The French Revolution* in 1791, which was subsequently withdrawn from publication, presumably by Blake himself; but he continued to supply the artist and poet with the engraving work on which he lived while producing his own illuminated texts. Johnson did not restrict himself to sponsoring the new generation of British writers. Under Fuseli's influence, he pioneered the translation of German Romantic writers into English: William Taylor of Norwich's translation of Goethe's *Iphigenia: A Tragedy* appeared in 1793, Sir John Stoddart's translation of Schiller's *Fiesco; or, The Genoese Conspiracy* in 1796 as well as works by 'Viet Weber' (G.P.L.L. Wachter).[13] Goethe, Herder, Schiller, Kotzebue and Kant were also reviewed in the *Analytical*.

Of all these diverse and exciting publications published by Joesph Johnson, many would have passed across Wollstonecraft's desk in the publishing process. She sometimes acted as a 'reader' of prospective publications,[14] sometimes she reviewed new works herself, as we shall see, or sent out them to experts in the field. This immersion in the white-hot productions of the scientific revolution and the passionate voices of the emerging Romantic movement not only completed Wollstonecraft's education but gave her the intellectual cutting edge to carve out her own originality.

The Dissenters' campaign and the press

It is no coincidence that both Johnson's and Wollstonecraft's busiest years were 1787–91 for this was the period of the Dissenters' propaganda campaign to abolish the Test and Coporation Acts, which prevented them from political participation or taking office under the Crown or in municipalities. Three attempts to introduce or pass such Bills would fail.

This kept Johnson's press busy. For example, during the third campaign in 1790, Johnson published the majority of the hundred pro-repeal tracts it generated as well as many which arose in response.[15] This controversy directly contributed to an increase in reading matter in the last twenty years of the century.[16] Rags-to-riches bookseller James Lackington ascribed his own rise in the world to his abandonment of Methodism, when he first began to read and to sell freethinking theology and secular books instead of orthodox religious fare. He stated 'The sale of books has increased prodigously with the last twenty years' for 'all ranks and degrees now READ'.[17] As long as it lasted the campaign united the working-class Dissenters with the wealthy Nonconformist manufacturers and merchants as well as the intellectuals of the academies. It politicized a generation, and coinciding as it did with the outbreak of the French Revolution which was welcomed by most British people in its early years, formed the seed-bed for later democratic and chartist politics.

The call for toleration of *all* creeds and sects, the central tenet of liberalism, was at the heart of the Dissenters' campaign. Joseph Johnson put his principles into practice by making it his policy to publish not only highly controversial theologians such as the Socinian Priestley, but pamphlets by their opponents as well: for example the Jewish writer David Levi; and the Calvinist John Johnson.[18] He also invited the Roman Catholic Alexander Geddes to become the chief reviewer of theology to scotch the notion that the *Analytical Review* would be merely a mouthpiece for nonconformists. Geddes, translator of the Bible for Catholics and a pioneer of Biblical criticism, was deeply involved in piloting the second Catholic Relief Bill, passed in June 1791.[19]

The apparent eclecticism of Johnson's publications resulting from this policy has led modern scholars to assume either that the publisher had no strong views or that his politics and religion were 'marginal' or 'eccentric': irrelevant to his business career as a publisher.[20] Certainly no publisher would survive long if he confined himself to authors with whose views he agreed; and Johnson was not a party man. But on the other hand the politics of the time are distorted by viewing them through a secular lens. Johnson was a committed Unitarian at a time when this was technically illegal, and seen as not only dangerous freethinking but almost tantamount to treason. He had not only published the 1773 apology and 1774 inaugural sermon of the theologian who founded the sect, Theophilus Lindsey; but arranged the renting of old auction rooms in Essex Street and personally obtained a licence for services to be held there in 1774, thus instituting the first Unitarian meeting house in Britain. A new building opened for worship on 28 March 1778. In 1783 a Society for Promoting the Knowledge of the Scriptures was established by the Unitarians which depended principally on Johnson to put out its publications. When the Unitarian Society was formed in 1791, he issued liturgical works for its congregations, listed in a 1796 catalogue.[21] Thomas Christie, the editor of the *Analytical Review* was the nephew of William Christie, Junior, Merchant at Montrose, from whose writings Lindsey said Unitarianism had taken its rise.[22] There was nothing marginal about this or about the Dissenters' campaign which intensified in the next decade. It struck at the very heart of the British constitution which was based on the indivisibility of the national church and kingdom. Priestley's pamphlet of 1785 comparing Unitarianism to gunpowder placed 'under the old building of error and superstition' horrified the establishment, as did attacks on the very notion of a state church by other of Johnson's authors, such as Robert Robinson and John Disney.[23]

By 1790, as the campaign intensified after Bills for the repeal of the Test Acts were defeated in 1787 and 1789, and the French Revolution ignited political radicalism, so the Rational Dissenters became politicized – and Wollstonecraft with them. They began calling not merely for toleration but religious liberty as a principle, a civil right.[24] This led to demands for greater political participation in a reformed constitution. When Edmund Burke, who had formerly sympathised with Dissenters, attacked Dr Price in *Reflections on the Revolution in France* (1790) a pamphlet war erupted, of which more later. Andrea Engstrom comments that Johnson published some of the most noted political activists of the day: Major John Cartwright, founder of the Society for Constitutional Information; John Horne Tooke, leader of the SCI; and Christopher Wyvill, Head of the County Association movement. In fact Johnson was a member of the SCI himself.[25] Though the incarceration of publishers of radical works gave him second thoughts regarding letting his name stand on the titlepage of Paine's *Rights of Man*, Johnson did not wash his hands of it but arranged for its publication through J.S. Jordan, and published the first part of Joel Barlow's *Advice To The Privileged Orders*, deemed next in the seditious stakes.

Women and journalism

By the end of the eighteenth century, not only had authorship become a profession but the age of the 'fourth estate' had arrived. In 1731

Edward Cave had launched the *Gentleman's Magazine* and employed the young Samuel Johnson to concoct political sketches. Journalists achieved the right to report on debates in parliament by 1772, and by 1780 there were 60 magazines being published in London.[26] Ever since the days of Steele's *Tatler* and Addison's and Steele's *Spectator*, women had been encouraged to read and correspond with periodicals to extend their education. This both included them within the 'public sphere' as described by cultural theorist Jürgen Habermas,[27] yet restricted them within a feminine niche. In early journals material had been presented as the chatter of a unifying authorial persona or essayist, sometimes female; with some magazines specifically targeting a largely female audience by their titles. There had been female editors: Eliza Haywood's *Female Spectator* (1744) was followed by Frances Moore Brooke's *Old Maid* (1755), and others such as Charlotte Lennox's *Lady's Museum* (1760).[28]

In fact, as Paula McDowell has argued, at an even earlier stage of print culture, from 1678 to 1730, women had been much more prominent than this in every aspect of Grub Street.[29] They had been active as printers, publishers and pamphleteers and came from a wide socio-economic spectrum. But the bourgeois 'public sphere', increasingly came to define itself by standards of politeness appropriate to male property-holders. McDowell makes the point that this was in order to distance the Whiggish discourse oppositional to absolutism from the radicalism and sectarianism that had flourished during and after the Civil War period. So after the days of Tory polemicist Mary de la Rivière Manley, who took Swift's place as editor of the *Examiner* in 1711, and the anonymous publication of Lady Mary Wortley Montagu's Whig paper, *The Nonsense of Common-sense* (1737), we hear nothing for the next fifty years of women editing ungendered periodicals, leave alone labouring-class female polemicist publishers.[30]

Therefore when Johnson launched the *Analytical Review* in 1788, Wollstonecraft understandably thought she was 'the first of a new genus' as a full-time journalist and editor's assistant to a major progressive journal. She was neither a *demi-monde* nor aristocratic politico like Haywood or Montagu, having arrived in Grub Street via the religious networks which linked the private and public spheres. Though her Newington Green circle was impeccably respectable, historical links can be traced back to the sectarian dissidence of the Civil War period in their intense religious pamphleteering and polemics. It could be argued that the revolutionary period of the 1780s/90s reignited the sparks of that earlier conflagration. Wollstonecraft's own language of 'vindications' and the 'bowels' of compassion has more than a whiff of it. Perhaps because of the history of female preachers in some Dissenting sects in the seventeenth century, the Unitarians, in particular, proved particularly hospitable to female intellectuals. The poet Anna Laetitia Barbauld emanated from Priestley's circle at Warrington; the feminist novelist Mary Hays from that of the Essex Street meeting house; and political journalist Ann Jebb was the wife of Anglican-turned-Unitarian John Jebb.[31] The process would continue in the early nineteenth century, with writers such as Harriet Martineau forming a link between the Unitarian climate which produced a Wollstonecraft and the Victorian evolution of a feminist political movement.[32]

Women writing for money

One reason for Johnson employing a female assistant was the rise in secular literature, especially prose fiction. It was women writers who dominated the novel from the 1780s right through to the 1810s.[33] 'This branch of the literary *trade* appears, now, to be almost entirely engrossed by the Ladies' commented the *Monthly Review* in 1773. William Lane established the Minerva Press to deal almost exclusively in fiction written by women and for women, and Curll, Bell and Hookham also specialized in women's novels. By the 1780s the 'dramatic, unparalleled surge' in women's fiction constituted an important new market in the book trade, requiring coverage in the periodicals.[34] Johnson needed a literature specialist for the new review. On her part Wollstonecraft could use journalism and translation work to to subsidize her writing career. This was as necessary then as now. Payment was a mere £10 to an unknown writer for the copyright of a book. Even popular novelist Charlotte Smith only earned £150 for a three-volume novel; though Frances Burney obtained £250 for *Cecilia* (1782), and best-seller Ann Radcliffe was reputedly paid £500 and £800 for *The Mysteries of Udolpho* (1794) and *The Italian* (1797) respectively.[35] As Cheryl Turner points out, it would be a herculean task for an unknown writer to attain the minimal respectable income of £50 p.a. simply by selling copyrights. Yet Johnson calculated Wollstonecraft was spending almost £70 p.a. merely on her siblings from 1788–1791. She was also driven by the necessity of paying back the debts she had amassed when her school had failed. Wollstonecraft had produced a phenomenal seven publications in these three years, which probably earned most of this amount, but her bread-and-butter income came from regular reviewing, which was paid at two to three guineas a 'sheet', a 'sheet' being sixteen printed pages.[36] Johnson would advance her money in expectation of this work.

When she had been working for Johnson less than a year, Woll-stonecraft boasted to Fanny Blood's brother George, '...in short my dear Boy, I succeed beyond my most sanguine hopes, and really believe I shall clear above two hundred pounds this year...I daily earn more money with less trouble' (*CLMW*, pp. 174–5). By 6 October 1791 she was still keeping herself and the family afloat: 'Accepting Mr J. I do not owe twenty pounds, this Winter I shall *try hard* to lessen the pounds that stand against me in his books' (*CLMW*, p. 201). Wollstonecraft was a pioneer for her generation, not just by writing professionally, but in having no other source of income. This was quite a feat even for a male professional writer: her contemporaries William Godwin and Samuel Taylor Coleridge were notoriously short of money and often cadged for handouts from wealthy admirers.

Despite boasting to her sister about her boldness in taking this step, 'You know I was not born to tread in the beaten track' (*CLMW*, p. 165), Wollstonecraft did not want it generally known. 'At the commencement of her literary career, she is said to have conceived a vehement aversion to the being regarded, by her ordinary acquaintance, in the character of an author, and to have employed some precautions to prevent its occurrence' commented Godwin (*MAVRW*, p. 68). Writing was becoming more acceptable for women supplementing inadequate incomes at home, but it was a different matter for a 'lady' to acknowledge keeping herself entirely by paid work. Charlotte Smith trumpeted her victimhood as a deserted wife to justify writing novels to support her children; while Jane Austen masked her clandestine writing life with a conventional domestic existence as the dutiful daughter of a clergyman; having too little commercial success to be embarrassed over her remuneration. But Wollstonecraft had abandoned the compromise of a quasi-familial writing life. She lived alone in the public world at the heart of 'the Trade'.

Yet Wollstonecaft's initial shame-facedness shows she was conflicted about this. She justified her way of life by conspicuous self-sacrifice: spending virtually all her earnings on her younger siblings; stinting herself to educate them and set them up in suitable professions. Though playing the parental role with her brothers and sisters, she reverted to wayward daughter with her new mentor. As she became intimate with him, she turned Johnson into her surrogate father, instead of merely an employer (*CLMW*, p. 178), and spent most of her free time in his company demanding he assuage her fears and guilt. He remembered:

During her stay in George Street she spent many of her afternoons & much of her evenings with me, she was incapable of disguise, whatever was the state of her mind it appeared when she entered, & the turn of conversation might easily be guess'd; when harrassed, which was very often ye case, she was relieved by unbosoming herself & generaly returned home calm, frequently in spirits. F [Johnson's closest friend, Henry Fuseli] was frequently with us.... She could not during this time I think expend less than £200 upon her brothers and sisters.[37]

At the end of 1790, when she went to consult the frail publisher about her problems as usual but found him seriously ill, she was distraught at the thought of losing him:

> I should be deprived of a tender friend who bore with my faults – who was ever anxious to serve me – and solitary would be my life...
>
> (*CLMW*, p. 199)

Her frequent jokes to her sisters about having become an old maid betray Wollstonecraft's wry awareness that her Bohemian way of life lessened her chances of an advantageous marriage. But by 4 September 1790 she readily admitted she loved the life of a journalist: 'I could not now resign intellectual pursuits for domestic comforts' (*CLMW*, p. 194). In words heavy with duty and the Protestant work ethic she justified following her chosen vocation of authorship to Johnson:

> While I live, I am persuaded, I must exert my understanding to procure an independence, and render myself useful. To make the task easier, I ought to store my mind with knowledge – The seed time is passing away. I see the necessity of labouring now – and of that necessity I do not complain; on the contrary, I am thankful that I have more than common incentives to pursue knowledge, and draw my pleasures from the employments that are within my reach. You perceive this is not a gloomy day – I feel at this moment particularly grateful to you – without your humane and *delicate* assistance, how many obstacles should I have had to encounter...
>
> (*CLMW*, p. 186)

The gentle publisher's '*delicate*' tact had smoothed the stony path of the proud 'Princess', as her friends nicknamed her, leading from the Wollstonecraft family's pathetic pretensions to gentility to a robust engagement with 'the Trade'.

Reviewing

The rapid expansion in print culture had produced a new demand for more regular and professional reporting of all the new books. Antonia Foster points out that today we take book reviewing so much for granted that it is difficult to imagine the startling effect when Ralph Griffiths pioneered in the *Monthly Review* the concept of sifting all new publications, the important texts being systematically reviewed through summary, extensive quotation and commentary, while lesser material was merely listed.[38] The *Monthly* reviewers represented themselves as friends: shepherding the reader through a forest of new works by indicating seminal passages; and making brief judgements based on supposedly shared aesthetic and academic standards. It was so profitable a policy that other publishers set up their own journals. These followed the *Monthly's* lead by calling upon a circle of experts in their chosen fields to become regular reviewers. These men of letters were attracted by the payment (but insisted on anonymity because of the 'Grub Street' taint) and by the power to shape contemporary taste and opinion. For, as well as individual subscribers, the periodicals went to all the learned societies, universities and academies, subscription libraries and book clubs. When Joseph Johnson launched the *Analytical Review* in May 1788, having no other editorial staff, he badly needed Wollstonecraft's assistance as well as that of its young editor, Thomas Christie, for this was perhaps his most ambitious venture and coincided with the period when he published the greatest number of titles of his career .

Wollstonecraft on the staff of the *Analytical Review*

It was no coincidence that the *Analytical Review* was launched at the commencement of the Dissenters' campaign and in the year of the anniversary of the 'Glorious Revolution'. Like Priestley's now defunct *Theological Repository*, and the Unitarians' Society for Promoting the Knowledge of the Scriptures (led by Lindsey, Disney, Jebb, Kippis, Price and others) which promoted an 'analytic' or objective method of interpreting the scriptures, it took a rational approach but extended it to secular as well as religious publications.[39] It was a weighty monthly of about 120 pages, with four months making up a volume (subscribers would have them bound), and three volumes a year. Major reviews could be a lengthy ten to twenty pages and run on through two or three issues, while lesser publications merited only a paragraph. That theology led the list of contents signalled its importance, followed by Philosophy (with Politics later becoming a separate section), the History of Academies, History, Biography, Law and Natural Knowledge, Botany, Chemistry, Medicine, the Mathematical Sciences, Music, Poetry and Miscellanies. This ordering suggests that at first Wollstonecraft's department of *belles-lettres* was deemed of lesser importance. However, from 1791 (perhaps because Wollstonecraft was taking more editorial responsibility during Christie's absences) there were fewer medical books and a greater preponderance of space was given over to travel writing, literature and political polemic.

Thomas Christie was of a scientific turn, though 'his mind constantly ran on topics of classical, theological and philosophical Literature'.[40] This tall, thin, charming and handsome young Scotsman had initially come to London in 1784 to study medicine and became a male midwife. He struck up a correspondence on natural history with John Nichols, editor of the *Gentleman's Magazine*. In 1787 he abandoned medicine and toured the country 'in search of general knowledge' and thereby introduced himself to all sorts of eminent writers. In 1788 he published a miscellany of essays, the third of which called for a society for the diffusion of knowledge to be set up, 'that should cause books to be composed for the particular purpose of instructing the unlearned, and that should print or circulate, in different regions, such performances as had a tendency to awaken the love of letters'.[41] He hoped the worship of saints would be replaced by the commemoration of Aristotle, Confucius, Locke and Newton and that enlightenment of the common people would accompany political reform. At this time Christie took on the editorship of the *Analytical*.

The full title was the *Analytical Review; or, the History of Literature, Domestic or Foreign, on an Enlarged Plan*: 'literature' meaning books in general. For Christie's aim was partly bibliographic: to give as complete and descriptive a listing as possible, and like Maty's *A New Review*, which had ceased in 1787, the *Analytical* announced its cosmopolitanism by providing a 'Literary Intelligencer of Europe' giving brief exerpts from foreign reviews, and declaring it would welcome articles in foreign languages or Latin. Christie wanted the *Analytical* to be an encyclopaedic 'repository for information' and furnished it with regular and copious indexes to fulfil this purpose.

Reviewers included James Currie, Henry Fuseli, Alexander Geddes, Joshua Toulmin, John Hewlett, Robert Anderson, John Aikin, Anna Barbauld, Lucy Aikin, Mary Hays, Alexander Chalmers and Anthony Robinson. William Cowper also contributed as did Christie himself.[42]

Wollstonecraft reviewed quite a wide variety of subject-matter, but specialized in literature, travel writing, morality, education and biography. She contributed particularly heavily to the *Analytical* in 1789 and 1790, where she shouldered the burden of providing literally scores of brief accounts of minor poetry, fiction and plays where she was paid little in relation to the vast of amount of reading entailed. As she became more experienced in1791 and 1792 she took on less of this drudgery but, as one would expect, increased the proportion of substantial articles on more important works. She must have taken on extra responsibilities when Christie was in revolutionary Paris for six months in 1789, and again in 1791 and 1792. Before she herself left for France late in 1792, Wollstonecraft was taking on much of the work of assisting Johnson in editing what had rapidly become the most radical monthly in London. It is significant that from January 1795 the *Analytical* was scaled down to six months a volume, probably a sign of how much the elderly Johnson missed Wollstonecraft's help. On her return in February 1796, she began contributing reviews again (initialled MI for Mary Imlay and then from May signed M) and continued until her death. When Christie tragically died while on a business trip to Surinam in October 1796, Wollstonecraft seems again to have undertaken some editorial tasks, for her letters show her visiting Johnson's shop, assigning books to reviewers and retrieving them.

In the Preface to the first number, Christie had been at pains to stress the scholarly objectivity and neutrality of the journal, to attract a broader ideological spectrum of readership than would be provided solely by the sectarian support of rational dissenters, who were small in number though intellectually influential. He declared that he had wanted a return to impartial summaries of books which allowed the reader to judge for himself, but had been forced to compromise with the modern preference for opinionated reviewers.

Unlike Christie, right from the beginning Wollstonecraft saw the role of journalist as an ideologue and shaper of opinion. She crowed to Joseph Johnson in 1788 over the flabbiness of the opposition:

> The Critical appears to me to be a timid, mean production, and its success is a reflection on the taste and judgement of the public; but, as a body, who ever gave it credit for much? The voice of the people is only truth, when some man of abilities has had time to get fast hold of the GREAT NOSE of the monster. Of course, local fame is generally a clamour, and dies away. The Appendix to the Monthly afforded me more amusement, though every article almost wants energy and

a *cant* of virtue and liberality is strewed over it; as always tame, and eager to pay court to established fame

(*CLMW*, pp. 179–80).

As a literary critic she believed in the value of an individual view to refine upon the consensus and make the reader rethink the basis of judgement:

There is always a floating estimate of an author's literary strength, after the measure has been shaken by a few strong hands, tolerably just: yet, the sagacity of an individual who dares to think for himself will ever enable him to point out certain tints that not only elucidate the character, particularly considered, but serve as rules for writers of inferior note.

(*WMW*, 7: 444)

Anonymity

In only the second number (June 1788) one contributor protests that it is impossible to be objectively 'analytical' about novels regurgitating 'the cant of sensibility' for 'ridicule should direct its shaft against this fair game' (*WMW*, 7: 208). This sounds very much like the satiric tongue of Mary Wollstonecraft. We cannot be certain as initially the reviews were unsigned. Christie may have wanted to do away with anonymity, to make his contributors accountable for any derogatory comments or puffing, for he did succeed in instituting the use of initials which were possibly traceable by the cognoscenti. Scholars deduce from evidence in her letters, the correlation of the absence of these initials with her travels abroad and on stylistic grounds that it is probable that the reviews signed M, W and T belong to Wollstonecraft, and her modern editors Janet Todd and Marilyn Butler ascribe to her also the unsigned articles leading up to one with those initials, though conceding that doubts may remain about some of these (*WMW*, 7: 14–18).[43] It was unusual for a contributor to have used their own initials in this era of anonymity. As Todd comments, Wollstonecraft was almost obsessively self-referential. Nevertheless, the convention of writing as an anonymous reviewer gave her the freeedom to cast off her gender: to write about boxing, a treatise on the functioning of the eye, natural history, music, and other topics usually considered masculine in addition to the 'feminine' subjects of literature, travel and education she specialized in. (She would bring out her first political polemic anonymously too.) She adopted the scholarly convention of the supposedly objective tone and plural voice of the journal-as-institution. This conferred a gravitas that would not have been accorded to a subjective individual response under a female by-line. She was a particularly stern reviewer of women's writing: refusing to operate the patronising double-standard in which men of letters traditionally refrained from adverse criticism. She took no prisoners: '... why is virtue always to be rewarded with a coach and six?'; '... the whole had a harmless lulling effect on us; but those whom it can keep awake, may read to the end...'; 'This kind of trash, these whipped syllabubs, overload young, weak stomachs, and render them squeamish, unable to relish the simple food nature prepares'; and even: 'Pray Miss, write no more!' (*WMW*, 7: 174, 192, 185). Nevertheless, using her own initials perhaps signalled a desire conflicting with the liberation conferred by anonymity that she should eventually be acknowledged the author, and known specifically as a woman journalist in order to set a precedent for others. Indeed a modern commentator, undeterred by the manly house style, describes her stance towards wayward female authors as 'maternal'; and (rightly) observes that her awareness of the interpenetration of gender and genre makes Wollstonecraft a pioneer of feminist criticism.[44]

The *analytical* as shaper of public opinion

Despite its cool rationalist obectivity in treating ideological opponents, the liberalism of the *Analytical* was apparent in its judicious but over-whelmingly positive reviews of Dr Price's sermon to the Revolutionary Society of 1789 (by Wollstonecraft); Paine's *Rights of Man* (1792), Wollstonecraft's *Rights of Woman* (1792) and Godwin's *Political Justice* (1793), the two latter being lead reviews.[45] Its religious reviewing was even more definitively radical. The ideological importance of the *Analytical* is shown by the fact that in 1791 the Church and King *British Critic* was launched specifically to combat its progressive Dissenting agenda, and then, when this proved clerical milk and water, Pitt lent secret government support to the launch of the brutal *Anti-jacobin Review* in November 1797 to finish the job. The imprisonment without trial, followed by a trumped up prosecution and further incarceration for six months of the elderly and impeccably respectable Johnson in 1798, for selling a pamphlet printed by another publisher containing a controversial remark that the poor would not be disadvantaged by a possible successful French invasion, was a mark of desperation. It only succeeded in adding fuel to the radicals' fiery demand for liberty of the press. Pitt and Canning's spleen probably derived from fear of the *Analytical*'s support for the United Irishmen, and then its reviewing of Daniel O'Connell's *State of Ireland* in September 1798.[46] With the imprisonment of the publisher following on from the deaths of Christie and then Wollstonecraft, the *Analytical*'s circulation fell to 1500, compared with 4550 for the *Gentleman's Magazine*; 3500 for the *British Critic*; and 3250 for the *European Magazine*.[47] By the end of 1798 Johnson had to surrender the *Analytical* to other hands, where it soon foundered. In February 1799 the *Anti-Jacobin Review* celebrated by publishing a cartoon by Thomas Rowlandson, 'A Charm for a Democracy, Reviewed, Analysed, & Destroyed'. This showed the *Analytical* 'fallen never to rise again', mourned by prominent liberals while O'Connell's manifesto, the works of Joel Barlow and other incendiary texts are being heaped to ignite the bonfire under a cauldron of sedition under the eye of the devil and evil spirits.

The significance of the *Analytical Review* for posterity did not lie solely in its campaigning for liberal causes like the abolition of the slave trade and the extension of civil and political rights. As Walter Graham states:

> The *Analytical Review* reflected the romantic or sentimental drift of literature during the 1790s better than any other periodical; in particular, it...did more than any of its contemporaries to sentimentalize the writing about external nature. Especially good examples of this progressive tendency may be seen in the long and appreciative articles on the "picturesque" studies of William Gilpin and discerning treatments of Wordsworth's *Evening Walk and Descriptive Sketches*.

He goes on: 'Because of its forward looking tendency in politics and literature it is unquestionably one of the most important periodical sources for the student of the eighteenth century'.[48] Graham does not mention that the appreciative reviewer of Gilpin was actually Mary Wollstonecraft. But then even Wollstonecraft scholars have paid little attention to her journalism. Critical comments on her reviews are usually confined to her views on women's fiction, especially in relation to her own novels. Her reviews tell us as much about her role as a leading woman of letters as her own creative writing, however. Mary Wollstonecraft was the chief literary reviewer in the periodical most closely involved with the 'Romantic' currents of thought evolving out of and in reaction to the Enlightenment. A closer look at her articles will show that, though she is often thought of as a rationalist, Wollstonecraft was at the heart of the new Romantic fascination with nature, the primitive and the exotic – and especially with the construction of the self, the role of the writer and the creative process.

The writer as genius: the English moralist and the continental sentimentalist as contrasting role models

The first substantial review that Wollstonecraft was assigned and which was placed second article was a commentary on Dr Johnson's sermons in September 1788 in the Divinity section (*WMW*, 7: 36). Indeed, one of her very first short notices the month before had been an emotional (defiantly *un*analytical) response to the sermon he had written for the funeral of his wife published soon after his own death (*WMW*, 7: 32). She went on to review a selection of Johnson's periodical essays (*WMW*, 7: 48), and Arthur Murphy's *Essay on the Life and Genius of Samuel Johnson* (1792) (*WMW*, 7: 443) as well as a compilation of biographical sketches of Johnson (*WMW*, 7: 446), and the second instalment of Johnson's sermons, [*AR*, 5 (September 1789), pp. 64–7].[49] As James Basker has pointed out, Wollstonecraft's whole ouevre is peppered with allusions to Johnson which showed her familiarity with virtually every one of his works.[50]

Dr Johnson was a role model for every aspiring professional writer, and especially a moralist such as Wollstonecraft in her early days. His influence was particularly strong at the end of the 80s when she found his Christian stoicism consolatory when grief-stricken for Fanny (*CLMW*, 178–9) and was frustrated in her lack of intellectual fulfilment. In 1787 she had begun an allegorical tale 'The Cave of Fancy', modelled on Johnson's *Rasselas* which Godwin published in *Posthumous Works*; she had recommended Johnson's *The Adventurer* as more suitable reading than novels for girls in *Thoughts*; and she included five pieces by Johnson in *The Female Reader*.[51] As Basker points out, Wollstonecraft seems to have seen in Johnson the writer as suffering Romantic hero enduring depression and neglect, and herself as a female equivalent (despite their being on opposite sides of the religio/politico fence). He represented her long-held religious beliefs counselling stoic endurance. This did not prevent the doughty critic criticizing his inability to appreciate the Miltonic sublime in poetry (*WMW*, 7: 446) and his 'gloomy...narrow' religion of fear (*WMW*, 7: 36); and castigating his biographer for indiscriminate praise.

If Johnson represented the gold standard in English letters for the aspiring author to emulate, then France had produced the good doctor's antithetical opposite – the most dangerous of role models, especially for a woman writer. For if the stoicism of the Tory moralist had permeated Wollstonecraft's didactic works, it was the influence of that 'rascal' as

Johnson called him, Jean-Jacques Rousseau, who had inspired the
fictionalized autobiography of *Mary: A Fiction*. In the same batch of
reviews for volume II (May 1788) in which she had reviewed *The Beauties
of the Rambler, Adventurer, Connoisseur, World and Idler*, Wollstonecraft
was also considering two collections of selected writings of that very
different tortured genius, across the channel, supposedly driven to the
brink of madness by his detractors. She went on to contribute an
important long review of the publication in1784 of the second part of
Rousseau's *Confessions* in April 1790 (article 4), then commented on the
third volume of this in March 1791 (*WMW*, 7: 228; 362), as well as
evaluating two defences of Rousseau, by Madame de Staël (*WMW*,
7:136) and M. Guigne (*WMW*, 7: 409) respectively, and a spurious
'sequel' to *La Nouvelle Héloïse* (*WMW*, 7: 283). The April 1790 review
was first in the field, leading the way in a critical revaluation of Rousseau
by English radicals, according to modern scholarship.[52] Chiding 'cold
critics' for their ridicule of the *Confessions* and intolerance of the philosopher's unconventional religion and morality, Wollstonecraft made an
impassioned defence not only of Rousseau's integrity but of the genre
of modern autobiography itself:

> in short without screening himself behind the pronoun WE, the
> reviewer's *phalanx*, the writer of this article will venture to say, that he
> should never expect to see that man do a generous action, who could
> ridicule Rousseau's interesting account of his feelings and reveries –
> who could, in all the pride of wisdom, falsely so called, despise such
> a heart when naked before him.
>
> Without considering whether Rousseau was right or wrong, in thus
> exposing his weaknesses, and shewing himself just as he was, with all
> his imperfections on his head, to his frail fellow-creatures, it is only
> necessary to obseve that a description of what has actually passed in
> a human mind must ever be useful.
>
> (*WMW*, 7: 228–9)

However, 'what has actually passed in a human mind' is often the
aesthetic opposite of the didactic, and with her author-educator hat on
Wollstonecraft could not recommend exerpts of the freethinking Rousseau
as suitable reading-matter for young people (*WMW*, 7: 49) – in complete
contrast to her advocacy of the conservative Christian, Johnson. In his
autobiography *Confessions* and sentimental novel *La Nouvelle Héloïse*
Rousseau wrote 'from the heart' with 'the felicity of genius' about sex,
but 'for youth':

such delineations of human frailty appear to us...improper, because
they inflame the passions, and furnish excuses for sensual indulgence
before either the mind or body arrive at maturity

(*WMW*, 7: 409).

Yet as an obsessively autobiographical writer trying to exorcize her
own demons Wollstonecraft's personal identification with Rousseau
was stronger than with Johnson. 'He rambles into the *chimerical* world
in which I have too often [wander]ed – and draws the usual conclusion
that all is vanity and vexation of spirit. He was a strange inconsistent
unhappy clever creature – yet he possessed an uncommon portion of
sensibility and penetration' she had written Everina in 1787 (*CLMW*,
p. 145). Rousseau represented for Wollstonecraft her repressed passions,
particularly when she was suffering from unrequited love for the married
Rousseauist Henry Fuseli in the early 90s. When she and Godwin began
an affair in1796, in notes making assignations they euphemistically
coded their lovemaking as 'talking philosophy'. When she was twitting
the pedantic Godwin on his stilted loveletters – ['Don't] 'choose the easiest
task, my perfections...' – Mary sent him the second volume of *La Nouvelle
Héloïse* because she did not give her rationalist lover credit for as much
'philosophy' [i.e. eroticism] as Rousseau (*CLMW*, 331). Later after a tiff
with Godwin, she offered to part, declaring dramatically, in an allusion
to *Les Rêveries du Promeneur Solitaire*: 'and I – will become again a *Solitary
Walker*' (*CLMW*, 337).

For a woman writer to emulate Rousseau was to court controversy, yet
because female intellectuals were by definition breaking with convention and inviting censure and scorn, they were particularly drawn to
identify with his Romantic heroizing of the egoist/artist. De Staël and
Wollstonecraft would both be held up throughout the nineteenth century
as examples of the deleterious influence of Rousseauistic sentimentalism
because they had publicly followed their hearts and flouted sexual
convention. However, her caustic 1789 review of the young de
Staël's first published work, a 'timid' eulogy of Rousseau, demonstrates
Wollstonecraft's view that a good critic should not be an apologist for
any writer, for true genius is flawed and all the more magnificent for
being seen entire:

How little, indeed, do they know of human nature, who by their
injudicious candour labour to destroy all identity of character;
endeavouring to root out tares, to soften apparent defects, they may
seem to rub off some sharp corners, rude unsightly angles; but could

they really succeed in their childish attempt, they would only level original prominent features, and stupidly active, transform a sublime mountain into a beautiful plain.

(*WMW*, 7: 136)

Her metaphor of a mediocre artist toning down natural ruggedness here shows Wollstonecraft judging Rousseau by his own primitivist criteria. She elevates the Burkean masculine sublime (proto-Romantic) over the feminine beauty of order and regularity in aesthetics (Neoclassical). The female critic, she implies, needs to leave the shelter of convention if she is to recognize genius in others and to develop her own individualism.

The picturesque

Her friendship with Henry Fuseli had introduced Wollstonecraft to the company of other artists.[53] She knew John Opie well (he was rumoured to be in love with her), corresponded with Joshua Cristall, and must have known Fuseli's friend William Blake who illustrated *Original Stories*. She contributed an article in the *Analytical* on Sir Joshua Reynolds' discourse on Thomas Gainsborough, who had raised the profile of landscape painting (*WMW*, 9: 157); and she was the most prominent reviewer in the monthlies on the aesthetics of landscape – the concept of the picturesque. As a girl, she had attended the literary circle at Beverley of William Mason, the friend of Gilpin. Wollstonecraft foregrounded, very soon after publication and at length, the 'ingenious and instructive' second edition of Gilpin's *Observations on the River Wye* (1789) in September 1789 (*WMW*, 7: 160), which would go through five editions by 1800 and prepare the ground for the Romantic poetry of Wordsworth. She was equally quick off the mark with *Observations, Relative Chiefly to Picturesque Beauty, Made in the Year 1776, on Several Parts of Great Britain, Particularly the Highlands of Scotland* (1789) in January 1790 (*WMW*, 7: 196); and *Remarks on Forest Scenery, and other Woodland Views...Illustrated by the Scenes of New Forest in Hampshire* (1791) in August 1791 (*WMW*, 7: 386); and *Three Essays: on Picturesque Beauty and on Sketching Landscape...* (1792) in September 1792 (*WMW*, 7: 455).

Gilpin is significant for the development of Romantic currents of thought because he, like Edmund Burke in *A Philosophical Enquiry into the Origin of the Sublime and Beautiful* (1757), repudiated neo-classicism by emphasizing the subjective response of the viewer confonted by natural grandeur. An Anglican clergyman, Gilpin elevated nature over human culture: viewing landscape as a divine work of art. Paradoxically, at the very time agrarian improvers were enclosing 'wastes' and industrialization was despoiling the land, Gilpin's tours inspired a nationalistic pride in the wilder regions of the British isles: his own lake district, as well as Wales and Scotland. Examples of rural poverty were often either aestheticized or airbrushed out of the picture.

'The art of travelling is only a branch of the act of thinking' pronounced Wollstonecraft in her review of William Hamilton's tour of Antrim (*WMW*, 7: 277), and she approves writers like Gilpin who have 'some decided point of view, a grand object of pursuit to concentrate their thoughts, and connect their reflections' (*WMW*, 7: 161) in contrast to the desultory topographical accounts of rich idlers. Gilpin's attempt to formulate 'the principles of picturesque beauty' is laudable, though Wollstonecraft points out the difficulties in conveying an emotional response: 'sentiments which are lively, in proportion to the sensibility of the person who feels them, are ever evanescent, and almost incommunicable.... So much depends on the original frame, present mood, and other adventitous circumstances, an author cannot always expect to find his reader disposed to enter into his feelings' (*WMW*, 7: 161–2). Gilpin's drawings are helpful pointers, but 'a want of nerve and boldness in the lines' renders them closer to beauty than the sublime. Gilpin stressed that sketches must be done 'on the spot' from life and Wollstonecraft's incipient Romanticism shows in her preference for these impressionistic 'plain shadowy drawings' over tinted 'prettiness, and a high manner of finishing' them later (*WMW*, 7: 197), [that is, the new fashion for watercolours]. This was comparable to her preference for a spontaneous prose style. She castigated the artist J. Hassell, a follower of Gilpin, for 'the affected phrase' and 'prettiness' in accounts of tours calculated 'to pamper the imagination [especially of female readers] and leave the understanding to starve' (*WMW*, 7: 279); while Samuel Ireland was simply 'florid' and 'fustian' (*WMW*, 7: 447).

Cultural others

Wollstonecraft was always an indefatigable reviewer of travel books and tours at home or abroad, whether vehicles for sentimental effusions or cultural critiques. One of her earliest substantial reviews had been of Arthur Costigan's *Sketches of Society and Manners in Portugal* in August 1788 (*WMW*, 7: 29) for which she was well qualified by her visit to Fanny in Lisbon. She also wrote at length on Hester Lynch Piozzi's *Observations and Reflections Made in the Course of a Journey Through*

France, Italy, and Germany (*WMW*, 7: 109); John Meares' voyages from China to America (*WMW*, 7: 332); Ireland's tour of Holland (*WMW*, 7: 300); Duclos's travels in Italy (*WMW*, 7: 354); Le Vaillant's travels in Africa (1796) (*WMW*, 7: 479), and briefly on journeys in the West Indies (*WMW*, 7: 355); Kamtschatka (*WMW*, 7: 345), Australia and many other countries. Wollstonecraft demonstrates the Romantic turn from classical models to a new awareness of exotic, orientalist or anti-quarian cultural others, in her fascination with travels but also with translations and mythology. In July 1790 her enthusiastic review of Sir William Jones'translation from the Sanskrit of the drama *Sacontalá* – 'we have perused with so much pleasure' – was lead article, for writing on Indian culture and history was very prominent in the *Analytical* (*WMW*, 7: 271) in these years of the trial of Warren Hastings. Its 'artless touches of nature, which come home to the human bosom in every climate, will be found a delicious regale', she promised. The following month saw her sympathetically surveying Dr Sayers' *Dramatic Sketches of the Ancient Northern Mythology* in which he attempted to 'write in the ancient manner' with only limited success (*WMW*, 7: 286).

The campaign for the abolition of slavery was gathering momentum when Wollstonecraft began her career as a journalist and would only stall with the declaration of war with revolutionary France. She was moved by the bestselling slave autobiography *The Interesting Narrative of the Life of Olaudah Equiano, or Gustavus Vassa, the African: Written by himself* (1789), in which 'Many anecdotes are simply told, relative to the treatment of male and female slaves, on the voyage, and in the West Indies, which make the blood turn its course (*WMW*, 7: 100). But the sardonic critic noted some polishing of the naïve original had occurred and complained 'The long account of his religious sentiments and conversion to methodism, is rather tiresome'. Lieutenant-Colonel Jardine in his *Letters from Barbary, France, Spain, Portugal etc* (1788) thought the Berbers degenerate and ripe for colonization (*WMW*, 7: 108) and de Brisson, who had been a captive in North Africa, attested to their ferocity (*WMW*, 7: 241). But Wollstonecraft was pleased to find Le Vaillant in his African travels (1796) scotched the usual horror stories of brutal African customs and oppression of their women, praising 'the domestic virtues and moral sensibility' of the Hottentots in the Cape, at least those uncontaminated by 'rapacious whites, from whose bosoms commerce has eradicated every human feeling' (*WMW*, 7: 480). As early as December 1788, she tackled the notion just beginning to be thrown up by the Enlightenment rage for classification that differences of skin colour and appearance proved that God had divided humans into separate species or 'races', when she gave a long and enthusiastic account of Samuel Stanhope Smith's *Essay on the Causes of the Variety of Complexion and Figure in the Human Species* (1788). Smith took a naturalist's approach to the human being, arguing from many examples that God had not created different species of human (the hypothesis of polygenesis) but simply endowed mankind with the 'power of accommodating itself to every zone' over a long period of time. This hypothesis of monogenesis could sometimes be used to explain racial dissimilarities from European physiology in terms of degeneracy, but Smith is one of those who stresses the adaptibility of the human body to different climates and circumstances as a sign of God's grace.[54] Wollstonecraft endorsed this, and also carefully distinguished between the concept of a common innermost human nature and culturally-produced national characteristics: 'The untutored savage and the cultivated sage are found to be men of like passions with ourselves: different external circumstances, such as the situation of the country, forms of government, religious opinions, etc have been traced by the ablest politicians as the main causes of distinct national characters' (*WMW*, 7: 50). She also reviewed *The Negro Equalled by Few Europeans* (1790) by Joseph Lavall, a story 'invented to give the author an opportunity to depict ... the misery those poor wretches endure who languish in slavery', which she warmly recommended to young people despite remarking tartly 'It would have been more interesting if it had been less romantic' (*WMW*, 7: 282).

Novel writing

Despite all her cavils against the 'truly feminine novel', which has 'no marked features to characterize it' so that 'the same review would serve for almost all of them' (*WMW*, 7:82), it is obvious from her reviews that Wollstonecraft read them all – for her sins. They gave her plenty of opportunity for tongue-lashing: 'Much ado about nothing. We place this novel without any reservation at the bottom of the second class'; 'We smiled at the numbers death swept away' (*WMW*, 7: 83); '...the gentlemen as well as the ladies faint, lose their senses, are dying one hour, and dancing with joy the next', 'As tender embraces do not occur in every page, the reader has time to breathe between each fond scene' (*WMW*, 7: 119). But her puritan fears of popular fiction 'as a principal cause of female depravity' (*WMW*, 7: 459) were only the other side of the coin of her awareness of its huge power to influence the public, and she was always ready to concede that 'to write a good novel requires uncommon abilitites' (*WMW*, 7: 66).

So when she was attempting to write a second novel herself in 1796–97, and finding the writing problematical, we find her reviews particularly considered and insightful. Indeed, at the end of her writing life it is evident that Wollstonecraft found herself in the infuriating position of being a better critic than she was writer of novels. Her fellow female 'Jacobins', Mary Robinson and Elizabeth Inchbald, were producing novels of protest which mixed the improbabilities of romance convention with social criticism. Robinson's own early life would influence the story of Wollstonecraft's protagonist in *Wrongs of Woman*. Wollstonecraft admired 'the spirit of independence, and a dignified superiority to whatever is unessential to the true respectability and genuine excellence of human beings' in *Robinson's Angelina* (1796), whose 'principal object is to expose the folly and the iniquity of those parents who attempt to compel the inclinations of their children into whatever conjugal connections their mercenary spirit may choose to prescribe' (*WMW*, 7: 461). Mrs Inchbald's 'improbable' adventures also 'become interesting in proportion as they exhibit the conflicts of feeling and duty', and Wollstonecraft notices the piquant mixture of sentimental 'naivete' and 'judicious satirical sallies' in dialogue that had worked so well in her stage plays (*WMW*, 7: 463). In her earlier review of Inchbald's *A Simple Story*, Wollstonecraft had fumed that though like her own Mary, Matilda was 'educated in adversity', she failed to become a strong role-model: 'Why do they [female writers] poison the minds of their own sex by strengthening a male prejudice that makes women systematically weak?' (*WMW*, 7: 370). More mellow now, she regrets that Mary Robinson develops her plots too rapidly 'to allow incidents gradually to grow out of it which are the fruit of matured invention' (*WMW*, 7: 486). As with Charlotte Smith, the drive to earn money compromises the art. Wollstonecraft commented sadly of Smith: 'It is to be lamented that talents like hers have not had a more genial sky to ripen under' (*WMW*, 7: 485).

In dealing with Frances Burney's *Camilla* (1796) Wollstonecraft insists 'an analytical account ... would not do it justice' for 'we are in justice bound to say that we think it inferiour to the first-fruits of her talents, though we boldly assert, that Camilla contains parts superiour to any thing she has yet produced' (*WMW*, 7: 465). Perhaps it is not surprising that Wollstonecraft should show herself adept at scenting out the weaknesses as well as pointing up the strengths of a moralistic novel of the conduct-book type. Anne Mellor has suggested that Wollstonecraft, like other female literary critics of the Romantic era (Joanna Baillie, Anna Barbauld, Elizabeth Inchbald, Clara Reeve and Anna Seward) subscribed to a coherent aesthetic theory quite distinct from 'Romantic' individualism. They were didactic, pedagogical and concerned to balance rationality with the claims of emotion; upholders of a mimetic theory of art rooted in the realistic portrayal of the quotidien.[55] This seems accurate if we confine our attention to Wollstonecaft's comments on fiction. Nevertheless, we have seen that her other interests as a reviewer were often strongly proto-Romantic, and Wollstonecraft was certainly as self-referential in her own writing as the most egoistic of Romantic individualists. Though she often validated realism, her own fictions do not focus on the quotidien in the manner of Burney or Austen, but are 'philosophical' novels of ideas – a genre more popular on the continent than in Britain. That she perfectly understood the way the fantastic worked in the mind of the reader is demonstrated by her insightful account of Ann Radcliffe's Gothic romance, *The Italian* (1787):

> The nature of the story obliges us to digest improbabilities, and continually to recollect that it is a romance, not a novel, we are reading; especially as the restless curiosity it excites is too often excited by something like stage trick. – We are made to wonder, only to wonder; but the spell, by which we are led, again and again, round the same magic circle, is the spell of genius. Pictures and scenes are conjured up with happy exuberance; and reason with delight resigns the reigns to fancy, till forced to wipe her eyes and recollect with a sigh, that it is but a dream.
>
> *(WMW*, 7: 485)

This shows that Wollstonecraft could probably have agreed with Clara Reeve in *The Progress of Romance Through Times, Countries, and Manners etc* (1785) that 'romances are neither so contemptible nor so dangerous a kind of reading as they are generally represented', being a kind of 'heroic fable' in elevated language whose tradition can be traced back to classical times (p. 111), in contrast to the the novel which 'gives a familiar relation of such things, as pass every day before our eyes'.

In fact, surveying her career as a reviwer has demonstrated that Wollstonecraft's fear of the fictional, and of false sensibility – overtly expressed in her pedagogic works – was merely the other side of the coin of her deep personal fascination with the inspirational power of the creative imagination and with the romantic myth of the misunderstood author. As an autodidact, with no university education in the classics, she benefitted from openness to other cultural influences: she learned French and German, travelled in Europe and revelled in accounts of exotic climes and manners. If she was impatient with formulaic stilted romances destined as female reading-fodder, then it was because they were unnatural. Or as we might say today, not Romantic enough.

4
'An Amazon stept out': Wollstonecraft and the Revolution Debate

> And lo! an Amazon stept out,
> One WOLSTONECRAFT her name,
> Resolv'd to stop his [Burke's] mad career,
> Whatever chance became.
>
> An oaken sapling in her hand,
> Full on the foe she fell,
> Nor could his coat of rusty steel
> Her vig'rous strokes repel.

(William Roscoe, 'The Life, Death and Wonderful Achievements of Edmund Burke: a new ballad', 1791)

> Thus WOLLSTONECRAFT, by fiery genius led,
> Entwines the laurel round the female's head;
> Contends with man for equal strength of mind,
> And claims the rights estrang'd from womankind;
> Dives to the depths of science and of art,
> And leaves to fools the conquest of the heart;
> Or mounts exulting through the fields of space,
> On faith's strong pinions, to the throne of grace.

(John Henry Colls, *A Poetical Epistle Addressed to Miss Wollstonecraft,
Occasioned by Reading her Celebrated Essay on the Rights of Woman,
and her Historical and Moral View of the French Revolution*, 1794)

The Dissenters' campaign for full civil rights coincided with the outbreak of the French Revolution in 1789. The nonconformist bourgeois liberalism of Price, Priestley and Burgh, based on Locke and the equality of all men in the sight of God, became spiced with a heady new radicalism. Gone was the Whiggish myth that reform only meant a return to an earlier better-balanced constitution. Thomas Paine, William Blake and William Godwin, all from artisan-class Dissenting roots but having abandoned institutional religion, boldly proclaimed that the rights of all men were natural and inalienable. The reform of parliament and the constitution was just the beginning of the progress they imagined. The plight of the rural poor and the new urban and industrialized working class cried out for social and economic reform. Lower-class agitators such as Thomas Spence and Daniel Eaton arose and publicized their communitarian schemes for redistributing land or wealth in ballad sheets and broadsides.[1]

Joseph Johnson's dinners demonstrated the overlap between old-generation 'True Whigs' and the new radicalism. Round the publisher's table with the Dissenters sat agitators for parliamentary reform, John Horne Tooke and John Thelwall; cobbler-turned-novelist and play-wright Thomas Holcroft; American poet and pamphleteer Joel Barlow; philosophical anarchist William Godwin; and – most importantly – corset-maker-turned-bridge-builder and major polemicist of the American revolution, Thomas Paine. Paine, together with another of Johnson's authors, the Welsh Deist David Williams, author of *Letters on Political Liberty* (1789), was honoured with French citizenship for his political writings and elected on to the National Convention to help draft a new constitution for France. Thomas Christie undertook to translate it into English and Johnson published it in Britain. Christie became a close friend of Paine, whom he met in revolutionary Paris. From 1791 to 1792, when Paine was in London, Wollstonecraft was a regular visitor of his.[2] In January 1792 Christie became a founder member of the London Corresponding Society, set up by shoemaker Thomas Hardy, whose aim was to spread reformist ideas amongst the lower classes in all British cities.[3] The more controversy, the more publications generated. We can see why the Pittite administration would label the Johnson circle as 'Jacobins' or emulators of the revolutionaries and would seek to check the outpourings of his press.

William Godwin tells us that the radical ideas of the French Revolution had a traumatic effect on Mary Wollstonecraft's thinking: 'The prejudices of her early years suffered a vehement concussion. Her respect for establishments was undermined' (*MAVRW*, p. 72). But one of her friends, we don't know who, reacted by retreating into religious conservativism: 'At this period occurred a misunderstanding upon public grounds, with one of her early friends, whose attachment to musty creeds and exploded absurdities, had been increased, by the operation of those very circumstances, by which her mind had been rapidly advanced in the race of independence'. At this point Wollstonecraft's Newington Green mentor, Dr Richard Price was attacked in print by Edmund Burke in *Reflections on the Revolution in France* (1790). This event became a catalyst. Everyone had to stand up to be counted.

The pamphlet war known as the 'Revolution Debate' was the fiercest political controversy in print culture since the commonwealth period. Its significance should not be downplayed merely because no second English revolution ensued. Its very existence testifies to an appetite for participation in the public sphere which seemed only to increase with feeding. It grew so gargantuan it struck terror into the establishment. Dissenters, women and the unpropertied classes – having no civil rights – made the most of print culture, which was democratic capitalism in action. The outpouring of texts from the press was the shocking proof not just that the reading public had expanded to include women and the working classes, but that woman and artisans were not passive consumers – they had the pen in hand and brought the most famous orator and statesman of the day to book. Print had got out of control. It could disseminate ideas even to the illiterate by means of chapbook excerpts and ballads. The writing was on the wall. However long deferred, the day would inevitably come when political rights would be extended to all.

A Discourse on the Love of Our Country

On 4 November 1789 Richard Price preached this sermon to the Revolution Society, which met to commemorate the bloodless 'Glorious Revolution' of 1688, when the Catholic James II had been deposed in favour of Protestant William of Orange. Price used the occasion to call for the repeal of the Test and Corporation Acts, and his providential belief in progressive reform of the British constitution was renewed by the breaking news of the revolution in France which he welcomed in the passionate conclusion some thought blasphemous:

> What an eventful period is this! I am thankful to have lived to see it, and I could almost say, *Lord now lettest thou thy servant depart in peace, for mine eyes have seen thy salvation.* I have lived to see a diffusion of knowledge which has undermined superstition and error. I have lived to see the rights of man better understood than ever, and nations panting for liberty, which seemed to have lost the idea of it. I have lived to see thirty millions of people, indignant and

resolute, spurning at slavery and demanding liberty with an irresistible voice...

Richard Price, *A Discourse on the Love of Our Country*, (1789)

Sermons spawned political tracts as a genre. When published they bore the signs of their origin as speech-acts: they were short, written in the first-person and, very directly addressed the auditor/reader. So Price begins by asking conversationally, that on this anniversary of 'our delivery at the Revolution from the dangers of Popery and arbitrary power', if he should 'be led to touch more on political subjects than would at any other time be proper in the pulpit, you will, I doubt not, excuse me'.[4] Wollstonecraft, in her review of it for the *Analytical* described his style as 'simple, unaffected ... the heart speaks to the heart in an unequivocal language' (*WMW*, 7: 185). Her own polemics would adopt a comparably informal style, evoking speech. Price's published text, which went through six editions in a year, used many capital letters, dashes and underlining to indicate the emphases of the original oratory, and especially the impassioned passages, termed 'hwyl' in Welsh, when the preacher was possessed by a visionary spirit.

What infuriated Edmund Burke enough to summon up all his oratorical skill in reply to Richard Price? Price preached that the true patriot should not irrationally love his country right or wrong, but use his reason to actively interrogate whether or not it followed the path of virtue. He told his flock that it was their right and duty to pursue truth for themselves: 'Our first concern as lovers of our country must be to enlighten it'. Enlightenment was the difference between dignified human beings and subjects who 'crouch to tyrants ... as if they were a herd of cattle': 'Shew them they are *men* and they will act like *men*' (Price, p. 181). In this formulation education is the only distinction worth making: rank, gender, religious affiliation, and race lose their relevance. And every individual can educate himself/herself if there is freedom of the press.

Price hails the philosophers of the English and the French Enlightenments for disseminating among their fellow creatures 'just notions of themselves, of their rights, of religion, and the nature and end of civil government' (Price, p. 182). He credits their 'writings' with inspiring 'those revolutions in which every friend to mankind is now exulting'. But he warns that the oppressors, the priests and tyrants, are bound to respond with attempts to censure and control the spread of print culture: 'They know the light is hostile to them, and therefore they labour to keep men in the dark. With this intention they have appointed licensers of the press ...'. His own sermon boldly challenges such censorship. For Price informs the congregation that sometimes their consciences will forbid them obeying civil laws:

> For it has oftener happened that men have been too passive than too unruly, and the rebellion of Kings against their people has been more common and done more mischief than the rebellion of people against their Kings.... Civil governors are properly the servants of the public and a King is no more than the first servant of the public, created by it, maintained by it, and responsible to it ...
>
> (Price, p. 185).

Price seemed a demagogue to Burke, who thought the role of a man of the cloth was to inculcate a quietist ideology of obedience and acceptance of suffering in his flock. Mary Wollstonecraft, having abandoned her earlier belief in resignation to the divine will of providence, would affirm the doctrine of civil disobedience even more strongly than Price in a 1792 review for the *Analytical*: '[T]he most sacred duty of humanity [is] to oppose authority, which cannot be ordained by God' (*WMW*, 7: 424).[5]

Burke's *Reflections of the Revolution in France*

The personal attack by Burke on Price as 'a man much connected with literary caballers, and intriguing philosophers'[6] came as a shock to the public. It was seen as a betrayal by the Dissenters, for the Whig statesman had once been sympathetic to their cause, supported the American Revolution, and was a friend of Paine's. The public was mystified by Burke's melodramatic evocation of the French royal family beset by a murderous mob and his predictions of anarchy and slaughter, when at this time many who had visited the country could testify to its relative peacefulness and moderation. The truth was that Burke was only interested in France insofar as the revolution provided him with raw material to create a cautionary tale to frighten the British away from following suit. He now saw the Rational Dissenters not just as the thorn but as the spear in the side of the paternalistic National Church. He wanted to turn the Whigs against the new radicalism led by Rational Dissenters and scupper the campaign for repeal of the Test Acts.[7] He made the embarrassing revelation that the Revolution Society had adjourned to the London Tavern after Price's sermon, where the preacher had moved that congratulations be sent to the French National Assembly; and that one of the toasts drunk was to 'The Parliament of *Britain* – may it become a National Assembly' (*Reflections*, p. 7). Burke went on to explain in Parliament on 11 May 1791 that he had written *Reflections* to counteract 'malignant factions', which attempted 'by clubs and others, to circulate pamphlets and disseminate doctrines subversive of the prerogative, and therefore dangerous to the constitution' (*Reflections*, p. 33)

Dissenters, the national church and control of print culture

There was a great emphasis in the first half of *Reflections* on this dangerous circulation of controversial ideas through books and associations. The second stressed the role Burke wished to preserve for the national church of controlling education through schools and universities. As Mary Wollstonecraft began to read and respond, perhaps originally in order to review it, she found herself pouring out a passionate rebuttal which turned into a political polemic itself. This was hardly surprising, as she herself represented exactly the sort of autodidact reader and educational writer Burke despised: who believed she had found, and would spread, enlightenment through participation in the public sphere. *Reflections* opens by casting aspersions on the Society for Constitutional Information, which circulated progressive books, charging it with fomenting revolution under the cover of charity. The Whiggish Revolution Society had been infiltrated with 'new members' (*Reflections*, pp. 55–6), Burke suggested. It wasn't simply the notion of parliamentary reform to which Burke objected, but the way 'this seditious, unconstitutional doctrine is now publicly taught, avowed, and printed' (*Reflections*, p. 76). He sarcastically pictured Price and the Revolution Society strutting down to the London Tavern to make their toasts 'with a proud consciousness of the diffusion of knowledge, of which every member had obtained so large a share in the donative, [and] were in haste to make a generous diffusion of the knowledge they had thus gratuitously received (*Reflections*, p. 117).

Burke mocked Price's dangerous espousal of individualism. Price refused to endorse any single form of worship as the only true faith, and he encouraged heterodox believers to set up their own churches: 'His zeal is of a curious character. It is not for the propagation of his own opinions, but of any opinions. It is not for the diffusion of truth, but for the spreading of contradictions' (*Reflections*, p. 63). Burke realized that if such views spread so that sectarianism was abandoned and thoroughgoing religious toleration were adopted, then a multiplicity of sects and religions would result. If all beliefs were to be equally respected, this would call for a secular state, not one bound up with a monopolistic National Church whose communicants were the only citizens allowed entry to university, the professions and participation in local and national government. Burke looked back nostalgically to the days when the church had controlled access to literacy:

> The nobility and the clergy, the one by profession, the other by patronage, kept learning in existence.... Happy if learning, not debauched by ambition, had been satisfied to continue the instructor, and not aspired to be the master! Along with its natural protectors and guardians, learning will be cast into the mire, and trodden down under the hoof of a swinish multitude.
>
> (*Reflections*, p. 130)

This latter telling phrase, revealing Burke's fear of an educated lower class thinking for themselves and refusing to tug forelocks, helpfully provided eye-catching titles for radical propaganda, such as Thomas Spence's *Pig's Meat, or Lessons for the Swinish Multitude* (1793–95).

Burke urged that the Church of England was no mere manmade institution to be tampered with. It was sacred because divinely ordained by God:

> He willed therefore the state – He willed its connection with the source and original archetype of all perfection.... Church and state are ideas inseparable in [British] minds.... Our education is in a manner wholly in the hands of ecclesiastics, and in all stages from infancy to manhood.
>
> (*Reflections*, pp. 148–9)

Burke's opposition to the French Revolution particularly centred on the fear that atheistical 'philosophical fanatics' would have French church property appropriated, and that a secular 'Civic education' on a Rousseauistic lines would be adopted by the national Convention (*Reflections*, p. 197). He feared British sympathizers would want to emulate them. His Irish background perhaps accounts for Burke's particular sensitivity to the role of the Church of England in maintaining the Ascendancy and the union of England with Ireland, as well as with Scotland and Wales, in the face of Catholic and Dissenting disaffection. Protestant Britain had needed a Catholic enemy to promote unity at home while competing for trade and colonies. Yet here was France perhaps divesting herself of Popery and emulating the

British constitution, and North London progressives such as Price preaching cosmopolitan ideals denouncing the sort of patriotism he deemed merely 'a love of domination, a desire of conquest, and a thirst for grandeur and glory, by extending territory and enslaving surrounding countries' (*Reflections*, p. 179).

Reflections was published on 1 November 1790 and sold at 5s. The excitement of events across the channel combined with the puzzle of Burke's *volte face* made it compulsory reading, and extracts were immediately published in the *Public Advertiser*. Such was the excitement that 7,000 copies were sold in the first week alone; and 19,000 in the year following in Britain and another 13,000 in France where it had been quickly translated.[8] By September 1791 it had run through eleven editions (*Reflections*, p. 15), and been translated into German and Italian. Horace Walpole, Frances Burney, Edward Gibbon and many Pittites praised it effusively but Fox, Sheridan and the Whigs, at whom it was aimed, were not impressed, and neither was their patron, the Prince of Wales. The radicals were scornful: Horne Tooke dubbed the book 'the tears of the priesthood for the loss of their pudding'. Many cartoons appeared caricaturing 'Don Dismallo' or 'The Knight of the Woeful Countenance' and his quixotic lament for the lost age of chivalry. *Reflections* sparked an unprecedented pamphlet war. There were over seventy responses.[9] One of the very first was Wollstonecraft's, on 29 November.[10] It was published anonymously, and only nineteen days later the second edition priced at 2s 6d was on sale with her name on the title page.

A Vindication of the Rights of Men

Godwin records that Mary had 'seized her pen in the first burst of indignation, an emotion of which she was strongly susceptible. She was in the habit of composing rapidly' (*MAVRW*, p. 73). Her advertisement explains that 'Many pages...were the effusions of a moment; but, swelling imperceptibly to a considerable size, the idea was suggested [presumably by Johnson] of publishing a short vindication of *The Rights of Men*' (*WMW*, 5: 5). The title boldly affirmed support for the French Declaration of the Rights of Man, as would Paine's subsequently. For the sake of speed, she sent off the sheets to the printer as she wrote them, but this gave her no opportunity to revise. Godwin felt the book was impertinent: 'a too contemptuous and intemperate treatment of the great man' (*MAVRW*, p. 73). However, Wollstonecraft felt no constraint in expressing her anger. Godwin tells the following anecdote, which casts an intriguing light on Johnson's understanding of Wollstonecraft's volatile egoistical temperament and how best to deal with it:

> When Mary had arrived at about the middle of her work, she was seized with a temporary fit of torpor and indolence, and began to repent of her undertaking. In this state of mind she called one evening, as she was in the practice of doing, upon her publisher, for the purpose of relieving herself by an hour or two's conversation. Here the habitual ingenuousness of her nature, led her to describe what had just past in her thoughts. Mr Johnson immediately, in a kind and friendly way, entreated her not to put any constraint upon her inclination, and to give herself no uneasiness upon the sheets already printed, which he would cheerfully throw aside, if it would contribute to her happiness. Mary had wanted stimulus. She had not expected to be encouraged, in what she knew to be an unreasonable access of idleness. Her friend's so readily falling in with her ill-humour, and seeming to expect that she would lay aside her undertaking, piqued her pride. She immediately went home; and proceeded to the end of her work, with no other interruptions but what were absolutely necessary.
>
> (*MAVRW*, pp. 73–4)

Her first political polemic demonstrates how composing those scores of reviews for the *Analytical* had paid off in shaping Wollstonecraft's style, which was the direct, forceful eloquence of the crusading journalist not the disciplined reasoning of a logician. Modern critics have described it as disorganized, but an impression of spontaneity was acceptable in such political pamphlets. It was also a deliberate strategy to contrast 'honest' indignation with the calculated oratory Burke had been sweating over for some time. Her training as a reviewer had taught her to pay close attention to the style of the text she was judging, and she signalled in her advertisement that she would demystify Burke's rhetorical tricks: '[M]y indignation was roused by the sophistical arguments, that every moment crossed me, in the questionable shape of natural feelings and common sense' (*WMW*, 5: 5). She used her critic's merciless eye for spotting and quoting – out of context – any overblown bombast. She would even parody the victim text, and use techniques of irony and satire, to expose its motivation. Her own contrasting stance or persona was carefully chosen to persuade the reader of her authority and integrity.

Burke, of course, had followed a comparable path when answering Price. As Price argued for the supremacy of reason, his opponent sought to imply the preacher was an egoistical rationalist by interspersing into his own arguments 'spontaneous' digressions full of natural feeling. His frame device was a letter to a 'very young gentleman at Paris, who did him the honour of desiring his opinion' on the revolution (*Reflections*, p. 53), based on an actual request by Charles-Jean-François de Pont.[11] The informality of a letter would enable him to write personally, with the reader stepping into the subordinate role of the enquirer, endowing Burke with an advice-giver's paternal authority. Burke had announced: 'Indulging myself in the freedom of epistolary intercourse, I beg leave to throw out my thoughts, and express my feelings, just as they arise in my mind, with very little attention to formal method' (*Reflections*, p. 60). In fact, Burke was the most eloquent practitioner of the age in what is now called the 'New Rhetoric', which had assimilated recent ideas from the Scottish Enlightenment on taste, beauty, sublimity, and psychology: adapting the orality of traditional classical rhetoric to the production of English prose for print culture.[12]

Wollstonecraft's tactic was to address an ad hominem reply addressing Burke in the second person, also in the form of a letter. In this as in the second Vindication, Wollstonecraft used the first-person pronoun, and D.L. Macdonald's stylistic analysis demonstrates that she tends to refer to herself as an isolated individual or a representative of humanity rather than as part of a group.[13] She was an outsider, and made a virtue out of necessity in foregrounding her own lack of status in comparison to 'a man whose literary abilities have raised him to notice in the state' (*WMW*, 5: 7). Unlike that sophisticated man of letters, she was just a plain, honest beginner: 'I have not yet learned to twist my periods, nor, in the equivocal idiom of politeness, to disguise my sentiments'. Burke is frequently buttonholed as 'Sir', while his antagonist quizzes him from a moral point of view, admitting with mock humility that her ideals are 'simple, unsophisticated' (*WMW*, 5: 9).

Since she wrote anonymously, as when she reviewed, there was an assumption of masculinity in her frequent play on the words 'manly' and 'men': 'You see I do not condescend to cull my words to avoid the invidious phrase, nor shall I be prevented from giving a manly definition of [the rights of men]' (*WMW*, 5: 7). This was part of an ongoing strategy in which Burke was constantly associated with the feminine and the speaker with the masculine (e.g. *WMW*, 5: 21, 23, 24). His feelings are 'ornamental' art, concocted for a feminine performance: '[T]he Ladies, Sir, may repeat your sprightly sallies, and retail in theatrical attitudes many of your sentimental exclamations' (*WMW*, 5: 8). In fact the book is permeated by this association of the speaker's republican ideals with true manliness and Burke's courtliness with effeminacy and foppery. This gendered view of different forms of government had been adopted by French philosophes such as Montesquieu, Voltaire and Rousseau as well as the Scottish Enlightenment philosophical historians such as John Millar, who had influenced commonwealthmen Priestley and Price:

> Yes, Sir, the strong gained riches, the few have sacrificed the many to their vices; and, to be able to pamper their appetites, and supinely exist without exercising mind or body, they have ceased to be men.
>
> (*WMW*, 5: 10)

There was an unconscious slippage or play on words regarding gender in this formulation, for – though the philosophes had specifically blamed the undue influence of women at court for aristocratic effeminacy – in the context of Wollstonecraft's humanitarian discussion of universal rights, 'manliness' signifies 'humankind', and when she discusses education, manhood can signify gender-neutral adulthood and the attainment of reason:

> Is it among the list of possibilities that a man of rank and fortune *can* have received a good education? How can he discover that he is a man, when all his wants are instantly supplied, and invention is never sharpened by necessity.
>
> (*WMW*, 5: 42)

It was also a traditional weapon of satire to denigrate one's opponent's manhood. This had been used in classical times, when Juvenalian satire included savage personal abuse including casting aspersions on the victim's sexual potency. Wollstonecraft only hints at the latter, but roundly denounces the 'skulking, unmanly way' Burke boasts of his impartiality when he has secured a pension by his pen (*WMW*, 5, 13); and the 'unmanly servility' produced when 'men of some abilities play on the follies of the rich' (*WMW*, 5: 24). Her barbs would be given another twist of ridicule when Burke's 'manly' opponent was revealed to be a woman – in the publication of the second edition with Wollstonecraft's name on the title page. Wollstonecraft and Johnson might have planned it this way as a publicity stunt. The *Analytical Review* enjoyed the joke, crowing: '[H]ow deeply must it wound the feelings of a *chivalrous knight*, who owes the fealty of "proud submission and dignified obedience" to the fair sex, to perceive that two of the boldest of his adversaries are women!' [referring to Wollstonecraft and Catharine Macaulay].[14] As with her reviews, anonymity allowed Wollstonecraft to write as robustly as a man, and gained her views a fair hearing without prejudice; while revealing her identity later allowed her book to be re-read in the light of her sex. Some passages constituted what we would now term a feminist critique of Burke's aesthetic treatise, *A Philosophical Enquiry into the Origin of Our Ideas of the Sublime and the Beautiful*. She had on her first page rejected these binaries in favour of discrete moral absolutes, declaring moral truth the essence of the sublime and simplicity the only criterion of beauty. She went on to analyse the implication of Burke's gendering of his paired aesthetic categories:

> You may have convinced them [women] that *littleness* and *weakness* are the very essence of beauty; and that the Supreme Being, in giving women beauty in the most super eminent degree, seemed to command them, by the powerful voice of nature, not to cultivate the moral virtues that might chance to excite respect, and interfere with the pleasing sensations they were created to inspire'
>
> (*WMW*, 5: 45).

This contains the germ of the insight she would develop in *Rights of Woman*.

Wollstonecraft had fun parodying Burke, for example substituting Dr Price for Marie Antoinette as the object of reverence. 'I could almost fancy that I now see this respectable old man, in his pulpit, with hands clasped, and eyes devoutly fixed, praying with all the simple energy of unaffected piety...' (*WMW*, 5: 18). This brought down to earth Burke's courtier-like reverie on the French queen: 'I saw her just above the horizon, decorating and cheering the elevated sphere she just began to move in, – glittering like the morning star...'. Wollstonecraft comments that however Utopian are Price's political visions, at least they are grounded in Christian belief rather than making an erotic idol of rank. She appropriates Burke's imagery of veils and drapery,' You have been behind the curtain...' (*WMW*, 5: 21) and lets in the light on his Gothic melodrama of the queen stripped of the trappings of status: 'On this scheme of things a king *is* but a man; a queen *is* but a woman; a woman *is* but an animal, and an animal not of the highest order' (*WMW*, 5: 25). On behalf of women she repudiates the Burkean homage to chivalry, 'because such homage vitiates them, prevents their endeavouring to obtain solid personal merit; and, in short, makes those beings vain inconsiderate dolls, who ought to be prudent mothers and useful members of society' (*WMW*, 5: 25). Chivalry was not much in evidence in his depiction of poor women who marched the king and queen from Versailles to Paris on 5–6 October as 'furies' in 'the abused shape of the vilest of women'. She punctures his cartoon-like rhetoric: 'Probably you mean women who gained a livelihood by selling vegetables or fish, who never had any advantages of education...' (*WMW*, 5: 30).

Linguistically, Wollstonecraft puts Burke in the position of the perhaps-about-to-be-violated queen, promising 'with manly plainness' (*WMW*, 5: 36) to 'strip you of your cloak of sanctity' and 'to shew you to yourself, stripped of the gorgeous drapery in which you have enwrapped your tyrannic principles' (*WMW*, 5: 37). For all this reverence for royal families was not in evidence during the recent regency crisis. Burke had then rushed round collecting statistics from mental hospitals to prove how unlikely it would be for George III to recover from his insanity, and help get him locked up so the Prince, Burke's own patron, would take the reins (*WMW*, 5: 26). In a Swiftian lightning reversal, she insinuates that the lachrymose Burke is mad himself. Adapting Burke's own words describing the French revolution as a 'tragi-comic scene', she describes what he would see if he looked into the 'wild anarchy' of his own mind, which lacks the rudder of moral reason in its artificial manipulation of the emotions: 'You would have seen in that monstrous tragi-comic scene the most opposite passions necessarily succeed, and sometimes mix with each other in the mind; alternate contempt and indignation; alternate laughter and tears; alternate scorn and horror' (*WMW*, 5: 28).

Paradoxically, Wollstonecraft's own enthusiasm – her 'eager warmth and positiveness' was noted by the *Monthly Review* – was put to the use of satirizing Burke's sensibility and imagination as mere literary fictions.[15] To counter imagination from the standpoint of sober truth, she asserted her own authenticity by adopting a religious rather than literary mode: a first-person spiritual confession or testimony of her beliefs.

> If virtue be an instinct, I renounce all hope of immortality; and with it all the sublime reveries and dignified sentiments that have smoothed the rugged path of life: it is all a cheat, a lying vision; I have disquieted myself in vain; for in my eye all feelings are false and spurious, that do not rest on justice as their foundation, and are not concentred by universal love.
>
> I reverence the rights of men. – Sacred rights! for which I acquire a more profound respect, the more I look into my own mind; and, professing these heterodox opinions, I still preserve my bowels

[compassion or pity – 17th-century usage]; my heart is human, beats quick with human sympathies – and I FEAR God!
. . . It is not his power that I fear – it is not to an arbitrary will, but to an unerring *reason* I submit . . .
This fear of God makes me reverence myself.

(*WMW*, 5: 34)

She specifically rejects here Shaftesbury's linking of the emotions with an innate moral sense, and the subjectivity of the Burkean sublime which puts the fear of God on the same spectrum as awe for temporal authority. For Wollstonecraft, still a Lockean thinker, it is the power of reason not the passions which distinguish us from the brutes (*WMW*, 5: 40), and transfigures what, in a Miltonic phrase, she calls 'the human face divine' (*WMW*, 5: 27).

Wollstonecraft puts her ideals of justice and human rights on a moral basis, for, like the Rational Dissenters, she is fighting a crusade against a corrupt state which impedes the freedom of the individual to make truly moral choices and to participate in improving society. However, Rational Dissenters such as Richard Price did not threaten the rule of property, or the existing social hierarchy.[16] Wollstonecraft's position has become more radical than theirs, for she asserts '[T]he property in England is much more secure than liberty', while the property of the working man 'is in his nervous arm' and may be easily stolen from him (*WMW*, 5: 15). 'Hereditary property' and 'hereditary honours' impede progress; and Burke's respect for age-sanctioned precedents would logically mean he would have crucified Jesus, rather than follow Christ's revolutionary ideas (*WMW*, 5: 14). Primogeniture distorts filial and conjugal love into property deals and increases the gap between wealthy and poor. The liberty of the poor is sacrificed to the property of the rich in game laws, press gangs and capital punishment for petty theft.

Wollstonecraft reserves the climax of her book for an impassioned demand for a more equal society. It is Burke's contempt for the poor which most rouses her indignation: '[Y]ou seem to consider the poor as only the livestock of an estate' (*WMW*, 5: 17). His cynical response to their suffering is that they 'must be taught their consolation in the final proportions of eternal justice'. She pictures a rich landowner adopting the vogue for the picturesque initiated by Burke in cultivating 'sweeping pleasure-grounds, obelisks, temples, and elegant cottages as *objects* for the eye', but ignoring the peasantry. 'Why cannot large estates be divided into small farms?' she demands. If the rich can enclose the commons, 'Why might not the industrious peasant be allowed to steal a farm from the heath?' (*WMW*, 5: 57). Though she does not develop this hint, the rhetorical question allies Wollstonecraft with the extremely radical land reform movement of the late eighteenth century. The artisan communist propagandist Thomas Spence, whose lecture of 1775 was reproduced in numerous pamphlets, and Professor William Ogilvie, author of *Essay on the Rights of Property in Land* (1781), both argued for a redistribution of property to improve the lot of agricultural labourers, though coming from opposite ends of the class system. Paine's *Agrarian Justice* (1797) was so moderate by comparison that Spence wrote *Rights of Infants* (1797) to disparage it.

Then Wollstonecraft turns to the misery of the unemployed in London with a pessimistic vision of class division which surely helped inspire Blake's famous poem 'London':

Where is the eye that marks these evils, more gigantic than any of the infringements of property, which you piously deprecate? Are these remediless evils? And is the humane heart satisfied with turning the poor over to *another* world, to receive the blessings this could afford? ...
Surveying civilized life, and seeing, with undazzled eye, the polished vices of the rich, their insincerity, want of natural affections, with all the specious train that luxury introduces, I have turned impatiently to the poor, ... but, alas! what did I see? a being scarcely above the brutes, over which he tyrannized; a broken spirit, worn-out body, and all those gross vices which the example of the rich, rudely copied, could produce. Envy built a wall of separation, that made the poor hate, whilst they bent to their superiors; who, on their part, stepped aside to avoid the loathsome sight of human misery.

(*WMW*, 5: 57–8)

For the poor are shackled by what Blake called 'mind forg'd manacles'. When Wollstonecraft compares the outrages committed on the French royal family on 6 October to the misery and vice haunting our steps every day she feels that threats of hellfire pale into insignificance, for 'Hell stalks abroad' in today's London. In her evocation of the lashed slave in the colonies and the worker dying unmourned in the work-house Wollstonecraft parodies Burkean tearful sensibility with a double row of dashes signifying the overflow of emotion demanding 'more than tears'.

Reception

Wollstonecraft's book caused a stir and made her name. A foretaste of sexist vitriol to come was the insinuation by the Anglican Dr Edward Tatham in *Vindication of Burke's Reflections* (1791) and *Letters to Burke on Politics* (1791) that Wollstonecraft's anger against press gangs was on account of her friendship with 'honest mechanics' with whom she was on the most intimate terms![17] The Tory *Critical Review* also described her as 'too nearly approaching to the levelling principles of the present times'. The reviewer warned her that if she 'assumes the disguise of a man' she must not expect chivalrous treatment, while the *Gentleman's Magazine* doubted whether such a good pamphlet could really have been written by a 'fair lady'.[18] But the *Analytical* prophesied its 'lively and animated remarks, expressed in elegant and nervous language...[would be read] when the controversy which gave rise to them is forgotten'.[19] Dr Price, in a letter of thanks she kept all her life, assured her that he had 'not been surprised to find that a composition which he has heard ascribed to some of our ablest writers, appears to come from Miss Wolstonecraft'.[20] Catharine Macaulay expressed herself 'pleased at the attention of the public to your animated observations' in thanking Wollstonecraft for her complimentary copy, and proposed they should correspond (*MWRL*, p. 167). Liverpool art lover William Roscoe, later to write a biography of Lorenzo de' Medici, wrote a mock-heroic poem in celebration of her and commissioned her portrait to be painted. On 6 October 1791 she wrote to tell him she did not think 'it will be a very striking likeness; but, if you do not find me in it, I will send you a more faithful sketch – a book that I am now writing, in which myself, for I cannot *yet* attain to Homer's dignity, shall certainly appear, head and heart – but this between ourselves...' (*CLMW*, p. 203). Her confidence burgeoning, she was already at work on *Rights of Woman*.

Other pamphlets

Wollstonecraft's was not just one of the first but one of the best half dozen of all the replies to *Reflections*. The vast majority of responses to *Reflections* were critical of Burke, but they expressed a range of views: from the moderate Whig views of James Mackintosh or Capel Lofft; or the historical perspective of 1688 by the 'True Whig' Catharine Macaulay; to the masterly defence of the Dissenters by Joseph Priestley or the philosophical anarchy of William Godwin, which envisaged the eventual withering away of all government. Thomas Christie, as someone who had lived in revolutionary Paris for six months, was in a position to correct many of Burke's factual inaccuracies in his response. The editor of the *Analytical* concentrated on defending Price's support for enlightenment through print culture:

> I think a clergyman acts properly, who sometimes preaches a sermon in favour of *the liberty of the press*, and teaches his audience the high value of that inestimable privilege; for the propagation of truth is the most sacred and peculiar duty of the ministers of the gospel. But truth cannot be propagated where the press is restrained...[21]

He went on to draw attention to the fact that the new French constitution guarantees as natural and civil rights: 'Liberty to every man to speak, write, print and publish his thoughts, without the writings being subjected to censure or inspection before their publication'.[22]

Paine's *Rights of Man*

But the most startling of all the replies to Burke was that of Thomas Paine, the first part of which had appeared on 22 February 1791 for 3s and sold out within hours. Like Wollstonecraft, Paine asserted 'the divine origin of the rights of man at the creation'.[23] Every new generation was born with these sacred – because God-given – inalienable rights. They should become transformed into civil rights by the contract with government which Locke had described. But Paine denied that each new generation should be bound by precedents from the past. Opposed to 'hereditary legislators' and the 'aristocratical law of primogenitureship' (*Rights of Man*, p. 104), he declared: 'Lay then the axe to the root, and teach governments humanity' (*Rights of Man*, p. 80). In simple, clear language he spoke to the common man, rather than the intelligentsia. He was less concerned with defending Price and the Dissenters' campaign than supporting the French Revolution and demystifying 'the puppet-show of state and aristocracy' in Britain (*Rights of Man*, p. 81). In the course of demolishing a scurrilous government-sponsored attack on Paine's private life, Wollstonecraft wrote in the *Analytical* in October:

> [H]is writings prove him to be a man of strong sense, and his arguments must be answered before they lose their force: the dirt thrown on his character will not stick to political axioms'
>
> (*WMW*, 7: 396).

Paine was determined to make the publication of his book a testing-ground for the rights of free speech, opinion, conscience and association: rights which became embodied in the first amendment to the American Constitution that same year.[24] As we have seen, Joseph Johnson originally printed the book but at the last minute lost his nerve and Godwin, Holcroft and Brand Hollis helped Paine to arrange its distribution under the imprint of J.S. Jordan. Because the price was relatively high at 2s 6d, the government initially let it go. Paine gave his profits to the Society for Constitutional Information; and waived royalties when permitting provincial printers to make copies because he wanted to disseminate the book as widely and cheaply as possible to reach the common man.[25] Jordan published a new edition three days after the first; by 30 March a third appeared; by May a sixth, when 50,000 copies had been sold. The book was translated into French and German.

When he produced an even more revolutionary second part of *Rights of Man* on 16 February 1792, which concentrated on the inequity of wealth, Paine planned to print 100,000 copies of each part to test the liberty of the press. Paine himself estimated that the sale of the complete edition reached 'between four and five hundred thousand' within ten years of publication, making it the most widely read book of all time. His modern biographer, Keane, calculates that one out of every ten literate Britons bought it, without taking pirated copies into account. A network of reform societies had arisen to distribute it throughout Britain. Opposition to this reform movement was not confined to a new eruption of polemical pamphlets. In July 1791 a 'Church and King' mob destroyed the house, library and laboratory of Dr Priestley, as loyalism began to mobilize. Pitt's government now moved to suppress any cheap incendiary texts distributed to the working classes: the price was crucial in whether the publisher was prosecuted. By May 1792 a Royal proclamation was issued against 'wicked seditious writings printed, published and industriously dispersed' and a summons was served on Paine (*Rights of Man*, ed. Henry Collins, p. 36). Legend has it that Blake warned Paine to leave the country. He was certainly in France by the time he was declared an outlaw.

Rights of Woman

Godwin tells us of the writing of *Rights of Woman* that, above all, Wollstonecraft wanted her book to bring about change:

> She considered herself as standing forth in defence of one half of the human species, labouring under a yoke which, through all the

records of time, had degraded them from the station of rational beings, and almost sunk them to the level of the brutes. . . . the rich as alternately under the despotism of a father, and a husband; and the middling and the poorer classes shut out from the acquisition of bread with independence . . .

(*MAVRW*, p. 74)

By 2 January 1792 Wollstonecraft had completed what she thought of as the first volume of *Rights of Woman*, though no second part was ever published. It comprised a substantial volume and was priced at 6s. She confessed to Roscoe:

I am dissatisfied with myself for not having done justice to the subject. – Do not suspect me of false modesty – I mean to say, that had I allowed myself more time I could have written a better book, in every sense of the word, the length of the Errata vexes me. . . . I intend to finish the next volume before I begin to print, for it is not pleasant to have the Devil [printer's assistant] coming for the conclusion of a sheet before it is written.

(*CLMW*, p. 205)

A second edition was published in 1792 which was reprinted in 1796. In this, Wollstonecraft, emboldened by success, more confidently affirmed the equality of the sexes, when adjusting her expressions. Her book sold only a few thousand copies, nothing in comparison with Paine. Yet *Rights of Woman* was a *cause célèbre* and became known throughout Europe.

Godwin asserted that she wrote *Rights of Woman* in six weeks. His view that the book was hurriedly-written, poorly organized and repetitive has passed into literary history. Undoubtedly, Wollstonecraft's masterpiece was produced by the revolutionary moment, and, passionate in temperament, she [and Johnson] wanted to get it out quickly. But, unlike Godwin, she was not interested in conforming to scholarly conventions. Her vehemence and personal tone are a conscious attempt to reproduce in literary style a persuasive political speech. This was an acceptable form of rhetoric in this type of polemic. As an author she had always attempted to use her personal experience as a witness to her sincerity. This reflected her Puritan heritage of spiritual testimonies. Her method was to state the 'few, simple principles' of her argument, and then elaborate these by way of many detailed examples and anecdotes from her real experience. This does involve occasional restatement, but it is a rhetorical method of reinforcement rather than mere disorganized planning. It also utilizes that dialectic between real and ideal, which characterized the subjective language of sensibility.[26]

Another difficulty that faced her, as a pioneer 'feminist', was how to address the reader: whether to direct her argument solely at her own sex, or speak to men as well. In her analysis of the text, Amy Smith has found that Wollstonecraft consciously attempted to engage with men and women at different stages of her argument, to bring about her proposed 'REVOLUTION in female manners'.[27] Even when she addressed women, she sometimes spoke sternly from a distance, and at others rallied them in sisterly solidarity. Her use of pronouns therefore varied from second to third to first person plural, and the changes in gear contribute to a lack of fluency and smoothness. But she was more interested in effecting change through writing than proving she could write correctly and elegantly.

Her immediate precursor in addressing the role of woman was the celebrated historian of the English Revolution and Civil War, Catharine Macaulay Graham, whose *Letters on Education: with Observations on Religious and Metaphysical Subjects* (1790) Wollstonecraft had reviewed in a long leading article for the *Analytical*. She had approved Macaulay's progressive dictum that 'the same rules of education in all respects are to be observed in the female as well as to the male children' (*WMW*, 7: 313). But the most thought-provoking section must have been the proposition that there is 'No Characteristic difference in sex', which denied that intellectual abilities and characteristics were innately different in boys and girls. Wollstonecraft comments: 'The Observations on this subject might have been carried much farther' (*WMW*, 7: 31). Like Macaulay, she would treat the subject as a moral and philosophical question. But unlike the older woman, Wollstonecraft had moved on from rational dissent and Whiggery to relate the status of women to the question of rights for all, on an individual democratic basis.

Many have noticed that in using the singular 'woman' Wollstonecraft's title deliberately echoed that of Paine. She had got to know Paine in 1791–92 and was firmly identifying herself as a fellow radical. Braithwaite suggests that passages on hereditary distinctions in *Rights of Woman* are echoed by the arguments of Paine's second part of the *Rights of Man*, which he was then engaged in writing. This undoubtedly reflects their conversations of the time.[28] Wollstonecraft's Paineite title was enough for Hannah More, who refused to open the book. Paine wrote for the common man and Wollstonecraft's second vindication was aimed at the middle class, but both were beyond the pale – for neither the working

classes not women were expected to enter the public sphere, in which only educated men of letters wrote on politics.

Out of all the texts generated by the Revolution debate, *Rights of Woman* was one of the most radical affronts to liberalism as the preserve of a male property-owning elite.[29] Authority based on gender was, like rank, a hereditary prejudice to be swept away. Worse, Wollstonecraft challenged the economic slavery of women:

> From the respect paid to property flow, as from a poisoned fountain, most of the evils and vices which render this world such a dreary scene to the contemplative mind. . . . There must be more equality established in society, or morality will never gain ground, and this virtuous equality will not rest firmly even when founded on a rock, if one half of mankind [be] chained to its bottom by fate . . .
>
> (*WMW*, 5: 211)

Wollstonecraft commented that females had no stake in the nation – 'denied all political privileges, and not allowed, as married women, excepting in criminal cases, a civil existence, [women] have their attention drawn from the interest of the whole community to that of the minute parts' (*WMW*, 7: 256). She demanded political rights: '[W]omen ought to have representatives, instead of being arbitrarily governed without having any direct share allowed them in the deliberations of government' (*WMW*, 7: 217). Women were routinely ignored in calls for universal manhood suffrage by reformers both in Britain and in revolutionary France. *Rights of Woman* was dedicated to Talleyrand, who served on the National Assembly, and specifically asked him to reconsider his rejection of equal secondary education for both sexes in his plan for public education in the new republic.[30] She counters Rousseau's denial of citizenship to women on the basis that they cannot perform military duty. Her comparison of women to soldiers (e.g. *WMW*, 5: 92, 216), and description of wives and mothers as 'active citizens' suggests that the birthing and nurturing of new citizens is an equivalent civic sacrifice. This implies a challenge to the new republic's assumption that women constitute 'passive' not 'active' citizens with full civil rights.

These 'feminist' aspects did not take up much space in *Rights of Woman* and were dismissed as Utopian nonsense even by her most sympathetic progressive contemporaries and indeed the generation to come. More important for the present than the call for civil rights was Wollstonecraft's extended philosophical and moral argument for the intellectual equality of women. For Wollstonecraft, it was the God-given

gift of reason to both sexes, not property, that guaranteed independence and was the basis of human rights. It was difficult even for Pittites to demonise the puritan female philosopher when she so insistently allied the possession of reason to the attainment of virtue. Her impassioned call for women to become full moral agents in the world rather than to be solely immersed in the life of the body was rooted in protestant orthodoxy and could not easily be refuted. Superficially, the book didn't look so very different from many harmless pleas for better female education. Yet what seemed in one way merely an extension of enlightenment ideals, in fact constituted an attack on the most fundamental assumption of civic humanism: that a man's authority over his family, itself hierarchically ordered by age and gender and endorsed by the laws of inheritance, was natural and fixed. The implications of feminist individualism for the property laws, and for the dynastic system of politics and patronage in Georgian Britain were simply unthinkable.

The book's ideal of woman as a self-supporting intellectual gave it a certain self-referentiality. That was why Wollstonecraft had described it as a self-portrait to Roscoe. Wollstonecraft called for women to be educated not 'as a preparation for life', still the justification for needlework being taught girls in schools until the 1960s, but for 'advancing gradually towards perfection' (*WMW*, 5: 122), in other words for immortality. To attain true virtue, 'passive obedience' to convention must be rejected. Instead, women must have the independence to actively take moral decisions, according to their conscience, in order to live the good life. They must judge and be judged by the same standards of absolute moral value as men. This emphasis anticipates the existentialist feminism and transcendence of the body of twentieth-century philosopher Simone de Beauvoir.

Wollstonecraft styles herself 'a philosopher' and 'a moralist' (*WMW*, p. 103), and she is justifying her own authority as a writer when she asserts that women are equal to men in their 'power of generalizing ideas, of drawing comprehensive conclusions from individual observations'. But she notes that culturally women are more submerged in the material world than men: '[E]very thing conspires to render the cultivation of the understanding more difficult in the female than the male world' (*WMW*, 5: 123). The role of a female radical writer is therefore vital to challenge women's 'habitual slavery to first impressions', for 'when an author lends them his [sic] eyes they can see as he saw...' (*WMW*, 5,186). Though 'vanity and vexation close every enquiry' for the strenuous intellectual, 'disappointed as we are in our researches, the mind gains strength by the exercise, sufficient, perhaps to comprehend the

answers which, in another step of existence, it may receive...' (*WMW*, 5,178).

To be capable of truly independent thought, women must first have economic independence: 'to earn their own subsistence' (*WMW*, 5: 155). They must be free to make decisions for themselves and for their children; their actions not always mediated through their relationships with fathers or husbands:

> The being who discharges the duties of its station is independent; and, speaking of women at large, their first duty is to themselves as rational creatures, and the next, in point of importance, as citizens, is that, which includes so many, of a mother'
>
> (*WMW*, 5: 216).

Wollstonecraft approved of motherhood as a meaningful and dignified civic role, in a republic where society would recognize and reinforce the domestic cultivation of virtue. In fact, she placed the family at the heart of political reform – 'the unit of the social and moral reproduction of society'.[31] An egalitarian marriage bringing up boys and girls equally was fundamental to building a new society on rational principles.

In contrast to 1970s feminists, it was sexual passion she deplored as a snare, in which 'becoming the slave of her own feelings, [woman] is easily subjugated by those of others'. 'The being who can govern itself has nothing to fear in life; but if any thing [be] dearer than its own respect, the price must be paid to the last farthing' (*WMW*, 5: 171). The irrational tribute society pays to women's beauty is unmerited, like its respect for wealth (*WMW*, 5: 126). But 'the woman who has dedicated a considerable portion of her time to pursuits purely intellectual, and whose affections have been exercised by humane plans of usefulness, must have more purity of mind, as a natural consequence, than the ignorant beings whose time and thoughts have been occupied by gay pleasures or schemes to conquer hearts' (*WMW*, 5: 193).

She had opened the book by citing the romantic myths of Prometheus and Pandora as idealizations of revolutionary individuals who dared to steal the 'celestial fire of reason' to challenge the status quo of hereditary power. But it is the seductive modern myth of nature she warns the reader against. The idea that the state of nature was a primitive golden age was propagated by Rousseau, inspiration of the French revolutionaries and English liberals alike in their critique of the *ancien régime*. But Wollstonecraft perceived that idealizing nature could be potentially conservative, especially with regard to women. Rousseau's chapter on

female education in *Émile*, like the republican Milton's portrayal of Adam and Eve, complacently depicted feminine traits of submissiveness and weakness as 'natural' rather than culturally produced. It is this blindness of the male radical tradition towards the oppression of women she principally seeks to correct.

It is because she writes from the unique overlap she herself has created between radical politics and the conduct book genre that Wollstonecraft is able to spot the inconsistencies in progressive liberalism and Christian moralism alike. She states unequivocally that 'all the writers who have written on the subject of female education and manners from Rousseau to Dr Gregory, have contributed to render women more artificial, weak characters, than they would otherwise have been' (*WMW*, 5: 91). But she also shows how even the best women writers have been complicit with the male-centred ideology of 'natural' femininity, citing Anna Barbauld, Mrs Piozzi, Madame de Staël and the Countess de Genlis. She contends that soldiers, supposedly the epitome of masculinity, are just as vain, mercenary, and concerned with surfaces as women, demonstrating that manners maketh men and women (*WMW*, 5, 92). Obsession with their appearance is culturally-produced in subalterns with no power over anything else and who scramble for preferment.

Effeminacy characterizes the unnatural state of anyone, aristocrat or woman, who pursues pleasure and does not work (*WMW*, 5: 120, 125–7, 157). Wollstonecraft wants women to give up their empire over men and join the meritocracy: 'When do we hear of women who, starting out of obscurity, boldly claim respect on account of their great abilities or daring virtues?' (*WMW*, 5: 127). She is bitter that 'the woman of the greatest abilities, undoubtedly, that this country has ever produced... [Catharine Macaulay] has been suffered to die without sufficient respect being paid to her memory', but confident that 'posterity... will be more just' (*WMW*, 5: 174–5). She concludes the book by comparing women with Dissenters: both are sections of the community denied civil rights and university education; both have been accused of cunning and petty machinations (*WMW*, 5: 265). Their 'prim littleness' and scheming behaviour is only the product of powerlessness and exclusion.

Reviews of *Rights of Woman* were mainly respectful, but many male readers were chary of it. Dr John Aikin's review of *Rights of Woman* was lead article in the March number of the *Analytical*, with the second part of Paine's *Rights of Man* playing second fiddle, and was so long it had to be continued in July. He praised the author's 'discernment in seeing through that trick which our sex for ages has played off upon her's, and her courage in avowing sentiments which are a kind of heresy in female

circles'.[32] Nevertheless, he attempts to evade the significance of the title, avowing *Rights of Woman* is only 'an elaborate *treatise* of *female education*' though of the utmost importance, and demurs at what he obviously sees as hopelessly utopian ideas such as extending political representation to women or co-education after the age of nine. A similar line was taken by William Enfield in the *Monthly Review*, which chivalrously saluted the growing number of female intellectuals in the Georgian age, and genuflected in the harmless direction of a more rational scheme of female education. However Enfield failed to understand, let alone endorse, any of Wollstonecraft's most original insights into the relationship between the psychological characterization of femininity and the oppression of women. *Rights of Woman* was positively received by the *Literary Magazine*, the *General Magazine*, the *New York Magazine* and the *New Annual Register*. Only the pro-government *Critical* asserted the intellectual inferiority of women, and worried that after Wollstonecraft a woman might have such a high opinion of her mental capacity that she would not lower 'the dignity of her virtue' to childcare and 'descend to the disgusting offices of a nurse'.[33]

Mixed responses circulated even within radical circles. Wollstonecraft's old friend Thomas Taylor coupled her with Paine in his mean-spirited parody, *A Vindication of the Rights of Brutes* (1792). Even Godwin himself, in his *Memoirs of the Author of a Vindication of the Rights of Woman*, felt obliged to concede that many of the sentiments of this 'very bold and original production' were 'of a rather masculine description', with occasional passages of 'a stern and rugged feature' (p. 75). He had met Wollstonecraft for the first time at Johnson's on 13 November, 1791, in company with Paine, where the talk had been of monarchy, Tooke, Dr Johnson, Voltaire, pursuits and religion. They had formed a mutual antipathy for one another and argued most of the evening. Though he conceded she was an original thinker, he found her writing beneath his notice because it was too ungrammatical and careless in its expressions (*MAVRW*, p. 80). Anna Barbauld responded to Wollstonecraft's attack on her poem praising femininity, 'To a Lady, with some painted flowers', by writing 'The Rights of Woman' which preferenced romantic love over 'separate rights'. She probably circulated it in manuscript, but did not publish the poem. However, Blake was inspired by *Rights of Woman* to compose his *Visions of the Daughters of Albion* (1793). John Henry Colls and George Dyer published their paeans of praise for the vindicator of women's rights, and her friend, the Cornish working-class artist, John Opie painted another portrait of Wollstonecraft proudly with her book and quill.

The book burned like a slow fuse through the networks of 1790s women writers. Anna Seward confided to her diary that the book was startling and provocative. Sarah Trimmer, though conceding that 'Miss Woolstonecraft [sic] is a woman of extraordinary abilities', smugly congratulated herself on having 'found so much happiness in having a husband to assist me in forming a proper judgement...that I never wished for a further degree of liberty or consequence than I enjoyed'.[34] Hannah More categorically refused to read the book, commenting '[T]here is, perhaps, no animal so much indebted to subordination for its good behaviour as woman.'[35]

In August 1792 Wollstonecraft received an ardent letter of support from Unitarian Mary Hays, who, daringly for a woman, had published a theological pamphlet *Cursory Remarks*, in answer to Gilbert Wakefield's *Enquiry into the Expediency and Propriety of Public Worship*. She would become a follower of Wollstonecraft and submit her manuscripts to her for comment; later writing her own feminist treatise. Mary Robinson, in her *Letter to the Women of England on the Injustice of Mental Subordination* (1799), would also avow herself 'of the same school' as that 'illustrious British female' (Wollstonecraft). In her *Letters from the Mountains* (1807), Anne Grant records her excitement at reading the 'dangerous' *Rights of Woman* in 1794. She had written in her diary that it was 'so run after here [Glasgow], that there is no keeping it long enough to read it leisurely'.

The most exciting response of all was perhaps the visit of her dedicatee, Talleyrand, to her lodgings, not long after the first edition had been published. Fuseli's biographer cattily records that because of her frugal lifestyle, there was hardly any furniture to sit on, and Wollstonecraft had to offer the French minister his meagre glass of wine in a teacup.[36] At this time she shocked conventional minds with her Bohemian unbound mass of auburn hair and her adoption of the coarse dress and thick stockings of a milkmaid, to express her feminist contempt for fashion and her revolutionary principles. Wollstonecraft doubtless discussed with Talleyrand the French plans for a national education system, and tried to persuade him to implement secondary education for girls.

Wollstonecraft enjoyed her celebrity, showing off to her sister that '[M]y book &c &c has afforded me an opportunity of settling *very* advantageously in the matrimonial line, with a new acquaintance; but entre nous – a handsome house and a proper man did not tempt me' (*CLMW*, p. 210). By June she was planning to visit France with the Fuselis and Joseph Johnson, for she expected to be introduced to many thinkers and writers there. The early days of the revolution had brought some of

the improvements in women's legal status that Wollstonecraft supported. Marriage had been made a civil contract and divorce legalized. Primogeniture had been abolished so that sons and daughters had equality in inheritance. Women were now allowed to testify in court, and to sue for support from the fathers of illegitimate offspring.[37] Even more exciting, the revolution had provided a discursive place, where women freely published their writings, made speeches, took part in street politics, organized clubs, and hosted salons, according to their class. Wollstonecraft wanted to be part of it. Her book was already translated and published in Paris and Lyons, 'and praised in some popular prints' (*CLMW*, p. 213). It would also be translated into German by Saltzmann. But after they had set off, the friends had to change their plans when it became obvious that England was on the brink of war with France. Then came the horrifying news of the September massacres, when mobs of sansculottes armed themselves and butchered half of all the priests and suspected royalists in the prisons of Paris. The Burkean nightmare seemed to be coming true. Undeterred, Mary had to see what was happening for herself. Eventually she travelled alone on 8th December, 1792.

Fuseli

Wollstonecraft had written nothing but reviews for nearly a year. Privately, she was battling against inner demons, for she had suffered unrequited love for her close friend the Swiss artist Henry Fuseli for some time. He was a bisexual; twenty years older than her; short, white-haired, sharp-tongued and eccentric. Hazlitt said, 'His pictures are... like himself, with eye-balls of stone stuck in rims of tin, and muscles twisted together like ropes or wires'.[38] His paintings often explored the forbidden realms of the psyche; they could be erotic and disturbing; some of his private collection were pornographic. As an artist he was 'sensationalist, pretentious...and sometimes fatuous, but dynamic, memorable and adventurous'.[39] Marginalia in Horace Walpole's catalogue of Fuseli's exhibition of 1785 reads: 'shockingly mad... mad... madder than ever...quite mad'! The only artist considered even madder than Fuseli was his friend William Blake.

It was Fuseli's Rousseauistic view of woman, which dictated his marriage in 1788 to a submissive, lower-class and uneducated artist's model, Sophia Rawlins. Wollstonecraft's arguments with Fuseli had helped her work out her attack on Rousseau. Fuseli, in his turn, was influenced by the 'termagent', as he once described her. Throughout the 1790s his work explored the range of female identity and experience: from the

Miltonic Eve and Sin, to the heroic Brittomart and queenly Titania; from courtesans to Milton's wife and to domestic scenes of his wife with her needlework. This was 'to a great extent generated by Wollstonecraft acting as the "positive" pole to Mrs Fuseli's no less potent "negative"'.[40]

Blake relished the artist's religious scepticism, doodling in his notebook:

> The only man that e'er I knew
> Who did not make me almost spew
> Was Fuesli: he was both Turk & Jew –
> (MS notebook, 1808–11)

However, Godwin detested him and attributed Mary's satirical side to the bad influence of Fuseli's cynicism. After her death he wrote to Joseph Johnson who had criticized his portrait of the Swiss artist in *Memoir of the Author of Vindication of the Rights of Woman*:

> As to his cynical cast, his impatience of contradiction, or his propensity to satire, I have carefully observed them: & I protest the sincerity, of my judgement, that the resemblance between Mary's traits of this kind to his, was so great, as clearly to demonstrate that one was copied from the other.[41]

In fact, Wollstonecraft's love of satirical humour was evident in her girlhood, but it was presumably not a sufficiently 'feminine' aspect of her character for Godwin's taste.[42]

Fuseli had undoubtedly been flattered by her ardent hero-worship and stimulated by her intellectual companionship. But things came to a head when Wollstonecraft proposed to Mrs Fuseli a *menage à trois* in which his wife would be Henry's sexual lover and Mary his intellectual companion.[43] Mrs Fuseli threw her out and from henceforth she was no longer welcome at their house. Wollstonecraft wrote the artist many love-letters some of which he unchivalrously refused to open and then, even more caddishly, refused to return. But eventually, she had to accept her dismissal.

In 1790 Wollstonecraft had needed the jolt of revolutionary ideas to dispel her Christian stoicism, in order to move her philosophy forward: to viewing social injustice as intolerable – something to be tackled in this world. This had produced her *Vindications*. Now in her sojourn in France she was about to discover that sexual desire was not so easily quelled in favour of friendship or platonic love as she had assumed in

her puritan youth, and advocated in her books. Her determination to work out her principles of conduct anew, without recourse to patriarchal conventions would bring her much suffering. But her bravery and refusal to compromise would also develop her feminist thought beyond that expressed in *Rights of Woman*, and far beyond the ken of most of her contemporaries.

5

'The true perfection of man': Print, Public Opinion and the Idea of Progress

Up until now, the history of politics...has been the history of only a few individuals: that which really constitutes the human race, the vast mass of families living for the most part on the fruits of their labour, has been forgotten...it is only the leaders who have held the eye of the historian.

(Condorcet, *Sketch for a Historical Picture of the Progress of the Human Mind*)

'The quarrels of popes and kings, with wars or pestilences, in every page; the men so good for nothing, and hardly any women at all – it is very tiresome: and yet I often think it odd that it should be so dull, for a great deal of it must be invention'.

(Catherine Moreland on history. Jane Austen, *Northanger Abbey*)

The newly born republic was proclaimed on 22 September, 1792 or 'year 1 of Liberty'. It was depicted in a popular print as a newly-spawned infant Hercules: arising from the skirts of a brawny female sans-culottes, an earthy parody of the Virgin Mary. France was already at war with the monarchies of Russia, Prussia and Austria, whose armies had initially been repulsed. The early Utopian phase of the revolution was over. Dumouriez, the victorious French commander, was solicited by the advocates of revolution in Belgium and Holland to lend them his support.[1] Now the revolution was to be spread abroad.

The National Convention began to split into two amorphous groupings: the Jacobins, led by Robespierre and nicknamed 'the mountain' because they sat in the highest seats, who were in alliance with the Parisian 'sans culottes'; and the Girondins, whose chief support came from the provinces. The latter, at first in the ascendancy, deplored the violence of the September massacres – yet had not taken action to stop them. The Girondins were particularly messianic in urging a patriotic crusade 'for universal liberty' against the absolutist powers, but the 'Mountain' was against war. Then an iron chest was discovered containing letters showing Louis XVI scheming against the republic, and the king was arrested for treason.

Wollstonecraft had recently arrived, and was staying in a six-storey gloomy empty mansion, no 22 Rue Meslée, belonging to her sister's old headmistress. Her first letter to Joseph Johnson on 26 December was dramatic:

> About nine o'clock this morning, the king passed by my window, moving silently along (excepting now and then a few strokes on the drum, which rendered the stillness more awful) through empty streets, surrounded by national guards, who, clustering round the carriage, seemed to deserve their name. The inhabitants flocked to their windows, but the casements were all shut, not a voice was heard, nor did I see any thing like an insulting gesture. – For the first time since I entered France, I bowed to the majesty of the people, and respected the propriety of behaviour so perfectly in unison with my own feelings. I can scarcely tell you why, but an association of ideas made the tears flow insensibly from my eyes, when I saw Louis sitting with more dignity than I expected from his character, in a hackney coach going to meet his death, where so many of his race have triumphed. . . . I have been alone ever since; and, though my mind is calm I cannot dismiss the lively images, that have filled my imagination all the day. – Nay, do not smile, but pity me; for, once or twice, lifting up my eyes from the paper, I have seen eyes glare through a glass-door opposite my chair, and bloody hands shook at me. . . . I am going to bed – and for the first time in my life, I cannot put out the candle.
>
> (*CLMW*, p. 227)

Note the Gothic style of this letter. Wollstonecraft, like the on-the-spot reporter she was, lost no time in conveying vivid personal impressions of this historic moment. This suggests she went to France specifically to gather material for a book. She planned to write to Johnson for later publication a series of letters 'On the Present Character of the French Nation'. Her choice of the letter form, which refracted reality through subjective impressions, was doubtless suggested by the runaway success of Helen Maria Williams's seemingly artless effusions, *Letters Written in France* (1790).

Helen Maria Williams

Williams had cheekily appropriated Burkean sensibility for the revolution. She declared that living in France was 'like living in a region of romance'; and that 'The French revolution is not only sublime in a general view, but is often beautiful when considered in detail'.[2] To the horror of British conservatives, she denied any atavistic attachment to her native land: claiming she had 'strongly caught the contagion of French patriotism'. New instalments were added annually, and Williams became an essential source of information on the revolution for the British, despite her radical politics. Poet, novelist and travel-writer, she too had emerged from Dissenting circles, her mentor having been Revd Andrew Kippis. She had now made her home in France. She would soon set Wollstonecraft an example of revolutionary sexual mores by living openly with her married lover, the Unitarian businessman, John Hurford Stone, formerly a member of the Newington Green congregation. Even after his divorce they never married.

Wollstonecraft had 'warmly recommended' Williams's novel, *Julia, a Novel: Interspersed with Some poetical Pieces* (1790) and very favourably reviewed *Letters Written in France, in the Summer, 1790 etc* (1790) in the *Analytical*. She lost no time in making contact with this hostess of an important salon where British visitors mingled with the most eminent Girondin circle, including Madame Roland and Pierre Vergniaud. By 24 December she wrote to Everina: 'Miss Williams has behaved very civilly to me and I shall visit her frequently, because I *rather* like her, and I meet french company at her house. Her manners are affected, yet the *simple* goodness of her hearts (sic) continually breaks through the varnish, so that one would be more inclined, at least I should, to love than admire her. – Authorship is a heavy weight for female shoulders especially in the sunshine of prosperity' (*CLMW*, p. 226). The two most radical British women writers of their age made a piquant contrast: Wollstonecraft the austere feminist philosopher; and Williams the gushing sentimentalist.

Execution of the king

The execution of the King on 21 January 1793 was a traumatic moment, dividing constitutional monarchists such as Mirabeau from wholehearted republicans. Though the Girondins were republicans, not all were democrats. Some looked back to the classical model, as the Americans had, which was founded on slavery and did not include universal suffrage. The Girondins believed in *laissez-faire* economics, not a regulated economy, and were often fiercely individualist. Some argued for a federal model rather than the highly centralized state that many Jacobins envisaged necessary to express the 'general will'.

With the foundation of a republic in France, British radicals also had to reassess their political ideals. They were forced to realize that republicanism could be adopted by first-world nations as well as new states in the Americas. In the second part of *Rights of Man*, Paine pointed out that representative democracy could be used to ground the entire state, rather than simply act as a constraint on the executive, as in Whig thinking.[3] From now on the British consensus that looked back to the 1688 settlement as an ideal balance bedevilled by an overweening monarchy was gone. Those who continued to support the French or to argue for reform at home were isolated: seen as extremist democrats by the majority whose new fear was 'mobocracy'.

Letter introductory to a series of letters on the present character of the French nation

The only other surviving letter which Wollstonecraft seems to have sent to Johnson for the projected publication was one dated 15 February 1793, which was not published until after her death in the *Posthumous Works of the Author of a Vindication of the Rights of Woman* in 1798. Unlike Williams, who celebrated commerce and the disappearance of snobbish contempt towards business,[4] Wollstonecraft feared the new bourgeois ruling class would be as corrupt as the courtly:

> I would I could inform you that, out of the chaos of vices and follies...I saw the fair form of Liberty slowly rising, and Virtue expanding her wings to shelter all her children! I should then hear the account of the barbarities that have rent the bosom of France patiently, and bless the firm hand that lopt off the rotten limbs. But, if the aristocracy of birth is levelled with the ground, only to make room for that of riches, I am afraid that the morals of the people will not be much improved by the change, or the government rendered les venal.
>
> (*WMW*, 6: 444)

Hitherto she had considered the middle class 'to be in the most natural state', leading the age of commerce towards a new society. But now they have seized power in France, as a moralist, she begins sceptically to question whether unfettered capitalism is indeed true liberty; whether freedom *from* government control constitutes the ultimate in reform. Again she tests the boundaries of liberalism.

The September massacres also forced utopian thinkers to face the question of revolutionary violence. Wollstonecraft confesses that she is beginning to lose her confidence in 'my theory of a more perfect state' (*WMW*, 7: 445). Her Christian faith had been rooted in the belief of Price and Priestley that individuals cultivating virtue would thereby spontaneously produce a perfect society. So disillusion with the revolution brought with it religious doubts: '[S]tart not, my friend, if I bring forward an opinion, which at the first glance seems to be levelled against the existence of God! I am not become an atheist, I assure you by residing at Paris'. Questioning why God allowed such horrors as Paris had seen that Autumn, she was gripped by a mood of Romantic nihilism, speculating whether 'evil is the grand mobile of action' in this world. This despairing mood was only temporary, but the history of the French revolution she wrote next would be the most secular of her books so far. Indeed, her turn to history was itself symptomatic of late Enlightenment investment in that discipline, as a replacement for theology, in the search for meaning in viewing society. She must have kept the rest of her observations as notes for her ambitious history of the revolution, the most carefully planned and composed book she ever wrote.

The Girondins and the public sphere

Wollstonecraft and Williams found the Girondins took women's ideas seriously within the confines of their salon culture. The philosopher Marie Jean Antoine Nicholas de Caritat, Marquis de Condorcet (a close associate of Paine's) was a feminist who favoured female suffrage and advocated education for both sexes. Manon Roland was an *eminence grise*, writing her husband's political speeches and discreetly influencing policy whilst keeping in the background. Nevertheless, the new constitution had not granted women citizenship and Thomas Christie actually commended it for retaining Salic law and 'not raising them [women] out of their natural sphere'.[5] The 'Mountain', was shortly to turn against women's 'meddling' in politics altogether. When they seized power under Robespierre, the Jacobins became anti-feminist and dissolved the women's clubs led by Claire Lacombe and Pauline Léon they had previously supported.

Though Paine and Wollstonecraft belonged to no party, they, Christie and others of the Johnson circle, gravitated particularly to the anglophile Girondin grouping, who were intellectual heirs of the Encyclopaedists, emphasizing reason, stoicism and individual liberty.[6] Paine, James Mackintosh, Horne Tooke and the Scottish poet John Oswald already had close links with them.[7] Indeed, many of the Girondins were writers and journalists, so there were close parallels with the Joseph Johnson circle in London. Their leader Jacques-Pierre Brissot was a newspaper man as were many of his colleagues.

Gary Kates's study of the origins of the 'Girondins' shows them to be a loose group of friends, many of whom from 1790–91 had met as a club, 'the Cercle Social', which had been formed to bring about reform and universal brotherhood.[8] The most important members of the 'Cercle Social' were crusading journalist and close friend of Paine, Nicolas Bonneville; the radical Bishop of Caen, Abbé Claude Fauchet; propagandist writer Jacques-Pierre Brissot; Minister of the Interior, Jean-Marie Roland; mathematician and philosopher, Marquis de Condorcet; and physician François-Xavier Lanthénes. Believers in Enlightenment, they wanted to disseminate radical ideas through the printing press, which Condorcet in 1782, had described as 'that preserving art, which safeguards human reason...the patrimony of all nations'. The group saw printing as facilitating democracy in large countries, which hitherto had only been feasible in city-states in classical times. Quite consciously they used print culture and salons to promote what Jurgen Habermas has termed the 'public sphere' of opposition to absolutism.

The press and the genesis of the revolution

The minor writer Brissot and journalists Jean Louis Carra and Antoine-Joseph Gorsas had all begun as active political propagandists in the *ancien régime*. In 1788 Brissot had founded the club 'Les Amis des Noirs', to campaign against slavery. Wooden printing presses were still being used in France, but this backwardness in technology did put publishing in the reach of activists of moderate means. The events leading up to the revolution in 1789 forced the king to grant freedom of the press from prior censorship. After the revolution, the National Assembly abolished the privileges of the Book Guild, which was defunct by 1793. Many orthodox booksellers went bankrupt when the damn of monopolistic royalist regulations burst and the underground world of unofficial culture and radical propagandists such as Brissot swept into the light of day. The number of known printers quadrupled and booksellers tripled.[9] Over six hundred journals or pamphlets were launched. Eighty per cent of the papers were ephemeral propaganda but some, weekly or daily, commanded a distribution of at least 10,000, and were probably read by four times as many. By 1790 there were some 335 newspapers: mainly partisan and sometimes scurrilous responses to the tempo of the times.[10] The sale of weighty classics of the cultural heritage – and indeed books in general – fell off. Instead, an unprecedented democratization of the printed word made communication direct and instantaneous. Newspapers disseminated information on daily events and mobilized public opinion. As Carla Hesse put it: 'Enlightenment now transformed from a body of thought into a new set of cultural practices.'

In his *Letters on the Revolution* (1791), Thomas Christie recommended the most respectable and conservative of the now bewildering array of French newspapers to British readers who wanted to know the real state of French affairs, giving prices, descriptions and an indication of partisanship.[11] He suggested dailies such as M. Garat's *Journal de Paris* which commented on the proceedings of the National Assembly in suitably analytical fashion; or the *Gazette Nationale ou Moniteur* published by wealthy publisher Panckouke, who had survived from pre-revolutionary days; and weeklies such as *Mercure de France* edited by the Swiss conservative Mallet du Pan; or the constitutional royalist Mirabeau's *Courier de Provence*; and the twice-weekly *Gazettin*. The French government itself effectively boosted circulation of factual journals such as *Le Moniteur* by ordering copies for employees and the army.[12] Wollstonecraft would use it as a source of information for her history.

Brissot, meanwhile, had established a popular paper, the *Patriote Français*, to which Madame Roland and her husband and other Girondins contributed. Its explicitly pedagogical aim was to provide the People with political enlightenment. Its subscription of thirty-six livres a year would have put it beyond the reach of the sansculottes, however. By 1790–91 the 'Cercle Social', established by Brissot and the idealistic Fauchet, had forged links with like minds from the provinces, particularly the Gironde. As Kates has shown, the 'Cercle Social' then formed an association, 'Confédération des Ami de la Vérité', and a publishing company, 'Imprimerie du Cercle Social' to print its works campaigning against slavery and for radical causes. For example, it published the work of the Dutch feminist Etta Palm d'Aelders. Bonneville edited its regular paper, *Bouche de fer*, supposedly the contributions found in the club's letterbox. The group did not have to reconcile the interests of a commercial publisher with their intentions, for the writers themselves had established the publishing house and thus formed a ready-made pressure group. Kates emphasises that the Girondins 'were not only a preponderant influence in the Imprimerie du Cercle Social, they constituted its core and leadership'.[13]

By the time Wollstonecraft arrived in Paris in December 1792, Roland and his circle of friends dominated the new National Convention. The 'Mountain' were particularly fearful of the way, between August 1792 and January 1793, Roland, as Minister of the Interior, had begun using Government money and patronage to subsidize the Girondin press, reminding them of *ancien régime* practices.[14] Hugh Gough has shown how he channelled money into setting up Jean Baptiste Louvet's *La Sentinelle*; then inaugurated a fund administered by Lanthenas to support writers and journalists sympathetic to the Girondins, such as Gorsas. This was wound up after Jacobin protests. The 'Mountain' had reason to be afraid. Their own newspapers, such as Jean-Paul Marat's *Journal de la République Française*, Jacques-René Hébert's *Père Duchesne*, and Maximilien de Robespierre's *Journal des Hommes Libres* could not compete with the Girondins's *Annales Patriotiques* with a circulation of 12,000, or Gorsas's *Courrier*, the *Patriote Français*, or the Cercle Sociale's other publications, which were distributed to a network of provincial clubs.

The line between the media and the government became a dangerously blurred one in the new National Convention, when a significant number of journalists, writers and pamphleteers who already exercised enormous influence through their publications became deputies.[15] Girondin writers Brissot and Carra now argued as vitriolically face to face in the debating chamber with rival left-wing journalists such as Marat and Camille Desmoulins, as they did in print over responsibility for the September massacres and the trial of the king. Such was the power of the press to command public opinion, and so commanding the Girondins' lead in print culture, that on 9–10 March when the enragés of the Paris commune turned against the 'conspiracy' of the Girondins to control the revolution, they smashed the presses of Brissot's *Patriote Français* and Carra's *Annales Patriotiques*.[16] After the demise of the Girondins in May 1793, Robespierre and successive governments clamped down on the press altogether, instituting greater censorship than the monarch had ever thought of.

From January 1793 until they were expelled from the convention in May, the Girondins combined propagandising in print with meetings in regular salons, where they ineffectually tried to unite themselves into a political party, organizing voting and infiltrating committees. Women were present, though sometimes men separated to discuss political tactics. M.J. Sydenham comments: 'It indicates how fine was the distinction between normal social activities and political liaisons, and suggests that private political discussion was the natural corollary of an attempt at government by ill-organized and interminable debate'.[17] This frenetic combination of writing, discussion and socializing suited Wollstonecraft. She enjoyed the urbanity of French life and hinted to Eliza that she already had an admirer (*CLMW*, pp. 228–9) – perhaps an unintended outcome of a bad habit she admitted to of absent-mindedly replying 'Oui, oui' to cover up her lack of fluency in French!

Wollstonecraft and the Girondins

Wollstonecraft 'renewed her acquaintance with Paine', and through him became 'personally acquainted with the majority of the leaders in the French revolution' (*MAVRW*, pp. 83–4). This statement of Godwin's has been declared an exaggeration by Todd (*MWRL*, p. 215). But its lack of specificity is surely due to his fear of revealing in 1798, at the height of the reactionary backlash, the fact that Wollstonecraft mixed socially not only with leading Girondins, whose martyrdom in the Terror subsequently conferred on them the inaccurate label of moderates; but later with the two politicians principally associated with setting up the Committee of Public Safety, the engine of the Terror. Her lover's business at Le Havre would be conducted with the connivance of the Jacobin regime. Though she had more in common with the Girondins, Wollstonecraft debated her ideas over a range of political opinion.

Moncure Conway, biographer of Paine, lists the Brissots, Nicholas Bonneville, the Rolands, Joel Barlow, Mary Wollstonecraft and her future lover, Captain Imlay, as regular visitors at Paine's lodgings – the mansion formerly occupied by Madame Pompadour – which he shared with the Christies and other friends.[18] Mary soon became the close friend of Thomas Christie's wife Rebecca. From his first visit in 1789 Christie had been on intimate terms with the Comte de Mirabeau, the Abbé Sieyès, Jacques Necker and other moderate liberals on the political scene. In 1792 he had been employed by the National Assembly on translating the new constitution into English.

Wollstonecraft wrote to Everina on the 24 January 1793: '[M]y spirits are fatigued with endeavouring to form a just opinion of public affairs' (*CLMW*, p. 225). Meanwhile, back in Britain, Wollstonecraft's name was habitually being linked with Paine's. On 20 January Eliza wrote to

Everina that in West Wales, where she was a governess, the reactionaries not only loathed 'Tommy Paine whose effigy they burnt at Pembroke the other day, nay talk of immortalizing Miss Wollstonecraft in the like manner'.[19] On 1 February Republican France declared war on Britain.

Plan for national education

By early February Wollstonecraft had been co-opted to draw up a plan of national education for consideration by the committee appointed by the new constitution (*CLMW*, p. 230). National education was absolutely central to making something lasting out of the revolution. Everyone agreed on that. Emancipated citizens of the new republic needed a 'liberal' education – not to be spoon-fed superstition. But whether the state should take over from the Church in institutionalising public education; whether that education should be wholly secular; whether compulsory to foster egalitarianism and collectivity; or whether free enterprise should be allowed to provide a variety of schooling; whether the syllabus should be vocational or ideological: were questions which could not be resolved. Though up until 1795 there was a general consensus on the establishment of elementary education for all, the inclusion of the female sex remained contentious; while secondary schooling for girls was not taken seriously at all. Hence Wollstonecraft's invitation. It seems difficult to credit, but Mirabeau, Brissot, Saint-Just, and – less surprisingly – Bonaparte, all wanted girls to be taught at home on the model of Rousseau's Sophie.[20]

Talleyrand's report and Bill, published in 1791, had argued that education was crucial in weakening social inequity and so primary schooling should be universally provided for all classes and both sexes, though not made compulsory. Boys destined for the professions could then continue to the fee-paying district school, which would offer scholarships to deserving cases. Talleyrand had not been able to envisage any secondary education for girls except vocational training for orphans and the poor. Though Wollstonecraft had read the plan 'with great pleasure' she accused Talleyrand of treating female education 'in too cursory a manner' in her dedication of *Rights of Woman* to him (*WMW*, 5: 65). She had no idea, of course, that the report had been secretly co-authored by his lover, Germaine de Staël.[21] Wollstonecraft hopefully seized upon the momentary insight he had experienced (or more likely that Staël incorporated), when he had admitted there was an anomaly:

> That half the human race should be excluded by the other half from all participation in government, that they should be natives in fact

but foreign by law to the soil where they were born, that they should be owners of property without influence or representation, are political phenomena which in abstract principle seem impossible to explain.[22]

However, the utilitarian argument that intellectual education would be wasted on those predestined for familial/manual labour seemed obvious to most people in France. Brissot in *Patriote Français* had given the Talleyrand plan cautious support but rejected any female education at all, while Camille Desmoulins in *Révolutions de Paris et de Brabant* accepted it at primary level. Perhaps Talleyrand explained this to Wollstonecraft when he met her in London.

The next national education plan, drawn up by Condorcet's Committee on Public Instruction, had been discussed by the Convention in December 1792. Much more radical, it completely divorced education from religious indoctrination, providing free instruction and vocational training at all levels, paid for from public funds. This would be of utilitarian benefit to the economic prosperity of the state. Moral and religious education was a matter for the private sphere of the home. Despite his own feminism, there had still been no provision for secondary education for girls, because Condorcet feared it would be too controversial.[23] The Condorcet plan caused a storm of controversy amongst the Girondins themselves, let alone their opponents, because the ambitious notion of state education was feared as a dangerous extension of the power to shape public opinion through print culture. What this shows is a splitting within liberalism. While those of a Utilitarian leaning wanted to enshrine the new secular faith in Enlightenment by setting up state educational institutions which would benefit the whole nation, individualists feared the increase of centralised power and defined freedom in terms of less government.

Though we have no evidence that Wollstonecraft ever met Condorcet, she must have known his writings, and Paine would have been a mutual contact. It seems she was consulted at the point when the Committee went back to revise its proposals in response to the Convention's objections. These included the charge that its envisaged national Society for Arts and Sciences was elitist and would replace the tyranny of priests with an oligarchy of intellectuals. The Strasbourg mathematician Professor Arbogast coordinated revision of the plan in Spring 1793 and it was approved by the Committee on May 28.[24] This was within days of the Jacobins's seizure of power and expulsion of the Girondins from the National Convention. However, the committee on Public Instruction was an ongoing project 'that had accompanied the Revolution from its very beginnings, when Talleyrand and Sieyès had been important members, right through to the Terror, producing enormously long and ambitious plans'.[25] R.R. Palmer points out that the Jacobin Bureau de Consultation's subsequent education proposal was merely an amended version of Arbogast's revision of the Condorcet plan, taking into account a similar proposal brought forward by the Council of Paris. It was published in August 1793 as *Reflections on Public Instruction*, and Arbogast continued to serve on an expanded Education Commission that Autumn. Palmer notes that *Reflections on Public Instruction* included provision of secondary education for girls. The influence of Wollstonecraft here seems probable. Ironically, the ethical emphasis of her own educational writings had less affinity with Condorcet's utilitarian emphasis on vocational instruction and more with Robespierre's Rousseauistic vision of bringing together (in Schama's words) 'those two pillars of the moralized republic: the school and the family' through ideological socialization.[26] Her posthumously-published sixpenny primer *Lessons for Children*, for example, teaches a young child to read simple sentences reflecting everyday family situations, chosen to develop the child's moral independence and stressing that only the immaturity of her ability to reason prevents her equal standing with adults of the household and the world at large.

American adventurers in Paris

Wollstonecraft had already met at Joseph Johnson's dinners the American poet and polemicist Joel Barlow. He was now in Paris, and was made a French citizen, being highly valued by the Girondins for his writings in defence of the revolution. His wife Ruth became another close friend. Rather like the late-1970s hippies-turned-yuppies, Barlow and his fellow Americans such as Colonel Blackden and Mark Leavenworth were keen to combine their commitment to liberty with a buccaneering speculation in business. Barlow drew J.P. Brissot into his land speculation company, peddling emigration schemes to America, which then failed. The Comte de Volney commented that though Barlow wasn't a deliberate crook, his 'trite, idle and inflated rhetoric...had condemned 500 meritorious families to hardship and misery'.[27] Another such American adventurer was Gilbert Imlay, to whom Mary was introduced but instantly disliked (*MAWRW*, p. 85).

Events moved fast as Winter turned to Spring: military defeats and the defection of Dumouriez, which cast doubt on the loyalty of all the Girondins; the uprising against the republican government and brutal crushing of the peasants of the Vendée; a deepening economic crisis.

The Convention reacted by creating a centralized system to extirpate counter-revolutionary plotting. A Revolutionary Tribunal was established, and on 6 April the Girondin Henry-Maximin Isnard proposed a Committee of Public Safety be appointed.[28] The first denunciations would soon multiply into the Terror which would engulf the Girondins themselves. Against this unpromising background, Mary Wollstonecraft fell head-over – heels in love with Gilbert Imlay. Godwin visualized her recovering from depression following her unreciprocated love for Fuseli, and blossoming into her first experience of mutual love and sexual passion:

> Her sorrows, the depression of her spirits, were forgotten, and she assumed all the simplicity and the vivacity of a youthful mind. She was like a serpent upon a rock, that casts its slough, and appears again with the brilliancy, the sleekness, and the elastic activity of its happiest age. She was playful, full of confidence, kindness and sympathy. Her eyes assumed new lustre, and her cheeks new colour and smoothness. Her voice became chearful; her temper overflowing with universal kindness; and that smile of bewitching tenderness from day to day illuminated her countenance, which all who knew her will so well recollect, and which won, both heart and soul, the affection of almost every one that beheld it.
>
> (*MAVRW*, p. 88)

There are many testimonies to Wollstonecraft's charm and powers of conversation in Paris. Her friend Count Schlabrendorf, who became rather smitten, said that 'Her face, so full of expression, presented a style of beauty beyond that of merely regular features.' Archibald Hamilton Rowan remembered that 'Her manners were interesting and her conversation spirited, yet not out of her sex'.[29] The Prussian naturalist, Johann Georg Forster, who met her in April 1793, told his wife that she was very charming and sociable.[30]

Gilbert Imlay

Gilbert Imlay was a tall, charming American in his late thirties who had had several amours, and – rumour had it – was the ex-lover of Helen Maria Williams. He was probably born about 1754 in New Jersey. He had been a lieutenant in the American war of independence, though he later styled himself 'Captain'. If Captain Arl-ton in his novel *The Emigrants* (1793) is a self-portrait, then he had a ruddy open complexion and animated blue eyes with 'an open and manly countenance'. He was 'frank and ingenuous with men and diffident with ladies', but when intimate could be 'highly facetious and entertaining'. Arl-ton is rather boyish and impetuous, inclined to get into scrapes.[31] Wollstonecraft imagined Imlay a Rousseauistic Daniel Boone, confiding to her sister: 'Having been brought up in the interiour parts of America, he is a most natural, unaffected creature' (*CLMW*, p. 251). Actually, he had been a land speculator in 1780s Kentucky, as associate of the notorious General James Wilkinson, presumably fictionalised as General W- in *The Emigrants*. By 1787 Wilkinson was a double agent – working for the Spanish in a conspiracy to separate Kentucky and the Southwest from the United States, while scheming to foster Louisiana's independence from Spain with the connivance of America. About this time Imlay fled, leaving his creditors behind him, and next appears in Europe in the 1790s as a travel writer and adventurer.[32] Mary Wollstonecraft seems to have had little idea of Imlay's shady background. Godwin emphasized that she 'reposed herself upon a person of whose honour and principles she had the most exalted idea' (*MAVRW*, p. 88).

Americans such as Joel Barlow and Gilbert Imlay saw free enterprise as the cornerstone of revolutionary freedom: 'a rebellion against the claims of privilege, monopoly and despotism'.[33] Imlay's well-received travel book, *Topographical Description of the Western Territory of North America* (1792) paints the West as an Eden ripe for settlement. Such books inspired the Romantic poets Southey and Coleridge's plan for Pantisocracy; the Welsh antiquarian and poet Iolo Morganwg's dream of an expedition to find the descendants of the legendary Welsh Prince Madoc amongst the native Americans; and many other idealistic schemes. The Utopian language was designed to encourage the emigration of such Dissenters and radicals who despaired of reform in Britain and wanted to found a New Jerusalem. Today, we might think such dreams uncannily echoed the imperial projects of Old Europe in their civilising mission and scant regard for the natives. Imlay probably also wrote the book as propaganda for a revived Louisiana scheme, in which the Spanish-American adventurer General Miranda had successfully interested Dumouriez in 1792.[34] The Girondins dreamed of taking possession of their own piece of the New World Empire and were keen to ally themselves with the American republic. To further this latter end, Brissot had produced his own travel book, *Nouveau Voyage dans les Etats-Unis*, translated into English by Joel Barlow in 1792. Wollstonecraft had reviewed it for the *Analytical Review* in September 1791. Brissot declared his object was to learn from the mores of the Americans how to preserve the liberty the French revolution had seized, for 'one can gain liberty without morals but one cannot keep it' (*WMW*, 7: 390). Though Wollstonecraft had sardonically pointed out the 'pardonable partiality' of his 'enthusiastic eulogiums', she respected 'the sacred overflowings of an honest heart' and endorsed his wish to emulate the religious toleration, easy gender relations and efforts of the Quakers to abolish slavery he found in America.

At least eight plans were presented to the government from 1792 to 1793 on taking possession of Louisiana, and Gilbert Imlay's was the one initially taken most seriously, as he had the ear of Brissot.[35] He set out the commercial advantages the territory would bring France; and argued that the expedition should be undertaken by American citizens to draw the United States into the war in support of France, and to deflect Spain from participating in a European war against republican France. But in March 1793 the Ministry rejected the scheme and instead appointed a committee to travel to America to organize the expedition. Barlow, but not Imlay was a member of this committee. This sudden disfavour was possibly because Imlay was found to be engaging in shady financial dealing. But the expedition was abandoned when the Jacobins seized power at the end of May.

Girondins lose power

A young man named I.B. Johnson, wrote to Godwin after Wollstonecraft's death, recalling having seen her frequently at his friends the Christies' or Thomas Paine's Paris lodgings between April and September 1793. At that time she was writing her 'account of the French revolution', he recalled. The company had included Paine; Girondin deputies such as Pierre Roederer; the president of the National Convention, Henry-Maximin Isnard who inaugurated the Committee of Public Safety; and notorious demagogue Bertrand de Barère, publisher of *Point de Jour*. The latter, infamous for advocating that the tree of liberty be watered with the blood of tyrants, was soon treacherously to denounce the Girondins. He joined the Jacobins and organized the Terror, becoming the main voice of the Committee of Public Safety. Barère would eventually betray Robespierre in his turn. Other regular guests included the German adventurer Baron Trenck; and natural philosopher Georg Forster, who was a member of the Jacobin club and had been part of the provisional adminstration of Mainz when it was taken by the republic. The feminist campaigner Théroigne de Méricourt sometimes joined them for dinner. Johnson remembered:

> About the time the Jacobin party had attained the summit of their power, we used to pass our Evenings together very frequently either in conversation or any amusement[that] might tend to dissipate those gloomy impressions the state of affairs naturally produced. Miss Wollstonecraft was always particularly anxious for the success of the Revolutn & the hideous aspect of the then political horizon hurt her exceedingly. She always thought, however, it would finally succeed.[36]

It is easy to deduce even from these few words the agonized realization of Wollstonecraft and her Girondin friends that their grasp of the republic was slipping away, and that violence and anarchy were to begin.

Vitriolic arguments in the National Convention found the Girondins arguing against Jacobin proposals to regulate corn prices and wages, and, under their new president Isnard, they attempted to stamp out the deployment of militant bands of Parisian sans-culottes whose direct action undermined the authority of the Convention. The crisis came at the end of May when Robespierre encouraged the will of the 'sovereign people' to manifest itself by the enforced removal and house arrest of leading Girondins by armed bands. Madame Roland entrusted her manuscripts to Helen Maria Williams, as did the Countess de Genlis when they were imprisoned. Wollstonecraft visited Manon Roland in gaol.[37] Hercules replaced Marianne as the symbol of the Republic, marking a masculinist Jacobin reaction against women's participation in politics. Manon Roland and the feminist Olympe de Gouges were soon to be guillotined, as well as Marie Antoinette. Théroigne de Méricourt was stoned by a mob and lost her mind.

The British expatriates were doubly distrusted as enemy aliens and Girondin allies by the nationalistic Jacobins. But the love-struck Mary Wollstonecraft did not flee any further than Neuilly-sur-Seine, a village just outside Paris. On 13 June, she warned her sister not to discuss politics for 'all letters are opened'. Her head was still full of schemes of emigrating to America with Imlay and even taking her sisters with them. She wrote to Eliza 'I am now at the house of an old Gardener writing a great book; and in better health and spirits than I have ever enjoyed since I came to France' (*CLMW*, p. 231). On 24 June she wrote again: 'I am now hard at work in the country, for I could not return to England without proofs that I have not been idle' (*CLMW*, p. 232). She was saturating herself in research for her history of the revolution, and needed a carriage to bring all the books she had to take with her. She used to meet Imlay at the barrier, a tollgate in the city wall, and this was where their baby would be conceived. She playfully threatened him: 'You *must* be glad to see me – because you are glad – or I will make love to the *shade* of *Mirabeau'*, whose character and motivation she was then working on. Sometimes, she would sneak into Paris early in the morning to breakfast with Ruth Barlow, or spend the occasional day visiting such friends as were left, such as the Swiss Madeleine Schweitzer, or the Swede, Gustav, Graf von Schlabrendorf. One day she walked into Paris, and to her horror 'the blood of the guillotine appeared fresh on the pavement. The emotions of her soul burst forth in indignant exclamation, while a prudent bystander warned her of her danger, and intreated her to hasten and hide her discontents' (*MAVRW*, p. 89).

Such outbursts of the outspoken Wollstonecraft persuaded Imlay to register her as his wife at the American embassy so that she would have the protection of American citizenship. She moved back to Paris to live with him and took his name in private life, though her books were still published under 'Mary Wollstonecraft'. Godwin commented that Mary had refused to marry Imlay because this would make him legally responsible for her debts and her family's financial embarrassments. She felt that they had made a sacred commitment to one another which did not need a legal ceremony to make it binding – not 'having clogged my soul by promising obedience &c &c' (*CLMW*, p. 253). Imlay's views were probably expressed by the character P.P. Esq. in *The Emigrants*, arguing in extenuation of his extra-marital relationship with Lady B—:

> What, shall two beings who have justly inspired a confidence in each other, who feel an affinity of sentiment, and who perceive that their happiness or misery are so materially connected, that to separate them would prove fatal to both, not to consider themselves superior to prejudices which are founded in error, and which would lead them to ridiculously sacrifice a real and substantial, for an imaginary good; and when too no person can be injured by the unity?
>
> (II: 49)

Idyllically happy despite Imlay's frequent absences, she would threaten him: 'If you do not return soon – or, which is no such mighty matter, talk of it – I will throw your slippers out at window, and be off – nobody knows where' (*CLMW*, p. 242). Wollstonecraft now embraced sexual pleasure as enthusiastically as she had once expressed puritan disdain for it in *Rights of Woman*. When a Frenchwoman boasted she had no sexual feelings, saying: 'Pour moi, je n'ai pas de tempérament', Wollstonecraft answered confidently: 'Tant pis pour vous, madame. C'est un défault de la nature' (*MWRL*, p. 236).

The terror

The Terror now began: putting an end to politics and inaugurating a bloody dictatorship in Paris which exterminated all opponents, real and imaginary. Schama comments that the Jacobins 'warred against commercial capitalism' in the Terror, particularly targeting the mercantile and commercial elites and their ports and cities.[38] These of course were the provincial areas and urban interests represented by the Girondin deputies. The question of *laissez-faire* belief in a free market versus a regulated economy which could help the poor was one which particularly deepened the divisions between the Girondins and the Jacobins. The dissemination of print was a capitalist venture too, of course. Indeed, the advocacy of a free press by the writers and propagandists at the heart of the Girondin social circle was itself emblematic of the interrelationship between their form of Enlightenment liberalism and their belief in free trade and the deregulation of the market.

That Autumn the Jacobin administration turned against the British expatriates and rounded them up. Helen Maria Williams, Stone and the Christies were temporarily gaoled before they escaped France. Wollstonecraft visited them all and von Schlabrendorf in prison (*MWRL*, p. 240). In her panic, Williams had destroyed the manuscripts with which she had been entrusted. Madame Roland, on learning the news, had cried: 'I wish they had thrown me into the fire instead!' Thomas Paine, under deep suspicion for having voted against the execution of Louis XVI for humanitarian reasons, suffered long imprisonment in the Luxembourg. He narrowly escaped the guillotine and would not be released, broken in health, until the fall of the Jacobin regime late in 1794. This was ironic, as Paine's ideas for a welfare state, abolition of poverty and distribution of property set out in part 2 of *The Age of Reason* were more Jacobin than Girondin.

The guillotine was working ceaselessly by October, and Wollstonecraft could never forget 'the anguish she felt at hearing of the death of Brissot, Vernigaud and the twenty [Girondin] deputies, as one of the most intolerable sensations she had ever experienced' (*MAVRW*, p. 90). Some Girondins emulated Roman republicans by committing suicide before they were arrested. 'The French will carry all before them – but, my God, how many victims fall beneath the sword and the guillotine!

My blood runs cold, and I sicken at thoughts of a Revolution which costs so much blood and bitter tears' Wollstonecraft wrote (*CLMW*, p. 257).

Imlay and Barlow had moved their operations to Le Havre and were keeping in with the new Jacobin administration and making plenty of money by blockade running. By November, Wollstonecraft realized she was pregnant and wrote to Imlay: 'I have felt some gentle twitches, which make me begin to think, that I am nourishing a creature who will soon be sensible of my care. This thought has not only produced an overflowing of tenderness to you, but made me very attentive to calm my mind and take exercise, lest I destroy an object, in whom we are to have a mutual interest, you know' (*CLMW*, p. 237). She soon joined him, and from January to September 1794 they lived in Le Havre 'with great harmony' (*MAVRW*, p. 90). She had sent off part of the MS of her history by 3 February 1794 and asked Joel Barlow to get her *Le Journal des Débats et des Décrets* to provide factual information, telling Ruth to let him know: 'I am now more seriously at *work* than I have ever been yet, and that I daily feel the want of my *poor Books*' (*CLMW*, pp. 249–50). By 10 March she was able to tell Everina dramatically 'I have just sent off great part of my M.S. which Miss Williams would fain have be [sic] burn, following her example – and to tell you the truth – my life would not have been worth much, had it been *found.*' It was a race as to whether the history would be delivered before the baby. On 27 April she wrote to Ruth Barlow: 'I am still very well; but imagine that it cannot be long before this lively animal pops on us – and now the history is finished and everything arranged I do not care how soon' (*CLMW*, p. 253). Her daughter was born on 14 May and named Frances after Fanny Blood.

Writing history

An Historical and Moral View of the Origin and Progress of the French Revolution; and the Effect It Has Produced in Europe (1794) is perhaps Wollstonecraft's most ambitious and yet underrated work. She wrote only one volume, despite promising 'two or three more' in the Advertisement. Like Williams, who was writing her own account of the downfall of the Girondins whilst in exile in Switzerland, Wollstonecraft was facing up to the necessity of analysing what had gone so horrifyingly wrong in France. This was a dangerous task for one writing secretly during the Terror, the time when Paine recalled 'Pen and ink were then of no use to me; no good could be done by writing, and no printer dared to print'.[39] So she confined herself to commenting on the less contentious events up to 1790, which are, however, implicitly interpreted through the bloody lens of 1794. This meant that her book would be a retrospective analysis of the same events which had inspired Burke's *Reflections*: another contribution to the revolution debate. This ruled out 'feminine' epistolary on-the-spot reportage like Williams's, for Wollstonecraft hadn't been living in Paris then. Her title stresses the scholarly distance yet particular perspective implied by 'view'. In other words she would adopt the stance of a modern opinionated historian. Her most considered and least journalistic work, Tom Furniss describes the *French Revolution* as 'one of the most profound discussions of revolutionary politics to emerge out of the Revolution Controversy'.[40]

As a pioneering *female* historian, Wollstonecraft was again following in the footsteps of Catharine Macaulay. The latter's Whig *History of England* (1763–83) had been meticulously researched from primary sources in the British Library, to refute Tory interpretations of the seventeenth-century English revolution. Traditionally, history books had been expensively produced for the educated man of affairs, by gentlemen scholars who had their own private collection of manuscripts and publications. It was a prestigious, masculine field. Karen O'Brien has traced the evolution of a broader, more popular market for history during the later eighteenth century, and Wollstonecraft's *French Revolution*, priced at a reasonable though not cheap 7s, catered for this. The new readership produced the rise of the authoritative 'philosophical' historian of the Scottish Enlightenment.[41] Wollstonecraft was familiar with the works of Hugh Blair, Adam Smith, David Hume and William Robertson. She did not choose, however, as might have been expected, the genre of comparativist histories of manners deemed more 'feminine' in terms of audience (though none had actually been written by women). Like Macaulay she attempted the detailed 'masculine' analysis of political events in one country at one significant moment of change. She was a 'philosophical' historian in the sense that she interspersed her narrative of events with passages of critical commentary on the dialectic between constitutional change and the stage France had reached in civilisation.

Girondins, public opinion and the question of progress

Jane Rendall has pointed out that 'the French Revolution presented a powerful challenge to all those who wrote in the spirit of Scottish philosophical history, who identified it as "a case study in the history of the progress of modern society"'.[42] But the descent of the revolution into Terror presented an even greater challenge to the Utopian theories on social perfectibility of the Girondin circle than to the empiricist Scots. Condorcet – while in fear of his life – vindicated perfectibility in his *Sketch of the Progress of the Human Mind* (1795) – written at exactly the same time as Wollstonecraft's *French Revolution,* just prior to his arrest and death, probably from suicide. The invention of printing was for Condorcet the transformative moment in history, inaugurating intellectual progress. Condorcet predicted an ongoing dialectic between knowledge and liberty in the production of an enlightened public opinion, which he described as 'a tribunal, independent of all human coercion'.[43] Education was to be the key in rectifying inequality instead of exacerbating it, and philosophers of different nations would work for perfectibility of the human race, motivated by universal philanthropy.

Georg Forster the Prussian botanist and travel writer whom Wollstonecraft befriended in Paris, had late in 1793 also thrown himself into writing a series of letters on the revolution, *Parisian Sketches.* Forster died before his account was completed. Like Condorcet, Forster argued that though the leaders of the revolution had been reprehensible, they were helpless to oppose the force of public opinion, the will of the people.[44] No longer led by intellectuals and propagandists, the revolution had *become* public opinion in action. It was an uncontrollable unstoppable fever, and the naturalist Forster compares it to a force of nature obeying only the laws of its own necessity. Having witnessed the Terror, no one could wish the experience of revolution on any other country, but he continued to believe that other nations could learn from it in instigating their own progress to perfection.

Wollstonecraft had herself inherited a Utopian providentialism from the intellectual climate of Rational Dissent and this was heightened by her contact with the Girondin idealists. For example, in her history she cited the Girondin Protestant pastor Jean Paul Saint-Etienne Rabaut's *The History of the Revolution in France.*[45] Rabaut declared messianically that the revolution was the result of the 'light of knowledge which had penetrated every class of citizens in this kingdom, to a greater degree than it hath illumined other nations'. It was therefore a test case for the world: '[O]urs was the cause of the whole human race' (Rabaut, *History of the Revolution in France,* III, 276–7).

Despite all that had happened since Rabaut had written in 1792, Wollstonecraft, too, clung to her belief in progress simply through Enlightenment. The book opens with a ringing affirmation of it. The intellectual overthrow of mental tyranny had triumphed through enlightenment science and especially 'the fortunate invention of printing', which 'rapidly multiplied copies of the productions of genius...bringing them within the reach of all ranks of men'.[46] 'When learning was confined to a small number of the citizens of a state' the people could be held down by their own superstitious religious fears or respect for rank (*French Revolution*, p. 19). Not any more.

Enlightenment and the imagination

The democracy of print allows individuals to publicly challenge the ideologies of the ruling classes. Wollstonecraft is deeply suspicious of the susceptibility of the imagination to glamorous myths and long-held customs which enslave the populace. 'Mystery alone gives full play to the imagination, men pursuing with ardour objects indistinctly seen or understood' (*French Revolution*, p. 196). The 'imagination...becomes the inflated wen of the mind' when imbued with what Marxists would later term false consciousness: 'We must get clear of all the notions drawn from the wild traditions of original sin: the eating of the apple, the theft of Prometheus, the opening of Pandora's box...we shall then leave room for the expansion of the human heart.... One principal of action is sufficient – Respect thyself.... The image of God implanted in our nature is now more rapidly expanding; and, as it opens, liberty with maternal wing seems to be soaring...' (*French Revolution*, pp. 21–2). The Christian myth of the Fall and its classical equivalents sap the ardour and curiosity of Promethean individuals aspiring like Eve and Pandora after knowledge, filling them with guilt and fear of external authority. Wollstonecraft's humanist credo 'respect thyself' reverses the roles. It is mankind's creative mind which most reflects the divine. Wollstonecraft's maternal imagery combines the dove of the Holy Spirit with the Goddess of Liberty in a vision of the human spirit unshackled, flying out across the world and soaring free and heavenwards.

We can see here how central and slippery the concept of the imagination is for Wollstonecraft – representing as it does both the passive capacity of the auditor to be seduced by myths, yet also the active Godlike power of the creative author to think for oneself. Wollstonecraft anticipated Germaine de Staël in her realization that the form a nation's arts take is related to its particular stage of political development. Her Puritan sternness about fantasy, like that of Marxism later, is rooted in suspicion of the supersitition and fatalism which oiled the works of hierarchical, feudal societies; and underpinned the plots of their beguiling romances. Fantasy (sometimes confusingly interchangeable with 'imagination'), according to Wollstonecraft, is most natural in ancient benighted primitive societies which produced the best poetry of the ages; though also the product of idle and restless ignorant dreamers, such as women or romantic crusaders of the middle ages. 'The perfection of the arts' in classical republics is also suspect, because fatalistic Greek tragedy, for example, was used to overawe and amuse the people in a civilization based on slavery and the bondage of women (*French Revolution*, pp. 110–12). Like Rousseau, she castigates the French addiction to theatre: the showy product of an aristocratic society whose wars were theatrical exhibitions, and whose courtly pageantry is a harlot's ornaments put on to seduce the peasantry (*French Revolution*, pp. 26–30). Taste was but 'the antidote to *ennui*' until 'the reign of philosophy succeeded to that of the imagination' (*French Revolution*, p. 229). This implies that the age of Enlightenment brought a greater rational control of emotional responses to ideas; that religious and social ideologies could now be brought under conscious scrutiny and questioned. Making 'imagination' and aesthetic beauty synonymous with the 'romantic' age of unthinking beliefs is obviously pejorative; modernity is preferred with its sciences and philosophy of social improvement.

John Whale perceptively comments that Wollstonecraft's vision of progress articulated in the *French Revolution*, 'implies the replacement of the imagination as a sign of a particular and exclusive aristocratric culture – a narrowly defined notion of taste – by a vision of the imagination as an expansive moral capacity which can control economic and technological developments and stop them degenerating into a new aristocracy of wealth'.[47]

Public opinion

In modern times the French 'dared to think for themselves', reading avidly 'the productions of a number of able writers, who were daily pouring pamphlets from the press', for example the philosophical researches of 'the abbé Sieyes and the marquis de Condorcet' softened by 'the unctuous eloquence of Mirabeau' (*French Revolution*, pp. 44–5). The revolution was the direct result of Enlightenment, and heralded a glorious dawn. However, like Forster, Wollstonecraft concedes that this heady power of public opinion paradoxically became extremely dangerous when it outgrew a subordinate role. Soon 'the liberty of the press...was a successful engine employed against the assembly' itself. Wollstonecraft argues: 'The countenancing of this abuse of freedom was ill-judged', citing Rabaut's account of the 'prodigious manufacture of pamphlets...poems, songs, epigrams, satires, tragedies' sold at the doors of the Assembly (*French Revolution*, p. 186). The Constitution should have been quickly framed rather than everlasting debate allowing the escalating voices of public opinion to rival those of the legislative assembly itself. This paved the way to direct action and Robespierre's takeover:

> It was the indispensable duty of the deputies to respect the dignity of their body – Instead of which, for sinister purposes, many of them instructed the people how to tyrannize over the assembly; thus deserting the main principle of representation, the respect due to the majority.
>
> (*French Revolution*, p. 212)

In voicing this contradiction between her continuing belief in Enlightenment through print culture, yet recognition of the fearsome destabilizing power of the influence of the press, Wollstonecraft was not alone. The Girondin journalist Louvet himself had denounced: 'this eternal domination of writers over . . . the magistrates, the people's representatives, the leading public officials'.[48] But another journalist-revolutionary – that expert in regime change, and survivor of them all, Barère – relished the role of the press as inquisitor of all government:

> Do you wish for an eye that watches at all times the legislators, the directory, the ministers, the judges, the administrators, the magistrates of the people, and the commissaries of government? Are you in want of an arm to arrest and denounce abuses of all kinds, and tyranny everywhere? – All these are effected by the liberty of the press. . . . There is no medium between the liberty of the press and the inquisition of the press.[49]

But a constitutionalist such as Wollstonecraft had realized that liberating the press from royalist control had meant that, as a species of capitalism, it could be manipulated by the wealthy and pressure groups. Her long-term political aim was the emancipation of the lower-classes from landlords and capitalists as well as from deference to monarchs and priests. An unregulated press had proved a thorn in the side of the fledgeling republic's attempt to build the New Jerusalem. The power of the press to mobilize public opinion and thereby hobble representative government is still today one of the most contentious features of modern democracies, and discussed in the social theories of Theodor

Adorno and Jürgen Habermas. Wollstonecraft was one of the first British radical writers to highlight this contradiction at the heart of the 'public sphere'.

Education before emancipation

Wollstonecraft's vindication of representative government leads to another dilemma. How broad should the electorate be? To strike a balance between the French predilection for revolution and the English preference for stability, Wollstonecraft advocates 'a gradual change of opinion'. For '. . . just sentiments gain footing only in proportion as the understanding is enlarged by cultivation, and freedom of thought, instead of being cramped by the dread of bastilles and inquisition' (*French Revolution*, p. 70). The French have jumped the gun by fixing 'on a system proper only for a people in the highest stage of civilization' (*French Revolution*, p. 162). Steven Blakemore comments that her 'argument of paradise deferred is a classic explanation for revolutions that inexplicably fail to follow theory and has been repeatedly used for the past two centuries'.[50] But gradualism is not some sort of a revisionist compromise for Wollstonecraft, rather a desperate bid to retain forward movement. She writes in dread of a counter-revolution. For 'All sudden revolutions have been suddenly overturned, and things thrown back below their former state' (*French Revolution*, p. 183). The 'sovereignty of the people, the perfection of the science of government [is] only to be attained when a nation is truly enlightened' (*French* Revolution, p. 193). Hence the necessity of implementing public education before instituting full political democracy. Wollstonecraft was messianic in her vision of the future enlightenment of the whole population through education for all.

> It is a palpable error to suppose, that men of every class are not equally susceptible of common improvement: if therefore it be the contrivance of any government to preclude from a chance of improvement the greater part of the citizens of a state, it can be considered in no other light than as a monstrous tyranny, a barbarous oppression, equally injurious to the two parties, though in different ways. For all the advantages of civilization cannot be felt, unless it pervades the whole mass, humanizing every description of men – and then it is the first of blessings, the true perfection of man.
>
> (*French Revolution*, p. 220)

Always conscious of the ironic disjunction between the Utopian future she envisages and the dark night of the Terror in which she writes, Wollstonecraft admits:

> It is perhaps, difficult to bring ourselves to believe, that out of this chaotic mass a fairer government is rising than has ever shed the sweets of social life on the world. – But things must have time to find their level.
>
> (*French Revolution*, p. 47).

Though aristocratic governments of the past have degenerated through luxury and been overthrown, she denies history is necessarily cyclical, for if 'the great majority of society' is exercising body and mind 'to earn a subsistence' the whole body politic will continue healthy (*French Revolution*, p. 22).

This extraordinary metaphor of balancing the mental and bodily health of each individual making up the nation runs through the whole book. Wollstonecraft's doctrine was that each individual should work using both brain and body for the sake of their corporeal and spiritual health and that of the body politic which makes up the nation. Startlingly democratic, it evokes the Jacobin ideal of redistributing intellectual and physical labour throughout the whole population instead of dividing it through class. The *ancien régime* was 'a gigantic tyranny...draining away the vital juices of labour to fill the insatiable jaws of thousands of fawning slaves and sycophants...' (*French Revolution*, pp. 32–3). 'The people could no longer bear bleeding – for their veins were already so lacerated' (*French Revolution*, p. 43). The French lagged behind in technological advance because their 'cast-like division [of classes]... destroying all strength of character in the [nobility] and debasing [the lower classes] to machines' produced no drive to improve the material comfort and independence of ordinary people (*French Revolution*, pp. 230–1).

Commerce and the redistribution of wealth and labour

Necessary too was 'the unshackling of commerce' for 'the prosperity of a state depends on the freedom of industry', so 'that talents should be permitted to find their level' (*French Revolution*, p. 226). Wollstonecraft, like the Girondins, applauded François Quesnai and the physiocrats for their vision of economics as a sort of natural law. The physiocrats had influenced the thinking of Adam Smith to whose work she often refers, and the Comte de Mirabeau. Wollstonecraft supported policies such as free trade, doing away with monopolistic and bureaucratic impots, and substituting instead an indirect taxation system, weighing less heavily on the poor (*French Revolution*, p. 19). She repeated the physiocrat doctrine that all wealth originated with the land. But she gives it her own egalitarian spin by commenting on the deleterious effect on the workers of modern industrial capitalism:

> Commerce also, overstocking a country with people, obliges the majority to become manufacturers rather than husbandmen; and then the division of labour, solely to enrich the proprietor, renders the mind entirely inactive
>
> (*French Revolution*, pp. 233–4).

Taking issue with Adam Smith's dictum that labour should be divided into repetitive tasks to achieve greater efficiency,[51] she makes an impassioned plea for the worker to be considered as a whole and independent individual, exercising both body and mind:

> The time which a celebrated author [Smith] says is sauntered away, in going from one part of an employment to another, is the very time that preserves the man from degenerating into a brute; for every one must have observed how much more intelligent are the blacksmiths, carpenters, and masons in the country than the journeymen in towns.... The very gait of the man, who is his own master, is so much more steady than the slouching step of the servant of a servant....
>
> The acquiring of a fortune is likewise the least arduous road to pre-eminence, and the most sure; thus are whole knots of men turned into machines, to enable a keen speculator to become wealthy; and every noble principle of nature is eradicated by making a man pass his life in stretching wire, pointing a pin, heading a nail, or spreading a sheet of paper on a plain surface.
>
> (*French Revolution*, p. 234).

That Wollstonecraft could make this searing indictment of industrial capitalism sixty years before Dickens's *Hard Times* shows her radicalism and independence of thought. She realized that political economics was the key to social equality and argued for a direct tax on property rather than indirect duties on goods. 'No government has yet established a just system of taxation' she commented, giving facts and figures to prove it. One daring suggestion shows her to be interested in advanced ideas of land reform and redistribution. She argued that, at the dawn of the French revolution:

> An able, bold minister, who possessed the confidence of the nation, might have recommended with success that taking of the national property under the direct management of the assembly; and then endeavoured to raise a loan on that property...
>
> *(French Revolution, p. 181).*[52]

Like early communist Thomas Spence, she envisaged that a true republican society would become rural in nature: 'as the charms of solitary reflections and agricultural recreations are felt, the people, by leaving the villages and cities, will give a new complexion to the face of the country' *(French Revolution, p. 229).* As in *Rights of Men*, she introduces a bold reverie inspired by wandering the landscaped gardens of a palatial mansion, imagining the land divided up to 'build farms', substituting the people's prosperity for the landowner's picturesque. Such an attack on property puts the radical Wollstonecraft well beyond the pale enclosing Whigs and moderates. She acknowledges the utopian nature of this vision by adopting the novelistic language of sensibility in an account of the moralizing author, the 'pensive wanderer' visiting the empty palace of Versailles, which still radiates its own deadly aura of tyranny:

> The very air is chill, seeming to clog the breath; and the wasting dampness of destruction appears to be stealing into the vast pile on every side.
>
> *(French Revolution, p. 85)*

Sexual politics

Wollstonecraft's political thinking had always been coloured by metaphorical representation of the independence of republicanism as 'manly', while the dependence fostered by feudalism was 'feminine'.[53] This was a commonplace of the discourse of civic humanism. Simply applying this perspective to the social oppression of her own sex in *Rights of Woman* had brought her to distinguish between conventional femininity – berated as false consciousness – and being an independent female human being. The paradox is that the trope which brought her to her greatest feminist insight now has her stigmatising the whole French nation as effeminised by their long oppression under absolute monarchy. She therefore adopts a 'masculine' stance: contemptuously comparing a Frenchman to a woman, whose character is passively formed by conforming to the expectations of the prevailing ideology (p. 230). Compare the Protestant pastor Rabaut on this 'effeminacy of the soul' of the French, which he links to the 'false maxims' of the Catholic South, in comparison with the enlightened philosophy emanating from the universities of the Protestant North (Rabaut, *History of the Revolution in France*, I, 24).

Disturbingly for modern socialist-feminists, Wollstonecraft is so determined to separate her own intellectual feminism in *Rights of Woman* from the street politics of lower-class women in the revolution, that she deliberately rivals Burkean opprobrium in her portrayal of the march of the sans-culottes women to Versailles. No longer the sturdy market traders of *Rights of Men*, now they are 'the lowest refuse of the streets': their action orchestrated by their betters 'not the effect of public spirit' (*French Revolution*, p. 197; also see p. 207). As such women are uneducated and doubly oppressed by conventional ideologies of rank and gender it doesn't seem possible to Wollstonecraft that they could embody the independence she always associates with intellectual enlightenment. Vivien Jones has noted how her linear rationalist narrative is disrupted by novelistic paradigms from Gothic fiction when dealing with such crises of revolutionary direct action.[54] Marie Antoinette is depicted as a stock victim and the Duke of Orleans as a typical aristocratic villain manipulating the mob, in Wollstonecraft's melodrama of counter-revolutionary plotting.

The nature of ideological change

When she turns to the most difficult question of all, why violence erupted, Wollstonecraft put her finger on the central paradox about ideological change – that it never comes untainted by the past. So the form the revolution took was paradoxically shaped by the theatricalism of *ancien régime* ideology. 'The character of the French...had been so depraved by the inveterate despotism of ages, that even amidst the heroism which distinguished the taking of the bastille, we are forced to see that suspicious temper, and that vain ambition of dazzling, which have generated all the succeeding follies and crimes' (*French Revolution*, p. 123). Servility has destroyed the 'noblest sentiments of the soul.... Ought we then to wonder, that this dry substitute for humanity is often burnt up by the scorching flame of revenge?' (*French Revolution*, p. 126). Inner moral development had not accompanied the outward development of manners.[55] So at each stage, and with reference to all the events in 1789 from the calling of the Estates General to the instituting of the new National Assembly and beyond, Wollstonecraft showed that the history of the revolution was the product of a dialectic between progressive concepts and the remnants of old ideologies these would replace. The friction and conflict inevitably led to outbreaks of violence and even massacres.

Wollstonecraft did not shirk the most contentious question posed to a radical like herself: whether the end justified the means and whether violence was ever justified. Though she strongly urges that the progress of reason will ameliorate all governments in the fullness of time, she also admits that in a very few cases of extreme degradation, the violent overthrow of tyranny is justified (*French Revolution*, pp. 45–6). Though she resolutely faces the most difficult issues that the philosophical historian tries to judge, Wollstonecraft's faith in the principles of the revolution and belief in its eventual success is never in doubt.

Reception

Though this was the most scholarly of her publications Wollstonecraft had brought in an element of personal testimony, even using novelistic techniques occasionally. Contemporary reviews all commented on this innovative style for a history. The *British Critic* complained '...it is more florid than the tone of the subject allows; mixing too much that of the novelist with that of the historian; the dignity of whose matter very ill accords with tinsel and tawdriness'.[56] But the *English Review* thought it 'animated, vigorous, and various. She is not afraid to make use of any word, or metaphor, or other figure, that may convey to the mind of the reader, with energy and precision, the precise point in question' – though the reviewer did draw the line at her graphic extended simile of the Terror as an attack of diarrhoea purging the body politic.[57] The *Monthly Review* felt: 'She writes this wonderful chapter in the history of the world, not like an annalist, but like a philosopher'. The new work afforded 'many new proofs of the writer's superior literary merit. The vigour of her imagination appears throughout the work in the metaphorical cast of her language'.[58]

The *Analytical Review* devoted the lead article to this 'work of uncommon merit' in December 1794, continued in January 1795. The reviewer described the author as qualified for such an ambitious undertaking 'in a degree which in a woman may appear to male vanity highly astonishing', having produced a book which will 'command the serious attention of the moralist and statesman' with its 'energy of diction and... richness of imagery', 'solidity and depth of thought' and 'strong traits of original genius'.[59] The success of Wollstonecraft's history was sufficient to warrant another edition in 1795.[60]

Other writers by then began to bring out rival philosophical analyses of the revolution, usually from more conservative perspectives. Dr John Moore's Whiggish *View of the Causes and Progress of the French Revolution* (1794) was described by the *Analytical* as 'neither stongly marked with the characters of originality, nor distinguished by any extraordinary depth of reflection'.[61] It was deemed a colourless 'grey' work by a later *Analytical* reviewer, who described Anti-jacobin propagandist William Playfair's *History of Jacobinism, Its Crimes, Cruelties and Perfidies, etc.* (1795) as a 'black' view of the republic, in complete contrast to the idealistic white of Mary Wollstonecraft: an 'unreserved defender of the revolution'.[62] John Adams, president of the United States, agreed, annotating his edition:

> This is a lady of a masculine masterly Understanding.... The Improvement, the exaltation of the human Character, the perfectibility of man, the Perfection of the human Faculties are the divine Objects which her Enthusiasm beholds in beatificism. Alas how airy and baseless a fabrick![63]

* * *

As the heat of Summer 1794 declined, the swelling agonies of the Terror were at last lanced by the denunciation and execution of Robespierre himself and a final bloodletting. Wollstonecraft attended a revolutionary fête celebrating the interrment of Marat's body in the Panthéon, on 21 September, and decided to get Fanny a sash commemorating Rousseau. A provisional government restored the liberty of the press. Wollstonecraft welcomed this joyfully, writing on 23 September: '... they write now with great freedom and truth, and this liberty of the press will overthrow the Jacobins, I plainly perceive' (*CLMW*, p. 264). By 1st October she again attributed regime change to the power of print: 'The liberty of the press will produce a great effect here – the *cry of blood will not be vain!* – Some more monsters will perish – and the Jacobins are conquered. – yet I almost fear the last flap of the tail of the beast' (*CLMW*, p. 267).

6
The Commercial Traveller, the Imagination and the Material World

The art of travelling is only a branch of the art of thinking
Mary Wollstonecraft, *Analytical Review* 7 (1790)

(*WMW*, 7: 277)

Though she temporized her political despair by taking the long view in her history of the French revolution, Wollstonecraft's ideals had been blasted by the Terror. She had got through by channelling all the force of her Utopianism into her relationship with Gilbert Imlay: envisioning it as an Edenic partnership of equals. Long before the French Revolution, she had idealized friendship as an earthly aspect of divine love in her Platonic early novel, *Mary: A Fiction*. The moral universe was the only dimension that mattered to her, so Wollstonecraft recognized no artificial divisions between public and private spheres. When her ideals became politicised during the revolution, she still saw *fraternité* as love for one's fellow man in active daily life as well as social policy. As she lost her orthodox religious faith, she practised *fraternité* less in terms of the familial duties and personal charity which had driven her in the 1780s to make such strenuous efforts to assist her siblings and the Bloods, and to take in an orphan child. However, socialization and conversation remained for her, as for Godwin back in London, an essential component of the good life as well as of one's literary vocation. Moral questions needed to be tested out in discussion and against the pulses of daily experience before they were disseminated to the wider world through print. The authority of moral laws was to be challenged. Fraternal and sexual relationships would now reflect the emotionally honest commitments of individuals decided moment by moment.

Fraternity, the material world and the creative imagination

Sexual experience had blown away the puritanism with which Wollstonecraft had treated physical love in *Vindication of the Rights of Woman*. As her religious beliefs turned towards humanism, she developed more and more her existing but conflicted belief in the importance of the human imagination.[1] A sort of secular soul, it mimicked the divine in its ability to mediate between the material world (including the body) and the realm of mind – and thus apprehend a spiritual unity throughout the universe. This led her towards an idealized or 'Romantic' view of the creative imagination, and of authorship. Wollstonecraft's concept of the imagination became both frankly erotic and intensely spiritual and she tried to share it with Imlay. On 12 June 1795 she wrote to him that imagination was the catalyst converting appetite into love: the 'unison of affection and desire, when the whole soul and senses are abandoned to a lively imagination, that renders every emotion delicate and rapturous' (*CLMW*, p. 291). She sacralized her erotic desire for him:

> Thy lips then feel softer than soft – and I rest my cheek on thine, forgetting all the world. – I have not left the hue of love out of the picture – the rosy glow; and fancy has spread it over my own cheeks, I believe, for I feel them burning, whilst a delicious tear trembles in my eye, that would be all your own, if a grateful emotion directed to the Father of nature, who has made me thus alive to happiness, did not give more warmth to the sentiments it divides...
>
> (*CLMW*, pp. 238–9)

She revelled, too, in motherhood and the physical pleasures of breast-feeding, boasting to Ruth Barlow that 'My little Girl begins to suck so *manfully* that her father reckons saucily on her writing the second part of the R-ts of Woman' (*CLMW*, p. 256).

But Gilbert Imlay interpreted the new revolutionary sexual mores in a somewhat less mystical and high-minded manner than Wollstonecraft, and explained that he needed a variety of lovers to express his zest for life spontaneously. A fraternal partnership of equals, both performing parental roles and furthering their egalitarian ideals in creating a commune in rural America was no longer on the agenda. Imlay had sold the dream to many, but Mary was one of the last to wake up.

Rejection by Imlay

All her attempts to interest him in the baby's development proved fruitless. As early as 19 August it was clear to Wollstonecraft that their attachment was no longer mutual (*CLMW*, p. 259), and by September Imlay had left for London. He pleaded business as the excuse for not returning after the stipulated two months. Wollstonecraft recalled bitterly the chivalric championship of women expressed in his novel *The Emigrants*: 'Reading what you have written relative to the desertion of women, I have often wondered how theory and practice could be so different...' (*CLMW*, p. 279). She had moved from Le Havre back to Paris, and throughout a miserable winter of shortages and rationing wrote to him incessantly as she had Fuseli. Her loveless childhood had rendered her incapable of tolerating rejection. Refusing to acknowledge any rival but commerce, she declared 'you are embruted by trade' and begged him to bring back his 'barrier-face', the welcome which had met her when she used to walk from Neuilly to the Paris tollgate with a basket of grapes (*CLMW*, p. 263). But all Imlay offered now was financial support. He was evasive about the future but lacked the courage to make a clean break.

Wollstonecraft hated the prospect of being economically dependent on a man who had ceased to care for her, and realized she should resume her literary career. She reminded her erstwhile lover: 'And let me tell you, I have my project also' (*CLMW*, p. 271). She was probably then intending to write another volume of her history of the revolution. On 30 December she reiterated, 'I am determined to try to earn some money here myself...for the little girl and I will live without your assistance, unless you are with us' (*CLMW*, p. 273). On 10 February she had received 3000 livres, perhaps from Johnson for her *French Revolution*, and declared she would take another bond from the same source, 'and then endeavour to procure what I want by my own exertions' (*CLMW*, p. 278).[2]

But Imlay had tired of the strong woman whose independent mind had once presented a challenge to his masculine charm. He disabused her of her romantic notions of their living the good life in poverty or settling in America, for he wanted money and the comforts it brought. She in her turn was reluctant to leave the republic and return to a rabidly 'anti-Jacobin' London – at that juncture putting radical writers and publishers such as playwright Thomas Holcroft and lecturer Thomas Thelwall on trial for treason. Joseph Johnson had been cross-examined in court about his role in publishing Thomas Hardy and John Horne Tooke.[3] Paine had been outlawed while in France, and Helen Maria

Williams's lover, John Hurford Stone, declared a 'seditious and wicked traitor' *in absentio* during the Stone brothers' trial for fomenting revolution in Britain. Wollstonecraft could easily imagine herself the butt of the loyalist mob, the female equivalent of Tom Paine. '[A]m I only to return to a country, that has not merely lost its charms for me, but for which I feel a repugnance that almost amounts to horror...!' (*CLMW*, p. 280). She doubtless also dreaded the ignominy of her friends and family witnessing the disintegration of the relationship with Imlay, so recently announced in triumph. She had no choice, however, as Imlay and Joseph Johnson – alternative sources of financial support – were both in London. She arrived back in Britain on 11 April 1795.

Imlay had rented a house for her in Charlotte Street, Soho, but his reception of Wollstonecraft was 'cold and embarrassed' (*MAVRW*, p. 94). In the face of the stark reality of his rejection, she could not sustain the fantasy of their ideal love she had continued to spin in her letters during their long separation. She sank deep into depression, exacerbated by poor health after a lingering lung infection. By 22 May she wrote: 'It seems to me that I have not only lost the hope, but the power of being happy. – Every emotion is now sharpened by anguish. – My soul has been shook, and my tone of feelings destroyed' (*CLMW*, p. 288). She who had made independence the cornerstone of her beliefs now graphically demonstrated abject dependence on her ex-lover. She attempted suicide by swallowing laudanum. Presumably a note to Imlay alerted him, for Godwin declares it was 'perhaps owing to his activity and representations, that her life was, at this time, saved. She determined to continue to exist' (*MAVRW*, p. 94). The way that Godwin expresses this resolution is typically precise. For Wollstonecraft did not merely passively survive; she decided to resume living. To live for her meant to take a considered moral action to shape her own destiny. She decided immediately to undertake a voyage to Scandinavia, accompanied only by the year-old baby Fanny and her young French nurse, Marguerite. As early as the 10 June she was writing from Hull, where she soon found herself a cargo vessel bound for Elsinore willing to take passengers.

Scandinavia

What was the purpose of this extraordinary decision? As Godwin commented, it was one 'worthy of the strength and affectionateness of her mind' (*MAVRW*, p. 94). She intended to attempt single-handedly to extricate her ex-lover from the business entanglement which he had made the excuse for staying in London. Incapable of 'feminine' wiles herself, she naively hoped that by removing the obstacle supposedly preventing his return to the continent, she would bring about their reunion – and by these Herculean efforts on his behalf even rekindle Gilbert's love. Imlay presumably strung her along, for she originally hoped he would meet up with her in Germany. The letter he wrote for Wollstonecraft to take, conferring power of attorney upon her, spoke gushingly of her as 'my best friend and wife' and 'my dear beloved friend and companion' in whose 'talents zeal and correctness' he entrusted the management of these affairs.[4] Imlay must have been relieved to obtain a breathing space, and by a means which might even bring him commercial benefit. He must also have genuinely respected her abilities, to put such an important business affair in her hands. As the famous revolutionary writer, whose *Rights of Woman* had been translated into Italian, French and German (and she used her own name on her travels, not Imlay), Wollstonecraft would gain entry to the highest Scandinavian circles, and get the ear of influential people. If she were successful, both in business and love, Wollstonecraft hoped she and Fanny would benefit from the resulting financial settlement.

Another reason for the journey was therapeutic. Travel was believed to help cure depression, and Gilpin's theory of the picturesque, which Wollstonecraft had helped to popularise, advocated the power of contemplating the landscape to restore order to the mind. Popular medical treatises such as William Buchan's *Domestic Medicine, or the Family Physician* (1769) and Thomas Trotter's *A View of the Nervous Temperament* (1807) particularly associated melancholia with 'masculine' literary genius, with which Wollstonecraft consciously identified.[5] They advised change of air, exercise, taking spa waters and bathing: all of which she tried, to restore her health, with some success.

Lastly, but not least in importance, Wollstonecraft hoped her travels would provide material for the book she needed to write to re-establish her literary career and achieve economic independence: 'I had a dislike to living in England; but painful feelings must give way to superior considerations. I may not be able to acquire the sum necessary to maintain my child and self elsewhere' (*CLMW*, p. 310). When she was pouring out her troubles to her old fatherly friend, Joseph Johnson, the publisher responded with a practical suggestion, he commissioned a travel book. Passionate and restless like her father, Wollstonecraft had already travelled quite extensively for a woman: to Ireland, Portugal and France. As chief reviewer of the genre for the *Analytical*, she knew all the latest publications. Travel writing appealed to her utilitarian, pedagogic side in its accumulation of useful knowledge, but also to her Protestant predilection for the autobiographical, as it constituted first-hand observation and commentary.

The projected book would particularly attract Johnson's scientific readership, for Sweden was a key destination for the study of natural history, being the birthplace of Carl Linnaeus himself.[6] It would equally interest his liberal clientèle: for Sweden's *coup d'état* and regicide, and the Scandinavians' refusal to join the allied powers against the French republic, gave the lands of the midnight sun a political fascination. The question on everyone's lips was whether Sweden could become an alternative model to that of France. Could Enlightenment bring a smoother transition to equality in a *less* advanced society? Or would reform merely replace feudal oppression with ruthless capitalism and complacent materialism? The extraordinary book that Wollstonecraft was about to write should be seen very much as the product of the Non-conformist English Enlightenment circles of which Johnson was centre and chief publisher. Natural history and political change were not discrete but related areas of intellectual concern in this milieu. The scientific study of nature in Warrington and by the Lunar Society and others, the development of Unitarianism and natural religion, Utopian belief in individual perfectibility and social enlightenment had together created an intoxicating image of progress as juggernaut. But the Terror stopped it in its tracks. Now idealists such as Wollstonecraft reacted by reenvisioning the natural world as one spiritualised organic system, and the individual human imagination as a sacred yet relatively powerless element in the immense and mysterious forces determining change.

Work in progress

Claire Tomalin has plausibly suggested that Johnson may also have given Wollstonecraft other literary work: perhaps a translation of the memoirs of Madame Roland to correct, which would appear in 1795.[7] This is significant. For the confessional style of *Letters from Norway* should also be seen in the context of Roland's and other self-justificatory Girondin autobiographical accounts, appearing in the wake of the Terror which had claimed their authors' lives or their political hopes.

By 18 July Wollstonecraft had written to Imlay from Tonsberg, where she had to pass three or four weeks alone in a quiet inn, that she had begun some work, probably the journal which formed the basis of *Letters from Norway* (CLMW, p. 306). The published version, which would come out early in 1796, showed an obliqueness and writerly sophistication greater than in any of her previous texts. Wollstonecraft's fictionalised letters addressed to an absent lover created that mystery in narrative which stimulated her readers' curiosity, by deliberately withholding full explanations of either her personal relationship with the narrattee or the specific business which took her to Scandinavia. She merely hinted enigmatically at a deteriorating relationship and inveigled against the corrupting influence of commerce, without emphasizing the irony (obvious only to Imlay) of the fact she was herself on business, and business mired in intrigue. Two years later readers would find out the full shocking story of Wollstonecraft's suicide attempts and lack of a legal marriage to Imlay when they read Wollstonecraft's letters to her former lover amongst the posthumous works and alongside Godwin's frank *Memoirs*. Readers might then view the author of the travels as a victim either of the oppression of women in society or of the delusions of her own revolutionary freethinking, according to their politics. But they continued in the dark about her business in Scandinavia until the late twentieth century.

The business of the journey

Not until Gothenburg historian Per Nyström's pioneering research was it revealed that Wollstonecraft's project was to recover a lost treasure ship owned by Gilbert Imlay. The 'Maria and Margaretha' (named after Mary and her maid) was evading the British blockade by sailing under the neutral Danish flag, while carrying Bourbon silver bars and plate worth £3500 destined for Scandinavia. This was an astonishing amount of money, and far more than Imlay was personally worth. He must have raised it by speculation, perhaps with help from the Jacobin government itself, to pay for a cargo, probably of corn and iron, for import into the beleaguered French republic. This would be provided by Imlay's agent, the Finnish wholesaler Elias Backman, in Gothenburg.[8] Had Imlay been a British citizen, he could have been executed for treason for aiding France in this way. So no wonder if neither Wollstonecraft nor Godwin revealed the nature of the business trip to the increasingly loyalist reading public. Wollstonecraft was given power of attorney by Imlay to take on the conduct of a lawsuit which Backman had inaugurated against the ship's young captain, Peder Ellefsen, who claimed the brig had sunk together with the treasure. It certainly disappeared without trace. Wollstonecraft was assuming charge of a case 'taken up on the highest political levels in Denmark and Sweden' (Noström: 21–2).

Ellefsen was the black sheep of a well-known family of ship owners and ironmasters, who used their wealth to protract the trial and influence the outcome. Backman, on the other hand, was associated with the revolutionaries who had opposed the autocracy of the Swedish king Gustav III, and assassinated him in 1792. Backman had then fled to France where he moved in Jacobin circles. The new administration in Sweden meanwhile refused to join Britain and Russia in the war against the French republic, and, together with Denmark under prime minister A.P. Bernstorff, they declared their neutrality, while encouraging liberal reforms at home. Backman returned and was appointed by George Washington as American consul-general in Gothenburg, the first in Europe. Although only a modest merchant, he had good connections because of the (pro-French) political context of his business dealings. The financier and ironmaster Carsten Anker wrote to the Governor of Kristiansand in support of Backman, and the Danish government was prompted to set up a Royal Commission to investigate the case in January 1795. It was found that the captain had superintended the removal of the silver from the brig, and turned the ship itself over to the mate, presumably as the price of silence. Ellefsen was arrested the next month and his formidable family complicated the case by challenging the appointment of one of the commissioners. By the time Wollstonecraft set out, Imlay had decided to cut his losses, for he empowered her to make an out-of-court settlement with Ellefsen if she thought fit.

Wollstonecraft's journey was planned around the case. She first needed to make contact with Backman. When her ship was unable to dock at Arendal in Norway or Gothenburg in Sweden she persuaded the captain to break the usual rules and let sailors row her to a nearby lighthouse, probably at Nidingen in the Kattegatt, where she bribed them to go further along the rocky coast to procure a pilot. Wollstonecraft found her little female party lodgings in a cottage on the dramatic Onsala peninsula. She then proceeded to Gothenburg; arriving on 27 June and staying for a fortnight with Backman. She left baby Fanny and her nurse behind (*Letters from Norway*, p. 260),[9] when she and Backman travelled to Strömstad. The purpose was to meet merchant Christoffer Nordberg and district judge A.J. Unger who had made the preliminary enquiries about the ship. They stayed with Nordberg and made 'a little voyage to Norway' by ferry for pleasure and visited the fortress of Fredriksten. Backman then returned home, while Wollstonecaft set off for alone for Tönsberg to consult judge Jacob Wulfsberg, the commissioner to whom Ellefsen had objected, on the grounds that he was a former agent of Backman's. Tönsberg was higher up the coast than Stromstad, and she embarked immediately she returned from Norway at five in the morning, stopping only for a dish of coffee. On the way there, she stopped at Larvik on 14 July for discussions with the lawyers acting in the case. She finally arrived at Tonsberg late at night on 16 July, ready for her business meeting the next day. Though she was 'seriously employed in this way' she also enjoyed the outdoor life: 'I walk, I ride on horseback – row, bathe, and even sleep in the fields; my health is consequently improved' she told Imlay (*CLMW*, p. 307). But discovering she had to wait in Tönsberg at least three weeks, she wished she had brought the baby whom she was badly missing (*Letters form Norway*, p. 270).

Wollstonecraft next journeyed west to Risör, the home of Ellefsen, by road and by sea. On her way, she called again at Larvik to meet the 'locusts' (lawyers) with 'visages deformed by vice' as she colourfully described them. She was warned that the further westward she travelled, 'as traffic takes the place of agriculture' the 'more cunning and fraudulent' she would find the inhabitants (*Letters from Norway*, p. 290–1). The sea was rough and the coast wild. After having to take refuge at Portør for a night the boat at last entered the forbidding seaport of Risør. Massive cliffs met her eyes, in a cleft of which the houses were crammed with hardly space to scramble between them. Its main trade, Wollstonecraft surmised, was contraband (*Letters from Norway*, p. 295) and her account of the place communicated a sense of disgust for entrepreneurial trickery that targeted Imlay as well as Ellefsen. We don't know if she spoke to Ellefsen himself or his family in this the climax of her commercial travelling, but she did arrange a meeting with the British vice-consul. On 22 August she set out on her return journey to Tonsberg, and boarded the ferry to Moss. She went north to Oslo, where she was the guest of the entrepreneur and fellow of the British Royal Society, Bernhard Anker, the brother of the ironmaster who had supported Backman and pressed for an inquiry into the loss of the treasure ship. After visiting the cascade and fortress at Fredericstadt, and checking out whether any sea-captains had ever seen the Kraken, Wollstonecraft took a boat to Stromstad, not arriving until one in the morning.

In a fever of impatience to see Fanny after an absence of six weeks, Wollstonecraft returned to Gothenburg on 25 August, having experienced many adventures on the road. She had seen something of the hard-drinking, rough and tumble of peasant life and coped alone with the vagaries of the post-horse system in remote countryside, once sleeping in a stinking hovel packed with human flotsam. By now, she was weary of travel, but for the sake of business – both Imlay's lawsuit and her own literary project, she made her way South through Denmark to Copenhagen, accompanied by Marguerite and Fanny, after having visited the falls at Trolhaettae. In the capital, she was feted by high society – even being received by prime minister A.P. Bernstorff himself. Perhaps her caustic account of his 'cautious circumspection which treads on the heels of timidity' (*Letters from Norway*, p. 331) suggests that he was infuriatingly noncommittal with reference to the case. She later journeyed to Korsör, from whence she crossed the Great Belt and the Little Belt to Schleswig, and made her way overland towards Hamburg. From there she returned to England, landing at Dover on 4 October, four months after leaving London. Letters Wollstonecraft had received from Imlay while in Scandinavia had made it brutally clear he had no intention of living with her ever again. Within less than a week of her return to England she would make a second and this time a determined attempt at suicide. More of this later.

We don't know exactly what had been the outcome of Wollstonecraft's business visits, but it can hardly be coincidence that two days after she returned to Britain, on 6 October, a ship named 'Maria and Margaretha' and owned by Elias Backman signed on a crew at Gothenburg. Imlay did send another friend, John Wheatcroft, to Scandinavia that Autumn. He travelled with a passport approved by the Committee of Public Safety and signed by Sieyès. A year later in November 1797, a court hearing closed when the plaintiffs failed to come forward with a further statement after Wulfsberg was disallowed. Further records of the Commission are mysteriously absent as if the whole thing had ground to a halt or been hushed up. It seems certain that someone succeeded in arranging a private deal for the Ellefsens to pay compensation to Imlay in return for dropping the case against Peder. From the timing of the reappearance of the ship, this was more likely to be Wollstonecraft than Wheatcroft, who probably concluded the deal. One thing is certain: Mary received none of the proceeds.

Travel writing and *Letters from Norway*

Scandinavia made a relatively unusual destination for a travel book. *Letters from Norway* capitalized on antiquarian interest in Anglo-Saxon history and Norse mythology generated, for example, by Bishop Percy's translation of Paul Henry Mallet's *Northern Antiquities, or, A Description of the Manners, Customs, Religion and Laws of the Ancient Danes and Other Northern Nations Including Those of Our Own Saxon Ancestors* (1770), and Daines Barrington's *Orosius* (1773) – Alfred the Great's translation into Anglo-Saxon of Orosius's history of the world. Interest in Nordic culture was part of a Romantic repudiation of classicism and the aristocratic grand tour, and flourished in the nationalist climate the war created.

Wollstonecraft had read the most authorative previous account by Archdeacon Coxe, *Travels into Poland, Russia, Sweden and Denmark* (1784), which was written in an objective, scholarly manner, complete with a bibliography of sources, and tables of facts and figures regarding the population, laws, army and navy. Though Coxe acknowledged the existence of picturesque scenery, he suppressed mention of his own feelings. In a telling phrase, he stated that the cataracts of Trolhaetta were 'too sublime to be accurately described' (III, 293). Wollstonecraft would refer dismissively to Coxe, casting doubt on one or two of his factual statements. She would also provide what he could not – a much greater emphasis than had ever been seen before in travel writing on scenery description and the author's lyrical response to the sublime.

This turn towards the Romantic sublime drew upon the aesthetic theories of Burke and Gilpin; and on a literary equivalent of putting the figure of the artist in the corner of the picture in eighteenth-century topographical poetry.[10] For Nigel Leask, the significant milestone in the direction of romanticized travel writing had been *Voyage Round the World* (1777) by Wollstonecraft's friend the naturalist Georg Forster, who in his youth had accompanied Captain Cook on his second voyage. In his preface Forster had dismissed mere collections of facts, commenting that it was necessary 'to be acquainted with the observer, before any use could be made of his observations'. Forster went on to become an important essayist; friend of and influence on Goethe, Alexander von Humboldt and the formative figures of German Romanticism, especially Friedrich Schlegel.[11] As Leask remarks, it is extremely likely that his thinking influenced Wollstonecraft's Advertisement, where she admits her inability to 'avoid being continually the first person – "the little hero of each tale"'; yet 'perceived that I could not give a just description of what I saw, but by relating the effect different objects had produced on my mind and feelings, whilst the impression was still fresh' (*Letters from Norway*, p. 241).[12]

The point about the new 'affective realism' or, as Adam Smith termed it, 'indirect discourse' in prose narrative, was not to denigrate truth-telling, but rather to confer greater authenticity by contextualising facts. Because of the instability of travel writing as a genre, and its vulnerability to charges of plagiarism and tall-tale-telling, stylistic strategies for authentication had evolved: such as casting oneself as a 'philosophic traveller', citing personal experience, and revealing oneself to have the melancholy temperament which signified 'acute mental ability'.[13] Wollstonecraft used all of these, even flagging up the significance of her Hamletian pose by a remark on melancholy as 'the malady of genius' (*Letters from Norway*, p. 329).

Nevertheless, by no means did she reject the authorial stance of authoritative gatherer of facts. Indeed, she provided her own notes with statistics on Scandinavian industry, economy and taxes. She had no time for the merely entertaining travel book, such as Matthew Consett's *A Tour Through Sweden, Swedish Lapland, Finland and Denmark in a Series of Letters* (1790) and Andrew Swinton's *Travels into Norway, Denmark and Russia 1788–1791* (1792). *Letters from Norway* typifies the intensity of the struggle Leask describes in Romantic-period travel writing to integrate literary and scientific discourses, 'rather than embodying the achieved triumph of imagination over knowledge'.[14] Indeed, for Wollstonecraft the whole point of imagination lies in its synthesising and universalising power respecting different branches of knowledge – of science, society, morals, aesthetics.

Wollstonecraft pitched her own narrative at the reader familiar with Scottish Enlightenment universal histories. These were largely derived from travel accounts, whose authors she rebuked for reproducing national stereotypes, which are 'rarely just, because they do not discriminate the natural from the acquired difference'. Cultural differences were 'much more numerous and unstable' than the effect of climate and more difficult to analyse (*Letters from Norway*, p. 266). 'The most essential service' that travel writers 'could render to society, would be to promote inquiry and discussion, instead of making those dogmatical assertions which only appear calculated to gird the human mind round with imaginary circles, like a paper globe which represents the one he inhabits'. The traveller should be cosmopolitan, and rather than assuming his/her own nation's superiority in culture, should comment on and compare the societies visited, in an impartial spirit which we would now call sociological.

In the case of *Letters from Norway*, the autobiographical reflections on the melancholy voyager's state of mind were not irrelevant to this purpose. Wollstonecraft alludes in the opening pages to 'the horrors I had witnessed in France, which had cast a gloom over all nature' (*Letters from Norway*, p. 247). This contextualizes her despair as grounded in the battering her personal and political ideals had taken in the Terror. Linked to this political background is the spiritually restorative role of 'spontaneous pleasure' in nature, which gives 'credibility to our expectation of happiness' – improvement in this world and the next. Contemplating Nature allowed 'the enthusiasm of my character' ... 'to be lighted up afresh'. The landscape thus has a dual role: it is studied as the environment shaping a specific society in all its particularity; but its beauty also gives the melancholy observer hope that human progress will partake of the regenerative force of nature.

Women and travel writing

The book's greatest novelty, of course, lay in its being written by a woman. Originally, travel writing had been the preserve of the aristocrat on his Grand Tour, a diplomat or colonizer; the objectivity of whose observations was guaranteed by a distanced prose style and securely grounded in male British ruling-class identity. However, travelogue had been interbreeding with the novel form since the days of Defoe. Smollett, Fielding and especially Sterne had all introduced narrative forms from fiction into their travels books, especially autobiographical anecdotes.[15] The growing tendency towards an informal epistolary style, and inclusion of quotidien details in place of a knowledge-based geographical survey, allowed the first women writers to enter the field.

Wollstonecraft had reviewed Hester Lynch Piozzi's *Observations and Reflections, Made in the Course of a Journey Through France, Italy and Germany* (1789), and regretted the 'frivolous, superficial remarks' that this merely entertaining type of travel-writing entailed (*WMW*, 7: 109). It was not that she dismissed 'the knack of epistolary writing, the talent of chatting on paper', for she claims it as a 'truly feminine' style, in contrast to the studied wit and vanity of Pope's letters. But she is much more enthusiastic about Helen Maria Williams's effusive *Letters written in France* (1790) because it has a crusading purpose. '[S]uch an air of sincerity', being put to political use, 'leads us to hope that [the Letters] may remove ... a *few* of the childish prejudices' about the revolution (*WMW*, 7: 322).

Wollstonecraft attempted in her own travel-writing to unite the seductive 'feminine' epistolary style with the traditional and more intel-lectually prestigious role of traveller-philosopher, whose observations added to the extension of knowledge in the Enlightenment ideal. She wasn't content with the lesser novelty of merely *being* a woman travel writer like Piozzi: Williams had shown her one could write as a woman too. Yet Wollstonecraft was unwilling to create in her authorial persona a sentimental stereotype of femininity like the gushing Williams, who asked Stone and Christie to contribute chapters when she needed to include commentary on the 'masculine' subjects of military campaigns and constitutional politics. Wollstonecraft solved the problem innova-tively by creating a new feminist quest narrative, which is still the prototype of plots in twentieth-century fiction by Margaret Atwood,

Paule Marshall and other women writers. The narrative opens with the speaker in a 'normal' feminine role as lover and mother, but she leaves her baby and servant behind in her intrepid journey into a wild landscape and at the same time into her own psyche. Mother nature [16] helps her peel away the carapace of gendered socialization and regenerate her spiritual sense of self, preparatory to returning to face society again. Wollstonecraft's persona is a heroic voyager who reverses the usual gender roles: she is a female Hamlet sick of life; a tragic Dido who leaves her Aeneas at home while making a business trip.

It was a bold move, too, for the epistolary quasi-novelistic frame gradually to reveal the woman writer to be a mother in the process of being abandoned by the child's father. The precedent for this was Charlotte Smith, whose *Elegiac Sonnets* hinted at the speaker's marital unhappiness, and who advertised in her novels' prefaces the fact that she was a deserted wife bringing up her children on the proceeds of her writing, in order to attract sympathy and minimize the stigma of writing for money. But Wollstonecraft's revelation was much more shocking, coming from Europe's most famous vindicator of the rights of woman. Her tacit admission in this book of her betrayal by an unworthy lover, and the failure of their revolutionary sexual partnership constitutes a modern form of tragedy, in its 'endeavour to render moral failure into art by public avowal'.[17] It was an early example of Romantic art's preoccupation with the tragedy of revolutionary ideals betrayed.

The epistolary form

The letters which she actually wrote to Imlay and the fictionalised letters of the travel book are quite distinct. The latter were based on a journal written for publication, as the author herself stated. She declared that reading, writing and travelling must always be guided by a specific aim:

> As in travelling, the keeping of a journal excites to many useful enquiries that would not have been thought of, had the traveller only determined to see all he could see, without ever asking himself for what purpose.
>
> (*Letters from Norway*, p. 256)

Wollstonecraft transformed her journal into an epistolary form when she returned to London. Having requested the return of her letters from Imlay, she incorporated a few passages from the actual letters. However she quite deliberately retained the impressionistic style of the on-the-spot journal: 'I have been writing these last sheets at an inn in Elsineur, where I am waiting for horses' (*Letters from Norway*, p. 318). She did not bother to check quotations or bolster her assertions by research: for example, 'A sensible writer has lately observed, (I have not his words by me, therefore cannot quote his exact words)'; or 'It would be easy to search for the particulars of this engagement in the publications of the day; but... this manner of filling my pages does not come within my plan...' (*Letters from Norway*, pp. 255, 262). The published account deliberately combined such present-tense impressions of spontaneity with past-tense retrospective narrative to reflect the way the mind of a writer moves between experiential sense impressions and the rationalizing consciousness of second thoughts.

Where the travelogue had been carefully crafted was, in the words of Mary A. Favret: 'to deliberately rewrite and replace the original love letters, transforming Wollstonecraft's emotional dependence and personal grief into a public confrontation with social corruption'.[18] Wollstonecraft made her personal betrayal symptomatic of the degeneration of the Girondin high ideals into *laissez-faire* capitalism. Indeed, one could go further. Wollstonecraft could be said to be wreaking her revenge on her ex-lover by publicizing not only his caddish desertion of her and his daughter, but the near-fraudulent nature of his conman commerce: strongly hinting he deliberately tricked the British into reimbursing him for confiscated but unsaleable cargo (*Letters from Norway*, p. 304).

Wollstonecraft plays on the ambiguous status of the letter as supposedly private communication, yet open to publication in the form of epistolary novel, travels, or political polemic. She skilfully evokes sympathy by beginning and returning to the sentimental role of deserted lover/ mother while concomitantly sketching a self-portrait of the heroic independent woman, travelling alone, conducting business and 'asking men's questions' (p. 248), and questing in a manner one can only describe as Byronic: 'Wrapping my great coat around me, I lay down on some sails at the bottom of the boat, its motion rocking me to rest...' (p. 268).

The reversal of gender roles she had utilized in her Juvenalian onslaught on Burke's masculinity in *Rights of Men*, is more subtly implied in *Letters from Norway*. Nevertheless it is still central to her own stance as a 'masculine' active searcher for truth, writing back to a static male correspondent 'feminised' and immured by dependence on sensual and material gratification. Wollstonecraft made much more sophisticated use of the technique of buttonholing the reader alongside the male addressee than she had in castigating Burke. She could seduce, inform, and praise an ex-lover as well as reproach or harangue him according to her changing mood. The effect is that an individual Eloïse's or Dido's complaint to her absent lover (*pace* Ovid, Pope, Rousseau) can meta-morphose into a general indictment of the widespread betrayal of the revolutionary ideal of fraternity, which invokes and involves the reader. For example, on missing her baby left behind in Gothenburg, ('my little cherub', 'my Fannikins', 'my babe, who may never experience a father's care or tenderness'), she addresses Imlay directly using the second person: '*You* know that as a female I am particularly attached to her – I feel more than a mother's fondness and anxiety, when I reflect on the dependent and oppressed state of her sex' (*Letters from Norway*, p. 269; my italics). Mother love (itself a reproach to the absent father) is here exceeded by the protective zeal of the feminist, and the politicised appeal on behalf of all women extended to the reading public at large.

On the other hand, the general political enquiry underlying the *Letters* – whether the modern age of commerce and industrial revolution will help or hinder progress towards social equality – can just as frequently narrow down to a personal barb at the narratee – the epitome of a former idealist who has sold his soul by profiteering. Supposedly gen-eralised comments on speculators who 'term all virtue, of an heroic cast, romantic attempts at something above our nature' are interrupted by an aside:

> But you will say that I am growing bitter, perhaps personal. Ah! Shall I whisper to you – that you – yourself are strangely altered . . .
>
> (*Letters from Norway*, p. 340).

It is left for the maternal female philosopher to keep the flame of idealism burning: but also to qualify her heady account of mystic communion with nature with an earthy materialism: mentioning the smell of rotten herrings manuring the fields, and the ironworks powered by the sublime cascades she contemplates. As Mitzi Myers comments, the personal and social themes flow one into another, joined by a supposedly artless yet actually sophisticated use of associationism, in conveying the thought processes of the speaker.[19]

Portrait of the author contemplating a landscape

As a writer famous throughout Europe, Wollstonecraft was in a position to foster interest in her personality. Her name was a selling point, a literary commodity. Not only did she hint at biographical revelations, but in confessional passages she analysed her own character. She used the second person ambiguously, so the reader takes the role of an intimate companion: 'You have sometimes wondered, my dear friend, at the extreme affection of my nature – But such is the temperature of my soul.... For years have I endeavoured to calm an impetuous tide – labouring to make my feelings take an orderly course. – It was striving against the stream' (*Letters from Norway*, p. 280). Accepting for the first time in print, just how passionate was her nature, Wollstonecraft even compared herself to Maria of Sterne's *Sentimental Journey Through France and Italy* (1769) whose extreme sensibility turned her mind. She also alluded quite openly to her pleasure in her awakened sexuality. This willingness to acknowledge aspects of her character which would be harshly judged by conventional mores followed in the path of Rousseau's *Confessions*, but was extraordinarily brave – and unrivalled among women writers of her time.

Her analysis of her own responses to the sublime scenery showed a self-reflexive interest in the creative mind which would make this travel book into a seminal Romantic text, inspiring two generations of British poets. 'Nature is the nurse of sentiment... yet what misery, as well as rapture, is produced by a quick perception of the beautiful and sublime... when every beauteous feeling and emotion excites responsive sympathy, and the harmonized soul sinks into melancholy, or rises to extasy, just as the chords are touched, like the aeolian harp agitated by the changing wind' (*Letters from Norway*, p. 271). Feeling she was 'destined to wander alone', she cried: 'Why has nature so many charms for me – calling forth and cherishing refined sentiments, only to wound the breast that fosters them? How illusive... are the plans of happiness founded on virtue and principle; what inlets of misery do they not open in a half-civilized society?' (*Letters from Norway*, p. 298).

The obvious prototype for such a frankly autobiographical account of the author's turn to nature was again Rousseau – in *The Reveries of the Solitary Walker* (1782–89). That had opened with a dramatic declaration of the author's complete alienation from his fellow *philosophes*: 'I am now alone on earth, no longer having any brother, neighbour, friend, or society other than myself.' Wollstonecraft elevates the breach between herself and Imlay into a kind of philosophical crisis, too.[20] The bonds of friendship, of fraternity, have been broken in their relationship by him as by the leaders who betrayed the revolution. Nevertheless, while Wollstonecraft's deliberate allusions to Rousseau's misanthropic botanist invoke a comparison, at the same time they underline her difference from him. He was dismissive of book education, and latterly wrote only for his own eyes, for Rousseau would have us believe the *Reveries* were not intended for publication. For Wollstonecraft, though, writing has a social utility particularly vital for a rural or primitive culture: 'The reflection necessary to produce even a certain number even of tolerable productions, augments ... the mass of knowledge in the community' (*Letters from Norway*, p. 256).

Like Rousseau she paints herself as the melancholy genius whose extreme sensibility is too overwrought for repose: 'What is this active principle which keeps me still awake?' (*Letters from Norway*, p. 248). Like him, she 'then considered myself as a particle broken off from the grand mass of mankind; – I was alone'. But in an immediate correction (and critique) of this solipsistic excess, she continues: 'till some involuntary sympathetic emotion, like the attraction of adhesion, made me feel that I was still part of a mighty whole, from which I could not sever myself...' (*Letters from Norway*, p. 249). Unlike Jean-Jacques, Wollstonecraft uses nature as a retreat in the religious sense – she will and continually does return to society, her spiritual roots refreshed and her desire for reform unquenched.

The creative imagination

There are 28 references to the imagination in this text. Wollstonecraft defined imagination in a letter to Imlay of 22 September 1794 as:

> the mother of sentiment, the great distinction of our nature, the only purifier of the passions – animals have a portion of reason, and equal, if not more exquisite, senses; but no trace of imagination, or her offspring taste, appears in any of their actions. The impulse of the senses, passions, if you will, and the conclusions of reason, draw men together; but the imagination is the true fire, stolen from heaven, to animate this cold creature of clay, producing all those fine sympathies that leads to rapture, rendering men social by expanding their hearts, instead of leaving them leisure to calculate how many comforts society affords.
>
> (*CLMW*, p. 263)

This passage shows that Wollstonecraft did not envisage the creative imagination and society as a binary opposition. Imagination was the Promethean spark which rendered men *social* – bringing them together (as a community of readers for example) in a shared sympathy which promotes collective endeavour. She saw imagination and society developing each other dialectically: 'the world requires...the hand of man to perfect it; and as this task naturally unfolds the faculties he exercises, it is physically impossible that he should have remained in Rousseau's golden age of stupidity' (*Letters from Norway*, p. 288). So in no way was she a Rousseauistic romantic primitivist. The sluggish peasants of Sweden have 'little or no imagination...or curiosity' (*Letters from Norway*, p. 245), for advancement of the arts and sciences is needed to develop the faculty through education (*Letters from Norway*, p. 251). She is shocked that the Norway has no university, and there is no curiosity after scientific knowledge which would bring much-needed industrial improvement (*Letters from Norway*, p. 276).

Imagination partakes both of reason and feeling: '...my very reason obliges me to permit my feelings to be my criterion...the cultivation of the mind, by warming, nay almost creating the imagination, produces taste...' (*Letters from Norway*, p. 289). The author does not write for his/her own satisfaction or for posterity. S/he must share the fruits of her/his imagination, for it is 'intercourse with men of science and artists, which not only diffuses taste, but gives that freedom to the understanding without which I have seldom met with much benevolence of character on a large scale' (*Letters from Norway*, p. 302). So there is cause for hope of progress in Scandinavia for the press in Denmark and Norway is free and a public sphere established. The 'least oppressed people of Europe' are on the road to freethinking, and can discuss French publications without fearing to displease the government – unlike the British (*Letters from Norway*, p. 276).

Ideally, there should be a corresponding dialectic between the improvement of the material world and social reform, for 'Without the aid of the imagination all the pleasures of the senses must sink into grossness' (*Letters from Norway*, p. 250). Seaports devoted solely to commerce and good living produce 'an absence of public spirit' (*Letters from Norway*, p. 274). The ultimate horror is Risør. To live there is to be 'bastilled by nature', and while the author found her own solitude there desirable, as 'my mind was stored with ideas', she 'shuddered at the thought of receiving existence, and remaining here, in the solitude of ignorance' (*Letters from Norway*, p. 295).

The material world and the perceiving mind

In contemplating the earth, Wollstonecraft saw a sacred work of art, 'the huge dark rocks, that looked like the rude materials of creation forming the barrier of unwrought space' (*Letters from Norway*, p. 245).

The human creative imagination most aspires to the divine when the senses link the soul to a mystic apprehension of its material beauty:

> With what ineffable pleasure have I not gazed – and gazed again, losing my breath through my eyes – my very soul diffused itself into the scene – ... seeming to become all senses ...
>
> (*Letters from Norway*, p. 280)

Aesthetic pleasure is not confined to the cerebral here, it is eroticised, sensual. A few lines further on she situates herself bodily in the landscape, tasting the mountain spring, bathing, rowing, and scooping out a jellyfish from the water (*Letters from Norway*, p. 281). Elizabeth Bohls describes this as anti-aesthetics, for Wollstonecraft does not suppress her gender, sexuality and bodily presence as in conventional scholarly discourse of the picturesque. In other passages the observer treats her awe at the sublime chaos of the falls together with the references to the human industries centred on them (*Letters from Norway*, p. 316). As with Marx in the next century, Wollstonecraft's political agenda was driven by a Utopian desire to unite material needs of both the individual and the body politic with spiritual improvement.[21] And the sensual imagination was the key faculty synthesising reason with emotion in the act of creation – of authorship imaged as procreation:

> In solitude the imagination bodies forth its conceptions unrestrained, and stops enraptured to adore the beings of its own creation.
>
> (*Letters from Norway*, p. 286)

But even as the author mimics the divine creation, she questions whether her cherished autonomy, her individualism will survive the death of the body, asking herself: 'Life, what art thou? Where goes this breath, this *I*, so much alive?' (p. 279). Drifting along in her boat, she muses:

> I cannot bear to think of being no more – of losing myself – though existence is often but a painful consciousness of misery; nay, it appears to me impossible that I should cease to exist, or that this active restless spirit, equally alive to joy and sorrow, should only be organized dust ...
>
> (p. 281)

Yet when she contemplates the timeless forests, she perceives decay and annihilation as forces conditioning an amoral battle for survival: roots torn up by the storms become the shelter of the next generation; saplings struggling for existence, next to the fragile 'grey cobweb-like appear-ance of the aged pines'; in an endless cycle of creation and destruction (*Letters from Norway*, p. 310). Later, the sight of soldiers at Sleswick cas-tle – armies being the epitome of hierarchical society and this one 'in thrall to 'German despotism' – inspires a proto-Darwinian vision of nature in which the significance of the individual is swept away:

> It is the preservation of the species, not of individuals, which appears to be the design of the Deity throughout the whole of nature. Blossoms come forth only to be blighted; fish lay their spawn where it will be devoured: and what a large portion of the human race are born merely to be swept prematurely away. Does not this waste of budding life emphatically assert, that it is not men, but man, whose preservation is so necessary to the completion of the grand plan of the universe? Children peep into existence, suffer and die; men play like moths about a candle, and sink into the flame: war, and 'the thousand ills which flesh is heir to,' mow them down in shoals, whilst the more cruel prejudices of society palsies existence, introducing not less sure, though slower decay.
>
> (p. 336).

Though this bleak view does not predominate in *Letters from Norway*, the fact that Wollstonecraft can articulate it so feelingly, demonstrates that she has absorbed, perhaps from Forster, a newly pessimistic notion of progress as an impersonal and not necessarily benign force of nature, much less susceptible to change by the efforts of individuals.

Reception of *Letters from Norway*

Letters from Norway, reasonably priced at 4s, must have come out very early in 1796, for it was reviewed in the February issue of the *Analytical*. Wollstonecraft resumed her reviewing work in the same number, under the initials MI. The *Analytical* pointed out Wollstonecraft's extraordinary versatility:

> After the repeated proofs which the ingenious and justly admired writer of these letters has given the public, that her talents are far above the ordinary level, it will not be thought surprising that she should excel in different kinds of writing
>
> (*Analytical Review* 23, Feb. 1796: 229).

She had already published fiction, political polemic, conduct literature, educational works, philosophical history and now attempted the
genre of travel. It was as if her restless intellect could not pause to
complete projects or consolidate her expertise, but sought ever more
challenges.

The book was extremely controversial, for as the *English Review* put it,
'Wollstonecraft...appears to us in the light of a female Rousseau'
whose sensibility was 'tinctured with melancholy', and many reviewers
speculated on her uncertain marital status. The *English Review* warned
the unsuspecting reader of 'her democratic ferocity, even to something
like a defence of assassination'; and unfeminine frankness in discussing
Swedish permissiveness of young people's sexuality. The book was
perceived as more dangerous than *Rights of Woman* because it wasn't
a polemic. It was entertaining; the reviewers all agreed on its high literary
quality. Through subjective evocations of sublime scenery, it would
dazzle unsuspecting readers. Wollstonecraft's landscape painting wasn't
harmless: it undermined orthodox belief in revealed religion by implying
one could communicate with God through nature. The Anglican *British
Critic* conceded that not until now had Wollstonecraft demonstrated
she could join 'a *masculine* understanding [with] the finer sensibilities
of a female' evident in an improved though 'bombastic' prose style. But
the reviewer would not be doing his duty if he permitted her 'to pursue
triumphantly her Phaeton-like career' without castigating the Deism or
natural religion he detects underlying her book. 'Has she maturely
weighed the analogy which subsists between the book of nature and the
word of God?' If she acknowledged the authority of the latter, she would
find the 'refuge from sorrow' she craved.[22] Samuel Taylor Coleridge had
a similar reaction, for in his notebook for Autumn 1796 he planned an
'epistle to Mrs Wolstonecraft [sic] urging her to Religion'.[23]

Letters from Norway had been translated into German and published
in Hamburg and Altona as early as January 1797, according to the
Monthly Magazine. It was also translated into Swedish and Dutch, and in
1806 extracts were translated into Portugese (*MWRL*, p. 485). A second
edition would be called for in 1802. It was a great critical success and
Johnson brought out a new edition of the *Rights of Woman* on the
strength of it. It inspired other travels to Scandinavia. Jacques-Louis de
La Tocayne's *Ma Promenade en Suède et en Norvège* (Braunschweig, 1801)
and Edward Daniel Clarke's *Travels in Various Countries of Europe* (1819–23)
felt bound to refer to *Letters form Norway*. Thomas Brown, professor of
Moral Philosophy at the University of Edinburgh was even inspired to
write a poem, *The Wanderer in Norway* (1814).

Wollstonecraft's travel book was a seminal text for the development of British Romantic writing. It became the prototype for liberal writers in reflexively examining their own role as artists through meditative passages, in the course of traversing landscapes and cultural sites which allow them to reflect obliquely on the loss of their political hopes. Wordsworth adapted the British tour to a similar purpose, though permeating it with a Burkean evocation of English tradition and continuity.[24] But it was exiled or oppositional writers who were her true heirs. Madame de Staël in *Corinne, or Italy* (1807) and Byron in *Childe Harold's Pilgrimage* (1812–18) would follow Wollstonecraft in using a love-story framework upon which to hang a European travelogue, while developing the figure of the suffering artist/idealist into a full-blown symbol of the individual alienated from his/her own country.

'On poetry and our relish for the beauties of nature'

Wollstonecraft resumed her former London literary life by 1796. Perhaps partly because of her return, Johnson felt confident enough for a new venture. In March, together with Richard Phillips, he launched a lively new miscellany: the *Monthly Magazine*. This was edited by John Aikin, who had taken over much of the literary reviewing on the *Analytical* when Wollstonecraft departed. Less heavy than the *Analytical*, it aimed at a broader audience. It comprised many short sparky pieces, in the form of letters to the editor, generating debate and passing on information. Wollstonecraft may have helped with editorial work. She also contributed a piece on poetry, of which she was an enthusiastic reader, as her numerous *Analytical* reviews testify. The 'Hints' or maxims in the manner of Rochefoucauld, which Godwin transcribed in *Posthumous Works* from her manuscript notebooks, contain many reflections on the poetic imagination, the sublime and on originality or genius. No. 31 reads:

> It is the individual manner of seeing and feeling, pourtrayed by a strong imagination in bold images that have struck the senses, which creates all the charms of poetry. A great reader is always quoting the description of another's emotions; a strong imagination delights to paint its own. A writer of genius makes us feel; an inferior author reason.
>
> (*WMW*, 5: 276)

Wollstonecraft distilled her thinking on the creative imagination into her short excursion into literary theory: an essay which appeared under the initials WQ in the third volume of the *Monthly Magazine* (April 1797, 279–82).[25] A different version was reprinted in her *Posthumous Works*, probably revised and edited by Godwin, as she was unlikely to have prepared it for publication elsewhere.[26] I therefore quote from the original article, in Wollstonecraft's distinctively vigorous style.

Wollstonecraft begins with a paradox. In contemporary society it has become fashionable to praise country life and the beauties of nature, but this taste has been acquired from books, not actual experience, and the people who most articulate it live in 'crowded cities'. She goes on to consider what makes 'natural' poetry: deciding that the verse 'written in the infancy of society' is 'the transcript of immediate emotions'. Wollstonecraft prided herself on her own originality as a thinker and as a writer, and, for her, inspiration should come directly out of actual experience:

> At such moments, sensibility quickly furnishes similes, and the subli-mated spirits combine with happy facility – images, which spontan-eously bursting on him, it is not necessary coldly to rack the understanding or memory, till the laborious efforts of judgment exclude present sensations, and damp the fire of enthusiasm.

Wollstonecraft does not naively imagine the author produces his (sic) text in a textual vacuum, however, for he draws upon a well-cultivated mind. Sensibility must be combined with the understanding, but rational consciousness sublimated; so that under the influence of 'strong feelings', the poet's sorrow will be 'artlessly, yet poetically' reproduced in words.

Worrying away at the implications of this oxymoron, Wollstonecraft acknowledged that the quality of the verse thus produced is bound to be uneven. Revisions would be necessary 'during the cooler moments of reflection', even though 'at the expence of those involuntary sensations, which, like the beauteous tints of an evening sky, are so evanescent, that they melt into new forms before they can be analyzed'. The meta-phorical language of ancient cultures had been absorbed from a natural environment permeated with authentic spiritual significance. But modern (that is, Augustan) poets have been burdened by a dead weight of clichés from print culture; an education based on imitation of the classics according to stultifying rules; and the mythology of a dead culture. 'But, though it should be allowed that books conned at school may lead some youths to write poetry,' such verse 'will seldom have the energy to rouse the passions which amend the heart.'

Wollstonecraft then returns to consider why people need poetry at all. Why read about a scene from nature, rather than contemplate it for themselves? Such readers lack primary imagination. Applying the jargon of the picturesque, she describes how the poet functions to remind the flaccid mind how to look at nature and teach it what to feel:

The poet contrasts the prospect, and selecting the most picturesque parts in his camera, the judgement is directed, and the whole attention of the languid faculty turned towards the objects which excited the most forcible emotions in the poet's heart...

For Wollstonecraft, contemporary readers are passive. Their 'gross minds are only to be moved by forcible representations' and sensations. They are not themselves introspective, and are not interested in developing their own imaginative or philosophical faculties. The poet must rouse them, especially 'when civilisation and its canker-worm, luxury, have made considerable advances'. 'In the present state of society, the understanding must bring back the feelings to nature...'.

She concludes with a daring analogy which likens the merely sensual reader to a passive Imlay and the original author to an active Mary. The sensibility which 'makes a man relish the tranquil scenes of nature, when sensation rather than reason: imparts delight, frequently makes a libertine of him'. For he prefers 'the sensual tumult of love a little refined by sentiment' to 'the calm pleasures of affectionate friendship, in whose sober satisfactions, reason, mixing her tranquillizing convictions, whispers, that content, not happiness, is the reward of virtue in this world'. In other words, the author's role is not merely to seduce the reader's senses, but to be his intimate consolatory fraternal friend on the path to virtue. Wollstonecraft's short essay thus anticipated and surely influenced William Wordsworth's Romantic theory of poetry, expressed in the Preface to the 1800 edition of *Lyrical Ballads*; and perhaps another important Romantic manifesto: Joanna Baillie's 'Introductory Discourse' to the first volume of *Plays on the Passions* (1798).

Letters from Norway was the book that made Wollstonecraft a heroine for the coming generation: Coleridge and his friend Robert Southey sought her out. Coleridge's *Kubla Khan* would echo her imagery of the sublime chaos of creation, while Southey was inspired by her political heroism to write *Joan of Arc*. Sixteen years later, Percy Shelley and Wollstonecraft's daughter Mary would put Wollstonecraft in their Pantheon of Promethean intellectual rebels. The young writer Amelia

Alderson (later Opie) summed up the magnetism of Wollstonecraft's authorial persona in a letter to her, written on 28 August, 1796:

> Will you help me to account for the strong desire I always feel when with you, to say affectionate things to you? Perhaps it is because, you, like *Julie*, appear so capable of feeling affection that you cannot fail to excite it. I remember the time when my desire of seeing you was repres'd by fear – but as soon as I read your Letters from Norway, the cold awe which the philosopher had excited, was lost in the tender sympathy call'd forth by the *woman* – I saw nothing but the interesting creature of feeling & imagination, & resolved if possible, to become acquainted with one who had alternately awakened my sensibility & gratified my judgement – I *saw* you, & you are one of the few objects of my curiosity who in gratifying it have not disappointed it also. You and the *lakes of Cumberland* have exceeded my expectations...[27]

7

'We did not marry': the Comedy and Tragedy of Marriage in Life and Fiction

> Some said she was proud, some call'd her a whore,
> And some, when she passed by, shut the door;
> A damp cold came o'er her, her blushes all fled;
> Her lilies & roses are blighted & shed.
>
> "O, why was I born with a different Face?
> "Why was I not born like this Envious Race?
> "Why did Heaven adorn me with bountiful hand,
> "And then set me down in an envious Land?
>
> (From Williams Blake's 'Mary', Pickering MS)

> Then I saw mounted on a braying ass,
> William and Mary, sooth a couple jolly
> Who married, note ye how it came to pass,
> Although each held that marriage was but folly.
>
> (*The Anti-Jacobin; or Weekly Examiner*)

When she returned to London, Wollstonecraft found herself the figure-head of a circle of liberal women writers, all of whom were inspired to some degree by her revolutionary ideas and by her attempts to act on them in life. Two former actresses and established professional writers, the poet and novelist Mary Robinson and playwright and novelist Elizabeth Inchbald specialized in staging gender. The scandalous Robinson teased the public's fascination with her identity as the Prince Regent's ex-mistress by using various pseudonymous personae to corre-spond in verse with readers of the periodicals. The resolutely respectable Inchbald, author of *A Simple Story* (1791), was a pioneer in converting elements of stage melodrama into the 'Jacobin' novel of social protest. Inchbald socialized with the Siddons/Kemble theatrical circle, and the radical playwright Thomas Holcroft and his friend the anarchist philosopher William Godwin. The latter had become the chief spokesman for political radicalism in literary London after the publication firstly of his *Enquiry Concerning Political Justice* (1793) which demolished the moral basis of all governmental institutions, and secondly of his exciting novel of pursuit, *Caleb Williams* (1794), which targeted the justice system. The group read and commented on each other's work in progress with conscientious candour.

In letters, conversation and publications alike, this literary coterie posed philosophical questions about their life experiences while they also tested fictional situations by reference to real events. The disintegration of Mary Wollstonecraft and Gilbert Imlay's attempt to enact an egalitarian sexual partnership was eagerly discussed, and Wollstonecraft would be fictionalized and sometimes satirized in novels such as her erstwhile friend Amelia Opie's *Adelina Mowbray* (1804) as well as Anti-Jacobin fiction such as Elizabeth Hamilton's *Memoirs of Modern Philosophers* (1800).

When she had arrived back in London at the beginning of October 1795, Wollstonecraft was reduced to cross-questioning the cook at the lodgings her ex-lover had procured for her, to find where Imlay had installed his new mistress. She went to confront her and at long last became convinced there was no hope of continuing the relationship. On 10 October, she took a boat and rowed to Putney where it would be quiet enough to throw herself off the bridge unobtrusively. She walked up and down in the rain to make her clothes heavy, then jumped into the water, pressing her clothes around her to help her sink. She lost consciousness but was rescued and revived by onlookers. The event was reported in the *Times*, though the 'elegantly dressed' woman was not named. In a subsequent letter to Imlay Wollstonecraft asserted the attempt was not hysterical, but 'one of the calmest acts of reason' (*CLMW*, p. 317). She saw it as a revolutionary and heroic act of will. Godwin too would stress her 'cool and deliberate firmness' in *Memoirs*. He would, however, in the same work state that her 'exquisite and delicious sensibility' made her 'a female Werther' – alluding to Goethe's fictional suicidal lover (*MAVRW*, 88). As Todd comments, 'Both Wollstonecraft and her act were pushed back into a romantic or sentimental frame'.[1]

Mary Wollstonecraft's suicide attempts inspired not merely gossip but philosophical discussion amongst London literary circles, and a wider debate when Godwin's *Memoirs* came out after her death on whether suicide was justifiable; whether it could be seen as rational and heroic;

or was evidence of a tortured sensibility. In her own attempted fiction-alizations of the affair with Imlay and her failed suicide she was bedevilled by the question of genre. Unlikely as it may seem, in January 1796 she first wrote a dramatic comedy on the subject and unsuccessfully offered it to Covent Garden and Drury Lane (*MAVRW*, p. 101). Godwin records reading it on 2 June 1796.[2] Her aim was presumably to bring her philo-sophical insights about sexual politics to a wider audience by attempting a sentimental drama which aired moral issues, in the style of Holcroft or Inchbald. Wollstonecraft then decided on another populist genre: the 'Jacobin' novel. As will be seen, she was again confronted by formal problems in bending the genre to her crusading purposes.

Mary Hays and the Godwin coterie

It was the resumption of her friendship with Mary Hays which triggered Wollstonecraft's entry into the coterie centred on Godwin. Both were using fiction to explore the problem of determinism versus free will from a woman's point of view. But while Wollstonecraft was now moving towards an analysis of the social determinism of woman's role across classes, Hays focused on the psychological and the erotic formation of an individual protagonist. Hays was another female autodidact from Unitarian circles, whose religious beliefs had spurred her first excursion into print with a well-received theological pamphlet in 1791. Reading *Rights of Woman* had a profound affect on her and she not only wrote in 1792 to make contact with the author, but submitted her *Letters and Essays, Moral and Miscellaneous* for Wollstonecraft's scrutiny, when the latter was acting as Johnson's reader. Wollstonecraft's acerbic remarks on Hays's obsequiousness to male critics on 12 November 1792 had persuaded her new disciple to amend her preface – though the latter only substituted 'the sensible vindicator of female rights' as her authority for similar apologies for her inadequacies as an author. Wollstonecraft noted sternly that, despite these protestations, not only the preface but the pamphlet were 'too full of yourself', for 'till a work strongly interests the public true modesty should keep the author in the back ground – for it is only about the character and life of a *good* author that anxiety is active' (*CLMW*, p. 220).

But Hays had philosophical reasons for refusing to separate head and heart in her writing. Following Priestly, she rejected Cartesian duality, and became influenced by Claud Adrien Helvétius's view that material determinism or 'necessity' formed human character, asserting 'corporal sensibility to be sole cause of our actions, our thoughts, our passions'.[3]

On 14 October 1793 Hays wrote to William Godwin, asking to borrow a copy of his celebrated *Political Justice* whose price of three guineas she could not afford. This instigated a long, close friendship. Their epistolary discussions were particularly driven by what we would now call her 'feminist critique' of his extreme rationalism. For example, on 7 December, 1794 she protested at his cool recommendation of the 'annihilation' of the 'private affections' in favour of a less selfish philosophical love of mankind in general. A male scholar might hold such an ideal but the superficial education a woman receives 'renders a habit of severe investigation and abstract attention difficult to be attain'd'.[4] On 28 July 1795 she explained that in fact the more she improved her own intellectual education, the more frustrated she became with the restrictions society placed on women's ability to express 'the active, aspiring mind'.

> The strong feelings and strong energies which properly directed in a field sufficiently wide might – ah. What might they not have aided? – forced back, & pent up, ravage & destroy the mind that generated them!... Philosophy, it is said, should regulate the feelings, but it has added fervour to mine – What are passions, but another name for powers?

Hays was at this time suffering from unreciprocated love for another mentor, the leading radical Unitarian, William Frend, and explained to Godwin the sexual double standard which prevented women expressing their sexual desires naturally. On 1 October 1795 she argued that while 'the generality of men [were] dissolute', women were either prostituted 'to exchange their persons for a subsistence' in or out of marriage, or faced with the choice of 'stifling every natural affection' or 'exposing themselves to insult' for unconventional behaviour. On 20 November she made an exemplum of the case of Mary Wollstonecraft. Because it was suspected that the latter was an unmarried mother, some 'amiable' and 'worthy women' 'lamented that it would be no longer proper for them to visit Mrs.W.' Hays had stood up for her friend, remarking that 'Mrs. W-'s conduct [was only] a breach of *civil* institution which, no doubt, would bring with it, notwithstanding her superior fortitude and resources, civil inconveniences'. There was no need for further punishment. Hays's friends told her she was being naïve, but she still condemned 'the miserable substitute for virtue, called punctillio'.

Not long afterwards, Hays invited Godwin and his friend Thomas Holcroft to tea with Wollstonecraft. Doubtless she hoped a joint female assault on the current literary lion of radical circles would further the cause of women's rights. In a memo of the essential dates of his relationship with Wollstonecraft, amongst Godwin's papers, he records their 'rencontre' on January 8 1796, when Mary Hays effected their reconciliation despite his lingering resentment of Wollstonecraft's jibes at his expense five years previously.[5] On 11 January, Hays encouraged Godwin's chivalrous interest by commenting: 'I was glad to see her so lively tho' I knew her gaiety to be very superficial. She has been a great sufferer – with all her strength of mind, her sufferings have well nigh proved fatal – happy for her and happy for me she is yet preserved! I shall ever love her, for her affectionate sympathies, she has a warm and generous heart!' Three days later, Godwin's journal records he was dining in Mary's company, and on 26 January he was sufficiently intrigued to be '*reading* Wolstonecraft [sic]', presumably *Letters from Norway*. Reading was the way to his heart as he himself later admitted:

> If ever there was a book calculated to make a man in love with its author, this appears to me to be the book. She speaks of her sorrows in a way that fills us with melancholy, and dissolves us in tenderness, at the same time that she displays a genius which commands all our admiration.
>
> (*MAVRW*, p. 95)

Hays recognized that 'a strong sympathy of feeling & similarity in some respects of situation' existed between herself and Wollstonecraft, and she told Godwin on 6 February 1796 that the two women had confided in each other respecting their experiences of disappointed love. Godwin must have replied coldly, counselling stoic resignation, for Hays complained on 9 February that he didn't take either woman's emotions seriously enough. It may well have been Godwin himself who then suggested to Hays that she exorcise her demons through fictionalising her experience in a novel.

Letters from Norway was also an inspiration. Because the barriers between life and text, between public and personal writing were particularly permeable for women writers, it was they who became the vanguard for new writing which foregrounded its own textuality. But Hays went so much further than Wollstonecraft in incorporating the actual letters she had written to Godwin and to Frend into her narrative that Tilottama Rajan has coined the term 'autonarration' to describe the self-conscious juxtaposition of confessional material with fiction.[6]

Indeed, in the first half of 1796, Hays was not only writing private letters to her mentors, but also a series of polemical epistles for the *Monthly*

Magazine whose readers were engaged in a lively debate with her on the rights of woman and the philosophy of Helvétius: the effect of environment in shaping woman's intellectual character. Her epistolary novel drew on both these private and public letters, and attempted to give a social critique the emotional intensity of sentimental fiction, while its gesturing outside the text to the personal experience of the author signalled its authenticity. Rajan astutely points out that Hays overdetermines sexual love in *Memoirs of Emma Courtney* (1796): projecting onto it the 'desire for everything that is effaced from her own upbringing in a patriarchal society'.[7] Indeed the love object embodies all the privileges attached to masculinity the heroine wants for herself.

The comedy of courtship

Wollstonecraft's entry into Godwin's coterie, particularly after her final meeting with Imlay in April, turned the tragedy of her failed relationship into the curtain-raiser to a new comedy of courtship among the North London avant-garde. Firstly she received a proposal in an unsigned letter – apparently from the thrice-widowed Holcroft, who though 'chilled' sometimes by her manner was chivalrously touched by her situation and evidently inflamed by her open sexuality:

> In you I think I discover the very being for whom my soul has for years been languishing: one whom, the woman of reason all day, the philosopher that traces compares and combines facts for the benefit of present and future times, in the evening becomes the playful and passionate child of love.[8]

Mary presumably replied wittily enough to keep him at sufficient distance while retaining him as a close friend. Godwin himself was professing keen interest meanwhile, and he was a more stimulating sparring partner. They struck sparks from each other. Both were bold thinkers and oversensitive opinionated egoists. There was also the thrill of the chase. A middle-aged bachelor who looked every inch the pedantic philosopher, Godwin was sexually inexperienced, perhaps a virgin; yet somehow he managed to keep a circle of stellar female intellectuals competing for his attentions. The witty Elizabeth Inchbald was Wollstonecraft's most formidable rival, though Amelia Alderson was the youngest of the harem and very pretty, while Mary Robinson was one of the most celebrated beauties of the age. All these women as well as Hays and Wollstonecraft and the unhappily married Eliza Fenwick were established or would-be novelists discussing their work-in-progress with Godwin, and often engaging in a game of cerebral flirtation.

By 13 February Godwin had paid a visit to Wollstonecraft. On 14 April she took the unconventional step of calling on him alone. This was a significant upping of the ante. They began to see each other constantly, both alone and in company. In July, Godwin set off for a family visit to Norfolk, and when Mary twitted his epistolary flirtatiousness ('Do not make me a desk "to write upon" ' *CLMW*, p. 331) he was prompted to disobey, declaring daringly: '...that your company infinitely delights me, that I love your imagination, your delicate epicurism, the malicious leer of your eye, in short everything that constitutes the bewitching *tout ensemble* of the celebrated Mary'.[9] When he returned, both acknowledged 'a more decisive preference for each other.... It was friendship melting into love' (*MAVRW*, p. 104). But it was not until 13 August, according to Godwin's private memorandum, that there was an 'explication': presumably a mutual declaration of love. 'I had never loved till now' he wrote later (*MAVRW*, p. 105).

Even then there were sulks and stand-offs. Mary became passionate and may have frightened off the rationalist philosopher by taking the amatory initiative, for he withdrew from their new intimacy, coldly complaining on the 16 August that she had 'impressed upon me a mortifying sensation', perhaps of his sexual inadequacy, and she would have to accept him as only a 'puny valetudinarian'.[10] The next day it was her turn to admit herself 'mortified and humbled', wondering whether 'despising false delicacy... [she had] lost sight of the true' (*CLMW*, p. 337). She offered to resume the status of 'solitary walker'. Godwin admitted he was so ashamed of his behaviour that he would rather 'talk to you on paper than in any other mode'. He reassured Mary that 'I see nothing in you but what I respect & adore', and, on the prospect of losing her, became uncharacteristically overcome by emotion, confessing abjectly: 'For six to thirty hours I could think of nothing else. I longed inexpressibly to have you in my arms. Why did not I come to you? I am a fool.'[11] Relieved, Mary brought the temperature down, teasing him with an allusion to his ethos that universal benevolence was morally superior to personal ties: '...I cannot withhold my friendship from you, and will try to merit yours, that *necessity* may bind you to me' (*CLMW*, p. 338).

'We did not marry'

Godwin's journal entry 'toute' suggests that by 21 August they had consummated their love, and thereafter the methodical Godwin adopted a code of dashes and dots to record their lovemaking in his journal. But both continued to live, work and socialize separately, for both rejected conventional gender roles and Godwin believed that cohabitation and familial bonds compromised moral individuality and responsibility for one's actions. He commented later: 'We did not marry.... Certainly nothing can be so ridiculous... as to require the overflowing soul to wait upon a ceremony... to blow a trumpet before it, and to record the moment when it has arrived at its climax.... There were... other reasons why we did not immediately marry. Mary felt an entire conviction of the propriety of her conduct.... But [she] had an extreme aversion to be made the topic of vulgar discussion' (*MAVRW*, p. 105). Marrying her new lover would publicly acknowledge what was only strongly suspected – the fact that she had never married Imlay. She would be ostracized.

Marriage

But that was exactly what happened eventually. For in spite of or because of their adoption of some form of the rhythm method of contraception, by Christmas Wollstonecraft had fallen pregnant. Despite both their reservations about marriage the dirty deed was finally done on 29 March 1797, Godwin's journal laconically noting only 'Pancras'. This was the local church, and on 6 April they took a newly-built house together, no. 29 Polygon Buildings, though Godwin rented rooms nearby for his writing and stayed there every day until dinner time. He wanted to combine 'the novelty and lively sensation of a visit, with the more delicious and heart-felt pleasures of domestic life'; and pointed to the advantage of an arrangement ensuring 'the constancy and uninterruptedness of our literary pursuits' (*MAVRW*, p. 110). Mary was equally prosaic about their union, explaining baldly to Amelia Alderson on 11 April: 'I found my evenings solitary; and I wished, while fulfilling the duty of a mother, to have some person with similar pursuits, bound to me by affection.... Condemned then to toil my hour out, I wish to live as rationally as I can' (*CLMW*, pp. 389–90). To Godwin she admitted dryly: 'A husband is a convenient part of the furniture of a house... I wish you, from my soul, to be riveted in my heart; but I do not desire to have you always at my elbow' (*CLMW*, p. 396).

When the news of the wedding leaked out there was much mirth in artistic circles because Godwin had written so extensively against marriage in *Political Justice*, while Mary had argued so vehemently for woman's economic independence in *Rights of Woman*. Fuseli wrote sarcastically to William Roscoe on 25 May, 1797: 'You have not perhaps heard that the assertrix of female Rights has given her hand to the Balanciere of political Justice?'[12] Anna Barbauld noted 'numberless are the squibs that are thrown at Mr. Godwin . . . and he winces not a little on receiving the usual congratulations'.[13] Mrs Siddons and the jealous Elizabeth Inchbald, who was probably herself in love with Godwin, now publicly ostracized Wollstonecraft in a hurtful manner because it was now evident that hitherto she had been an unmarried mother. William Blake's poem 'Mary' may have been inspired by the obloquy she now experienced. But many of the Bohemian writers, artists and theatrical people in whose circle she and Godwin moved accepted Wollstonecraft as a moral idealist whose long period of grief for Imlay showed she had not lightly abandoned monogamy. Thomas Holcroft wrote: 'From my heart and soul I give you joy. I think you the most extraordinary married pair in existence'.[14]

The Wrongs of Woman, or, Maria; a Fragment

All the time this comedy of courtship and reluctant matrimony was going on, Wollstonecraft was at work on her novel of ideas which would constitute a critique on the institution of marriage! She and Godwin must have argued on the subject of marriage both theoretically (from their different philosophical points of view) and practically, with a view to resolving their secret affair. In his *Political Justice*, Godwin had secularized the uncompromising view of New England Calvinist theologian Jonathan Edwards that universal benevolence was morally superior to domestic affection, because impartial and not rooted in egoism and possessiveness. He stressed instead the utilitarian principle of the greatest good of society being paramount. This devalued the personal, familial ties Burke had declared to be the true root of patriotism. Wollstonecraft had also invoked the overriding importance of universal benevolence in *Rights of Woman* when she argued that women's social and maternal role is to inculcate 'the love of mankind' in general (*WMW*, 5: 66).[15] She was not so extreme as Godwin (no one was). He was against cohabitation altogether. Wollstonecraft wanted personal love to coexist with and strengthen an ethos of universal benevolence within the family. However, she does elevate friendship over all other affections (*WMW*, 5: 142) and parental love over sexual love because more conducive to social duty (*WMW*, 5: 189). Wollstonecraft's new novel was designed to show the injustice and immorality built in to marriage as presently constituted. When accompanied by Godwin's account of her own brutal childhood experiences in *Memoirs*, the institution of the family was revealed to be less a haven than an instrument of social repression.

Genre

Wollstonecraft's big problem was to adapt the genre to a purpose the opposite of that for which it had been developed. The eighteenth-century female-authored novel was primarily comedic: the plot driven by obstacles to courtship, and the conclusion a celebration of marriage embodying social harmony. So Wollstonecraft's would be an anti-novel. She never finished it. However, the opponents of Godwin and Wollstonecraft, who interpreted their championship of universal benevolence as an attack on domestic ideology, found the novel form ideally suited for attacking them. Charles Lloyd's *Edmund Oliver* (1798) would especially target the couple.[16]

Wollstonecraft saw the feminist potential in Gothic and opened with a striking image of her heroine's confinement in a 'mansion of despair' (*WMW*, 1: 85). The ruinous building (echoing Burke's image of the British constitution) here represents the institution of marriage: an 'asylum' which is a prison not refuge, and which might indeed drive you mad. '[T]he most terrific of ruins – that of a human soul' is caged within (*WMW*, 1: 91). The prison which is also a madhouse also suggests the false consciousness which binds a woman by her internalization of feminine duty. This impression is reinforced when, after the protagonist Maria's mental horizons have expanded by sharing life experiences with others, the bars and locks seem to melt away as the master of the bedlam flees (*WMW*, 1: 174). From both external oppression and from her 'mind-forg'd manacles' the *bildungsroman* heroine escapes by learning from her suffering, 'a train of events and circumstances' as Wollstonecraft explained in the notes for her preface (*WMW*, 1: 83).

The potent Gothicized image of the asylum/prison of the domestic interior has been going strong in feminist fiction ever since, from Charlotte Brontë to Charlotte Perkins Gilman and now Sarah Waters. However, Wollstonecraft's most important innovation was too daring even for most Victorian feminists. She would 'show the wrongs of different classes of women' (*WMW*, 1: 85) and she would link their fates together as equals. The life of Maria illustrated how the institution of marriage took away from an heiress her property, her civil rights, her power over her own body and custody of her child. Wives had the legal status of minors and could only look to the law for protection in the case of extreme violence or sexual perversion. Maria's lover, Darnford, declares that until divorces could be more easily obtained a strong female individualist could not be expected to endure such 'insufferable bondage':

Ties of this nature could not bind minds governed by superior principles, and such beings were privileged to act above the dictates of laws
they had no voice in framing, if they had sufficient strength of mind
to endure the natural consequence.

(WMW, 1: 172)

But the story of Maria's wardress, Jemima, considered the other side of
the coin. It graphically illustrated the fate of the unprotected illegitimate
female offspring in an unenlightened society – the fate to which the
suicidal Wollstonecraft had risked abandoning Fanny, and had now
decided to remedy by marrying Godwin. With no mother to love and
protect her, no surname and stigmatised as a bastard, Jemima, 'an egg
dropped on the sand' *(WMW*, 1: 110), is considered barely human, at
the very bottom of the social pyramid. '[A] slave, a bastard, a common
property': Jemima passes her childhood as a physically and sexually
abused household drudge, her youth as a common prostitute, and then
works as a washerwoman until, her health ruined, she becomes an anti-
social thief and embittered gaoler:

Thinking of Jemima's peculiar fate and her own, [Maria] was led to
consider the oppressed state of woman and to lament that she had
given birth to a daughter.

(WMW, 1: 120)

For the stories of the two women, and those of numerous minor characters universalise the economic basis of the oppression of women. The
inculcation of female chastity and fidelity in the institution of
marriage is unmasked as merely facilitating the perpetuation of primogeniture and male property rights. The poorest of paupers are always
women.

Equally daring, was Wollstonecraft's inclusion of sexual fulfilment as
one of the natural rights of woman. She juxtaposed a graphic account
of sex as a repellent marital duty for the bourgeois wife *(WMW*, 1: 139)
with the prostitute's 'horror of men' *(WMW*, 1: 113). This emphasizes
that there is no moral difference between marriage and prostitution as
both trade sex for subsistence. That her husband George Venables tries
to prostitute Maria to one of his creditors underlines the parallel. To
facilitate their sexual slavery, women are culturally conditioned to
think they cannot experience autonomous sexual desire. However,
when she rids herself of the false ideology of wifely 'duty', Maria is
shown not losing control but rationally choosing to consummate her

romantic love for her fellow inmate without shame or scruples (*WMW*, 1: 173). Acknowledging and acting on her own sexual desire symbolizes liberty for Maria. That is why the possibility of escape from the asylum offers itself after she has received Darnford 'as a husband'. Her new relationship with Darnford as well as with Jemima has an aura of Utopian egalitarianism within the prison because – just for the time being – these bonds of friendship are uncontaminated by the economic power structures of society. The vision it communicates of how things might be revives Jemima's hardened sensibility by regenerating her ability to weep (*WMW*, 1: 106). However, when they leave the asylum, reality returns: Darnford reverts to his libertinism and Jemima insists on receiving wages for her role as Maria's housekeeper.

Campaigning for easier divorce

Until the mid-nineteenth century, full divorce could only be obtained in England by an Act of Parliament, when evidence (usually of the wife's adultery) had been proved through a prior ecclesiastical court separation together with a successful action brought by the husband for damages against her lover for 'criminal conversation'.[17] Divorce in England, but not Scotland, was virtually a male monopoly, with only one successful bill brought by a woman (for incestuous adultery) by 1830. Wollstonecraft may well have obtained information on the marriage laws from a publication of Joseph Johnson: *The Laws Respecting Women as They Regard Their Natural Rights or Their Connections and Conduct* (1777). The anonymous compiler argued that while the ancient Britons had 'advanced women to rank and eminence' it was the feudal chivalric code, imported by the Normans, which had been 'fatal to the rights of woman'. The 'men became domestic despots, and though the politeness of such times may restrain them from gross acts of violence, yet they indulge themselves in a species of cruelty not less oppressive and painful, if the torture of a susceptible mind is superior to any bodily suffering', by which the author means the double standard of sexual morality in which wives are expected to tolerate infidelity (vii).

Wollstonecraft's arresting opening in the madhouse might well have been inspired by the number of contemporary case details given in *Laws Respecting Women* of females being confined in private asylums; so many that 14 Geo.III.c49 (1774) enacted that annual licences be granted to houses admitting ten or fewer 'lunatics' in the London area, and commissioners be appointed to visit them to check for irregularities (pp. 73–7). Here she would also have found the information that 'a man may lawfully own and retake his wife or child wherever he finds them' (p. 54), a fact of which she was doubtless fully aware from having assisted Eliza's escape from Bishop so many years earlier. She also doubtless made use of William Godwin's copy of *Trials for Adultery, or, the History of Divorce* (London: S. Bladon, 1779), and newspapers which gave prurient and detailed accounts of such legal cases. A 'Jacobin' novel like *The Wrongs of Woman*, which unmasked the economic springs of power, relied on the legal niceties of inheritance to drive its plot. Wollstonecraft was inspired by Godwin's *Caleb Williams* in her use of the nightmarish pursuit of Maria by her husband for the sake of her uncle's legacy.

The theme of 'the great difficulty there is in England of obtaining a divorce' (p. ix) had also been central to Gilbert Imlay's *The Emigrants* (1793), which contained fictionalised accounts of two crim.com. cases and concluded with a call for the reform of the British marriage laws (III: 180).[18] The novel was perhaps influenced by conversation with Wollstonecraft, whose family bore some resemblance to that of the British merchant depicted emigrating to America. The characters take different points of view on female adultery, with chivalrous Mr Il-ray attacking the British courts' tyranny 'over those helpless beings who have a claim upon our gratitude for our very existence, and whose weakness demands our most liberal support' (I: 67). His friend Captain Arl-ton, despairs of change, concentrating his hopes for social reform on the American republic (I: 103). America is the Garden of Eden where woman will be able to return to the laws of nature. When her uncle justifies his affair with a married lady repelled by the grossness of her drunkard husband, the British Caroline argues: 'However repugnant the laws respecting matrimony may be to the codes of nature, is of no consequence, compared to the tranquillity, safety and happiness of society' (II: 33). Her uncle replies validating the individual's right to happiness, probably voicing the author's views :

What shall two beings who have justly inspired a confidence in each other, who feel an affinity of sentiment, and who perceive that their happiness or misery are materially connected, that to separate them would prove fatal to both, not consider themselves superior to prejudices which are founded in error, and which would lead them to ridiculously sacrifice a real and substantial for an imaginary good; and when no person can be injured by the unity?

(II: 49)

However, the partial reform of the divorce laws and inheritance laws in republican France in women's favour had frightened the British off from themselves making divorce easier and more equitable. The 1790s saw a sharp rise in the number of parliamentary divorce bills and the judiciary reacted by imposing punitive damages in crim. con. cases as a deterrent against adultery. The judge in *Wrongs of Woman* was realistically depicted blaming the pernicious example of the French revolution for what he perceives as the moral degeneration of the times (*WMW*, 1: 181).

The Laws Respecting Women had been unusually radical in showing the spuriousness of the supposedly moral grounds for the injustice 'that a woman cannot obtain the same redress from the legislature against her husband, if she prove him incontinent'. It baldly pointed out the economic basis of the double standard on adultery: '[O]nly woman's infidelity can bastardise the issue'. The author concluded that the legislature does not concern itself with 'relieving a particular individual' but on the general principle of the great consequence which it is of to the community, that all property should be transmitted to the heir lawfully begotten...' and not 'to a spurious race' (p. 94). Middle class 'public opinion' endorsed the Evangelicals' argument that granting women divorces in order to marry their lovers would sanction and encourage adultery, and thus endanger male primogeniture. From 1771 to 1809 four bills to forbid a divorced wife from marrying her seducer were unsuccessfully brought before parliament. Thereafter, the conservative majority in the Lords inserted such a clause in every divorce bill, which was routinely struck out by the Commons.

Maria and divorce

This is the background against which Maria argues for the right to obtain a divorce from the hated Venables. She has quoted the words of her uncle to give masculine authority to the view that:

> The marriage state is certainly that in which women, generally speaking, can be most useful; but I am far from thinking that a woman, once married, ought to consider the engagement as indissoluble.... The magnitude of a sacrifice ought always to bear some proportion to the utility in view; and for a woman to live with a man, for whom she can cherish neither affection nor esteem, or even be of any use to him, excepting in the light of a house-keeper, is an abjectness of

condition, the enduring of which no concurrence of circumstances can ever make a duty in the sight of God or just men.

(WMW, 1: 147)

On the other hand, Maria is shown wanting the divorce in order to marry again. Maria has reluctantly decided, again on utilitarian grounds, as did Wollstonecraft with Godwin, that marriage is the lesser of two evils:

> Marriage, as at presently constituted, she considered as leading to immorality – yet, as the odium of society impedes usefulness, she wished to avow her affection to Darnford by becoming his wife according to established rules.
>
> *(WMW*, 1: 177)

Maria wants to fight the case against Darnford herself in order to refute the sexist concept of seduction (*WMW*, 1: 178). As *The Laws Respecting Women* commented about female adultery, 'the law always supposes compulsion and force to have been used because the wife is not supposed to possess a power of consent' (p. 53). However, neither was a woman allowed to participate in the court case as her legal existence was suspended during marriage, so Wollstonecraft shows Maria's written testimony being read out in court. That this is represented as permitted, as Elaine Jordan points out, is the one outright fantasy in the novel.[19] Maria's statement repudiating the conflation of adultery with seduction resists the law's denial of the wife's sexual autonomy; its male-only arrangements for one man to sue another for sexual trespass on his property.

Work in progress

Wollstonecraft must have begun the novel early in the Summer of 1796 for on 21 July she was sending 'the altered M.S' to Godwin for comments (*CLMW*, p. 331). He was reading *Mary: A Fiction*, her first novel, in the first week of August, presumably for comparison. By the 26 July she complained 'I seem to want encouragement – I therefore send you my M.S. though not all I have written' (*CLMW*, p. 342). But Godwin didn't take the hint to mitigate his usual robust candour. The story was all 'a feeling about nothing, a building without foundation' as far as he was concerned. She concentrated on the emotions at the expense of good plotting:

> Each new state of [the heroine's] mind ought perhaps to be introduced by a new and memorable incident; & these incidents might be

made beautifully various, surprising & unexpected, though all tending to one point. I do not want a common-place story of a brutal, insensible husband. [20]

On 4 September she replied, devastated by his stating that her manner of writing had 'a radical defect in it – a worm in the bud – &c', and in a profound 'depression of spirits' (*CLMW*, p. 345). Her belief in her whole identity was vested in authorship and he had challenged its foundation:

> I must either disregard your opinion, think it unjust, or throw down my pen in despair; and that would be tantamount to resigning existence; for at fifteen I resolved never to marry for interested motives, or to endure a life of dependence. . . . In short, I must reckon on doing some good, and getting the money I want, by my writings, or go to sleep for ever. I shall not be content merely to keep body and soul together – By what I have already written Johnson, I am sure, has been a gainer. And, for I would wish you to see my mind and heart just as it appears to myself, without drawing any veil of affected humility over it, though this whole letter is a proof of painful diffidence, I am compelled to think that there is some thing in my writings more valuable, than in the productions of some people on whom you bestow warm eulogiums – I mean more mind – denominate it as you will – more of the observations of my own senses, more of the combining of my own imagination – the effusions of my own feelings and passions than the cold workings of the brain on the materials procured by the senses and imagination of other writers – I am more out of patience with myself than you can form any idea of, when I tell you that I have scarcely written a line to please myself (and very little with respect to quantity) since you saw my M.S.

Wollstonecraft was doubtless just as strident in her own remarks on Godwin's play and essays for the *Monthly Magazine*, later published as *The Enquirer*, which she was commenting on at this time. And she did accept the philosopher's offer of grammar lessons. '[N]ow you have led me to discover that I write worse, than I thought I did, there is no stopping short – I must improve, or be dissatisfied with myself,' she wrote on 15 September (*CLMW*, p. 351). Nevertheless, her usual confidence deserted her. Godwin recalled:

> All her other works were produced with a rapidity, that did not give her powers time fully to expand. But this was written slowly and

with mature consideration. She began it in several forms, which she successively rejected, after they were considerably advanced. She wrote many parts of the work again and again, and, when she had finished what she intended for the first part, she felt herself more urgently stimulated to revise and improve what she had written, than to proceed, with constancy of application, in the parts that were to follow.

(*MAVRW*, p. 111)

In May 1797 she showed her M.S. to Godwin's friend, the radical artist and translator George Dyson, but his remarks, too, were 'a little discouraging' (*CLMW*, p. 391). Like Godwin, Dyson thought there wasn't much for Maria to make such a fuss about – not being allowed to refuse sex with her husband, however drunken, promiscuous and just plain boorish he became. But by now Wollstonecraft realized this supposedly 'objective' literary criticism of insufficient plot interest masked a lack of empathy in the male critic. If Dyson did not think 'the situation of Maria sufficiently important' she could 'only account for this want of – shall I say it? Delicacy of feeling by recollecting that you are a man . . . I should despise, or rather call her an ordinary woman, who could endure such a husband as I have sketched – yet you do not seem to be disgusted with him!!!'. She also defended her attempt to mix 'refined and common language' in Jemima's speech against the charge of vulgarity, and asserted that the character's 'strong Indignation in youth at injustice &c' was positive energy: a sign of 'superiority of understanding'. It is obvious that both her male critics found the novel rather strong stuff. They were uncomfortable with graphic representations in direct common language of the minutiae of women's lives in their sordid physicality. She, on the other hand, disdained indirection and allusion: 'I do not like *stalking horse* sentences'. Her fiction was too close to the bone in its sexual explicitness in both the analysis of middle-class 'marriage à la mode' and subplot of working-class life, especially coming from a female writer. Godwin extracted her explanation in this letter to Dyson of her intention to strive for psychological and social realism in the novel rather than a conventionally entertaining story and included it in the preface to the novelistic fragment when he published it after her death.

From February 1796 until May 1797 Wollstonecraft was reviewing for the *Analytical*, and concentrated almost exclusively on fiction in order to investigate the possibilities of the genre. She was now more willing than ever to admit that 'the writing of a good book is no easy task'

(*WMW*, 7: 486). However, it was not merely lack of confidence which stopped her completing the novel, it was her unwillingness to conform to literary convention. Wollstonecraft wanted to dispense with the sentimental clichés novelists usually used to depict adulterous women and prostitutes as the dupes of seducers. For example, Elizabeth Inchbald's *Nature and Art* (1796) was a melodrama describing a judge condemning to death a woman thief and prostitute whom he had unthinkingly seduced and ruined when a student. This was stagy but effective feminist propaganda against the sexual double standard, and Wollstonecraft herself found 'the story of Hannah Primrose...particularly affecting' even though the incidents of the story lacked probability (*WMW*, 7: 462–4). However, though she shared Inchbald's humanitarian approach to adultery and prostitution, Wollstonecraft wanted to give a much more authentic account of sexual slavery and to make the radical point that it didn't just affect a few unfortunate outcasts but married women too.

Memoirs and criminal biography

Wollstonecraft adopted the autobiographical mode which signalled authenticity. However, rather than focusing on one individual, as had Hays in *Memoirs of Emma Courtney* (1796), she attempted to universalise by splicing together the personal testimonies of the main characters, in an innovative adaptation of the *bildungsroman*. This juxtaposed male with female, bourgeois with lower-class experience and its plurality of first-person narratives lessened the authority of the third-person authorial voice. It also self-consciously drew attention to the textualisation of experience, and the role purposive reading and writing can play in emancipating the individual in contrast to the merely passive consumption of print, which may be a dangerous substitute for fulfilment. Books provide necessary employment for the imprisoned wife (*WMW*, 1: 89). The lending of them and the perusal of marginal notes forms a way of communicating for individual prisoners in their cells (*WMW*, 1: 93), an image which points up the way print culture draws separate readers together into a society of like minds. Books had made Darnford a republican (*WMW*, 1: 101). Even the illiterate servant Jemima, had once contributed to the republic of letters, for her literary master 'would read to me his productions, previous to their publication, wishing to profit by the criticism of unsophisticated feeling' (*WMW*, 1: 114). Maria also functioned as a naïve sounding board for her uncle to test his cynicism against (*WMW*, 1: 126), her love for Rousseau exacerbating her dreamy idealism.

From reading it is a short step to wanting to write an account of one's own experiences for posterity, as Maria does for her absent daughter (*WMW*, 1: 90). Unlike Lady Pennington's *An Unfortunate Mother's Advice to Her Absent Daughters* (1761) this memoir is an anti-conduct book. Wollstonecraft defers our reading these memoirs until chapter seven so that Maria's escape and her husband's search for her will follow on naturally from the autobiography of her early life. First Darnford and then Jemima tell their stories, and their auditors' reactions may guide the reader's response or prompt discussion. For example, there is the potential for irony when the republican Darnford's casual admissions of his fondness for 'the women of the town' (*WMW*, 1: 101–2) in his account of his adventurous life appeared only 'to be the generous luxuriancy of a noble mind' (*WMW*, 1: 100) to the naïve Maria's 'infantine ingenuousness' (*WMW*, 1: 104). The harsh reality of the prostitute's story following straight on leads the reader to take a less indulgent view of his libertinism. It is likely it was the complicated intersection of these narratives that caused Wollstonecraft to rewrite the first volume so often. The presentation of Henry Darnford (a portrait of Imlay) is the site of particular revision. Many passages suggest Maria is repeating her earlier delusion that trapped her into marriage in the first place: the fantasy of a perfect romantic love:

> A magic lamp now seemed suspended in Maria's prison, and fairy landscapes flitted around the gloomy walls, late so blank.
>
> (*WMW*, 1: 105)

On the other hand, it was the couple's creation of a loving enclave which included the jailer which so softened her defensive misanthropy that she volunteered her story and effected their escape. Darnford's enlightened views 'on the enslaved state of the labouring majority' (*WMW*, 1: 93) and comments that poverty shuts up 'all the avenues to improvement' (*WMW*, 1: 116), give Maria and the reader the hope that such a being as a male liberal who is also a feminist does exist. But – at least in the first draft – Darnford proves as disappointing as Rousseau in this respect. Though Darnford, like Imlay, argued that divorces should be more easily obtained (*WMW*, 1: 172), this sort of liberalization would facilitate the life of 'gallantry' he had recounted. When they live together, Maria realized that such men 'seem to love others, when they are only pursuing their own gratification' (*WMW*, 1: 176).

It seems, according to Godwin's editorial notes, that Wollstonecraft had been recently revising the novel to incorporate an important plot change: that Maria had met Darnford before they were both incarcerated ('This is extraordinary to meet you, and in such circumstances!' *WMW*, 1: 100). Godwin's notes that the 'copy which had received the author's last corrections breaks off in this place' and the pages which follow to the end of Chap. IV are printed from a copy in a less finished state'. Because this plot change 'appears to have been an after-thought of the author' the narrative which follows does not allude to the characters knowing each other (*WMW*, 1: 103). Godwin notes the place in chapter 5 where the most recently revised manuscript breaks off (*WMW*, 1: 116) and the older version resumes. Godwin then speculates whether or not the chivalrous fellow-lodger who prevents Venables capturing Maria in chapter 8 had been intended to turn out to be Darnford (*WMW*, 1: 163). His asterisks suggest an imperfect draft broken off at this point. He comments that in chapter 17 Darnford was portrayed in court as having acted rather more decisively than this in taking Maria away, so leaves the question open. Nevertheless, Daniel O'Quinn has argued that Godwin's editorial interventions push the narrative towards tracing this new plotline. The effect of the latter is to weaken Wollstonecraft's earlier critique of Maria's sentimental fantasies of romantic love, which were encouraged by reading Rousseau and imagining a St Preux figure would appear even before she had met her fellow-prisoner.[21] Though this is a valid comment on our reaction to the half-finished draft, it should be stressed that Godwin's notes were not written to construct a smooth narrative of the sentimental sort Wollstonecraft was resisting, he was primarily merely putting into practice the conventional editorial practice of respecting the author's latest intentions. Of course, had she lived, Wollstonecraft may well have scrubbed out the afterthought of Darnford as a chivalric acquaintance already known to Maria. However, had she instead completed the novel along those lines, she might have delineated the adulterous relationship more positively, giving it the less romantic and more rational quality of her new liaison with Godwin.

Wollstonecraft researched her novel of protest. She and Godwin went to the Bethlehem hospital to see for themselves what a lunatic asylum was like for authenticity of setting. She utilized the real-life reminiscences of acquaintances, for the story of Maria married at fifteen to the libertine George Venables echoes the memoirs of Mary Robinson, written for her daughter, which were not commenced until January 1798, and only published posthumously in a bowdlerized form in 1801.[22] Maria's escape from her husband and fears for her baby doubtless drew on her sister Eliza's separation from Meredith Bishop which Wollstonecraft had engineered. She may well have talked to prostitutes to make Jemima's story authentic. In 1787 Wollstonecraft had given financial help to Fanny Blood's sister Caroline, who had turned to prostitution, and thus knew the way the Poor Laws and parish regulations operated. She worked hard to make Jemima's story an authentic and disturbing account of what it was really like to live in poverty in contemporary Britain.

Illegitimate children, prostitution, divorce and the poor laws

1795 was a year of famine, a notorious high point of hardship for the poor. The agrarian and industrial revolutions had brought about a collapse of the economic position of the labourer. Then the Spleenhamland system of outdoor poor relief was extended to most of England and further aggravated the problem of pauperism as landlords reduced wages further because of the parish handouts. In 1796 Pitt threw out Samuel Whitbread's bill to introduce a minimum wage. Fearing riots and revolution, Hannah More in her *Cheap Repository Tracts* (1795–96), and William Paley in *Reasons for Contentment Addressed to the Labouring Part of the British Public* (1793) reminded the poor of their Christian duty to endure and to be content. The Evangelicals, were also fond of sexualising poverty; poor children were a problem produced by lower-class lack of restraint. Malthus was soon to bring out his *Essay on Population* suggesting labourers should marry late and limit their families. Illegitimate children and unmarried mothers became the particular butt of complaints about the burden on parochial poor relief, often wrapped up as moral concern.

Prostitutes were also blamed for corrupting men away from their family responsibilities. Patrick Colquhoun's *A Treatise on the Police of the Metropolis* (1796) found that though it was 'impossible to avoid dropping a tear of pity' for them, 'they cannot be supposed to experience those poignant feelings of distress, which are peculiar to women who have moved in a higher sphere'. The respectable population needed to be protected by removing them from public places, and submitting the sex trade to control and regulation. This could only happen if prostitution was tolerated by the law, as happened in some countries, such as India.[23] The author of *The Evils of Adultery and Prostitution; with an Inquiry into the Causes of Their Present Alarming Increase, and Some Means Recommended for Checking Their Progress*, which Wollstonecraft reviewed in 1792, had argued against licensed brothels, however; and thought the sexual double standard would be eradicated if male rakes were simply looked upon with the same aversion as prostitutes (*WMW*, 7: 457–9). The panic of the Evangelical 'moral majority' took the form of stigmatizing the adultery of the rich, as evidenced in the doubling of divorce bills, as well as the profligacy of the poor. Wollstonecraft's novel responded to all these interconnected controversies of the time regarding the economics and politics of sexuality.

Criminal biography

Jemima's story took a similar form to the popular eighteenth-century genre of memoirs (sometimes fictionalized) of criminals, published as sixpenny pamphlets. These had traditionally subscribed to one of two myths: a reforming point of view, seeking to reintegrate the criminal into the social and moral order; or an ambivalent and often frankly fictional celebration of the outlaw's subversiveness.[24] Though her aim is to plainly to show the reintegration of Jemima, Wollstonecraft's story is remarkably non-judgemental. She resists the paternalistic stance usually implicit in the first myth, for adversity has made Jemima stronger than either of the middle-class inmates whom her story enlightens, and she has saved enough money to obtain independence on her own terms, not through charity and certainly not through repentance. Wollstonecraft had written in 1792: 'Asylums and Magdalens are not the proper remedies for these abuses. It is justice, not charity, that is wanting in the world!' (*WMW*, 5: 140). As Vivien Jones has remarked, the radical force of Jemima's story lies not merely in its documentary detail but in presenting the middle-class heroine as equally an object of abuse, thus: 'reworking... the sentimental narrative's sentimental contract... Wollstonecraft's feminism disturbs the instrumental power of the classic humanitarian audience'.[25] Both women are tellers and both listeners to each other's narratives.

Jemima's story has an element of the second myth of criminal biography, for it shows a certain admiration for the prostitute as economic individualist and outlaw. Even whilst dragged 'through the very kennels of society' she values her independence 'which only consisted in choosing the street in which I should wander', hardened by having 'picked the pockets of the drunks who abused me'. Despite the danger and brutality, this independence is in some ways preferable to 'the yoke of service' to be endured in a brothel, where the madam is capitalist and the prostitute the worker (*WMW*, 1: 112–13). It is Jemima who effects Maria's escape, and, in the most fully projected conclusion, saves her life, not the other way round. Through womanly sympathy she makes a pact to become the 'second mother' of Maria's child, whereby they will both educate her 'to encounter the ills which await her sex' (*WMW*, 1: 120). Instead of adopting the romance conventions that depicted prostitutes as respectable girls tricked and seduced into bawdy houses, or depictions of illegitimate daughters touchingly reunited with their wealthy fathers, Wollstonecraft produced a realistic account in which Jemima comments: 'I have since read in novels of the blandishments of seduction, but I had not even the pleasure of being enticed into vice' (*WMW*, 1: 112).

Jemima's story, in fact, agrees in all its details with the findings of the most recent research into eighteenth-century prostitutes: that most were born into the poorest sections of the community; deserted by one or both parents; entered prostitution in their early teens; used alleyways rather than brothels; bought easily-available pills to attempt inducing abortions; and usually left the sex trade by their mid-twenties to pursue low-status menial employment or to marry. Many complaints were made that the parish watch failed to arrest prostitutes and the latter were accused of bribery in return for their complaisance.[26] Wollstonecraft adds the doubtless authentic detail that they extorted sexual favours in return for leaving the women to walk the streets. She had researched the subject like the journalist she was, perhaps by consulting William Jackson's six volume *The New and Complete Newgate Calendar* (1795?), for authentic accounts of female thieves and prostitutes.

Suicide, the individual and society

Wollstonecraft had only got about halfway through her novel when she died from complications following childbirth. In the last week of her life, on 29 August 1797 Godwin's journal records they were reading Goethe's *Werther* 'en famille'.[27] This suggests that Wollstonecraft may have been considering whether or not to fictionalize her own suicide attempt as its ending. She and Godwin may have been discussing possible conclusions to *The Wrongs of Woman*, for Godwin was reading Wollstonecraft's early novel *Mary: A Fiction* the following day, perhaps for comparison.

The novelistic fragment, posthumously published by Godwin, contained five slight sketches for the continuation of the story – '[S]imple as they are ... pregnant with passion and distress' commented Godwin (*WMW*, 1: 184). Although they all begin at the same point, they are not discrete alternatives as much as successive developments one from the other. So the 'mysterious behaviour' of Maria's lover in the second has become 'her lover unfaithful' in the fourth, pregnancy terminated by 'a miscarriage' in the third is then followed by suicide in the fourth. But the last and most developed sketch of the ending has the pregnant protagonist,

Maria, attempting suicide but saved by the wardress Jemima who has also discovered the first baby's death had been faked (*WMW*, 1: 182–4).

The choice between depicting the tragedy of her heroine's successful suicide of the fourth outline or her determination to fight on in the fifth went to the heart of a burning contemporary literary and philosophical issue. Goethe's novel of sentiment *The Sufferings of the Young Werther* (1774) scandalized orthodox Christians by romanticizing the suicide of the young lover as signifying his extreme sensibility. Was this a self-indulgent and morbid fascination with death? The novel and its numerous imitations and parodies (and Goethe himself wrote two of the latter) sparked a literary controversy over whether the act could be justified, and if so whether in terms of a rational and heroic act or the exquisite sensibility of the exceptional individual. The liberal novelist Charlotte Smith staged characters with different views discussing a suicide in *The Wanderings of Warwick* (1794). Germaine de Staël in *The Influence of Passions on the Happiness of Individuals and of Nations* (1796), would follow Goethe by justifying suicide in exceptionally passionate individuals when *in extremis*.

Most of the philosophers of the Enlightenment, including Hume, Montaigne and Voltaire had contributed to a major debate on whether the individual has the moral right to take his/her own life or has obligations to society, God or to himself which make it wrong. By the late eighteenth century, discussion was beginning to concern itself more with tracing observable causes in individuals and within societies.[28] There were political as well as moral connotations, when suicide was represented as the ultimate refusal to conform with a corrupt society. In the first version of Staël's novel *Delphine* (1802), the heroine is driven to commit suicide when hemmed in by social constrictions on the female sex. In *An Enquiry Concerning Political Justice* (1793) Godwin considered whether classical civilisation was right to admire Cato's suicide and admitted that his sacrifice was the lamp of republican virtue to succeeding ages of imperial tyranny (*MAVRW*, p. 136). Indeed, this was the view taken by several luminaries of the French revolution, who saw themselves as adopting the Stoic code of honour, in falling upon their swords to cheat the guillotine.

Obviously, whether Maria's desperate act was to be successful, or unsuccessful would predicate a tragic or comic outcome for Wollstonecraft's novel and she may have stalled on this. Secondly, her indecision about whether the suicidal Maria is pregnant or has miscarried demonstrates her awareness that there would be a horrified response to fictionalising an attempted suicide by a mother or pregnant woman. If her final and most developed outline represents her chosen ending then she decided to do it anyway. For the reader's shock at Maria's defiant statement that her body will make the unborn baby the most noble of tombs (*WMW*, 1: 183) would highlight the fact that 'universal' arguments about suicide, when discussing the respective obligations to oneself and to society, had failed to consider that the maternal individual was automatically assumed to put the needs of society – in the shape of her child – first. So representing the heroine's suicide attempt positively could be daringly individualist, exemplifying the triumph of her refusal to compromise her free will.

The generic question of whether to choose the tragic ending of suicide sketched in the fourth outline or the triumphant conclusion 'The conflict is over! I will live for my child!' of the final version went to the heart of what we would now call feminism in the novel. The romanticization of the heroine's death was more bleak, and perhaps more aesthetically satisfactory, but to embrace victimhood would imply the tragic impossibility of ever changing patriarchal society. This was the path taken by Staël and in the twentieth century by Jean Rhys. It was a question to bedevil Virgina Woolf in writing *Mrs Dalloway*. Tragedy would endorse romantic individualism rather than collective concern with women as a group. Yet the comedic route of devising a politically engaged uplifting conclusion following on from the anti-climax of the protagonist restored to life ('Violent vomiting followed', *WMW*, 1: 183) risked the sort of bathos recently deliberately invoked at the opening of Zadie Smith's *White Teeth*. Wollstonecraft also would need an alternative emblem to marriage to symbolize the forging of social bonds. Impressively, her final outline substituted the Utopian imagining of what did not yet exist – a coming together of women from different classes to bring about change. That Wollstonecraft began to sketch out this solution before her untimely death demonstrates again the originality of her mind.

When Godwin arranged his wife's literary remains in *Posthumous Works*, he followed *The Wrongs of Woman* in the first two volumes with the hints 'respecting the plan of the remainder of the work' culminating in Maria's exclamation 'I will live for my child!' The rest of volume two was filled with the first book of a series of reading primers, which Wollstonecraft had begun writing for Fanny in an exclamatory first-person conversational voice.[29] Then follow on her letters to Imlay, which Godwin compared to 'the celebrated romance of *Werther*' and found superior to Goethe. The effect is that one is invited to associate the fictional mother, Maria, with Wollstonecraft herself, inferring that the suicidal author, too, had decided to live (and write) for her child. The bitter irony that her life was then cut short following childbirth imbues all with tragedy. This arrangement of texts works to prioritise the maternal sensibility of the educationalist over the 'stern and rugged' feminist with whom Godwin was less comfortable.

The fragment reviewed

As editor, Godwin makes a case for considering that most Romantic of forms, the fragment, in its own right:

> There is a sentiment, very dear to minds of taste and imagination, that finds a melancholy delight in contemplating these unfinished productions of genius, these sketches of what, if they had been filled up in a manner adequate to the writer's conception, would perhaps have given a new impulse to the manners of a world.
>
> (*WMW*, 1: 81)

The *Monthly Review*, smarting from having noticed in her letters Wollstonecraft's scorn of its 'cant of virtue', thought the idea that a novel could change public opinion on such a matter proof of over-weening authorial vanity. Admitting the fragment was 'proof of her genius', the reviewer abhorred its 'argument against the institution of marriage'. He describes it as:

> a pernicious doctrine that a woman, when she deems herself ill-used by her husband, has the right to leave him and to select another man to supply the husband's place.... Religion is at an end if every female, who is *crossed in love*, or disappointed in her husband, is to be encouraged to commit an act of *suicide*.[30]

The *Analytical Review* took *The Wrongs of Woman* to be 'the vindication of [Wollstonecraft's] own sentiments and conduct', and judged it a 'very simple and probable story, founded upon daily occurrences and existing laws'. The reviewer particularly admired the 'justness of Jemima's story'. Though the style needed polishing in some places, the reviewer thought so highly of the novel that had it been finished 'we have no doubt that it would have been a pyramid on which her name might have been engraven for ages'.[31]

Postscript

> Mary, I've trod the turf beneath whose damp
> And dark green coverture thou liest! 'Twas strange!
> And somewhat most like madness shot athwart
> The incredulous mind, when I bethought myself
> That there so many earnest hopes and fears,
> So many warm desires, and lofty thoughts,
> Affections imitating, in their wide
> And boundless aim, heaven's universal love,
> Lay cold and silent!
>
> (From Charles Lloyd, 'Lines to Mary Wollstonecraft Godwin',
> from *Nugae Canorae*, 1819)

> Since the sex have been condemned for exercising the powers of
> speech, they have successfully taken up the pen: and their writings
> exemplify both energy of mind, and capability of acquiring the most
> extensive knowledge. The press will be the monuments from which
> the genius of British women will rise to immortal celebrity: their
> works will, in proportion as their educations are liberal, from year to
> year, challenge an equal portion of fame, with the labours of their
> classical *male* contemporaries.
>
> ([Mary Robinson], *Letter to the Women of England on the Injustice of
> Mental Subordination*, 1799, p. 91)

The way Mary Wollstonecraft died, and the manner in which her literary
afterlife began were both imbued with tragic irony. Just as she had
attained the relationship of mutual love between intellectual equals she
had always craved, and was revelling in the realities of the maternal role
she had theorized and philosophized for a decade, childbirth itself cut
short her life. Because she happened to die in 1798, when anti-Jacobin
feeling was at its height, her first biographer's groundbreaking frankness
about her life raised a cloud of scandal and satire which besmirched all
the respectful plaudits she had hitherto accumulated as a woman of letters.
Her reputation fell almost instantly into, if not obscurity, then such
pestilential shade that the next generation of women writers would not
dare to come near – at least publicly. Wollstonecraft's disciples, Marys

Robinson and Hays, did bravely produce their own 'feminist' treatises, testifying to her influence. However, Hays was constrained to bring out her *Appeal to the Men of Great Britain in Behalf of Women* (1798) anonymously and only alluded to Wollstonecraft without naming her.[1] Robinson adopted the pseudonym Anne Frances Randall for *A Letter to the Women of England, on the Injustice of Mental Subordination with Anecdotes* (1799), which on the first page honoured 'an illustrious British female, whose death has not been sufficiently lamented, but to whose genius posterity will render justice'.[2] But Robinson was crippled with a rheumatic or arthritic complaint, and was dead by 1800. The survivor of the trio, Mary Hays, was left to take the brunt of anti-Jacobin satire and then, like Godwin himself, quietly to disappear from the limelight of the literary scene.

Wollstonecraft's death

We owe our knowledge of all the intimate details of Wollstonecraft's protracted and painful death from septicaemia following childbirth to her husband's unprecedented frankness in *Memoirs*. Godwin laid all bare in his search for the medical truth. He was racked by doubts as to whether Mary could have been saved if treated differently or more quickly. Implicitly his account is a conscientious accumulation of the evidence, to put before an imaginary tribunal at which he himself stands in the dock. Should he have argued against his wife's faith in female attendants? 'I cheerfully submitted in every point to her judgement and her wisdom' (*MAVRW*, p. 112). Would another doctor have provided greater expertise? Had he done all he could in commandeering four of his friends to sleep in the house to be ready at any time to rush around North London to summon some of the foremost male specialists of the day?

While her widower agonized over whether conflict between traditional female or modern male medical practices played a part in Wollstonecraft's death, the less enlightened did not situate the event in terms of science and types of knowledge at all. They saw only the workings of providence. God was punishing the diabolical duo of Godwin and Wollstonecraft, avowed iconoclasts of domestic ideology, and particularly the impious vindicator of rights for woman, by striking her down in this particular way. The Revd Richard Polwhele marked her death by publishing a satire on Wollstonecraft's pernicious influence on women intellectuals, *The Unsex'd Females: A Poem* (1798). One of the author's notes comments:

> I cannot but think, that the Hand of Providence is visible... [in the way] she was given up to her "heart's lusts," and let "to follow her

own imaginations", that the fallacy of her doctrines and the effects of an irreligious conduct, might be manifested to the world; and as she died a death that strongly marked the distinction of the sexes, by pointing out the destiny of women, and the diseases to which they are liable...[3]

In her study of Wollstonecraft's death, Vivien Jones points out that, by the 1790s, a normal home birth was relatively safe. Understanding of pregnancy, labour and post-partum complications had advanced considerably throughout the century, so that from 1850 the statistics of deaths through childbirth would change little until the 1930s.[4] It is arguable whether this was solely due to the development of a medical specialism in obstetrics and gynaecology, or whether equally to the plentiful supply of female midwives. But Wollstonecraft and her 'feminist' supporters certainly felt that the uncertain social status of midwives had been exacerbated by male professionalization, and that there was a danger that male specialists could be over-interventionist by insufficiently valuing the experience of their female patients and midwives alike. The debate continues to this day.

Wollstonecraft saw childbirth in terms of (wo)manual labour not medical professionalism. 'She was sensible that the proper business of a midwife, in the instance of a natural labour, is to sit by and wait for the operations of nature, which seldom, in these affairs, demand the interposition of art' (*MAVRW*, p. 112). Childbirth was 'natural' to her enlightened eyes, and she wanted to dispel superstitious myths of the pain and fearfulness of the process so that mothers felt in control. As might be expected, she had chosen a female midwife for her home birth, rather than a man-midwife or one of the doctors at that time making obstetrics and gynaecology part of the male-dominated science of medicine. This was unconventional for a middle-class woman. She had boasted to her friends how quickly she had recovered her strength after Fanny's birth and she announced to Godwin she intended to come down to dinner the day after the birth. Not for her the usual 'lying in' for a month. The midwife, Mrs Blenkinsop, used the same language as Wollstonecraft of letting nature take its course, for on 30 August, 1797, her patient reported to Godwin, 'Mrs Blenkinsop tells me that I am in the most natural state, and can promise me a safe delivery – But that I must have a little patience' (*CLMW*, p. 411).

Her daughter Mary was born late that night, Wollstonecraft having been in labour since early morning. But two and a half hours later the midwife asked for her colleague, the physician and male midwife at the

Westminster New Lying-in Hospital at Lambeth, to be called in because the placenta had not been spontaneously delivered. Dr Louis Poignand arrived after another couple of hours, and performed the standard procedure of manual removal of the placenta. Unfortunately, it broke into pieces. Though Poignand believed he had removed it all, it later turned out that he was incorrect. Wollstonecraft was in excruciating pain, lost much blood and went into a series of fainting fits. Later, when her terrified husband entered her room, she greeted him with her captivating smile, telling him she would have died that night if she had not been determined not to leave him so soon after their marriage. Poignand later touchily withdrew his services after Godwin and Wollstonecraft asked the advice of their friend, the eminent Dr George Fordyce, who in turn recommended the physician and man-midwife Dr John Clarke. Clarke could do nothing by this stage but hope for the best. Godwin probably worried he should have called him in earlier, as Clarke was a leading specialist in obstetrics whose work was published by Johnson. However, he would not have been Wollstonecraft's ideal choice as he despised female midwives and thought women in labour 'obstructive' (*MWRL*, p. 454). Godwin's friend, the surgeon Anthony Carlisle, was also in constant attendance, but concentrated on moral support and advice on pain relief. He must have known that this was all that could be done.

On the third of September Wollstonecraft suffered a violent shivering fit, the onset of septicaemia caused by the decay of pieces of placenta left in the womb. 'Nothing could exceed the equanimity, the patience and affectionateness of the poor sufferer' (*MAVRW*, p. 116). But despite the very best in up-to-date male medical care and the careful nursing of her female friends, especially that of the Gothic novelist Eliza Fenwick, death was inevitable. Mary Hays wrote to Hugh Skeys, Fanny Blood's widower:

> Her whole soul seemed to dwell with anxious fondness on her friends; and her affections, which were at all times more alive than perhaps of any other human being, seemed to gather new disinterestedness upon this trying occasion.[5]

With hindsight Godwin probably agonized as to whether Poignand had been insufficiently experienced or skilful. Mrs Blenkinsop, too, had been rather slow to ask for assistance in the first instance. He probably wondered if Wollstonecraft's egalitarian choice of low-cost local practitioners from the Westminster New Lying-in Hospital, 'principally designed to relieve the Wives of poor industrious Tradesmen, or distressed

Housekeepeers...',[6] had been idealistic and over-optimistic for a woman of thirty-eight. But we would recognize today that manual removal of the placenta without anaesthetic or antibiotics would have been extremely dangerous and difficult whoever had performed it.

Wollstonecraft eventually died of puerperal fever at seven-forty in the morning of 10 September 1797. Eliza Fenwick wrote to Wollstonecraft's sister that 'in the very last moments of her recollection... [she said of Godwin] "He is the kindest best man in the world" ' (*MAVRW*, p. 164). The methodical Godwin was unable to write any words in his neatly-kept journal that night. After the precisely recorded time of death, there are three lines scoring the empty page – eloquent in their silence. He wrote to his old friend Holcroft, 'I firmly believe that there does not exist her equal in the world. I know from experience we were formed to make each other happy. I have not the least expectation that I can now ever know happiness again'.[7] He could not bear to attend the funeral, on 15 September in St Pancras, the same church where they had been married such a short time ago. Amongst his papers is his draft for the announcement of her death in the papers:

> On Sunday morning at Somer's Town, Mrs Mary Godwin, well known to the literary world by her original name of Wolstonecraft. She possessed uncommon power of mind: she was earnest in the investigation of truth: she was acute to detect and courageous to oppose every destructive prejudice. Calm, unassuming Inquiry was the Character of her Conversation: Affection and intelligence marked her conduct in the endearing duties of the friend, the parent and the wife. That she was esteemed and beloved, and that she is deeply regretted are words which express common Emotions. A few superior minds will imagine the Distress of her Friends, but the Associations of language cannot describe it.[8]

Memoirs of the Author of The Vindication of the Rights of Woman

Ironically, Godwin's pioneering biography, his tribute to Wollstonecraft's genius, was perceived not as a vindication but a denigration by its contemporary readers. Southey spoke for many when he commented that his former mentor, Godwin, showed 'want of all feeling in stripping his dead wife naked' (*MAVRW*, p. 11), by giving unprecedentedly frank details of her amorous and sexual relationships outside marriage, illegitimate child, suicide attempts and loss of conventional faith. Some modern feminist critics have agreed: charging Godwin's tactless candour on the one hand and his portrayal of his wife as a heroine of sensibility on the other with passing on an image of Wollstonecraft as wayward child of passion which put back the women's movement sixty years. Godwin is back in the dock.

Godwin had thrown himself into such a therapeutic orgy of writing that his editions of Wollstonecraft's literary remains and memoir of her life were published as early as January 1798. Even by November he was writing about the book as if completed, declaring to one correspondent: '[M]y principal source of materials for what I was writing was a variety of conversations that had passed between me and my wife'. He had also consulted Mary's friends, colleagues and relatives asking for letters and their remembrances, stating: 'I think the world is entitled to some information respecting persons that have enlightened & improved it'.[9] Some, such as Jane Gardiner (née Arden) and Joseph Johnson, responded warmly; while Everina and Eliza Wollstonecraft standoffishly refused to send their sister's letters; and Henry Fuseli taunted Godwin by opening a drawer full of them and shutting it again with a sneer.

On the day of Wollstonecraft's funeral Godwin had written to thank Anthony Carlisle for his support at his wife's bedside, and, though obviously craving his friend's reassurance regarding the strength and mutuality of the couple's love, also sternly enjoined him: 'But, above all, be severely sincere. I ought to be acquainted with my own defects, and to trace their nature in the effects they produce.'[10] This gives some clue as to the rigorous candour and objectivity underlying this ex-Calvinist's adoption of the confessional genre of life-writing. Readers would be staggered that the recently-widowed author could write without jealousy or rancour of his wife's consuming passion for another man, obviously the love of her life, and publish her private love letters (though their recipient was probably still alive), commenting approvingly on their literary merit.

However, Mitzi Myers rightly warns against exaggerating Godwin's naivety for he was already an accomplished biographer and pioneer in the genre.[11] She also notes that he was not so candid that he did not leave out such controversial matters as Wollstonecraft's precise role in her sister Eliza's marriage breakdown. We could add to this even more significant omissions. Godwin gave only a minimal reference to Wollstonecraft's political friendships and contacts in republican France; and no details at all of the 'business' which took her to Scandinavia: Imlay's blockade-running and his probable connections with the Jacobin government. This was completely understandable as 1798, the year of the Irish rebellion and an invasion scare, marked the height of anti-French feeling and fears of 'the enemy within'. But it does mean that despite its title, which, like her headstone, commemorated Wollstonecraft not as a wife and mother but as an author, *Memoirs* gives more prominence to her childhood, personality and sexuality (which her own Boswell believed had shaped her unique individuality) than to her politics. This may seem strange, coming from an anarchist philosopher usually caricatured as the embodiment of cold reason. But Godwin's belief in individualism had preceded his radicalism, and, despite his deconstruction of state power, he was equally suspicious of political collectivism and associations.[12] And even before his relationship with Wollstonecraft, he had revised *Political Justice* to correct his under-estimation of the importance of the emotions.

Now, as Myers astutely points out, he used the writing of her biography to 'bear witness to his new-found faith in feeling, domestic affections, and marriage'.[13] *Memoirs* would testify to his own intellectual and moral improvement through the influence of Wollstonecraft. Though, in response to the outcry which greeted the book, he did tone down sensitive passages slightly in the revised second edition, which was called for as soon as August, he also added substantially to his concluding portrait of their marriage and the way it had developed his thinking away from sterile rationalism. Though he was still chary of cohabitation, he now admitted that:

[T]he man who lives in the midst of domestic relations, will have many opportunities of conferring pleasure...without interfering with the purposes of general benevolence. Nay, by kindling his sensibility, and harmonizing his sensibility, and harmonizing his soul, they may be expected...to render him more prompt in the service of strangers and the public.

(*MAVRW*, p. 208).

He portrayed himself and Mary as exemplifying the complementarity of the sexes, though he was careful to emphasize that this was culturally conditioned, so as not to contradict Wollstonecraft's arguments in *Vindication of the Rights of Woman*:

A circumstance by which the two sexes are particularly distinguished from each other, is, that the one is accustomed more to the exercise of its reasoning powers, and the other of its feelings....Mary and myself perhaps each carried farther than to its common extent the characteristic of the two sexes to which we belonged.... her feelings had a character of peculiar strength and decision; and the discovery of them, whether in matters of taste or of moral virtue, she found herself unable to control. She had viewed the objects of nature with a lively sense and an ardent admiration, and had developed their beauties. Her education had been fortunately free from the prejudices of system and bigotry, and her sensitive and generous spirit was left to the spontaneous exercise of its own decisions. The warmth of her heart defended her from artificial rules of judgement; and it is therefore surprising what a degree of soundness pervaded her sentiments. In the strict sense of the term, she had reasoned comparatively little; and she was therefore little subject to diffidence and skepticism. Yet a mind more candid in perceiving and retracting error, when it was pointed out to her, perhaps never existed. This arose naturally out of the directness of her sentiments, and her fearless and unstudied veracity.

A companion like this, excites and animates the mind.... Her taste awakened mine; her sensibility determined me to a careful development of my feelings ...

(MAVRW, pp. 216–17)

This passage was an amplification of his earlier conclusion in the first edition, where he had summed up the difference between their minds as the contrast between the educated academic and the instinctual romantic genius:

The strength of her mind lay in intuition.... She adopted one opinion, and rejected another, spontaneously, by a sort of tact.... In a robust and unwavering judgement of this sort, there is a kind of witchcraft ...

(MAVRW, p. 121)

Though modern readers are quick to scent sexual stereotyping here, Godwin is actually echoing Wollstonecraft's own view that a genius possesses 'that quick perception of truth, which is so intuitive that it baffles research' (*WMW*, 5: 185). This concept of genius allowed for the co-existence of 'masculine' reason and 'feminine' passionate intuition in the same mind. Andrew Elfenbein suggests that Godwin linked his cross-gendered sense of Wollstonecraft's genius with an account of her erotic and her writing life as a development of feminisation: from her passion for Fanny Blood and her 'masculine', 'stern and rugged'

Vindications she progressed to the seductive sensibility of her Scandinavian travels and union with Godwin.[14]

Godwin, strongly influenced by Rousseau's *Confessions*, certainly portrayed Wollstonecraft as a romantic genius: an uneducated but original, brilliant, restless, brave, tormented, sometimes wayward free spirit, not to be judged by common standards. But the reading public could not handle the concept of a *female* Romantic genius. Indeed, as Helen M. Buss has remarked, the time had not yet come when a female subject was considered fit for a 'public honouring and institutionalization of her intellectual legacy. As a woman she can have only a private existence'.[15] The sexual double standard operated – and still does operate – so that while Rousseau's abandonment of all his children to the foundling hospital warranted some acknowledgement of his eccentricity, no amount of romantic genius could mitigate the loss of Wollstonecraft's 'reputation' that Godwin now unthinkingly publicized. Women themselves policed the code that female 'honour', once lost, was lost irretrievably, and that this overrode a woman's public authorial identity. This is shockingly illustrated in the reply sent to Godwin by Wollstonecraft's fellow 'Jacobin' novelist Elizabeth Inchbald in answer to his note announcing her death. Even on the day of Mary's demise Inchbald continued to justify her previous public ostracism of Wollstonecraft during a visit to the theatre: 'I did not know her. I never wished to know her: as I avoid every female acquaintance, who has no husband. Against my desire you made us acquainted'.[16]

Reviews and reaction

On 26 January 1799, Godwin received from Warrington an ill-spelt agonized letter signed 'A Lancashire Woman RW', which sums up the mixture of bewilderment, grief and disillusion which the *Memoirs* inspired in many ordinary readers:

> I perused it with avidity, the beg[inn]ing I [was] exceedingly gratified with, but felt hurt when I arrived at the place where all Woes commenced, A Woman of her exalted Mind forgets herself. every tongue is ready to condemn who can be Silent, not her own Sex I am sure she who shou'd have steped forward in asserting the rights of Woman, to so soon swerve from the Paths of Rectitutde is unfortunate to the last degree.... She could teach better a good deal than she did Practice Her Intulectual strength was superior to most either Male or Female...I am a true friend to my own Sex & sympathize with such

of them, who act with impropriety But do hope you will never make her Children acquainted with their deare Mother's misfortunes – Let all her amiable Qualities before them, they are worthy of their immulation her sorrows were more than often fall to the Lot of the generality of females...[17]

In complete contrast to this, Godwin also received a letter from W.G. Montfort of New York, on behalf of the democrat-republican vice-presidential candidate Aaron Burr, stating that he was 'a warm admirer of the life and writings of Mrs Godwin' and requesting permission that 'a polygraphic copy' of her portrait be made for him from that by Opie hanging in Godwin's study.[18] Burr went on to have his daughter brought up on Wollstonecraft's principles. But Burr, a sophisticated libertine, hardly typified the public reaction to *Memoirs*.

The *Analytical Review*, as might be expected, reviewed the *Memoirs* sympathetically. Anticipating the outcry which would follow, the reviewer stoutly defended his erstwhile colleague by pointing out the moral idealism underpinning her rejection of the outward forms of marriage, while conceding she was imprudent and naïve. She was 'another Heloïse' to an unworthy Abelard (Imlay). The reviewer complained, however, that the *Memoirs* were 'a bald narrative', giving 'no correct history of the formation of Mrs G's mind'. The present writer would concur with the *Analytical* in this, for, in his desire to stress her 'natural' genius, Godwin omitted details of Wollstonecraft's intellectual attainments and skimped on her professional literary life. 'We are neither informed of her favourite books, her hours of study, nor her attainments in languages and philosophy.... [W]e think too little is told us concerning the subjects of Mrs. G's study, and her manner of studying...'.[19]

A new periodical, the *Anti-Jacobin Review*, however, blamed the *Analytical* for leading Wollstonecraft astray in the first place: 'From the writers in that work she probably derived the anti-hierarchical and anti-monarchical doctrines, which it has been the uniform object of that Review to disseminate'.[20] The *Anti-Jacobin Review* was specifically launched, with government support, to scupper the *Analytical Review* and to terminate the publishing career of Joseph Johnson, who would by November be imprisoned on a trumped-up charge of selling a seditious pamphlet. Wollstonecraft's death and Godwin's tactless *Memoirs* were a stroke of luck which could not be passed up. Much of the first number was devoted to what one critic has described as Wollstonecraft's 'systematic defamation'.[21] Its review was acerbic, ridiculing Wollstonecraft's 'extravagant, absurd and destructive theories'. The level of subtlety may be gauged by its index reference on 'Prostitution' keyed to 'See Mary Wollstonecraft', which catalogues her 'amorous' exploits. It pronounced both Godwin and Wollstonecraft, 'by precept or example, as destructive of domestic, civil, and political society', and many of the substantial number of periodicals with a religious character followed its lead. The most the liberal *Monthly Review* could muster was to choke back a sob, more in sorrow than anger. Pausing to regret the absence of blushes suffusing the cheeks of her husband in relating such anecdotes of his wife, it cried: 'Peace to her manes! She was the child of genius, but of suffering: of talents, but of error!' The reviewer pronounced: 'No evil may result from recording the vow of love: but *many* evils *must* result from a contempt of marriage. It is one of the first institutions that are essential to social order'.[22]

Mary Hays wrote movingly in her obituary of her friend regarding the tragic irony that Wollstonecraft died just as she was entering into the happiest period of her life. Though she, like Godwin, portrayed Wollstonecraft as a female genius, she adopted the plural so as to suggest that there were other women (including Hays herself) whose natural force was being damned up, producing 'a destructive torrent' of strong passions which sweep them into collision with social convention:

> Woe be to these victims of vice or superstition, if, too ingenuous for habitual hypocrisy, they cannot stifle in the bottom of their hearts those feelings which should constitute their happiness and their glory: that sensibility, which is the charm of their sex becomes its bitterest curse; in submitting to their destiny they rarely escape insult; in overstepping the bounds prescribed to them, by a single error, they become involved in a labyrinth of perplexity and distress. In vain may reflection enable them to contemn distinctions, that, confounding truth and morals, poison virtue at its source: overwhelmed by a torrent of contumely and reproach, a host of foes encompass their path, exaggerate their weakness, distort their principles, misrepresent their actions, and, with deadly malice, or merciless zeal seek to drive them from the haunts of civil life.[23]

It was not only in the reviews that Godwin and Wollstonecraft were castigated, but in satires. As well as the misogynistic diatribe *The Unsex'd Females* by Revd Richard Polwhele, 'The Vision of Liberty' was anonymously published by C. Kirkpatrick Sharpe in *Anti-Jacobin Review* 9 (Aug. 1801), scoffed:

> William hath penn'd a waggonload of stuff,
> And Mary's life at last he needs must write,
> Thinking her whoredoms were not known enough,
> Till fairly printed off in black and white.

Wollstonecraft and Godwin were also lampooned so extensively in novels that these virtually constitute a school or sub-genre of their own. From about 1795, when the tide of reaction turned against revolutionary ideals, Godwin's philosophy, previously highly respected, had come under occasional attack. The same could be said of Wollstonecraft. But the *Memoirs* were now the signal for an open season on the couple. A rash of popular anti-Jacobin novels transformed the rationalist philosopher into a scheming machiavel, or contained pen-portraits or caricatures of Godwin, Wollstonecraft, Hays and others. They included: Jane West's *A Tale of the Times* (1799), Elizabeth Hamilton's *Memoirs of Modern Philosophers* (1800), George Walker's *The Vagabond* (1799), Charles Lloyd's *Edmund Oliver* (1798), the anonymous novels *St. Godwin* (1800), *The Citizen's Daughter* (1804), and *Dorothea, or a Ray of the New Light* (1801), Amelia Opie's *Adelina Mowbray* (1804), and Charles Lucas's *The Infernal Quixote* (1801).[24]

Some of these satires were genuinely engaging with Wollstonecraft's ideas even while they poked fun at their revolutionary idealism. But the Evangelicals took them more seriously still. Hannah More launched into apocalyptic mode in her *Strictures on the Modern System of Female Education* (1799), which was written specifically to counter Wollstonecraft, just as *Cheap Repository Tracts* targeted the ideas of Paine. Formerly, she had prided herself on not bothering to read *Rights of Woman* because 'there is something so fantastical and absurd in the very title'.[25] Now she thundered:

> 'The female Werter', as she is styled by her biographer, asserts, in a work intitled "The Wrongs of Women" that adultery is justifiable, and that the restrictions placed upon it by the laws of England constitute one of the *Wrongs of Women*.[26]

What really riled More was that such 'modern corruptors' of youth were not overcome by violent passions so much as coolly arguing for their gratification: '[C]ool, calculating intellectual wickedness eats out the very heart and core of virtue' (p. 49). On 28 April 1799 Mary Berry mischievously pointed out to a correspondent the irony that unlike the secular Maria Edgeworth, Hannah More and Mary Wollstonecraft 'agree on all the great points of female education'. In other words that both wrote out of their religious beliefs.[27] But of course because Wollstonecraft laid emphasis on a woman's moral individualism, whereas More urged her to cultivate obedience to authority, they came to opposite conclusions.

What all the controversy and satire demonstrates, above all, is how well-known Wollstonecraft's ideas were throughout society at this time. Indeed Mary Thale's study of London's public debating societies in the 1790s shows that they were not merely known to an educated elite but were debated by the workers too. Most of the speakers and auditors of these societies were lower class men with occasional female participants. When restrictions on free speech seemed to have been restored in 1795, and societies started up again, Wollstonecraft's ideas were amongst the first topics chosen for debate, and continued popular throughout the 1790s.[28]

Previously gender had only featured in humorous battles of the sexes. But now many societies wanted to debate such questions as 'Would it not be advantageous to the liberty and happiness of the world that women should equally partake all the rights and privileges of man?' But when a new crack-down on political meetings began in April 1798, Thale notes that the Westminster Forum amended the title of its 'feminist' debate after the first two nights, to imply censure of Wollstonecraftian notions. Whether this ominously demonstrates 'retrogression' and reaction, as Thale suggests, or was merely a tongue-in-cheek tactic to avoid trouble, is debatable. But a similar motive dictated the title of the very last known debate on any subject, comparing Wollstonecraft's moral influence to that of a notoriously promiscuous actress. Then the debating societies were entirely silenced by the Seditious Meetings Act of 1799.

Wollstonecraft was not without her supporters even at this dark hour. An anonymous pamphlet appeared, *A Defence of the Character and Conduct of the Late Mary Wollstonecraft Godwin, Founded on the Principles of Nature and Reason as Applied to the Peculiar Circumstances of Her Case, in a Series of Letters to a Lady* (London: James Wallis, 1803) whose chivalrous author (Sir Charles Aldis)[29] attempted to rebut the vitriolic outcry against her, as Godwin himself should have done when his *Memoirs* backfired (p. 53). Aldis described her as a 'rare genius *nigris simillime cygnis*' who submitted her actions only to the Almighty being rather than taking worldly wisdom into account (p. 36). Though as a historian, she was equal to Gibbon, her theory of moral agency was 'too much individualized to be capable of application to the general state of society' (p. 63) for laws and institutions are designed to benefit society at large, which does not consist of infallible persons. He infers that Wollstonecraft did not object so much to marriage 'as a political institution' as much as she desired the reform of current 'modes and laws' (pp. 95–6). But she was subject to criticism from her anonymous admirer because she gave insufficient regard to public opinion, whose approbation was necessary if she was to propagate her opinions more effectively.

Wollstonecraft in the nineteenth century

Given the rabidly loyalist climate which lasted as long as did the Napoleonic wars, it was not surprising that Wollstonecraft's ideas were not immediately canonized. Then, when peace came at last in 1815 and clamour for reform began to be heard again, Wollstonecraft's teenage daughter Mary eloped with one of her parents' young admirers, the married poet Percy Shelley. Shelley was notorious for his revolutionary views, having been sent down from Oxford for publishing an atheist pamphlet. This scandal, shortly followed by the suicide of both Fanny Imlay and Shelley's deserted and pregnant wife Harriet, together with the couple's friendship abroad with Wollstonecraft's aristocratic former pupil, Margaret Mountcashel, who had eloped in 1798 and lived with her lover under the name 'Mrs Mason', taken from *Original Stories*, provided anti-Jacobin wits with plenty of material. They satirized the poverty-stricken Godwin as having sold his eighteen-year-old daughter Mary and step-daughter Claire Claremont (mistress of Shelley's friend Lord Byron) to the aristocrat Shelley, and harped on the association between admiration for Wollstonecraft and female sexual permissiveness.

It was hardly surprising, then, that Wollstonecraft was rarely cited by nineteenth-century reformers and feminists. However, as Barbara Caine has argued, she was extremely well known by reputation.[30] Not only that, but, she remained a heroine to some. As Barbara Taylor's work has shown, the tracts and newspapers of the Owenite socialists regularly reprinted passages from the *Rights of Woman* from the 1820s until 1845, together with admiring commentaries.[31] Robert Owen, like Shelley, was an enthusiastic disciple of both Godwin and Wollstonecraft. Note also that Harriet Martineau refers in her autobiography to 'the admiration with which her memory was regarded in my childhood' amongst the Unitarian community.[32] The Unitarian circles, which had produced not just Wollstonecraft but a gallery of brilliant female 1790s intellectuals, Anna Barbauld, Helen Maria Williams, Mary Hays, remained the seed-bed and intellectual powerhouse of feminism as it would develop in the nineteenth century. Though numerically small, as we have seen, a disproportionate number of influential and powerful intellectuals were Unitarians, who constituted the driving force behind the dissemination of enlightenment through publishing, journalism and in debating societies. And it was through their participation in education and print culture that women would continue to infiltrate the public sphere, just as Mary Robinson had predicted they would (see epigraph). By the 1820s the secular wing, the Utilitarians, together with the Unitarians proper, were arguing for cheap books for all, for democratic access to secular state and university education, and public libraries. The universalism underlying rational dissent was proving too strong for the patriarchal attitudes of traditional Christianity which lingered even in Unitarian families. For, as Kathryn Gleadle has shown, by the 1830s it was again a Unitarian circle, led by William Johnson Fox of South Place Chapel, editor of the *Monthly Repository*, who mounted a 'relentless and spirited campaign on behalf of the rights of women'.[33] It was Fox who published Harriet Martineau's early writings. By the 1850s, the liberal feminists of the Langham Place group emerged, such as Barbara Leigh Smith, Bessie Rayner Parkes, Octavia Hill, Elizabeth Whitehead Malleson, Clementia Taylor. They also came from Unitarian families where Wollstonecraft's works were most likely to be available.[34]

The mid-century saw a paradox where the heirs of Wollstonecraftian radicalism, when they became influential public figures, more than ever needed to distance themselves from her disreputable reputation, even though some conservative women of letters could find it in their hearts to empathize with the poor romantic sinner who had helped clear the path for them. So Harriet Martineau, in her autobiography, declares she 'never could reconcile [her] mind to Mary Wollstonecraft's writings':

> Mary Wollstonecraft was, with all her powers, a poor victim of passion....I decline all fellowship and co-operation with women of genius...who injure the cause by their personal tendencies....The best friends of that cause are women...who must be clearly seen to speak from conviction of the truth and not just from personal unhappiness.[35]

Here speaks the mid-century Utilitarian feminist, pragmatically aware that the taint of free sexuality would scupper her political campaign. George Eliot, on the other hand, personally identified with Wollstonecraft *because* she saw her as a victim of social prejudice, as she was herself on account of her relationship with a married man. Eliot was surprised to find *Vindication of the Rights of Woman* so heavy and moralistic. It had been reissued in 1844, but apparently made little impact. Unsympathetic to Wollstonecraft's revolutionary politics, Eliot considered her as less of an artist because she was driven by ideology. In an essay of 1855, she judged Margaret Fuller 'as more of a literary woman, who would not have been satisfied without literary production; Mary Wollstonecraft, we imagine wrote not at all, for writing's sake, but from the pressure of other motives'.[36]

At this juncture, in 1857, Mary Shelley's daughter-in-law, who was a friend of Bessie Rayner Parkes and Barbara Leigh Smith, and a subscriber to their *English Woman's Journal*, decided it was time to rehabilitate the tarnished reputation of her husband's literary dynasty including his grandmother.[37] Lady Shelley entrusted family papers to the Unitarian writer and publisher Charles Kegan Paul, and this eventually resulted in *William Godwin: His Friends and Contemporaries* (1876) and a reprint of Wollstonecraft's *Letters to Imlay* (1879), with a prefatory memoir stressing that Wollstonecraft never entirely lost her religious faith. The pall was lifted and Wollstonecraft now became the subject of works of biography and criticism. At the end of the century when Victorian feminists put sexual freedom on their agenda they really began to take Wollstonecraft's ideas seriously. But Caine makes the important point that Wollstonecraft's ideas were not sufficiently programmatic to appeal to the suffragists: John Stuart Mill was more useful for them.[38] It was not until the twentieth century, when the limited aims of suffrage had been achieved, that Wollstonecraft's broader philosophical critique of the cultural and economic constraints on women would come into its own.

Both in the first and second waves of feminism, in the 1920s/1930s and 1960s/1970s respectively, feminists turned to Wollstonecraft: not as an archaic but as a vital, still-relevant thinker. 'She is alive and active, she argues and experiments, we hear her voice and trace her influence even now among the living, declared Virginia Woolf.[39] The story of Wollstonecraft's life was seized upon by feminist intellectuals, themselves experimenting with bohemian lifestyles, and became re-told as a tale of principle not illicit passion. The attack on conventional femininity in *Vindication of the Rights of Woman* helped inspire a 1970s feminism based on consciousness-raising and women's scrutiny of their life-experiences. The combination of an outpouring of feminist scholarship and the movement towards historicism in Romantic studies in the last twenty years has produced a new portrait of Wollstonecraft. Less recog-isably our contemporary, this eighteenth-century woman has an agenda so distinctly of its time – born out of religious as well as of political convictions – that we need scare quotes to call her a 'feminist' at all. By putting her back amongst her contemporaries, both male and female, in the literary and intellectual circles where her ideas were forged and her books read, this literary life has shown that writing, for her, was a vocation driven by intense moral fervour. Wollstonecraft laid down a tradition of feminism saturated in the word, in literacy and literature, in a participation in print culture and a concern with representation, whose effects are felt to this day.

Notes

1 'A genius will educate itself': Mary Wollstonecraft as Autodidact

1. William Godwin, *Memoirs of the Author of A Vindication of the Rights of Woman*, eds Pamela Clemit and Gina Luria Walker (Ontario and Letchworth, Herts: Broadview Press, 2001), p. 44. Henceforth cited in parenthesis as *MAVRW*.
2. *The Works of Mary Wollstonecraft*, ed. Janet Todd and Marilyn Butler (London: Pickering, 1989), 1: 124. All quotations are taken from this edition and will henceforth be cited in parenthesis.
3. Letterpress copy of letter dated 11 January, 1798. Abinger Archive. Dep.b.227/8.
4. See Matthew Mercer, 'Dissenting Academies and the Education of the Laity, 1750–1850', *History of Education*, 30:1 (2001), 35–58; and William St Clair, *The Godwins and the Shelleys: A Biography of a Family* (Baltimore, Maryland: The John Hopkins University Press, 1989), pp. 8–9.
5. Abinger Archive, Dep.b.214/3.
6. I am indebted to Michael Franklin for tracing the quotations except for William King, which was provided in Janet Todd's *The Collected Letters of Mary Wollstonecraft* (London: Penguin, 2003), p. 2. The latter only came out as this book was being revised.
7. Malcolm Andrews, *The Search for the Picturesque: Landscape Aesthetics and Tourism in Britain 1760–1800* (Aldershot: Scolar Press, 1989), p. 86.
8. Susan Gubar, 'Feminist Misogyny: Mary Wollstonecraft and the Paradox of "It takes One to Know One"', *Feminist Studies* 20:3 (1994), 453–73.
9. See Stuart Brown's entry in *The Dictionary of Eighteenth-Century British Philosophers*, eds John W. Yolton, John Valdimir Price and John Stephens (Bristol and Sterling, Virginia: Thoemmes Press, 1999), 2, 872–4.
10. Letter of 18 Feb 1784. Abinger archive, Dep.b.210/9.
11. William Robinson, *The History and Antiquities of the Parish of Stoke Newington in the County of Middlesex, Containing an Account of the Prebendal Manor, the Church, Charities, Schools, Meeting Houses etc* (London, 1842).
12. Abinger archive, Dep.c.604/1.
13. John Gasgoigne, 'Anglican Latitudinarianism, Rational Dissent and Political Radicalism in the Late Eighteenth Century', in Knud Haakonsen (ed.), *Enlightenment and Religion: Rational Dissent in Eighteenth-Century Britain* (Cambridge: Cambridge University Press, 1996), pp. 219–240, p. 224.
14. Gasgoigne, 'Latitudinarians, Rational Dissent and Radicalism', p. 231.
15. Barbara Taylor argues for the religious context of Wollstoncraft's feminism in 'The Religious Foundations of Mary Wollstonecraft's feminism', in Claudia L. Johnson (ed.), *The Cambridge Companion to Mary Wollstonecraft* (Cambridge: Cambridge University Press, 2002), pp. 99–118. Her impressive monograph on the subject, *Mary Wollstonecraft and the Feminist Imagination*

(Cambridge: Cambridge University Press, 2003) came out as this book was at the revision stage. Chapter 3 is essential reading on MW's personal faith.

16. I am indebted for my summary of Price's theology to D.O. Thomas, *The Honest Mind: The Thought and Work of Richard Price* (Oxford: Oxford University Press, 1977), chs 1–5.

17. Thomas, *The Honest Mind*, p. 201.

18. See Cheryl Turner, *Living By The Pen: Women Writers in the Eighteenth Century* (London and New York: Routledge, 1992), pp. 36–9.

19. *Thoughts on Education, Tending Chiefly to Recommend the Attention of the Public, some Particulars Relating to That Subject, which are not Generally Considered with the Regard their Importance Deserves* (Boston, 1749), p. 15.

20. Nancy Armstrong and Leonard Tennenhouse (eds), *The Ideology of Conduct: Essays in Literature and the History of Sexuality* (New York and London: Methuen, 1987), p. 4.

21. Gary Kelly, *Revolutionary Feminism: The Mind and Career of Mary Wollstonecraft* (Basingstoke and London: Macmillan – now Palgrave Macmillan, 1992), p. 31.

22. Hannah More, *Essay on Various Subjects, Principally Designed for Young Ladies*, 2nd edn (London: Wilkie, 1778), p. 3. All quotations are taken from this edition and henceforth cited in parenthesis.

23. See John Brewer, *The Pleasures of the Imagination: English Culture in the Eighteenth Century* (London: Harper Collins, 1997), p. 78.

24. Mary Poovey, *The Proper Lady and the Woman Writer: Ideology as Style in the Works of Mary Wollstonecraft, Mary Shelley and Jane Austen* (Chicago and London: University of Chicago Press, 1984), p. 49.

25. Quoted in Claire Tomalin, *The Life and Death of Mary Wollstonecraft* (Harmondsworth, Middlesex: Penguin, 1974), p. 75.

26. Katherine Sobba Green uses the term in connection with *Mary: A Fiction* in *The Courtship Novel, 1740–1820: A Feminized Genre* (Lexington, Kentucky: University of Kentucky Press, 1991), p. 96.

27. Brewer, *The Pleasures of the Imagination*, p. 193; see also: Jacqueline Pearson, *Women's Reading in Britain 1750–1835: A Dangerous Recreation* (Cambridge: Cambridge University Press, 1999).

28. Taylor, *Mary Wollstonecraft and the Feminist Imagination*, pp. 108–10. She comments that a strong Platonist element was discernible in Unitarian thought, especially in Price's moral philosophy and the writings of Anna Barbauld.

29. Taylor, *Mary Wollstonecraft and the Feminist Imagination*, p. 205.

30. *English Review*, 16 (1790), 465. See also *Monthly Review*, NS 2 (1790), 352–3.

2 'When the voices of children are heard on the green': Mary Wollstonecraft the Author-Educator

1. Linda A. Pollock, *Forgotten Children: Parent–Child Relations from 1500 to 1900* (Cambridge: Cambridge University Press, 1983), p. 269.

2. John Locke, *Some Thoughts Concerning Education*, eds John W. and Jean S. Yolton (Oxford: Oxford University Press, 1989), pp. 195–6.

3. *The Works of the Rev. Isaac Watts*, 7 vols (Leeds: Edward Baines, n.d.), VI: 359–60.

4. Mary V. Jackson, *Engines of Instruction, Mischief and Magic: Children's Literature in England from Its Beginnings to 1839* (Aldershot, Hants and Lincoln, Nebraska: University of Nebraska Press, 1989), p. 104.
5. Harvey J. Graff, *The Labyrinths of Literacy: Reflections on Literacy Past and Present* (London, New York and Philadelphia: The Falmer Press, 1987), p. 34.
6. Bette P. Goldstone, *Lessons To Be Learned: A Study of Eighteenth-Century English Didactic Children's Literature* (New York, Berne and Frankfurt am Main: Peter Lang, 1984), p. 43.
7. Mitzi Myers. 'Impeccable Governesses, Rational Dames, and Moral Mothers: Mary Wollstonecraft and the Female Tradition in Georgian Children's Books', in *Children's Literature*, eds Margaret Higonnet and Barbara Rosen (New Haven and London: Yale University, Press, 1986), 31–59.
8. Gary Kelly, *Revolutionary Feminism: The Mind and Career of Mary Wollstonecraft* (Basingstoke: Macmillan – now Palgrave Macmillan, 1992), p. 58. See also: Isaac Kramnick, 'Children's Literature and Bourgeois Ideology', in *Republicanism and Bourgeois Radicalism: Political Ideology in Late Eighteenth-Century England and America* (Ithaca and London: Cornell University Press, 1990), pp. 99–132; and M.O. Grenby, 'Politicizing the Nursery: British Children's Literature and the French Revolution', *The Lion and the Unicorn*, 27:1 (2003), 1–26.
9. Quoted by Grenby, 'Politicizing the Nursery', p. 1. Grenby also notes the Privy Council's investigation of Godwin's Juvenile Library, which an informer said was propagating 'the principles of democracy and Theophilanthropy', p. 2. His argument that 1790s children's literature was not political excludes the religious dimension of ideology.
10. Mrs Sarah Trimmer, *A Comment on Dr. Watts' Divine Songs to Children with Questions Designed to Illustrate the Doctrines and Precepts to Which They Refer; and Induce a Proper Application of them as Intruments of Early Piety* (London, 1789), p. iv.
11. G.E. Bentley, Jr, 'William Blake in France: The First Foreign Engravings after Blake's Designs', *Australian Journal of French Studies* 26 (1989), 125–47. I have obtained the information on the French edition from Bentley.
12. Reprinted in *Essays in Honour of William Gallacher*, eds P.M. Kemp-Ashraf and Dr J. Mitchell (Humboldt: Universität zu Berlin, 1966), pp. 339–340.
13. See Malcom Chase, *'The People's Farm': English Radical Agrarianism 1775–1840* (Oxford: Oxford University Press, 1988), pp. 21–2.
14. Susan Khin Zaw, 'The Reasonable heart: Mary Wollstonecraft's view of the relation between reason and feeling in morality, moral psychology, and moral development', *Hypatia*, 13:1 (Winter 1998), 78–117, 96.
15. Compare Wollstonecraft's emphasis on social conscience with the Cavinist concentration on personal salvation exhibited by Jane Taylor, author with her sister Ann of the phenomenally successful *Original Poems for Infant Minds* (1805), who wrote to a friend, 'I have sometimes thought that more might be done than is commonly attempted in education, to familiarize the idea of death to the minds of children, by representing it as the grand event for which they are born'. See *Memoirs, Correspondence and Poetical Remains of Jane Taylor*, 3 vols (Boston and Philadelphia: Perkins, 1835), I: 209.
16. Alan Richardson comments that Wollstonecraft acknowledges 'the inherently compromised nature of the fictionalized object lesson in the book's preface,

noting the vast superiority of proper habits "imperceptibly fixed" by daily experience', 'Mary Wollstonecraft on Education', in *The Cambridge Companion to Mary Wollstonecraft*, ed. Claudia L. Johnson (Cambridge: Cambridge University Press, 2002), pp. 24–41, p. 29.

17. Saba Bahar, *Mary Wollstonecraft's Social and Aesthetic Philosophy: 'An Eve to Please Me'* (Basingstoke: Palgrave Macmillan, 2002), pp. 138–9.

18. On Blake's illustrations as ironic commentary on the stories, see, Dennis Welch, 'Blake's Response to Wollstonecraft's *Original Stories*', *Blake: An Illustrated Quarterly*, 13 (1979), 4–15; Nelson Hilton, 'An Original Story', in Nelson Hilton *et al.* (eds), *Unnam'd Forms: Blake and Textuality* (Berkely: University of California Press, 1986); Jeffrey Parker, 'Text and Iconography in the Commercial Designs of William Blake', PhD thesis (University of South Carolina, July 1991). Orm Mitchell seems to me to exaggerate the irony in 'Blake's Subversive Illustrations to Wollstonecraft's *Stories*', *Mosaic*, 17:4 (Autumn, 1984), 17–34.

19. Edmund Burke, *A Philosophical Enquiry into the Origin of Our Ideas of the Sublime and the Beautiful* (Oxford: Oxford University Press, 1990), p. 63.

20. Zaw, 'The Reasonable heart', 91.

21. Thomas Pfau, '"Positive Infamy": Surveillance, Ascendancy, and Pedagogy in Andrew Bell and Mary Wollstonecraft', *Romanticism* 2:2 (1996), 220–42, 238.

22. *The Illuminated Blake* annotated by David V. Erdman (London: Oxford University Press, 1975), p. 80.

23. Pfau, '"Positive Infamy"', 238.

24. Patricia Howell Michaelson, *Speaking Volumes: Women, Reading, and Speech in the Age of Austen* (Stanford CA: Stanford University Press, 2002), p. 184.

25. Michaelson, *Speaking Volumes*, p. 189.

26. See Vivien Jones, 'Wollstonecraft and the Literature of Advice and Instruction', in *The Cambridge Companion to Mary Wollstonecraft*, ed. Claudia L. Johnson (Cambridge: Cambridge University Press, 2002), pp. 119–40, p. 130.

27. Abinger archive, Dep.B.210/3.

28. See Peter Haywood, *Joseph Johnson, Publisher* (Aberystwyth: College of Librarianship, 1976).

29. Alan Richardson, *Literature, Education, and Romanticism: Reading as Social Practice 1780–1832* (Cambridge: Cambridge University Press, 1994), p. 115.

30. On a comparison between the Anglican Sarah Trimmer's anthropocentric and theological treatment of nature and the Unitarian Barbauld's rational scientic view of the creation in their textbooks, see Aileen Fye, 'Reading Children's Books in Late Eighteenth-Century Dissenting Families', *The Historical Journal*, 43:2 (2000), 453–73.

31. *The Letters of Charles and Mary Anne Lamb*, ed. Edwin W. Marrs Jr, (Ithaca and London: Cornell University Press, 1976), II: 81–2.

32. *The Collected Letters of Samuel Taylor Coleridge*, ed. Earl Leslie Griggs (Oxford: Oxford University Press, 1956), I: 354.

33. Richardson, *Literature, Education, and Romanticism*, p. 115.

34. Mitzi Myers,'Pedagogy as Self-Expression in Mary Wollstonecraft: Exorcising the Past, Finding a Voice', in Shari Benstock (ed.), *The Private Self: Theory and Practice of Women's Autobiographical Writings* (Chapel Hill and London: University of North Carolina Press, 1988), pp. 192–210.

3 'The first of a new genus': Proud To Be a Female Journalist

1. Godwin is quoting the words of Johnson in his memorandum on MW sent to her widower after her death, 'A Few Facts', Abinger Archive. Dep.6. 210/3.
2. A.S. Collins, *Authorship in the Days of Johnson, Being a Study of the Relation Between Author, Patron, Publisher and Public 1726–1780* (London: Robert Holden & Co., 1927), p. 33. See also Victor Bonham Carter, *Authors by Profession* (London: Spottiswood Ballantyne Press, 1978).
3. J.W. Saunders, *The Profession of English Letters* (London and Toronto: University of Toronto Press, and Routledge and Kegan Paul, 1964), p. 160.
4. Gerald P. Tyson, *Joseph Johnson: A Liberal Publisher* (Iowa: University of Iowa Press, 1979), p. 36. On Johnson, see also Helen Braithwaite, *Romanticism, Publishing and Dissent: Joseph Johnson and the Cause of Liberty* (Basingstoke: Palgrave Macmillan, 2003) which was published as this book was in the revision process.
5. Helen Braithwaite informs me that Johnson's business letterbook shows that he only reluctantly acceded to growing requests from authors to have their works printed locally, preferring to handle all aspects of publication himself in London.
6. Thomas Rees, *Reminiscences of Literary London from 1779–1853* (London: Suckling and Galloway, 1896), p. 78.
7. Hall, 'Joseph Johnson', in James K. Bracken and Joel Silver (eds), *Dictionary of Literary Biography*, vol. 154, *The British Literary Book Trade 1700–1820* (Detroit and London: Gale Research Inc., 1995), pp. 165, 159.
8. Gerald P. Tyson, 'Joseph Johnson, an Eighteenth-Century Bookseller', *Studies in Bibliography*, 28 (1975), 2–16, 3.
9. Claire Tomalin, 'Publisher in prison', *TLS*, 12/2/94.
10. For this and other detailed information on Johnson's list, I am indebted to Carol Hall, 'Joseph Johnson', pp. 159–69, p. 159.
11. For other examples of Johnson's science list, see Braithwaite, *Romanticism, Publishing and Dissent*, p. 61.
12. Braithwaite, *Romanticism, Publishing and Dissent*, pp. 38–9.
13. Hall, 'Joseph Johnson', p. 167.
14. Durant, Supplement to *Memoirs of Mary Wollstonecraft Written by William Godwin* (London and New York: Constable, 1927), p. 175.
15. See Braithwaite, *Romanticism, Publishing and Dissent*, p. 96. See also Tyson, *Joseph Johnson: A Liberal Publisher*, pp. 93–7.
16. Nigel Cross, *The Common Writer: Life in Nineteenth-Century Grub Street* (Cambridge: Cambridge University Press, 1985), p. 12.
17. *Memoirs of the First Forty-five years of the Life of James Lackington, the Present Bookseller in Chiswell Street, Moorfields, London* (London: Lackington, 1791), pp. 167; 253–5.
18. Hall, 'Joseph Johnson', p. 161.
19. Reginald C. Fuller, *Alexander Geddes 1737–1802: A Pioneer of Biblical Criticism* (Sheffield: Almond Press, 1984).
20. For example, by Marilyn Gaull, in 'Joseph Johnson: Literary Alchemist', *European Romantic Review* 10:3 (1999), 265–78.
21. Tyson, *Joseph Johnson: A Liberal Publisher*, pp. 73, 147.
22. Theophilus Lindsay, *An Historical View of the State of the Unitarian Doctrine and Worship, from the Reformation to Our Own Times: With Some Account of the*

Obstructions Which It has Met With at Different Periods. (London: Joseph Johnson, 1783), p. 553. Thomas Christie refers to William Christie, Junior, as his uncle in a letter of 4 March 1785 quoted in J. Nichols, *Literary Anecdotes of the Eighteenth Century*, 9 vols (London, 1815), 9: 368.

23. Andrea A. Engstrom, 'Joseph Johnson's Circle and the *Analytical Review*: A Study of English Radicals in the Eighteenth Century', Unpublished PhD thesis of University of Southern California, August, 1986, p. 70.
24. Engstrom, 'Joseph Johnson's Cicle', p. 38.
25. Engstrom, 'Joseph Johnson's Circle', pp. 67, 84.
26. Collins, *Authorship in the Days of Johnson*, pp. 240–55.
27. See Jürgen Habermas, *The Structural Transformation of the Public Sphere: An Inquiry into a Category of Bourgeois Society*, trans. Thomas Burger with the assistance of Frederick Lawrence (Cambridge: Polity Press, 1992).
28. See Kathryn Shevelow, *Women and Print Culture: The Construction of Femininity in the Early Periodical* (London and New York: Routledge, 1989), pp. 151–67.
29. Paula McDowell, *The Women of Grub Street: Press, Politics, and Gender in the London Literary Marketplace 1678–1730* (Oxford: Oxford University Press, 1998), pp. 6–9. See also Hannah Barker, 'Women, work and the industrial revolution: female involvement in the English printing trades', in Hannah Barker and Elaine Chalus (eds), *Gender in Eighteenth-Century England: Roles, Representations and Responsibilities* (Harlow: Longman, 1997), pp. 81–100.
30. See Alison Adburgham, *Women in Print: Writing Women and Women's Magazines From the Restoration to the Accession of Victoria* (London: George Allen and Unwin, 1972), pp. 57, 88.
31. I am indebted to Helen Braithwaite for the example of Ann Jebb as another woman journalist from similar circles.
32. On the importance of these networks when they developed further in the next century, see Barbara Onslow, *Women of the Press in Nineteenth-Century Britain* (Basingstoke: Macmillan – now Palgrave Macmillan, 2000), p. 28.
33. E.J. Clery, Caroline Franklin and Peter Garside (eds), *Authorship, Commerce and the Public: Scenes of Writing, 1750–1850* (Basingstoke: Palgrave Macmillan, 2002), p. 6.
34. Cheryl Turner, *Living By The Pen: Women Writers in the Eighteenth Century* (London and New York: Routledge,1992), p. 39, and the *Monthly* Review was quoted on p. 31.
35. Turner, *Living By The Pen*, p. 114.
36. See Roper, *Reviewing Before the* Edinburgh *1788–1802*, (London: Methuen, 1978) p. 39.
37. Abinger Archive. Dep.B.210/3.
38. Antonia Foster, 'Review Journals and the Reading Public', in Isabel Rivers (ed.), *Books and Their Readers in Eighteenth-Century England: New Essays* (London and New York: Leicester University Press, 2001), pp. 171–90, p. 174.
39. Tyson, *Joseph Johnson: A Liberal Publisher*, p. 95.
40. Nichols, *Literary Anecdotes of the Eighteenth Century*, 9: 388.
41. [Thomas Christie], *Miscellanies: Literary, Philosophical and Moral*, 2 vols (London: J. Nichols, 1788), I: 213.
42. Roper, *Reviewing Before the* Edinburgh, pp. 22–3; Engstrom. 'Joseph Johnson's Circle', p. 102.
43. Mitzi Myers gives an up-to-date account of the problem of attribution as well as an excellent analysis of Wollstonecraft as a critic of sentimental fiction in

'Mary Wollstonecraft's Literary Reviews', in Claudia L. Johnson (ed.), *The Cambridge Companion to Mary Wollstonecraft* (Cambridge: Cambridge University Press, 2002), pp. 82–98.

44. Myers, 'Mary Wollstonecraft's Literary Reviews', p. 84.
45. Brian Rigby, however, sees the *Analytical*'s response to the French Revolution as much more 'cautious and measured' than I do, in 'The French Revolution and English Literary Radicals: the Case of the *Analytical Review*' in H.T. Mason and R. Doyle (eds), *The Impact of the French Revolution on European Consciousness* (Gloucester: Sutton, 1989) pp. 91–103. His view is comparable to that of Braithwaite, *Romanticism, Publishing and Dissent*, pp. 87–9, 94, 108.
46. Engstrom, 'Joseph Johnson's Circle', p. 182.
47. Walter Graham, *English Literary Periodicals* (New York: Octagon Books, 1966), p. 189.
48. Graham, *English Literary Periodicals*, pp. 220–1.
49. This review seems to have been accidentally omitted from Todd and Butler's *Works of Mary Wollstonecraft*.
50. James G. Basker, 'Radical Affinities: Mary Wollstonecraft and Samuel Johnson', in Alvaro Ribeiro, SJ and James G. Basker (eds), *Tradition in Transition: Women Writers, Marginal Texts, and the Eighteenth-Century Canon* (Oxford: Oxford University Press, 1996), pp. 41–55.
51. Helen Braithwaite notes that it may not be insignificant that Joseph Johhnson had become a principal part-owner in regularly-reprinted editions of the *Rambler, Adventurer, Connoisseur, World* by the 1790s (personal comment).
52. Edward Duffy makes this comment, though without noting Wollstonecraft's authorship of the article in *Rousseau in England: The Context for Shelley's Critique of the Enlightenment* (Berkely, Los Angeles and London: University of California Press, 1979), p. 34.
53. Durant suggests she wrote a review 'The Arts' in October 1788 describing Boydell's scheme for a series of paintings from Shakespeare. Durant, 'Supplement' to *Memoirs*, pp. 190–1.
54. See Scott Juengel, 'Countenancing History: Mary Wollstonecraft, Samuel Stanhope Smith, and Enlightenment Racial Science', *English Literary History*, 68:4 (2001), 897–927.
55. Anne K. Mellor, *Mothers of the Nation: Women's Political Writing in England 1780–1830* (Bloomington and Indianapolis: Indiana University Press, 2000).

4   'An Amazon stept out': Wollstonecraft and the Revolution Debate

1. See H.T. Dickinson, *Liberty and Property: Political Ideology in Eighteenth-Century Britain* (London: Weidenfeld and Nicolson, 1977), p. 253.
2. W. Clark Durant, Supplement to *Memoirs*, p. 225.
3. Jack Fruchtman, Jr, *Thomas Paine: Apostle of Freedom* (New York and London: Four Walls Eight Windows, 1994), p. 200.
4. Quotations, henceforth cited in parenthesis, are from D.O. Thomas (ed.), *Richard Price: Political Writings* (Cambridge: Cambridge University Press,

1991), where the typography of the sixth edition has unfortunately been modernized.

5. On Wollstonecraft's attempt to reconcile religious faith and radical principles, see Daniel Robinson, 'Theodicy versus Feminist Strategy in Mary Wollstonecraft's Fiction', *Eighteenth-Century Fiction*, 9:2 (Jan. 1997), 183–202, 197.

6. Quotations, henceforth cited in parenthesis, are taken from *The Writings and Speeches of Edmund Burke*, vol.8, The French Revolution 1790–1794, eds L.G. Mitchell and William B. Todd. (Oxford: Clarendon Press, 1989), p. 61.

7. See Braithwaite, *Romanticism, Publishing and Dissent*, pp. 101–2.

8. Information on the reception of *Reflections* has been obtained from L.G. Mitchell (ed.), *The Writings and Speeches of Edmund Burke*; and Gregory Claeys, 'The *Reflections* refracted: the critical reception of Burke's *Reflections on the Revolution in France* during the early 1790s', in John Whale (ed.), *Edmund Burke's* Reflections on the Revolution in France: *New Interdisciplinary Essays* (Manchester and New York: Manchester University Press, 2000), 40–59.

9. See James T. Boulton, *The Language of Politics in the Age of Wilkes and Burke* (Westport, CT: Greenwood Press, 1963), p. 83.

10. The first reply of all, by Major John Scott, the friend of Warren Hastings, appeared within a fortnight of *Reflections*.

11. Boulton, *The Language of Politics in the Age of Wilkes and Burke*, p. 75.

12. See Carey McIntosh, *The Evolution of English Prose, 1700–1800: Style, Politeness, and Print Culture* (Cambridge: Cambridge University Press, 1998), pp. 157–8.

13. D.L. Macdonald, 'The Personal Pronoun as Political: Stylistics of Self-Reference in the Vindications', in Helen M. Buss *et al.* (eds), *Mary Wollstonecraft and Mary Shelley Writing Lives* (Toronto, Ontario: Wilfrid Laurier University Press, 2001), pp. 31–42, p. 37.

14. *Analytical Review*, 8 (Dec. 1790), 416.

15. *Monthly Review* quoted by Boulton, *The Language of Politics in the Age of Wilkes and Burke*, p. 168.

16. John Seed, 'A set of men powerful enough in many things': Rational Dissent and Political Opposition in England, 1770–1790', in Knud Haakonssen (ed.), *Enlightenment and Religion: Rational Dissent in Eighteenth-Century Britain* (Cambridge: Cambridge University Press, 1996), pp. 140–168, 164.

17. Boulton, *The Language of Politics*, p. 186.

18. Quoted by Kelly, *Revolutionary Feminism*, p. 101.

19. *Analytical Review*, 8 (Dec. 1790), 416.

20. Quoted by Kelly, *Revolutionary Feminism*, p. 100.

21. Thomas Christie, *Letters on the Revolution of France and on the New Constitution Established by the National Assembly Occasioned by the Publications of the Right Honourable Edmund Burke MP and Alexander de Calonne, late Minister of State etc.*, 2 vols (London: Joseph Johnson, 1791), I: 12.

22. Christie, *Letters on the Revolution in France*, II: 7.

23. Thomas Paine, *Rights of Man*, ed. Henry Collins (London: Penguin, 1977), p. 88. All quotations will be henceforth in parenthesis in the text.

24. Fruchtman, *Thomas Paine: Apostle of Freedom*, p. 225.

25. John Keane, *Tom Paine: A Political Life* (London: Bloomsbury, 1995), p. 310. I have obtained my information regarding editions of *Rights of Man* from Keane.

26. See Syndy McMillen Conger, 'The sentimental logic of Wollstonecraft's prose', *Prose Studies* 10:2 (Sept. 1987), 143–58.

27. Amy Elizabeth Smith, 'Roles for Readers in Mary Wollstonecraft's *A Vindication of the Rights of Woman*', *SEL* 32 (1992), 555–70.
28. Braithwaite, *Romanticism, Publishing and Dissent*, p. 115.
29. See Kate Soper, 'Naked Human Nature and the Draperies of Custom: Wollstonecraft on Equality and Democracy', in Eileen Janes Yeo (ed.), *Mary Wollstonecraft and 200 Years of Feminisms* (London and New York, Rivers Oram Press, 1977), pp. 207–21, p. 210.
30. *Rapport sur l'instruction publique, fait au nom du Comité de constitution* (1791).
31. Sylvana Tomaselli, 'The most public sphere of all: the family', in Elizabeth Eger *et al.* (eds), *Women, Writing, and the Public Sphere 1700–1830* (Cambridge: Cambridge University Press, 2001), pp. 239–56, p. 241.
32. *Analytical Review*, 12 (March, 1792), 248; 13 (July, 1792), 481.
33. See R.M. Janes, 'On the Reception of Mary Wollstonecraft's *A Vindication of the Rights of Woman*', *Journal of the History of Ideas*, 39:2 (Apr.–June, 1978), 292–302.
34. Quoted by W. Clark Durant, in his Supplement to *Memoirs of Mary Wollstonecraft, Written by William Godwin* (London and New York: Constable, 1927), p. 215.
35. On this and other reactions to *Rights of Woman*, see Durant, Supplement to *Memoirs*, p. 216.
36. John Knowles, *Life and Writing of Henry Fuseli* (London, 1831), I: 165.
37. Suzanne Desan, 'Women's experience of the French Revolution: An Historical Overview', in Catherine R. Montfort, *Literate Women and the French Revolution of 1789* (Birmingham, Alabama: Summa Publications, 1994), pp. 19–32, p. 21.
38. Durant, Supplement to *Memoir*, p. 182.
39. Martin Myrone, *Henry Fuseli* (London: Tate Publishing, 2001), p. 75.
40. Peter Tomory, *The Life and Art of Henry Fuseli* (London: Thames and Hudson, 1972), p. 107.
41. Abinger archive, dep.b.227/8. Letterpress copy of letter 11 January 1798.
42. Godwin once wrote more frankly of Fuseli: 'He was the most frankly ingenuous and conceited man I ever knew. He could not bear to be eclipsed or put in the background for a moment. He scorned to be less than highest. He was an excellent hater; he hated a dull fellow, as men of wit and talents naturally do, and he hated a brilliant man, because he could not bear a brother near the throne. He once dined at my house with Curran, Grattan, and two or three men of that stamp; and retiring suddenly to the drawing-room, told Mrs Godwin that he could not think why he was invited to meet such wretched company', *The Collected English Letters of Henry Fuseli*, ed. David H. Weinglass (London, New York and Nendeln: Kraus International, 1928), p. 509.
43. Knowles, *Life and Writing of Henry Fuseli*, I: 168.

5 'The true perfection of man': Print, Public Opinion and the Idea of Progress

1. R.R. Palmer, *The World of the French Revolution* (London: George Allen and Unwin, 1971), p. 99.
2. Helen Maria Williams, *Letters from France* (Boston: Thomas, Andrews, West and Larkin, 1792), II: 3, 16.

3. Mark Philp, 'English Republicanism in the 1790s', *Journal of Political Philosophy*, 6:3 (1998), 235–62, 254.

4. Williams, *Letters from France*, II: 43.

5. Thomas Christie, *Letters on the Revolution of France and on the New Constitution Established by the National Assembly, Occasioned by the Publications of the Right Honourable Edmund Burke MP and Alexander de Calonne, Late Minister of State, etc.* (London: Johnson, 1791), I: 218.

6. Morris Slavin, *The Making of an Insurrection: Parisian Sections and the Gironde* (Cambridge, Mass., Harvard University Press, 1986), pp. 1–9.

7. Gary Kates, *The* Cercle Social, *The Girondins, and the French Revolution* (Princeton, NJ: Princeton University Press, 1985), p. 205.

8. Kates, *The* Cercle Social, *The Girondins, and the French Revolution*, pp. 178–93. See also, M.J. Sydenham, *The Girondins* (London: University of London, Athlone Press, 1961), ch.3.

9. See Carla Hesse 'Economic upheavals in publishing 1775–1800', in Robert Darnton and Daniel Roche (eds), *Revolution in Print: The Press in France 1775–1800* (Berkeley, Los Angeles and London: University of California Press, 1989), pp. 69–97.

10. For information on the periodical and newspaper press in the French Revolution I am indebted to: Emmet Kennedy, *A Cultural History of the French Revolution* (New Haven and London: Yale University Press, 1989), 317, 323.

11. Christie, *Letters on the Revolution*, I: 145–7.

12. R.R. Palmer, *The Improvement of Humanity: Education and the French Revolution* (Princeton, NJ: Princeton University Press, 1985), p. 84.

13. Kates, *The* Cercle Social, *The Girondins, and the French Revolution*, p. 193.

14. Hugh Gough, *The Newspaper Press in the French Revolution* (London: Routledge, 1988), pp. 90–2.

15. Simon Schama, *Citizens: A Chronicle of the French Revolution* (London: Penguin, 1989), p. 647.

16. Schama, *Citizens*, p. 714.

17. Sydenham, *The Girondins*, p. 97.

18. *The Life of Thomas Paine: with a History of His Literary, Political, and Religious Career in America, France, and England* (London: Watts, 1909), p. 183.

19. Abinger Archive, dep.b.210/7.

20. Palmer, *The Improvement of Humanity: Education and the French Revolution*, p. 81. I am indebted to Palmer for details on the successive plans for national education.

21. *Madame de Staël: Écrits retrouvés*, ed. J. Isbell and S. Balayé, *Cahiers staëliens*, 46 (1994–45), 12–17.

22. Palmer, *The Improvement of Humanity: Education and the French Revolution*, pp. 97–9.

23. Ibid., pp. 124–30.

24. Palmer, *The Improvement of Humanity: Education and the French Revolution*, p. 166.

25. Schama, *Citizens*, p. 828.

26. Ibid.

27. M. Ray Adams, 'Joel Barlow: Political Romanticist', *American Literature*, 9 (May 1937), 113–52, 117.

28. Schama, *Citizens*, p. 706.

29. Durant, Supplement to *Memoirs*, pp. 251, 253.
30. *George Forster's Werke: Samtliche Schriften, tagebücher, Briefe*, ed. Klaus-Georg Popp, vol. 17 Briefe 1792 Bis 1794 Und Nachträge (Berlin: Akademie-Verlag, 1989), p. 339. My thanks to Ann Heilmann for translating this.
31. Gilbert Imlay, *The Emigrants, or the History of an Expatriated Family, Being a Delineation of English Manners, Drawn from Real Characters, Written in America* (London: A. Hamilton, 1793), I: 88.
32. Oliver Farrar Emerson, 'Notes on Gilbert Imlay, early American writer', *PMLA*, 39:2 (1924), 406–39.
33. Samuel Bernstein, *Joel Barlow: A Connecticut Yankee in an Age of Revolution* (Cliff Island, Maine: Ultima Thule Press, 1985), p. 103.
34. Emerson, 'Notes on Gilbert Imlay, early American writer', 415.
35. On this plan, see Bernstein, *Joel Barlow: A Connecticut Yankee in an Age of Revolution*, pp. 94–5, and Emerson, 'Notes on Gilbert Imlay, early American writer', 415–19.
36. Abinger archive, dep.b.214/3. Letter to Godwin of 13 Nov. 1797.
37. Abinger archive, dep.b.214/3
38. Schama, *Citizens*, p. 787.
39. Conway, *The Life of Thomas Paine*, p. 182.
40. Tom Furniss, 'Mary Wollstonecraft's French Revolution' in Johnson (ed.), *The Cambridge Companion to Mary Wollstonecraft*, pp. 59–81, 69.
41. Karen O'Brien, 'The history market in eighteenth-century England', in Isabel Rivers (ed.), *Books and Their Readers in Eighteenth-century England: New Essays* (London and New York, Leicester University Press, 2001), pp. 105–34.
42. '"The grand causes which combine to carry mankind forward": Wollstonecraft, history and revolution', *Women's Writing*, 4:2 (1997), 155–72, 164.
43. Antoine-Nicolas de Condorcet, *Sketch for a Historical Picture of the Progress of the Human Mind*, tr. J. Barraclough (London: Weidenfeld and Nicolson, 1955), p. 100. Henceforth referred to parenthetically in the text.
44. Thomas P. Saine, *Georg Forster* (New York: Twayne Publishers, 1972), pp. 151–3. My account of *Parisian Sketches* is indebted to Saine.
45. Quotations are taken from: Jean Paul Saint-Etienne Rabaut, *The History of the Revolution in France*, translated by James White (New York: Greenleaf and Fellows, 1794) from henceforth cited in the text in parenthesis.
46. *WMW*, 6: 16. Henceforth referred to in the text as *French Revolution*.
47. John Whale, *Imagination Under Pressure, 1789–1832* (Cambridge: Cambridge University Press, 2000), p. 90.
48. Quoted by Jeremy Popkin, 'Journals: The New Face of News', in Darnton and Roche (eds), *Revolution in Print*, pp. 141–64, p. 164.
49. Bertrand de Barère, *An Idea of Government*, quoted in *Analytical Review* 27 (1798), 43.
50. Steven Blakemore, *Crisis in Representation: Thomas Paine, Mary Wollstonecraft, Helen Maria Williams, and the Rewriting of the French Revolution* (Madison and London: Fairleigh Dickinson University Press, 1997), pp. 96–7.
51. Gregory Dart mistakenly states she is agreeing with Smith, in *Rousseau, Robespierre and English Romanticism* (Cambridge: Cambridge University Press, 1999), p. 122.
52. William Ogilvie, a Professor at Aberdeen University, published *Essay of the Right of Property in Land* (1781), proposing that unpropertied citizens be

rented 40 acres of land. Common ownership would augment agrarian improvement and impede monopolies building up. Redistribution would be done gradually over a period of time. Thomas Paine, in *Agrarian Justice* (1795–96) proposed a fund be set up to compensate those who had cultivated the land for their dispossession of it. He was attacked for his moderation by Thomas Spence in *Rights of Infants* (1797). Spence asks for the social compact to be cancelled and land restored to the parishes to be rented out to farmers. He argues for the natural rights of all the human species to live off the land like other animals, for all wealth and improvements are produced by the work of the labouring classes. See M. Beer (ed.), *The Pioneers of Land Reform: Thomas Spence, William Ogilvie and Thomas Paine* (London: G. Bell & Sons, 1920).

53. See G.J. Barker-Benfield, 'Mary Wollstonecraft: Eighteenth-Century Commonwealthswoman', *Journal of the History of Ideas*, 50 (1989), 95–116.
54. Vivien Jones, 'Women Writing Revolution: Narratives of History and Sexuality in Wollstonecraft and Williams', in S. Copley and J. Whale (eds), *Beyond Romanticism: New Approaches to Texts and Contexts 1780–1832* (London and New York: Routledge, 1992), pp. 178–99.
55. See Daniel O'Neill, 'Shifting the Scottish paradigm: The Discourse of Morals and Manners in Mary Wollstonecraft's *French Revolution*', *History of Political Thought*, 23:1 (Spring, 2002), 90–116.
56. *British Critic*, 6 (1795), 29–36, 35.
57. *English Review*, 25 (1795), 349–52.
58. *Monthly Review*, 16 (1795), 393–402, 394, 402.
59. *Analytical Review*, 20 (December 1794), 337–47; 21 (January 1795), 13–17.
60. Braithwaite, *Romanticism, Publishing and Dissent*, p. 134.
61. *Analytical Review* 22 (July 1795), 21.
62. *Analytical Review*, 22 (November 1795), 458.
63. Durant, Supplement to *Memoirs*, p. 267.

6 The Commercial Traveller, the Imagination and the Material World

1. On MW's concept of the imagination, see Whale, *Imagination Under Pressure*, pp. 68–97.
2. Braithwaite notes that postal links had been suspended with the onset of war. Despite the Traitorous Correspondence Act , Johnson had twice managed to get money through to her in Paris in 1793. His own letters to her seemed to have been stopped or intercepted. *Romanticism, Publishing and Dissent*, p. 132 and note.
3. Braithwaite, *Romanticism, Publishing and Dissent*, p. 145.
4. Abinger archive, Dep.b.210/4
5. Beth Dolan Kautz, 'Mary Wollstonecraft's salutary picturesque: curing melancholia in the landscape', *European Romantic Review*, 13 (2002), 35–48.
6. On the significance for science and Enlightenment thought of travel accounts of Sweden see Brian Dolan, *Exploring European Frontiers: British Travellers in the Age of Enlightenment* (London: Macmillan – now Palgrave Macmillan, 2000), pp. 27–72, though only passing reference is made to Wollstonecraft.

7. Claire Tomalin, *The Life and Death of Mary Wollstonecraft* (London: Weidenfeld and Nicolson, 1974), p. 179

8. The following account of the case of the missing ship is taken from Per Nyström, *Mary Wollstonecraft's Scandinavian Journey* (Göteborg: Acta Regiae Societatis Scientarum et Litterarum Gothoburgensis, Humaniora 17, 1980). Afterwards cited in parenthesis in the text.

9. Todd states that she sent them back from Strömstrad on the basis of the letter to Imlay of 14 July 1795 but there seems no warrant for this (*MWRL*, pp. 323–5). References to *Letters from Norway* are taken from *WMW*, 6 and henceforth given in parenthesis.

10. On the origins of the turn to nature in travel writing, see George B. Parks, 'The turn to the romantic in the travel literature of the eighteenth century' *Modern Language Quarterly*, 25 (1964), 22–33, although Parks only makes passing reference to Wollstonecraft.

11. On reasons for the lack of recognition of the importance of Forster as an influential intellectual and as a supporter of the French revolution, see Peter Morgan, 'Republicanism, identity and the new European order: Georg Forster's letters from Mainz and Paris, 1792–1793', *Journal of European Studies*, 22 (1992), 71–100, though no mention is made of Wollstonecraft.

12. Nigel Leask, *Curiosity and the Aesthetics of Travel Writing 1770–1840* (Oxford: Oxford University Press, 2002), pp. 41–3.

13. Charles L. Batten, Jr, *Pleasurable Instruction: Form and Convention in Eighteenth-Century Travel Literature* (Berkeley: University of California Press, 1978), pp. 72–4.

14. Leask, *Curiosity and the Aesthetics of Travel Writing*, p. 9.

15. See Batten, *Pleasurable Instruction*, pp. 47–81.

16. For a psychoanalytic analysis of Wollstonecraft's use of a maternal stance with which to identify with nature, see Jeanne Moskal, 'The Picturesque and the affectionate on Wollstonecraft's *Letters from Norway*,' *MLQ*, 52:3 (1991), 263–94.

17. Sylvana Tomaselli, 'The death and rebirth of character in the eighteenth century', in Roy Porter (ed.), *Rewriting the Self: Histories from the Renaissance to the Present* (London and New York: Routledge, 1997), pp. 84–96, 96.

18. Mary A. Favret, *Romantic Correspondence: Women, Politics and the Fiction of Letters* (Cambridge: Cambridge University Press, 1993), p. 101.

19. See: Mitzi Myers, 'Mary Wollstonecraft's *Letters Written . . . in Sweden*: Toward Romantic Autobiography', *Studies in Eighteenth-Century Culture*, 8 (1979), 165–85, 181.

20. See Nancy Yousef, 'Wollstonecraft, Rousseau and the Revision of Romantic Subjectivity', *SiR*, 38 (Winter 1999), 537–57, 547.

21. Elizabeth A. Bohls, *Women Travel Writers and the Language of Aesthetics, 1716–1818* (Cambridge: Cambridge University Press, 1995), pp. 140–69. See also Whale, *Imagination Under Pressure*, p. 94.

22. Ward lists the reviews which appeared as: *Analytical Review*, 23 (1796), 229–38; *British Critic* 7 (1796), 602–10; *Critical Review*, ns, v.16 (1796), 209–12; *English Review*, 27 (1796), 316–21; *Freemason's Magazine*, 7 (1796), 196–97; *New Annual Register*, 17 (1796), 248–9; *Scots Magazine*, 58 (1796), 627–8.

23. *The Notebooks of Samuel Taylor Coleridge*, ed. Kathleen Coburn (London: Routledge and Kegan Paul, 1957), I: 259.

24. Mitzi Myers suggests Wollstonecraft anticipates Wordsworth's pilgrimage in *The Prelude* in search of a reintegration of self, nature and society, for: 'Underlying the seeming duality of personal and social motifs in the *Letters* is a continuous concern with human identity and self-realization, developed in counterpoint to the related themes of society's improvement and nature's values'. See Myers, 'Mary Wollstonecraft's *Letters Written...in Sweden*: Towards Romantic Autobiography', p. 166.

25. Printed for R. Phillips and sold by Joseph Johnson. The editor of the preface to the third volume boasts that it has already 'decidedly taken its station among those intended to favour the progressional improvement of mankind' but 'has displayed no partial adherence to any one set of opinions, but has freely admitted arguments on opposite sides'. The magazine was a miscellany which depended greatly on readers' 'original contributions', and called especially for information on 'the present state of this and other countries' (*Monthly Magazine*, 3:16 (Jan 1797), 251.

26. In '"A kind of witchcraft": Mary Wollstonecraft and the Poetic Imagination', *Women's Writing*, 4:2 (1997), 235–45, Harriet Devine Jump compares the two versions, pointing out that Godwin drastically reduced the high value Wollstonecraft placed on the faculty of the poetic imagination. The *Monthly Magazine* version is quoted here, as it seems to be Wollstonecraft's original, rather than the revised version reprinted in Todd and Butler's edition.

27. Abinger archive Dep.b.210/6.

7 'We did not marry': the Comedy and Tragedy of Marriage in Life and Fiction

1. For a full discussion of suicide and Wollstonecraft, see Janet Todd, *Gender, Art and Death* (New York: Continuum, 1993), pp. 102–19.

2. Abinger archive, dep.e.201–2.

3. See Gina Luria, 'Mary Hays: A Critical Biography', unpublished PhD thesis (New York University 1972).

4. Microfilm of the Correspondence of Mary Hays 1782–1837, Carl Pforzheimer Collection, New York Public Library. Hays's letters to Godwin quoted below are transcribed from this.

5. Abinger archive dep.c.604/2.

6. 'Autonarration and genotext in Mary Hays' *Memoirs of Emma Courtney*', *Studies in Romanticism*, 32:2 (Summer 1993), 149–76.

7. Rajan, 'Autonarration and genotext in Mary Hays' *Memoirs of Emma Courtney*', 156.

8. Abinger archive, dep.b.210/6.

9. Abinger archive, dep.b.210/4.

10. Ibid.

11. Ibid.

12. *The Collected English Letters of Henry Fuseli*, ed. David H. Weinglass (London and New York: Kraus International, 1928), p. 173.

13. Durant, Supplement to *Memoirs*, p. 314.

14. Durant, Supplement to *Memoirs*, p. 312.

15. Evan Radcliffe, 'Revolutionary Writing, Moral Philosophy, and Universal Benevolence in the Eighteenth Century', *Journal of the History of Ideas*, 54:2 (Apr. 1993), 221–40, 231–2.

16. Radcliffe, 'Revolutionary Writing, Moral Philosophy, and Universal Benevolence', 236.

17. See Lawrence Stone, *Road to Divorce: England 1530–1987* (Oxford: Oxford University Press, 1990), pp. 273–89, 327–46. I am indebted to Stone for factual information about the marriage laws of the time.

18. Gilbert Imlay, *The Emigrants, or the History of an Expatriated Family Being a Delineation of English Manners, Drawn from Real Characters, Written in America* (London: A. Hamilton, 1793). Quotations in parenthesis in the text. For an analysis of its views on women, see Liana Borghi, *Dialogue in Utopia: Manners, Purpose and Structure in Three Feminist Works of the 1790s* (Pisa: ETS, 1984).

19. Elaine Jordan, 'Criminal Conversation: Mary Wollstonecraft's *The Wrongs of Woman*', *Women's Writing*, 4:2 (1997), 221–34, 224. See this article for the legal background to the case against Darnford.

20. Quoted from the Abinger archive in Mitzi Myers, 'Unfinished business: Wollstonecraft's *Maria*', *The Wordsworth Circle*, 11 (1980), 107–14, 110. On 2 February 1796 he had written to another aspiring novelist: 'In a novel, do not trust to the independent attractions of the particular parts, but pay great attention to the concatenation & unity of the whole'. Abinger archive, dep.b. 227/8. Letterpress copy of letter to unknown recipient, perhaps Amelia Alderson.

21. Daniel O'Quinn, 'Trembling: Wollstonecraft, Godwin and the Resistance to Literature', *ELH*, 64:3 (1997), 761–88.

22. *Perdita: The Memoirs of Mary Robinson*, ed. M.J. Levy (London & Chester Springs: Peter Owen, 1994), p. ix.

23. Patrick Colquhoun, *A Treatise on the Police of the Metropolis* (London: Mawman *et al.*, 1796, repr. 1806), pp. 334–9. Quotations from the 1806 edition.

24. Lincoln B. Faller, *Turned to Account: The Forms and Functions of Criminal Biography in Late Seventeenth and Early Eighteenth Century England* (Cambridge: Cambridge University Press, 1987), p. 194. See also Philip Rawlings, *Drunks, Whores, and Idle Apprentices: Criminal Biographies of the Eighteenth Century* (London and New York: Routledge, 1992).

25. Vivien Jones, 'Placing Jemima: women writers of the 1790s and the eighteenth-century prostitution narrative' *Women's Writing*, 4:2 (1997), 201–20, 211.

26. See Tony Henderson, *Disorderly Women in Eighteenth-Century London: Prostitution and Control in the Metropolis 1730–1830* (London and New York: Longman, 1999), pp. 14–50.

27. Abinger archive dep.e.201–2.

28. Jack D. Douglas, *The Social Meanings of Suicide* (Princeton NJ: Princeton University Press, 1967), p. 5.

29. These are not bracketed with 'Letters on the Management of Infants' which was relegated to the final volume.

30. *Monthly Review*, 27 (1798), 325–7.

31. *Analytical Review*, 27 (1798), 240–5.

Postscript

1. Described by its modern editor Gina Luria as a gentler 'companion-piece to Wollstonecraft's *Vindication'*. The two works would be also similarly linked together by socialist feminist William Thompson in his *Appeal of One Half of the Human Race, Women, Against the Pretensions of the Other Half, Men, To Retain Them in Political and Thence in Civil and Domestic Slavery*, etc (1825). See introduction to *An Appeal to the Men of Great Britain in Behalf of Women* (1798, repr. New York and London: Garland, 1974), pp. 22–4.
2. Also published in 1799 was Mary Ann Radcliffe, *The Female Advocate. Or, An Attempt to recover the Rights of Woman from Male Usurpation* (1799).
3. [Richard Polwhele], *The Unsex'd Females: A Poem Addressed to the Author of the Pursuits of Literature* (London: 1798), note 44 to line 174. The quotations are from Godwin's *Memoirs*.
4. Vivien Jones, 'The Death of Mary Wollstonecraft', *British Journal for Eighteenth-Century Studies*, 20:2 (Autumn 1997), 187–206.
5. C. Kegan Paul, *William Godwin: His Friends and Contemporaries*, 2 vols (London: Henry King & Co, 1876), 1: 282.
6. Quoted by Jones, 'The Death of Mary Wollstonecraft', 197.
7. C. Kegan Paul, *William Godwin: His Friends and Contemporaries*, 1: 276.
8. Abinger Archive, Dep.b.227/8. Verso in another hand, 'Since her marriage I have seen her often & intimately, & for affectionate manners, kindness of heart & excellence of understanding I have never known a being at all to be compared to her'.
9. Both quotations from Abinger Archive, Dep.b.227/8. Letterpress copy of letter written in November, perhaps to Skeys; and another of 4 October, perhaps to one of Wollstonecraft's brothers, asking for information of her early life.
10. C. Kegan Paul, *William Godwin: His Friends and Contemporaries*, 1: 285–6.
11. Mitzi Myers, 'Godwin's *Memoirs* of Wollstonecraft: The Shaping of Self and Subject', *Studies in Romanticism*, 20 (Autumn 1981), 299–316.
12. See Robert Anderson, ' "Ruinous Mixture": Godwin, enclosure and the associated self', *Studies in Romanticism*, 39 (Winter 2000), 617–45.
13. Myers, 'Godwin's *Memoirs* of Wollstonecraft: The Shaping of Self and Subject', p. 311.
14. Andrew Elfenbein, 'Lesbianism and Romantic Genius: The Poetry of Anne Bannerman', *English Literary History*, 63:4 (1996), 929–57, 933.
15. Helen M. Buss, 'Memoirs Discourse and William Godwin's *Memoirs of the Author of A Vindication of the Rights of Woman'*, in Helen M. Buss, D.L. Macdonald, and Anne McWhir (eds), *Mary Wollstonecraft and Mary Shelley: Writing Lives* (Waterloo, Ont.: Wilfrid Laurier Press, 2001), pp. 113–26, p. 122.
16. C. Kegan Paul, *William Godwin: His Friends and Contemporaries*, 1: 277.
17. Abinger Archive, dep.b.227/8.
18. Ibid. Letter of 25 November, 1800.
19. *Analytical Review*, 27 (Mar. 1798), 238–40.
20. *Anti-Jacobin Review*, 1 (July 1798), 94–9.
21. Nicola Trott, 'Sexing the Critic: Mary Wollstonecraft at the turn of the century', in Richard Cronin (ed.), *1798: The Year of the Lyrical Ballads* (Basingstoke: Macmillan – now Palgrave Macmillan, 1998), pp. 32–67, p. 35.
22. *Monthly Review*, 27 (Nov. 1798), 321–3.

23. 'Memoirs of Mary Wollstonecraft', *Annual Necrology for 1797–8* (London: R. Phillips, 1800), pp. 454–6. Hays had also written an obituary in the *Monthly Magazine*, 4 (Sept. 1797), 231–3.

24. See B. Sprague Allen, 'The Reaction against William Godwin', *Modern Philology*, 16: 5 (Sept. 1918), 57–75.

25. William Roberts, *Life and Correspondence of Mrs Hannah More*, 3 vols (London: R.B. Seeley and W. Burnside, 1834), 2: 371.

26. Hannah More, *Strictures on the Modern System of Female Education* (1799, repr. Oxford and New York: Woodstock Books, 1995), p. 48, henceforth cited in parenthesis in the text.

27. Extracts from the journals and correspondence of Miss Berry: from the year 1783 to 1852, ed. Lady Theresa Lewis, 3 vols (London: Longmans, Green, 1866), 2: 91. Though the Victorian editor cites Wollstonecraft's *Thoughts on the Education of Daughters* in her note, it is more likely that Berry is actually referring to the *Rights of Woman*, Wollstonecraft's most famous publication.

28. Mary Thale, 'London Debating Societies in the 1790s', *The Historical Journal*, 32:1 (1989), 57–86, 82.

29. Attribution by Wendy Gunther-Canada, 'Mary Wollstonecraft's "Wild Wish": Confounding Sex in the Discourse of Political Rights'; '"The same subject continued": Two hundred years of Wollstonecraft Scholarship', in Mario J. Falco (ed.), *Feminist Interpretations of Mary Wollstonecraft* (Philadelphia, PA: Pennsylvania State University Press, 1996), pp. 61–83, 209–23.

30. Barbara Caine, 'Victorian feminism and the Ghost of Mary Wollstonecraft', *Women's Writing*, 4:2 (1997), 261–76. On Wollstonecraft's influence on twentieth-century feminists, see Cora Kaplan, 'Mary Wollstonecraft's reception and legacies', in Johnson (ed.), *Cambridge Companion to Mary Wollstonecraft*, pp. 246–70.

31. Taylor, *Mary Wollstonecraft and the Feminist Imagination*, p. 248.

32. *Harriet Martineau's Autobiography with memorials by Maria Weston Chapman* (London: Smith, Elder and Co, 1877), 1, 399.

33. Kathryn Gleadle, *The Early Feminists: Radical Unitarians and the Emergence of the Women's Rights Movement, 1831–51* (Basingstoke: Macmillan – now Palgrave Macmillan, 1995), p. 34.

34. Pam Hirsch, 'Mary Wollstonecraft: a problematic legacy', in Clarissa Campbell Orr (ed.), *Wollstonecraft's Daughters: Womanhood in England and France 1780–1920* (Manchester and New York: Manchester University Press, 1996), pp. 43–60, p. 53; Pam Hirsch, *Barbara Leigh Smith Bodichon: Feminist, Artist and Rebel* (London: Pimlico, 1998), p. 85.

35. *Harriet Martineau's Autobiography*, 1: 400.

36. 'Mary Fuller and Mary Wollstonecraft' (13 October 1855), *Essays of George Eliot*, ed. Thomas Pinney (London: Routledge and Kegan Paul, 1963), p. 201.

37. Pam Hirsch, 'Mary Wollstonecraft: a problematic legacy', pp. 55–7.

38. Caine, 'Victorian feminism and the Ghost of Mary Wollstonecraft', p. 271.

39. Woolf's 1929 essay on MW, reprinted in *The Common Reader* is quoted by Cora Caplan in 'Mary Wollstonecraft's Reception and Legacies', p. 246.

Index